NO RULES.
NO ADULTS.
NO WAY OUT.

WELCOME TO THE DARKWOODS.

Deep in a mystical wood, four clans of boys live in the treetops, their story lost in time and their pasts buried with it. Secrets hide among the shadows of a crocodile-infested river, winding through the heart of the forest and beckoning to explore what lays beyond.

Leonardo is a member of Raven Clan, the boldest and fiercest of the four groups, led by his ruthless older brother Aleksander. When clan hostilities build, Aleksander sends Leonardo on the river to defend Raven territory. Leonardo quickly learns that nothing is as it seems, and a series of inexplicable events—including the appearance of a ghostly lion and a mysterious Native girl, who calls Leonardo and his friends 'Lost Boys'—leads him to question everything he's ever known about the woods he calls home.

As the hostilities erupt into a fully-fledged war, Leonardo is forced to choose between loyalty and instinct; a choice that will seal the fate of Raven Clan and everyone he cares about.

THE LOST BOYS TRILOGY

Lost Boys
The Cove
The Dark

LOST BOYS

To: Austin

Welcome to the Darkwoods!

LOST BOYS

BOOK ONE OF THE LOST BOYS TRILOGY

RILEY QUINN

For permission requests, contact:

pr@rileyquinnofficial.com
www.rileyquinnofficial.com
www.westbaypublishing.ca

ISBN 978-1-7753730-1-8 (pbk) — ISBN 978-1-7753730-3-2 (epub)
ISBN 978-1-7753730-4-9 (mobi) — ISBN 978-1-7753730-5-6 (pdf)

407 pages
Text set in Baskerville

Cover design by Dan Van Oss

First Edition
1 2 3 4 5 6 7 8 9 10

For my family, who've been there on every step of this adventure.

"If you shut your eyes and are a lucky one, you may see at times a shapeless pool of lovely pale colours suspended in the darkness; then if you squeeze your eyes tighter, the pool begins to take shape, and the colours become so vivid that with another squeeze they must go on fire."

—*J.M. Barrie*

"Never say goodbye because goodbye means going away
and going away means forgetting."
—*J.M. Barrie*

CHAPTER 1

A mist liked to hang over the river in the early morning, cloaking the willow trees and masking them in silhouette. Dewdrops clung to the ferns and the underbrush, gleaming in the dawn light and dripping quietly into the river. That brought the fish, big and silver, rising from the bottom in search of the insects that skimmed over the water.

This was Leonardo's favourite time. The sun turned the mist gold, the air was fresh and humid, and everything still hung in the sleepy, untouched state of the night. It was as if the forest were just waking, and the shadows didn't watch him as closely as they did during the day.

Leonardo rested a hand on the edge of the boat, the weathered wood damp and spongy where dew had soaked into the raw splinters. From afar the boat looked graceful; slim and fluted at the bow where he sat, with a tall bowsprit and tail stem like a Viking

1

longboat. Up close it was a tired old creature, ancient and battered with scars on the boards and algae stains where the river sloshed against the prow.

It slipped through the morning with quiet purpose, the only sound the rhythmic clunk-splash of its eight oars, churning in perfect timing under young but practiced hands.

Two boys behind him broke the stillness.

"Pinch!"

"Yes, Moth?" said Pinch flatly.

Leonardo closed his eyes.

"Are you trying to lose a hand?" demanded Moth, his breath short between oar strokes.

"Um…"

"There are crocs in there."

"So?"

"Crocs eat hands."

"Moth," said Leonardo, glancing back. *Leave it alone. For once.*

Moth twisted to see him, a leaf trapped in his curly hair and his clothes skewed and rumpled. The rowers faced backwards on their benches, so making eye contact was an awkward feat to begin with, doubled by the fact that it was Moth attempting it.

"But—" *it's dangerous,* Moth's eyes said.

Leonardo raised an eyebrow. *And pointing that out will make him stop?*

Moth sighed and, for a moment, Leonardo actually thought he would drop it. The other boys down the length of the boat glanced at them cautiously, afraid to jinx it.

Then Pinch made a noise, annoyed that the squabble was dying, and Moth twisted back around to glare at him. Pinch wasn't a rower, and his hand still dangled overboard, daring a challenge. He formed the perfect opposite of Moth; sharp-edged and wiry in a black tee-shirt and combat boots, a tricorn hat sitting cockeyed atop his head. His eyes flashed with dark delight, long fingers stirring the water as it streamed past.

"Name one person you know who's had a croc eat their hand," said Pinch.

"Loads of people!" said Moth.

Leonardo sighed, turning forward again. He actually had a job to do, and it didn't involve babysitting his two friends.

"Like who?" said Pinch.

"Well... there's..."

"Liar."

"Halfwit."

"Liar."

"Guys," said Leonardo. Their bickering made it impossible to concentrate.

"Get your hand out of the water," said Moth.

"No," said Pinch.

"Why?"

"Because I'm busy."

Leonardo sighed. "Please don't ask."

"Doing what?" demanded Moth.

"Trying to catch a fish, stupid."

"And that's why you never ask," said Leonardo. Once, he'd found Pinch with a shirt-full of blackberries, placing them in a long line along the forest floor. When questioned, Pinch explained that he was attempting to catch a bear.

Life was simpler if you didn't ask.

3

"With your fingernail?" asked Moth.

"Fish are dumb," said Pinch. "They'll think it's a bug."

"No they won't."

"You would."

"That doesn't even..." Moth stopped. "Ohmygod, is that a croc?"

Leonardo glanced back, following Moth's gaze to the shallows near the riverbank. A dark shape drifted, half submerged. He squinted through the mist, on high alert. The boat sat low in the water, and while the sides came up just high enough to keep out a croc, the presence of the monsters still put everyone on edge.

"No," said Pinch.

"Yes it is!" said Moth. "Leo, look, it's—"

"A log," said Leonardo.

"Are you sure?"

"Yes."

"But—"

"Moth, my zone is forward." Leonardo peered over his shoulder and turned to the bow again. Aleksander had just appointed him point watchman, responsible for being the first eyes on any dangers ahead. He didn't want to be caught neglecting that duty. And crocodiles weren't the only threat on this river. The others were a lot smarter. And they carried weapons.

"Yeah," Pinch said to Moth. "And butt out of my zone."

"You're not even looking," said Moth.

"I don't have to," said Pinch. "I'm that good."

"Wait." Moth's danger voice was back. "It's moving."

"There's a current," said Pinch.

"Youknowwhat," said Moth. "If it eats your hand, don't come crying back to me."

Leonardo groaned. "Moth…"

For all that he considered Moth his closest friend, the other boy's plucky stubbornness could be exhausting.

"Why would I come crying to you?" said Pinch.

Leonardo sighed. And Pinch was even worse—give him a stick and he'd start poking everything in sight.

"Don't be an idiot," said Moth.

"That's rich."

"Crocs *eat* people, Pinch."

"Now it's whole people? I thought they just ate hands."

Someone groaned behind Leonardo. He glanced back as Jack and Will exchanged looks. Pinch still sprawled on his bench, hand dangling overboard. Conflict was a game to him, and annoying the rest of them just added to the fun.

It was an innocent kind of obnoxiousness, thought Leonardo. A way to function in a world that never fully understood him.

"Ohmygod, it's coming towards us," said Moth.

"It's. A. Log," said Pinch.

"You haven't even looked."

Aleksander is not going to like this. Leonardo felt his eyes on them from the back of the boat. His annoyance was like a laser-beam.

Leonardo opened his mouth to affirm that it was, in fact, a log, and end the squabble for good, but Pinch spoke first, twisting violently—supposedly to see the log—and making the boat rock.

"There," he snapped. "I looked. It's a log."

"But—"

"It has leaves on it, for crying out loud."

"Oh."

"God you're a halfwit," said Pinch.

Here we go.

"At least I'm a halfwit with two hands," said Moth.

"How many hands do you see?"

"Well, I see two middle fingers," said Moth.

"Oh, so you're not blind."

"Moth. Pinch. Cork it," Aleksander's voice came from the back of the boat, snapping everyone to attention. He stood atop the narrow bench that filled the tapered point of the stern. He called it the captain's platform, with more prestige than the rotting boards ever deserved.

Moth and Pinch fell silent. Leonardo tensed, along with every other boy in the boat.

"One day," said Aleksander, his tone sending a chill up Leonardo's spine, "the two of you will wake up and realize your tongues are gone."

Leonardo twisted to look at him, standing atop the bench. Aleksander's face remained perfectly calm despite the absurdity coming out of his mouth.

He's insane, thought Leonardo. It wasn't the first time he'd had the thought.

Pinch didn't miss a beat. "And what will you do with them?"

"Feed them to the crocs."

Someone laughed, then suddenly broke off. Aleksander had a precisely honed *shut up* face that could quiet even the most un-shut-up-able boys in the boat. Leonardo didn't have to turn around to know that the *shut up* face had made an appearance.

6

Aleksander didn't joke. He said absurd things on occasion, and his threats were in equal parts horrifying and ridiculous, but no one ever laughed. Laughter meant those threats quickly became less ridiculous and a lot more horrifying. Aleksander's fragile temper was infamous throughout the woods.

Pinch didn't push it further. Even he knew better than that.

Moth's knuckles grew white in Leonardo's peripheral, his oar slipping out of rhythm.

"Moth, your oar," said Leonardo under his breath. Aleksander wouldn't put up with a rogue oar for more than a stroke and a half.

"Eyes ahead, point-watch," snapped Aleksander. "You want to row?"

"No sir." Leonardo turned to look over the bow again. Aleksander said something about incompetency under his breath, only audible because the rest of the boat stayed deathly silent. Still, Leonardo always felt like those comments were intended to be heard.

Aleksander didn't say anything else—that he could hear—and neither did any of the boys rowing. They knew better than to call attention to themselves when Aleksander got like this. They just did their duty and hoped to finish the patrol unscathed. Leonardo did the same, leaning on the edge of the bow and fixing his gaze out over the river.

Point watchman was the highest rank below captain in the narrow boat. He'd been the left watchman until the old point-watch went missing, two days earlier. Aleksander gave him the promotion an hour after Davy's disappearance, and no one had said a word about it since.

There was no point pretending Davy would come back. Enough boys vanished in these woods that they had stopped searching for them. Leonardo shifted self-consciously on Davy's bench, glancing at the shadows between the trees. A pair of eyes watched him back, an owl in a hollow, half-hidden through the mist. The big yellow eyes followed them as the boat glided past, and a soft hoot carried over the slosh of oars.

Leonardo shuddered and looked away. The birds in these woods creeped him out. They were too knowing, too attentive. Ridiculous as it sounded, he felt like the owl was trying to judge which of them the woods would claim next. Davy wasn't the first to disappear, and Leonardo doubted he'd be the last. All Leonardo could do was fill his position and try not to draw attention to himself.

As the new Davy, he scanned the water and riverbanks ahead for crocodiles, floating debris, and most importantly, rival members from the other clans of boys that lived along the river. In these woods, attacks were as common as disappearances.

Hence the necessity of this patrol; every morning, every evening, and anywhere from two to eight times in between, depending on how paranoid Aleksander felt that day. Clan territories were serious business and protecting borders even more so.

Pinch held the position of right-side-watchman, and a boy named Jack had taken over Leonardo's job on the left. Their good eyesight and perceptiveness had earned them the jobs, and while rowers like Moth might envy them, being a watchman on the main patrol was far from the high life.

More like an endless reel of scrutiny and criticism, under the piercing gaze from the captain's platform.

8

"Point-watch," snapped Aleksander, yanking Leonardo out of his thoughts.

"Sir," said Leonardo.

"What's that on the left bank? Forty yards ahead."

The real question was, *why haven't you reported it yet.*

Leonardo answered without looking. "A black swan. Two actually."

He'd noticed them ten seconds earlier. No threat, and no one wanted to eat swan. Nothing to report.

Aleksander didn't respond. Most likely, he was already looking for something else that Leonardo might've missed.

Leonardo rolled his eyes. Aleksander had no idea how hard he worked, how he'd memorized every twist in the riverbank and studied every game trail and dry ravine in the woods until he could walk them blind. He'd done it all in a fruitless attempt to meet Aleksander's demands, but the bar seemed to float higher every time he came close to reaching it.

They rounded a bend in the river and Leonardo snapped back to duty.

"Tree cliffs," he called over his shoulder.

A pair of giant pines stood atop sheer rock walls, shaded green with moss and climbing vines. The river cleaved through the middle of it, running down from Hawk Clan's territory on the far side. The morning mist still hung heavy here, silhouetting strange shapes in the passage.

"Hold. Oars in," called Aleksander.

The oars clattered in their locks and the boat glided to a drift. Someone behind Leonardo gave a raven call, picked up by a few of the other boys. Leonardo stayed silent. Aleksander permitted this from the rowers, but his watchmen were expected to hold a higher standard. Stoicism earned respect, and if one thing was certain, it was that Raven Clan was to be respected.

The calls quieted down—even the rowers knew the length of their leashes—and a hawk cry sounded out through the mist. His eyes flicked to the sky, as always, unable to fully understand how that was a human-made sound. Then the prow of another boat appeared between the cliffs, a carved hawk staring out from atop the bowsprit.

"Hawk boat," he said, and glanced up at the raven carving above him, staring back at the Hawk boat with wooden-eyed intensity.

"Stay sharp," said Aleksander.

Tension ran up and down the ranks of Ravens. Every boy in the boat had fallen silent, and Leonardo knew their eyes were locked on their Hawk counterparts.

Leonardo scanned the clifftops. It was his responsibility to spot anyone up there planning an ambush. Slingshots could inflict a lot of damage from that height.

"Greetings, Hawk Clan," called Aleksander.

"Aleksander," a voice came from the mist-shrouded stern of the other boat, smug and self-important.

They glided between the cliffs and Aleksander used the rudder to bring them alongside. Hawk boys and Raven Clan boys grabbed hold, pulling the boats together. They clanked and came to rest, rocking in the water.

Leonardo cast a sidelong glance. Hawk Clan's leader, a boy considerably younger than Aleksander, stood on his own captain's platform a few feet to Leonardo's left, pudgy arms crossed and head tilted, a smirk between his apple cheeks. Leonardo watched him from the corner of his eye. If Aleksander saw him take his eyes off the clifftops for even a moment, he'd have Leonardo's head.

"Gallus," said Aleksander.

"Hullo."

"Any news?"

Gallus thought about it. "One of my patrols saw something...oh, which stream was it down? Can't remember. At the other end of our territory, anyhoo. Might've been one of the clans from up in the hills." He shrugged. "Didn't get a clear look."

Aleksander didn't respond right away. When he did, it was through a thin layer of patience. "So someone saw something somewhere that might've been someone."

"Correct-o."

Aleksander didn't reply.

"News on your end?" prompted Gallus.

"Fox Clan still refuses to make contact. A patrol saw a boat yesterday, but they retreated immediately."

Gallus made his lips like a duckbill while Aleksander spoke. Now he shrugged, a lock of moppy hair falling across his eyes.

"Foxes are halfwits. Here's my advice: ignore the shit out of them. Trust me, you'll be thanking me later."

"And why would I do that?" asked Aleksander.

"The stress! Listen to yourself, man. Fox this, Fox that. All they do is sit in their hole, eating blackberries and getting fat. Trust me, stop stressing about them and you'll forget they're even there."

"You underestimate them."

11

"Nah."

"Then you're a fool."

"Listen man, just trying to give you some advice." Gallus tapped his head. "Wisdom from the melon. Ignore it if you want. They're your neighbours, not mine."

"If your advice involves my clan dropping its guard, then do me a favour and keep it to yourself."

Gallus smiled his smug, apple-cheeked smile. "Careful now, don't want to go making enemies."

"I've made and defeated three enemies for every year you've been in these woods. Several of them have stood on the exact bench you're standing on right now."

Gallus smiled wider. "Lorenzo talked about you, back before he disappeared. I learned to swear, listening to him talk about you."

"I imagine you did."

"Oh yes. He called you—"

"I defeated him four…or was it five? Yes right, it was eight times. Eight battles, and Lorenzo lost them all."

Gallus waited for Aleksander to finish, then he tapped his head. "He didn't have the melon."

Aleksander paused and Gallus smiled, intentionally fake and strangely unsettling.

"We should be going," said Aleksander.

"Gotta go check that Fox border?"

"Among other things."

"You're not trying to find a way out are you?"

"There's no way out," said Aleksander. "You know that."

"Of course," said Gallus. "Adios."

"Oars down," called Aleksander, and the rowers swung into motion.

A strong magic pervaded the woods, and once a boy found himself trapped in it, he could walk for days without ever finding an end to the trees. Leonardo used to believe there was a way out, but over the years he'd come to realize the same truth as everyone else—only the woods chose who came and went.

CHAPTER 2

D id you see the way he was looking at me?" said Bates, a rower.

"Who?" said Robin, another rower.

"Whatshisface, with the green hat, I don't know his name."

"Oh yeah him," said Strato. A tuft of blonde hair stuck straight up under the strap of a backwards baseball cap. "He's a halfwit."

"Tell me about it," said Bates.

"Did you see the one playing with that knife?" asked Strato.

"No! Where was he?" asked Robin.

"Third from the back. Waving it out in the open like we're at war."

"We're always at war," said Robin.

"You know what I mean," said Strato, impatient.

"Hawks are dumb," offered Bates.

"Total halfwits," agreed Strato.

Leonardo stayed dutifully removed, scanning the riverbanks. He could feel Aleksander's eyes on his back and knew better than to stray from his post. Just because Hawk Clan was being civil today, it didn't mean that Bear Clan and Fox Clan would be the same.

Pinch and Jack kept just as alert, silent at their right and left watchman posts. All three boys were senior members, in their mid-teens. That was as specific as it got; there were no concrete ages within the clan boys. Time didn't spin quite right for them, and one boy would age fast while another did so extremely slowly.

There were even stories of boys who'd never gotten old. But those were just stories.

Leonardo had seen children grow to teens in what should've taken three times as long, and he'd seen boys stay exactly the same for years. Thus, the clan boys used two words to describe their ages: *Young* and *Getting old*.

Never *Old*, because that was when the disappearing happened. No one knew where the boys went when they got old and passed into adulthood. They just disappeared from the woods. One day you were getting old, the next you were gone. Old and vanished. Leonardo had lost many friends to the 'oldness', and almost all the boys who'd been in Raven Clan when he first arrived. Including Davy, the point-watch.

A lot of boys were afraid to grow old, but Leonardo was more curious than anything. He highly doubted that they just ceased to exist. After all, they had to have come from somewhere before they got here. Maybe they went back. Or maybe this was the first of many forests.

Two of the boys behind Leonardo started whispering.

"I'll bet Aleksander wanted that Hawk's knife," whispered Strato.

"It looked sharp," whispered Will. "I heard his shaving knife broke."

"That's my point, halfwit."

And suddenly everything made sense.

"You think that's why he's so pissed today?" asked Robin.

That's exactly why, thought Leonardo.

"Look at his face," whispered Moth, leaning back toward Leonardo.

"What?" whispered Leonardo, half turning.

"No, not now," hissed Moth. "He's looking. Ok, now."

Leonardo glanced back down the boat at Aleksander. His wavy hair hung down around his jawline, half-hiding an unmistakable shadow of stubble.

"How did I miss that?" whispered Leonardo, looking forward again as Aleksander glared at him.

"It explains his mood," said Moth.

Leonardo nodded. Aleksander waged a tireless war with his face, somehow convinced that if he looked young, he could trick the woods into believing it.

"He's getting old," whispered Moth.

Leonardo tensed. Aleksander had an uncanny ear for things like that.

He missed this one, and Leonardo whispered back, "I know."

"He's too hard on us," whispered Moth. "Half the clan are just boys, not…"

"Soldiers?" offered Leonardo. "Try telling him that."

16

Aleksander demanded perfection in his clan, indifferent to the fact that his youngest 'soldiers' were still in single digits and the oldest were only teens, at the pinnacle of unruliness and the barrel-bottom of discipline. They formed his war machine, and he expected all parts polished to gleaming.

Leonardo caught movement up ahead.

"Natives on the bank," he called.

"Armed?" asked Aleksander.

"Negative," said Leonardo. "Two women, two kids. They're carrying baskets."

"Stay sharp."

They passed the Natives, who glanced up from a jumble of flat rocks on the edge of the water. The baskets tottered, filled with clothing. Mostly rawhide, dyed and strung with beads.

Both sides watched the other, wary, until the Ravens rounded the next curve and rowed out of sight.

"Why do we share our territory with them?" someone asked. "Why don't we just kick them out?"

That was such a profoundly idiotic suggestion that Leonardo almost turned to look for the speaker. It sounded like Snout. But Rugby liked to imitate Snout sometimes, so it was hard to tell.

"Because they have men, with bows and arrows and spears," said Moth.

And they supply us with half our resources, thought Leonardo.

"So?" said the first speaker. Definitely Snout. "We could take 'em. We're Raven Clan."

"But they have girls," argued Strato. "You want to kick them out?"

"Who cares?" said Snout. "All we ever do is sail past."

17

"Who cares?" said Strato, incredulous. "*They have girls.*"

"And who knows?" added Bates. "Maybe one day we'll…"

"Never gonna happen." Robin.

"Why not?"

Moth answered, "*Because they have men, with bows and*—"

"Moth," said Leonardo under his breath. He could feel Aleksander's eyes on them again. Being extra annoying wasn't going to help anything.

But Strato was already responding. "Yes, Moth, we get it, but they're not savages. We trade with them all the time and they've never attacked us."

"*Aleksander* trades with them," said Moth, lowering his voice. "What do you think, he's going to let you come along?"

"Aleksander's a stick in the mud," replied Strato, just as quietly.

"Strato," Aleksander's voice cut crisp from the back of the boat. "The keel needs a cleaning. You're cleared of other duties for the rest of the morning."

"Yes sir. Sorry sir."

"Forget whose boat you were on?" asked Pinch, a wicked grin in his voice.

"You can join him," said Aleksander.

"What?!"

Leonardo sighed.

"I didn't say anything!" said Pinch.

"Yes, in fact you did. And you should be grateful I'm not making you scrub the boat yourself."

"Myself?" demanded Pinch. "But Strato called you—"

"Careful, right-watch."

"Yes sir." Pinch dropped silent.

Leonardo shook his head. Pinch needed to use his brain some-times, but Aleksander's moods were getting old as quickly as he was. The boys talked, they insulted each other, they spoke without thinking. It was how they worked. Grown-up, self-important Aleksander was a different species entirely. A hybrid; *adult* in every way but one.

The fact that he was still here.

Secretly, Leonardo suspected he was afraid to get old. Part of him wondered if it was that fear alone, and sheer force of will, that kept him from disappearing.

CHAPTER 3

Your big brother's in a good mood," said Moth as they walked up the beach.

"His underlings are slaving and miserable," said Leonardo. "Why wouldn't he be?"

They both glanced back at the longboat, dragged on the beach and tipped on its side so Pinch and Strato could scrape off the muck underneath. Aleksander stood in the shale nearby, watching, his delicate lips curled in the slightest hint of a smile.

"He feeds on unhappiness, doesn't he?" said Moth.

"Fear too," said Leonardo, stepping over a root and onto a beaten trail between the trees.

"Why is he still here?" Moth almost stumbled on the same root.

"Well, he's on the beach to feed, right? Or did you mean in the woods?"

"Woods. Leo, he's *old*." Moth said the last word hushed, looking back to make sure Aleksander wasn't listening. "He could have a beard if he wanted."

"I know." Leonardo shrugged. "Maybe it'll never happen. There *are* stories."

Moth shuddered. "Take that back."

"He is my brother…"

Moth raised an eyebrow.

"I know, I know, the geezer needs to go."

Secretly, Leonardo wasn't so sure. Aleksander may be terrible, but he was wickedly intelligent and he knew how to lead. Leonardo couldn't imagine anyone else in Raven Clan running a ship as tight as him.

Plus, he'd been acting strange lately, and not necessarily in a bad way. Promoting Leonardo to point watch, for instance. Aleksander didn't reward Leonardo. He punished him. It didn't take much; returning to camp a few minutes after dark could elicit days of extra duties.

A quiet voice in the back of Leonardo's mind wondered if he might be coming around. It would be a miracle among miracles, but old hope died hard.

"Better," said Moth. "What if he's like a god or something?"

"In his head, maybe," said Leonardo.

A screech split the air directly overhead and they both ducked, looking up. A bird hunkered on a branch above them, big and gold-feathered.

It croaked at them and they kept walking, turning a corner around a big ivy-covered tree trunk.

"But what if he is though? A god, I mean," said Moth. "Come

21

to punish us for some crime in our past life." He looked at Leonardo. "Maybe we were bank robbers."

Now Leonardo raised an eyebrow.

"I can see the headlines." Moth jumped up on a tree stump, waving his arms. "Kid robbers loot the bank, never caught."

Leonardo raised the other eyebrow, grinning up at Moth as a boy named Nym rounded the trunk from the other side. He squinted at Moth, then brought his hands together, bobbing in a quick bow to Leonardo.

"Your Highness," he said, grinning wide.

"I told you to stop doing that," said Leonardo.

"Apologies, my prince," said Nym. His dark hair was mussed up like usual, and his eyes flashed, bright blue and friendly. He had the kind of face that was instantly likeable, his slight build giving him a somewhat elfish appearance.

"*Nym.*"

"You're the king's brother. Shouldn't that make you a prince?"

"I'm no prince and Aleksander is certainly no king," said Leonardo.

"He basically rules the Darkwoods. Sounds like a king to me. Besides, if he *was* a king that would mean you'd be next to rule." He winked. "By the way, Moth, that stump is infested with ants."

"What!" Moth stumbled back off the stump, swatting at his legs.

Nym laughed, walking backwards down the trail.

"Liar," said Moth, realizing there wasn't a single ant on him.

Nym grinned. "Gotta keep you on your toes," he said, stepping over a root without looking.

"You're a halfwit," said Moth.

"Indeed," Nym kept walking, rounding the bend out of sight.

"Anyway"—Moth hopped over the stump—"you can't say it's not a possibility."

"What isn't?" Leonardo asked, still thinking about Nym's comments. Could he run a clan like Aleksander? He couldn't do the cruelty, or the ruthlessness. Did that make him weak? He knew what Aleksander would say.

He pushed aside a branch and let it snap back behind him. Dew spattered his arm and he rubbed it on his shirt.

"Bank robbers," said Moth.

"Right." Leonardo shook his head. "Wouldn't dream of it."

They walked into a stretch of woods where the trees spread out and the underbrush gave way to wide patches of dirt trampled from years of footsteps. They called it 'the clearing', even though there were too many trees and too much regrowth to really classify it as a clearing. But the rest of the forest was so dense that this space felt wide open in contrast.

They crossed to a thick tree with ladder rungs nailed to the trunk and started climbing for the canopy, where a wooden deck ringed the trunk. Big leafy branches rustled as they pulled themselves up, ducking under the overgrown greenery. Birdsong warbled from above, and a flock of sparrows took off as Leonardo pushed aside the branches.

A webwork of rope bridges sprawled out before him, connected to dozens of treehouses nestled in the crooks and forks of the trees. A hundred and twenty-two lanterns—Leonardo had counted them—hung from the smaller branches, swinging in the breeze, the brass old and weathered.

23

"You know, I can't remember where I lived before," said Moth as they crossed the bridge, pausing to watch the golden bird launch itself into the treetops, "But I bet it was nowhere near as cool as this place."

Leonardo surveyed the familiar treetops. Fleeting images of buildings and places came into his head sometimes, but they darted away whenever he tried to catch them. They all seemed out of sync, like forgotten bits of dreams, none of it as real as the woods. He wished he knew what it all meant.

Where did I come from?

Who am I?

The woods stole it all. It was a possessive thing, and it didn't like its children thinking about things it couldn't touch. Leonardo wasn't sure how he knew this; it was just the way the shadows leered at him, the way the breeze brushed his skin. And late at night, when the moon glared in through his treehouse window.

They wove their way to Moth's workshop, a particularly old treehouse nestled directly above one of the main bridges. A short ladder led to the hatch and Leonardo pulled himself up into a single room taken up by a sleeping roll and a collection of wooden carvings. Every inch of exposed floor was covered in wood shavings.

"Have I ever told you how weird this place is?" asked Leonardo, clearing a space with his boot.

"Every time you've been here," said Moth cheerily. "Have you seen my new carving?"

"The fairy?"

"No, I'm done with that one. Here, I'll show you the new one." He stepped past a trio of fairies and lifted a carving the

24

length of his forearm. The body was still blocky and the mane unfinished, but the intention was clear enough.

"A lion," said Leonardo.

"Correct-o," said Moth, in a perfect Gallus impression.

"Don't do that. Why a lion?"

"I don't know. I had a dream about one and decided to carve it. It was easy enough to do. Just a skinny bear with a tail. And a mane."

Leonardo tilted his head, examining the carving.

"You wouldn't understand," said Moth. "You have no imagination."

"Clearly."

"So…?"

"I don't think Aleksander's going to like it," said Leonardo.

"Because of Lion Clan?"

Leonard nodded.

"Yeah, I was thinking about that. Maybe I'll just keep this guy in here."

Lion Clan was once the greatest clan in the woods, but they had been disbanded long before Leonardo and Moth arrived. Long before Aleksander even. They were now in the realm of legend, in the exact seat where Aleksander wanted himself and Raven Clan to sit. Where most spoke of Lion Clan in reverence, he used contempt, and would continue to do so until Raven Clan took their place in the legends.

Aleksander had commissioned several carvings from Moth, all of them ravens. Leonardo couldn't imagine he would react well to knowing there was now a lion in his camp as well.

"Good idea," said Leonardo.

That was one part of Aleksander's leadership that he'd never agree with. Paranoia and fear-mongering didn't create loyalty, it created a clan of boys who only carried a Raven flag because the alternative meant becoming Aleksander's enemy. And historically, Aleksander's enemies didn't last long.

***

Moth sat against the wall, working on his skinny-bear's mane, and Leonardo leaned in the corner, watching him. They paused their conversation as footsteps rattled the ladder, then Pinch's head poked through the hatch, tilting to keep his tricorn hat from being knocked off.

It was too big, ratty from years of wear, and Pinch's most prized possession. He'd found it floating down the river one morning, God knew where from, and hadn't taken it off since.

It was the kind of hat that might look at home on a pirate's head, or a revolutionary's. And in that way, it couldn't have found a better owner than Pinch, with the smile of a cutthroat and eyes that sought war, all pale skin and combat boots and long fingers.

He straightened and gazed around the room, then stuck out a foot and deliberately tipped over one of the wooden fairy carvings.

"Hey!" Moth put down his lion and carving knife.

"Fight me." Pinch picked his way across to the window. He lifted up another fairy on the sill. "Why do you make so many of these things?"

"You know why," said Moth.

"'Cause you're a girl?"

"Screw off."

"Maybe later. Honestly Moth, they're horrifying." He held the fairy in Leonardo's direction.

"Look at these eyes. Could you sleep with these eyes on you?"

Leonardo shook his head, grinning. "I get nightmares being here in the day."

"Ha ha," said Moth. "You know I only sleep in here when I'm working on a project."

"Like that thing?" Pinch nodded to the lion beside Moth.

"No, like that thing." Moth pointed to a big stump in the back corner. Leonardo remembered seeing a few boys lifting it up from the clearing with ropes a day or two ago.

"Aleksander wants another raven," said Moth.

"I don't want to talk about Aleksander," said Pinch, poking a finger in each of the fairy's wooden eyes. A smudge of slime crossed his cheek like warpaint. Leonardo had forgotten about his and Strato's punishment.

"You're done the boat already?" he asked.

Pinch made a so-so gesture. "Strato offered to finish alone."

Moth snorted.

"I doubt that," said Leonardo.

"Well, he didn't say anything when I left."

Leonardo raised an eyebrow.

"What's he gonna do, tell Aleksander? You think he'd willingly go within a hundred feet of your brother?"

"It isn't really fair," said Moth.

"I don't even know what I'm being punished for! I didn't do anything. Besides, Strato's just a rower. Imagine if I got slime in my eyes and went blind."

"Oh no, not your precious watchman's eyes."

"Shut up."

"You shut up. And go away, I have work to do."

"More fairies?"

"Pinch," said Leonardo. "Leave him alone."

"I need to get it right," said Moth. "You said yourself, the eyes are wrong."

"I said they're horrifying," said Pinch.

"Which is wrong."

"*Which is wrong*," Pinch made a half-attempt at mimicking Moth's voice.

"Guys," said Leonardo, exasperated. "Do I need to send you to your rooms?"

They both ignored him.

"I saw one!" insisted Moth. "I need to make it."

"You saw a firefly."

"I did not."

"Did so."

"Did not."

Leonardo ground his palms into his eyes. Through the gaps in his fingers, dozens of wooden eyes watched the quarrel, fuzzy with old dust and prickled with wood shavings.

"There's no such thing as fairies," said Pinch.

"Yes there is! And I need to carve it before I forget what she looked like."

"It was years ago!"

"Not many. I still remember."

"Of course you do. Leo, back me up here; have you ever seen a fairy?"

They had been over this before. A lot of befores.

Leonardo sighed. "Let it go, Pinch. He's not making you carve them. And stop poking its eyes."

28

Pinch opened his mouth to say something and Leonardo quelled it with a sharp look.

Pinch quirked his lips, annoyed. "Sorry, Aleksander."

"Excuse me?" said Leonardo.

"Your face. Did you see it, Moth? It's the same one Aleksander gets. The *shut up* face, isn't that what you call it?" he asked Leonardo.

Leonardo set his jaw. "Yes. I know the one."

"You're doing it again! Look, Moth."

"Drop it, Pinch," said Moth. "You know he hates that."

"No. I just…" Leonardo shook his head. *I'm not my brother.*

Pinch frowned. "It's just a joke."

"I know," said Leonardo. He took a steadying breath. "Don't worry about it."

Blood doesn't mean anything. You're not becoming him. And no, that's not why he's suddenly promoting you, so don't even go there.

Pinch put the fairy back on the windowsill with her back to them. Leonardo didn't complain. That particular attempt did have disturbing eyes.

"Let's get something to eat," said Leonardo, trying to sound light. He looked at Moth, "Want us to bring you anything?"

"Only if you bring it," said Moth, just as light. Pretending for him. He looked at Pinch. "He'll spit in it."

"True," said Pinch, grinning. He was oblivious to it, and that alone eased Leonardo's mood a little.

CHAPTER 4

H urry up," called Puck. "Let's go. Strato, what are you doing? No, don't walk there, I just flattened that dirt. Moth, where's your sword? Strato, I said don't walk there! Oh good, Bates you're here. You can go loosen up by those pines."

Leonardo rounded a bend in the trail, coming out into a smaller clearing than the one below the treehouses. Puck, the boy who ran battle practice, walked around the clearing, directing every member of Raven Clan to which blade of grass they were supposed to stand on.

The entire clan was present, aside from Aleksander and his second-in-command, Ajax. They didn't play well with others.

Everyone else mulled around the area, chattering in the careless, disorganized scatter that Aleksander hated. Leonardo loved it. The buzz of energy, swords glinting in the sunlight, birdsong in the trees and the rustle of the leaves as the river splashed on the rocks behind a wall of underbrush.

"Strato! Get off the dirt!" snapped Puck, bee-lining for a kicked-up clod.

"Heads up!" shouted Pinch, firing an apple out of a tree with his slingshot.

Never has there been a stranger bunch, thought Leonardo, watching Bates attempt a karate kick on Robin and Nym.

They were a mixed-bag, tossed together by the magic of the woods. It dropped new boys randomly along the riverbanks, one every few weeks, few months, or few years. If they were in Raven Clan Territory, Raven Clan claimed them, named them, and helped them sort through the jumble of fading memories.

Some boys showed up claiming to be superheroes, or famous people who they most certainly were not. The woods left them with enough memories to know that undersized Will was definitely not a pro wrestler and Snout was the furthest thing possible from a pop diva. Strato had introduced himself by thirty different names in the first hour, and Bates had gone by at least forty before concluding he had no idea who he was.

Magic had a strange effect on the mind.

Leonardo was no different, and he'd been saved from the typical naming process—if shouting increasingly worse ideas could be called a process—by Aleksander.

They found him near the Hawk Clan border, back when Aleksander was still young, and the resemblance had been too strong to miss. They couldn't know for sure what the relation was, but the popular conclusion was brothers, and Aleksander—who'd never given the story of his own naming—insisted that a brother

31

of his needed a name of equal stature. Leonardo was chosen, possibly after Da Vinci, possibly just because Aleksander liked the name.

"Hey, halfwit," grunted Cato, pulling Leonardo out of his thoughts. The massive kid stood over him, blonde hair cropped right to his scalp.

Leonardo sighed. *Here we go.* "Morning, Cato."

"You look...extra..." Cato paused, trying to think of an insult. "*Stupid* today," he finished.

"Thanks," said Leonardo dryly.

"You're like a...dead fish," said Cato, chortling at his own wit.

Cato was Aleksander's other second-in-command. Another questionable choice. Leonardo had yet to figure out what he 'commanded' besides his fists. When he used them instead of his words, he was a formidable bully, and if Leonardo was leader, he wouldn't give him any more power than his size already awarded him.

Cato kept chortling as he continued across the clearing.

"Does that mean something?" asked Will, a younger boy standing near Leonardo.

Leonardo shook his head slowly. "Maybe he saw a dead fish this morning."

Will paused, thinking about this. "He doesn't like you very much."

"No," said Leonardo.

"He's kind of dumb."

"Yes."

***

32

"Listen up." Puck strolled through the centre of the clearing, hands on his hips. "We'll have four rounds. No byes today since we have sixteen competitors. Fight hard, boys; the safety of our borders depends on you staying sharp."

"What about you?" called Bates.

"I'm always sharp," said Puck. His pudginess might've cast doubt on this statement, but they'd all seen him fight, and no one questioned it. He wasn't the best in the clan, but he was close, and he was bossy enough to excel in the role of battle trainer.

"Leo and Strato, you're up first," said Puck.

Leonardo picked up his shield and walked out onto the freshly packed dirt. Within two fights, it would be rutted and kicked up, but Puck liked things just-so, and that meant stepping it down every day before training.

Strato drew his sword. Grime streaked his hair, thanks to the extra work Pinch had left him with. He looked irritable, casting dirty looks in Pinch's direction.

"You both know the rules," said Puck. "Keep it light. Nothing that'll keep your opponent off patrol or—"

"You could go on patrol without an arm," said Pinch, sprawled in the grass on the sidelines.

"Puck," interrupted Leonardo. "We know the rules."

"Good." Puck didn't want a fight either. Or at least, one he hadn't organized. "Go."

Leonardo jumped at Strato, catching him off guard, forcing him to throw up his shield and stop glaring at Pinch. His sword cracked against the wood and he reversed, slamming a second blow against the raven painted on Strato's shield. Strato threw him off and Leonardo shifted back, beginning to circle. Strato lunged and Leonardo knocked his sword away. The impact stung his hands on the leather grip.

He gritted his teeth and took a swing that Strato dodged.

Dammit. Leonardo always forgot how quick Strato was.

Leonardo blocked a slash with his shield and came at Strato again, forcing him back. Their swords rang through the clearing, echoing off the trees.

Leonardo caught him in the shoulder, then took an overhead swing that Strato barely blocked. Strato took a clumsy hack that Leonardo fended off, then Leonardo came at him with a barrage that Strato took on his shield. Sweat gleamed on both of their faces. Strato tried to sidestep him, and Leonardo hooked his ankle and tripped him.

Strato hit the dirt with a thump.

Leonardo put the tip of his sword on the leather padding over Strato's chest, breathing hard as he blinked away the sweat.

"Winner, Leo." Puck was already ushering them to the sidelines.

Leonardo sheathed his sword and offered Strato his hand. Strato clasped it and let Leonardo help him up. They crossed to where the other boys sat watching.

There were no hard feelings in these fights; Leonardo had beaten Strato enough times that it didn't really mean anything now. Strato made a point to sit away from Pinch, but it wasn't Leonardo's problem to solve, so he dropped to the grass beside Moth to watch the rest of round one.

Puck called Moth up last, in a fight against Will. Moth was

neither skilled at fighting, nor did he take any joy in competitions like this. Experience had made him proficient with a shield though, and he carefully blocked a few blows from Will, then let him win 'for experience'.

Everyone knew that Moth was just freeing himself from having to fight again. Catcalls followed him to the sidelines.

"Kid could use the practice," he said, sitting down next to Leonardo.

"Of course," said Leonardo. "Considerate of you."

Moth gave him the finger. Leonardo grinned.

His first ever fight had been against Aleksander, and it was more of a sword-beating than anything else. He'd come away bruised and miserable and saw for the first time how much joy his brother took in cruelty. The fact that they used dull swords in practice had only given Aleksander an excuse to be less careful, and he'd taken full advantage of it.

***

"Final round!" said Puck, looking and sounding like a circus ringmaster. "Is everyone ready?"

The crowd wasn't quite as enthusiastic. They were tired and stiff and they'd seen this show before, enough times that neither combatant winning would come as a big surprise.

Leonardo returned to the dirt patch, where Cato stood waiting, grinning at some unspoken joke. Maybe it was still the fish thing. He already had his sword out, and he twirled it as easily as a stick.

Their enmity might've been because Leonardo was the better swordsman and Cato was jealous, or it might've been because—

for all the physical size of his head—Cato had less brains than a pinecone, and relied on Aleksander to do all of his thinking. Cato's feelings towards everything were a carbon copy of Aleksander's.

Leonardo cracked his neck. Puck called, "Go!" and they crashed together, blades clanging in the afternoon sun.

Cato shared Aleksander's love for violence, and he came at Leonardo hard, jarring blow after jarring blow. Leonardo ducked under a slash at his head.

Shit. Too close.

He took a swing that Cato caught on his shield. He reversed a second swing that Cato blocked just as easily, then a third that he caught on his sword. Leonardo blocked a slash and nearly dropped his sword, his arm numbed from the impact. He stepped around Cato's shield side, forcing Cato to circle awkwardly with his tree-trunk legs, and lunged for his exposed shoulder. Cato blocked it and took a swing at Leonardo's head, which he deflected with his shield.

Leonardo sucked in a breath. That was even closer than the last one.

They hacked at each other in a crashing, clanging, grunting, teeth-rattling dance. No. Dance was the wrong word. It was a fight, and it was ungraceful, and it was messy, and it was real. Most of the boys kept it light in practice, but Cato had one mode—war.

Leonardo had no choice but to match it, as he'd been doing since the first time they'd crossed swords.

And as Cato had been doing since that day, he got more and more heated with every swing, until he shoved Leonardo backwards and raised his sword in a two-handed cleave. Leonardo saw his opening, twisted, and kicked Cato in the stomach before he could bring his sword down.

Cato stumbled back, the leather padding creaking as it stretched over his stomach. For a second, it looked like he was going to keep his feet, then gravity caught up. He went down like a building collapsing; slow at first, then his arms started to pinwheel, sword flashing in the sunlight, and he hit the dirt hard.

After his coughing and gasping subsided, Leonardo offered his hand, but Cato ignored it and pushed himself up, spit on the dirt, and stalked away. Anything less would've breeched custom.

Leonardo rolled his eyes and followed him back towards the main clearing. Leaving Aleksander alone in camp too long was a dangerous thing. He found insufficiencies at a per-minute rate, and the training session would've left him time to fill their entire afternoon with duties. Better to get started while the sun was still climbing.

CHAPTER 5

The next day started out deceivingly plain. In hindsight, Leonardo should've known better, since it was a full moon and things were rarely plain on a full moon. But regardless, he laced his boots and took his spot in the front of the boat, praying that Moth and Pinch played nicely today.

The Raven boat slipped through the mist, rowers quiet as they acclimatized to the waking world, watchmen blinking away sleep and fighting to keep their eyes sharp.

They navigated the narrow forks of the river in the lower portion of their territory, where it butted up against Fox Clan's. The border itself was defined by a small waterfall, with big black rocks polished smooth from the river running over them. It was more of a water-step than anything, easy enough to get a boat over, though they didn't attempt it. Getting the boat back up would be more complicated, and just like with Hawk Clan, borders were a careful subject in the Darkwoods.

Aleksander had them hold their position, back-paddling against the current in the wide bowl above the waterfall. Leonardo leaned around the prow to see into Fox territory.

The morning sun dappled through the mist, highlighting riverbanks crowded with brambles. Songbirds rustled in the underbrush, their sudden bursts of movement keeping him alert until a wooden prow slid around the bend downriver. A carved fox head stared out from atop the bowsprit, and the faces of the point watchman and the first two rowers leaned out over the side.

"Fox boat," said Leonardo.

Strato gave a raven call, which was picked up by the others, until it sounded like a flock of ravens was descending on the river.

The Fox boat stayed silent, only five feet of wooden hull peeking out from the brambles. The point watchman said something to someone further back in the boat, probably their leader. There were rumours that Fox Clan had a new one, but it was impossible to know for sure, since they never exposed enough of their boat to see the captain's platform.

"Silence!" snapped Aleksander. The Ravens fell quiet.

"Fox Clan!" he called. "Come talk at the border!"

The point watchman conveyed the message backwards. A moment later, the boat slid back out of sight, and the shadowed narrows became empty again.

Leonardo hadn't expected much else. This was becoming a typical encounter. Fox had always been skittish, but lately they'd become borderline reclusive. If Leonardo was leader, he'd send his two quietest Ravens into the bushes to follow that boat back to Fox's camp. Their caginess didn't sit well with him.

"They're scared of us," said Strato.

"Or not," said Moth.

"What does that mean?"

Aleksander answered, his tone shutting the window for any debate. "They're hiding something."

They finished their morning patrol and beached the boat, moving it up onto the shale so that the raven carving stared out over the river. This carving wasn't Moth's work, or anyone's they knew. The boat had been there longer than any of the boys, and the common belief was that the first ever clan boys had made it. No one knew exactly how long ago that was, but the stories went back over a hundred years.

***

It was mid-afternoon when Moth started shouting. He was in one of the watchtowers, which were really just treehouses with a strategic view. Leonardo was crossing the smaller clearing, practice sword on his hip, sweaty from a training session with an old tree trunk, and it took him a second to comprehend what Moth was yelling.

Lion?

Leonardo narrowed his eyes, hearing it clearly this time.

Lion.

By the time he hit the trees, Leonardo was at a full sprint, Moth's shouts echoing above.

Something came crashing through the bushes to his right and Leonardo twisted, drawing his dull blade as Pinch came bursting onto the path.

He faltered, seeing Leonardo's sword, and Leonardo jammed it back in his belt, letting out a breath. Never in his life had he been so happy to see Pinch.

"Let's go." They ran out beneath the rope bridges and tree-houses and rushed to the nearest ladder. Shouts filled the clearing as boys came running from the direction of the river and the trails surrounding the camp. Boots thudded against ladder rungs and the rope bridges creaked, swinging wildly.

At the top, Leonardo pulled himself onto the deck and rushed to the tower, Pinch behind him. Moth had stopped yelling and had most of his body leaned out a window, bracing his hands on the frame. He pulled himself back inside as they rushed in.

"It went into the bushes." He pointed out the window.

Aleksander burst through the door, curtain flapping in his wake. "Explain."

"There's a lion," said Moth. "Big one, with a mane and every-thing."

Leonardo thought of Moth's carving. The timing was un-canny.

"The lions died out years ago," said Aleksander.

"I know," said Moth. *"But there's a lion."*

"Impossible." Aleksander grabbed Moth's shoulder and tried to turn him.

Moth resisted, then sighed and twisted to face him. "Well, apparently not." He tried to look back out the window.

Aleksander turned him again.

"It wasn't a bear? Or a wolf?"

"It had a mane."

Aleksander didn't look convinced.

41

"I know what a wolf looks like," said Moth. "This was big, and it was yellow. It was a lion."

Aleksander turned to the group of boys gathered at the door. "Until we get more eyes on it, we have to be on guard. There could be a bear on the loose."

"Do we hunt it?" asked Strato, hand already on his sword.

"Yes," said Aleksander. "Senior clan members only."

"What about the rest of us?" asked Robin, a kid with a thousand freckles and a mess of vivid orange hair.

"Set up a watch around the camp. Take positions on bridges and decks. Yell if you see anything. I want all food removed from the cooking pits, but leave the pits burning."

"Why?" asked Cato.

"Because animals hate fire, halfwit." said Ajax. He wore a trench coat over his lanky frame, and his hair was long like Aleksander's, but flatter, and limp, like a thin brown mop.

"I want the torches lit too," said Aleksander. "And build fires near the edge of camp. Keep them contained. Don't burn the place."

He turned his eyes on Leonardo. "What's that?" He pointed at Leonardo's sword.

"My practice sword."

"Is this a practice bear?"

"If anything, it's a practice li—" Moth started, before Aleksander backhanded him across the mouth. Moth stumbled back, stunned.

"Is this a practice bear?" he said again.

"I came straight here," said Leonardo. "I was—"

"Get your sword and get to the ladder," said Aleksander. "Don't hold us up."

Leonardo looked at Moth, massaging his jaw and watching Aleksander warily. He turned without a word, pushed through Cato and Ajax, and ran across the rope bridges to the armoury, a squat treehouse with nails in the wall for shields and swords to hang. Boys' names were carved into the wood above them. The extras lay piled in the corner, next to woven baskets filled with pebbles for slingshots.

Leonardo grabbed his sword, the only one left on the wall, and tossed the practice one in the corner. He rushed back outside, jamming it through his belt.

The senior members had already gathered at the top of the main ladder. Besides himself, the patrol consisted of Pinch, Strato, Puck, Ajax, Cato, and half a dozen others, peering down at the trees and thumbing the handles of their swords. Aleksander might not believe Moth, but Leonardo could see the fear in the rest of their eyes, the visions of a giant tawny body and three-inch fangs playing through their minds.

The same visions played though Leonardo's head, and he swallowed as he stepped up to the ladder.

Aleksander stood on a root at the bottom, watching his troops descend.

"Stay close," he said once they were all down. "Twenty paces out is too far."

They fanned out into the underbrush, swords drawn and shields in hand. Behind them, younger clan members rushed down the ladders to empty the cooking pits. Leonardo crunched through the leaves, pressing through branches and feeling them swing back in place behind him.

The shadows outside of camp seemed deeper than usual, and Leonardo's heart raced as he crept through them, barely breathing.

Leonardo wasn't easily scared—most dangers paled in comparison to the one he lived with—but he felt very small seeking out the beast in the woods.

They spent the first hour searching with no results. Aleksander spent most of the time yelling up to the clan members on watch, who didn't see any more than the boys on the ground did.

Keeping track of his position proved difficult in the dense bush that surrounded the camp. Leonardo knew the game trails inside out, but in the thickets everything just became walls of green, and before long Leonardo realized he had gotten separated from the group.

He started to turn back when a stick snapped nearby. He froze, half of him wanting to call out, the other half knowing that if he did, he could draw whatever it was right to him.

Another stick snapped. Leonardo took a step backwards, holding his sword in front of him. The blood pounding in his ears was so loud it hurt.

The noises of the others drifted to him, distant and punctuated by Aleksander's shouted questions to the rope bridges. He felt like he'd fallen overboard and was watching his only hope at rescue sail away. He felt smaller than ever.

The bushes rustled in front of him and Leonardo stumbled back, his ankle rolling over a root. The bushes went still. He backed into a wall of sticks and realized he was cornered.

Someone called his name. They must've realized he was missing. Too late. He gripped his sword as a shape pushed through the leaves.

CHAPTER 6

The leaves parted and the lion stepped out. Only, it wasn't a lion, and history should've clued him in sooner.

"Pinch." Leonardo released his breath for the second time that afternoon. "What the hell are you doing?"

"Lion hunting. What the hell are you doing?"

"How did you get over here? Weren't you on Aleksander's right?"

Pinch shrugged.

"You're supposed to stay within twenty paces," said Leonardo.

"Touché. You do realize he's trying to scare it off, right?"

Leonardo frowned at him.

"Are you deaf?" Pinch pointed into the canopy. "How many times can one person check in with them?"

Leonardo turned as someone yelled his name again.

46

"And when he's not yelling at them, he's yelling at us," said Pinch.

"What are you saying?"

"Make lots of noise, scare off the lion, and everyone just thinks it was a bear. Oh, and keep everyone bunched together so we cover less ground."

Someone yelled his name again.

"Here!" Leonardo yelled back.

"Fuck," said Pinch. "Why'd you do that?"

Leonardo furrowed his brow.

"Never mind," Pinch shook his head. "Just think about it, you know I'm right."

Leonardo didn't answer. He was already thinking about it, and it made sense.

Underbrush snapped as Aleksander and the lion patrol came crashing towards them, making more noise than any animal could've.

"Well, I'm out," said Pinch. "See if I can actually find this thing. Maybe it'll come out just to shut your brother up." He bowed out, vanishing into the woods.

Leonardo guided the others to him. Aleksander was talking before he'd broken through the underbrush.

"What part of 'twenty paces out' was unclear to you?"

"I was just heading back."

"Were you?"

"It was an accident."

"There's no such thing."

"As accidents?"

"Just stay with the group."

Leonardo wanted to push it, but he held his tongue and did as told. He'd lived long enough in this clan to know his boundaries.

Another twenty minutes passed without a sight of the lion. Leonardo started to wonder if Moth had been mistaken. But then he remembered what Pinch had said, and he wasn't sure.

He wondered what it meant if the lion was real. They'd disappeared before even Aleksander's time. If they were back... Leonardo shuddered. The woods were about to become a lot more dangerous.

They discovered Pinch and reined him in from his marauding, and Aleksander continued to employ his best lion-deterring methods, which worked for the most part, until Strato came across a set of prints in the mud.

"Bear," said Aleksander immediately.

"Those are cat prints," said Strato.

Aleksander scowled at him. He had a version of his *shut up* face out, but the more heavy-duty *Another-word-and-you'll-regret-it* version.

"Let's keep moving," said Aleksander. "Unless we find more evidence, these mean nothing."

They trekked over the uneven land, forcing their way through walls of brush and hollows filled with brambles and vines and big silver flowers that smelled like spice. Hummingbirds buzzed past, and butterflies so big that their wingbeats sounded like flags flapping. Leonardo kept his head down, struggling hip-deep in thistles. By late afternoon, his arms and legs were scratched raw and his mood felt a lot like the growing shadows behind every tree. Dark and getting darker.

An insect bit the back of his neck and Leonardo swatted it

away, ducking under a low branch that snagged his shirt collar. He ripped it free, leaves shaking as the branch bobbed behind him. In moments like this, he almost wished he was leader, so he could end this absurd search. The lion was gone, if it had ever existed, and they would've been better off fortifying camp than chasing ghosts through the bushes.

But he wasn't leader, and he sighed as Aleksander ushered them onward. Boys crashed through the underbrush on either side of him, swearing and fighting to untangle themselves with every step. Leonardo came upon a giant pine and had to push through a stand of long grass to get around it, half-ducking under the claws of a hawthorn bush. He didn't notice the foot until he almost stepped on it.

Leonardo froze, one leg in the air and chest-deep in grass. The boot shot out of sight, and its owner scrambled through the fallen needles.

"Hey!" Leonardo dropped to the ground, ducking under the pine to see the boy crawling away. From the back, he didn't look like anyone Leonardo knew, but he was dressed like a clan boy, not a Native.

A spy.

"Get back here." Leonardo crawled after him, his knees knocking against roots as dead needles pricked his palms.

The other boy scrambled to his feet on the far side and ran into the bushes. Leonardo climbed out after him, shoving aside branches as he stumbled down a steep bank. Leaves whipped his face, rustling and snapping and filling the air with the smell of the bushes.

Then they both burst into a clearing filled with saplings and dappled sunlight. The boy glanced over his shoulder, racing around a bigger trunk and down into a ravine. He had a narrow face and small eyes, maybe twelve-ish. Leonardo sprinted after him, boots pounding on the spongy earth.

The boy cut around a bush and looped back up the bank. He scrambled up the slope, grabbing the undergrowth for purchase. Leonardo clawed up after him, thinking they were going to wind up right back where they had started.

At the top of the bank, the boy cut left, away from the pine and the hawthorn, and down another slope. He reached the bottom just as Strato stepped out of the trees. Strato froze, the boy froze, and Strato glanced up at Leonardo, scrambling down the slope. The boy darted right, into the bushes, and Leonardo yelled, "Stop him!"

Strato was already turning, and he plunged into the bushes, Leonardo only two steps behind them.

Strato yelled Puck's name, and more crashing echoed as Puck joined the chase. Leonardo wove through the forest, visibility cut to zero as he ducked and sprinted to catch up. His breathing came hard, raw scrapes stinging where the branches whipped him. He caught a glimpse of Puck just ahead, then they all burst into a clearing, split down the centre by a narrow brook. Strato leapt over the water and almost ran into Aleksander, rounding a clump of trees.

"What's happening?" Aleksander looked from Strato to Leonardo and Puck. All three boys turned in a circle, staring around the clearing. The woods had fallen silent. More boys from the lion patrol emerged, and Leonardo spit out an explanation as fast as he could.

"I've seen him before," said Puck. "He's from Fox, I'm sure of it."

"What is a Fox doing in our territory?" asked Strato.

"Spying," said Pinch.

"Enough," said Aleksander. "Split up. If he's hiding, we need to find him. If he's running, he'll have a boat. Ajax, go back to camp and launch a patrol, no one gets down the river."

They spent the rest of the afternoon searching for their new quarry, until they'd combed the forest for a kilometre in every direction. The sun had long set, and their torches burned low. Aleksander finally called off the search, to everyone's relief, and everyone agreed that if a lion or a Fox had been hiding in their territory, both were long gone now.

"Hey, what's this?" someone called from up ahead.

Hanging lamps flickered in the treetops overhead as Leonardo jogged to catch up, finding a group of boys gathered around a thorn bush, a clump of tawny hair snagged on a branch.

Aleksander pushed the boys aside. "Looks like—"

"Don't say bear," said Leonardo.

Everyone looked at him, then Aleksander. The air buzzed with anticipation. Leonardo knew he should shut up, play the good soldier, but he was tired and covered in scratches and didn't feel like listening to more denial.

Aleksander raised an eyebrow in warning.

"It's yellow," said Leonardo, pointing at the hair. "Bears aren't yellow."

Aleksander's face tightened. Leonardo held eye contact, blinking up at the taller boy. He felt dangerous, sharp, electric with all the absurdity Aleksander forced them to swallow. The exhaustion

51

of the afternoon made it bubble over, unstoppable and un-forgivable.

In his peripheral, Pinch's eyes flashed. His excitement was in clear contrast with the uncertainly on everyone else's face, eyes darting from Leonardo to his brother.

"Are you finished?" asked Aleksander, deathly calm.

"Depends," said Leonardo, glancing at the hair on the branch. "You willing to admit that's from a lion?"

Aleksander made a noise, somehow both angry and filled with dignified reproach. "Get up top," he snapped. "And don't bother to show for patrol tomorrow."

"Great," said Leonardo. "I'll sleep in."

"Leo," said Puck.

Leonardo glanced at him.

The other boys stared at Aleksander now, anticipating his response. Ajax looked just as excited as Pinch, but for entirely different reasons. Leonardo could see speculative punishments playing behind his eyes. And Cato ground his fist into his palm, playing out the execution of those punishments.

"You'll be cleaning out the underbrush below camp," said Aleksander, drawing disappointed looks from both of his minions.

If it sounded like a mild sentence, that was because neither boy had attempted to clear the tangled, thorny underbrush below camp. And besides, Aleksander was far too smart to miss killing two birds when he had a stone to throw.

"Too many hiding places?" guessed Leonardo.

"Get up top, Leonardo," said Aleksander.

"But…if I get rid of the hiding places and the lion comes back, everyone will see it."

Aleksander drew a long breath, feigning weariness. Leonardo knew he was actually reining in his anger, which could grow at the speed of a grassfire. When he spoke again, it was through a veneer of condescending impatience. "If a bear kills half of my clan," he said slowly, "Gallus and Hawk Clan will swoop in faster than the vultures."

"Or the lions," said Leonardo.

"Enough!" shouted Aleksander.

Puck had a hand on Leonardo's arm now, and even Pinch's grin began to fade.

Leonardo nodded and spun on his heel.

"I want it done by midday!" Aleksander called after him.

"Yes sir."

As soon as he was out of earshot, Leonardo grabbed a rock and hurled it into the dark. It whisked through the underbrush, rustling leaves. He grabbed another and threw it harder. It thwacked off a tree trunk.

One day. One day Aleksander would disappear off to wherever he was supposed to already be, and someone sane could take his place.

Never Ajax. Never Cato.

Leonardo often compared his own hypothetical choices to Aleksander's, but he'd never truly considered himself becoming leader. Raven Clan followed a very strict system of succession. The leader picked his successor and no one questioned it. Aleksander had yet to name who would lead once he disappeared, but Leonardo didn't have any illusions about his place in line.

If the leader failed to pick a successor before disappearing, it would go to a vote, but Leonardo had no interest in winning it.

53

His biggest fear was of turning into Aleksander, and following him as leader seemed like a good way to step in the wrong direction.

But if the option was Ajax…

Maybe you could lead without turning into him. Blood isn't fate; you can break the chain.

Leonardo shook his head. He needed to get some sleep.

CHAPTER 7

L eonardo had cleared the brush below camp once, years ago, and it had been miserable work.

It was nothing less today.

In the years since he'd cut them down, the bushes had grown back with a vengeance, sprouting thorns and tangling so tightly around the tree trunks that Leonardo had to use his sword to hack them away. All the scratches up his arms from yesterday's lion hunting opened again and bled by the time he was halfway done.

Blood isn't fate. Did he believe that? Yes, he had to, otherwise he was destined to become the one thing he'd sworn to never be.

He was cruel when he was younger than you are now. If the bad was in your blood, it would've shown up already. Besides, Aleksander has good qualities too. Maybe it's up to you which ones you follow.

So then, if Leonardo could stay *Leonardo*, would he be able to lead a clan like Raven? That posed a new question entirely, since half of Aleksander's power came from his ability to strike fear. The other half came from his mind, and Leonardo wasn't sure if any-one—much less himself—could match wits with an intelligence like Aleksander's.

Their only hope was if Aleksander started training a successor, and maybe this advancement to point-watch was the first step toward that.

Do you want it to be?

Leonardo chopped through a thick root. He had no idea.

Leonardo cleared right to the edge of camp and not an inch further, glancing up at the rope bridges as a guide. Only near the back of the clearing did he deviate from that line, where the bushes grew higher than his head and Leonardo had no interest in up-rooting them.

He got the work done by midday, as ordered, and left not a twig that Aleksander could complain about. By the time he was finished, a spider would struggle to hide below camp.

Covered in sweat, Leonardo washed out his cuts in one of the streams near camp, gritting his teeth against the sting. Moth and Pinch joined him, seeking respite from the heat of the morning.

"Can you do that downstream?" said Pinch, rolling up his pant legs and reclining with his ankles in the water. "I don't want your blood on my feet."

"I was here first." Leonardo shook the water off his hands and moved downstream of Pinch.

"So?"

"You could've sat over here," said Moth, who had chosen a rock upstream of Leonardo.

"But you're there," said Pinch, quizzical.

"Do you still think Aleksander was trying to scare off the lion?" asked Leonardo, crouching on the bank and splashing cold water on his leg, where he'd been sliced by the razor leaves of some kind of cotton-topped grass.

"Of course," said Pinch.

"Wait, what?" Moth twisted on his rock.

"Are you deaf too?" asked Pinch. "He was yelling up to you chickens on the rope bridges all day."

"Only senior members were allowed—"

"Boo hoo. If you'd been allowed, would you have come looking for the lion?"

Moth crossed his arms.

"No, you wouldn't have," said Pinch. "So cork it."

Moth huffed. "But why would Aleksander—"

"Because we're in a clan of halfwits."

Moth sighed, picking up a pinecone and throwing it into the stream.

"Pinch, elaborate," said Leonardo.

"You elaborate," said Pinch.

"Ok," said Leonardo. "Well, Aleksander is paranoid. He sees ghosts everywhere, and he thinks they're all out to get him."

"Ok…" said Moth.

"Pinch thinks that Aleksander sees the lion as an omen."

"Really?" asked Moth, suddenly interested.

Pinch shrugged.

"But he didn't believe me," said Moth, peeling the spines off another pinecone. "He treated me like an idiot for even suggesting there could be a lion."

"Right," said Leonardo. "Because he's afraid of what it could mean."

"Or," said Pinch. "He's afraid of what people could think it means."

Moth nodded, thinking. "According to the legends, the real lions and Lion Clan disappeared at the same time. It's not a far jump to see one returning as a sign that the other will."

"You think Lion Clan is coming back?" asked Leonardo. "They've been gone for years. And they weren't even in the Dark-woods. They were way down south."

"Aleksander is paranoid," said Pinch. "It doesn't need to be logical. He'd chase away the lion before his imaginary friends could gang up and start Lion Clan."

"Who has an imaginary friend?" Jack stepped out of the bushes and picked his way to the stream, hands clasped behind his back. A willowy type, Jack dressed in a tight-fitting tailcoat, his hair spiked into a great wave. He claimed it simply grew that way, but Leonardo—and most of the other boys—suspected that he used the clay on the stream banks.

Leonardo and Moth glanced at each other. Jack was far from the most tight-lipped member of Raven Clan, and telling him their suspicions about Aleksander could be catastrophic.

"Who has an imaginary friend?" Jack repeated.

"Moth," said Leonardo and Pinch in sync.

Moth's head whipped from Pinch to Leonardo, his mouth open.

"Is that so?" There wasn't a trace of sarcasm in Jack's voice. "Fascinating. What's his name?"

Moth regained his composure. With dead seriousness, he said, "Pinch."

Jack paused, then he started laughing.

Pinch looked at Leonardo and Leonardo grinned. Moth looked proud of himself, and Leonardo released a little of his breath.

That was quick thinking.

"What is Pinch doing this time?" asked Jack, folding his legs on the bank. He neither made a move to take off his boots or looked the slightest bit uncomfortable in the heat, despite the fact that he was wearing a full tailcoat.

The stream glistened a foot from him, but he didn't even glance at it. Leonardo had never met a person as unfazable as Jack.

"The usual. Terrorizing the children, mocking everyone else," said Moth.

"Indeed," said Jack. "Quite the adventure, our little lion escapade yesterday."

"Hey, you were in the other watchtower, weren't you?" said Moth, his tone suddenly sharp. "When I saw the lion."

Jack nodded.

"And you didn't see it at all?"

"The watchtower I was in faces the other way."

"But the back window…"

"I was looking out the front."

"What about after I yelled? You didn't go to the back?"

"It was gone by then."

"How long did it take you to cross the room?"

59

"Moth," said Leonardo, frowning.

Jack had stood back up, and Moth was on his feet too. He placed his hands on his hips.

"I panicked," said Jack. "I froze, and by the time I reached the window, it was gone."

"Really."

"Moth." Leonardo stood, ready to step between them.

"You wanna say something?" asked Jack.

"Should I?" asked Moth, uncharacteristically cutting.

"What's going on?" said Leonardo.

"Butt out of it," said Pinch, still sprawled with his feet in the water. "I want to see them fight."

"I just forgot," said Jack, hostility in his voice. "I have somewhere to be." He spun on his heel, tails flapping behind him, and marched into the trees.

"We live in the middle of nowhere!" Moth yelled after him.

Leonardo turned on him. "What's going—"

"He's the only one who could've proved the lion was real."

"So?"

"Aleksander made me look like an idiot, and that idiot could've proved him wrong."

Moth crossed to the stream's edge and sat on a rock, swatting angrily at a fly.

"But he didn't see anything," said Leonardo.

"He could've, if he was doing his job." Moth was back on his feet.

"He panicked, Moth."

"This is Jack, *Leo*. He doesn't panic. He's not capable of it."

A pinecone whizzed past Moth's head. He flinched and they

both looked at Pinch, slingshot in hand. He shrugged innocently, waving for them to continue.

"No one here's ever seen a lion," said Leonardo, still frowning at Pinch. "You can't expect—"

"Did you see him in the doorway?" asked Moth. "When you got to the tower I was in?"

Leonardo thought back. "Not specifically, no."

"He was with Page."

"So?"

"They ran up together."

And? That's not exactly new.

"Page was in the watchtower with him," said Pinch. "God you're slow."

"Oh," said Leonardo, understanding now.

It had long been rumoured that there was something going on between Jack and Page. Both boys were different from the rest of the clan and polar opposites of each other. Jack talked to everyone and Page talked to no one, Jack was unfazable and Page was so shy he was nearly invisible, Jack was extravagant and Page was quiet. But they were constantly together, the shadow and the sun, and the rumours had been spinning for years.

Leonardo didn't listen to many of Raven Clan's rumours, but he had his own suspicions. He'd felt Jack's eyes on him several times when he had his shirt off, and the boy's hair alone was evidence enough.

"He was distracted while he was supposed to be on duty," said Moth. "He probably wasn't even at the window. When he heard shouting, he went to the front window first, and by the time he got to the back, the lion was gone."

61

"So you're saying," said Pinch. "That if there was a girl standing in your watchtower, you would just keep on staring at the trees. Never turn from your duty. Moth the stoic—"

"That's why we don't have girls."

"We don't have girls," said Pinch. "Because we're the unluckiest bunch of halfwits that has ever set foot anywhere."

"They have to be somewhere," said Strato, emerging from the same trail Jack had vanished down.

"Did I miss the party memo?" demanded Moth.

"The Natives," said Pinch, replying to Strato.

"Yeah, but they have guys too. The ratio is still off. There have to be a bunch of girls somewhere in this forest, just like all of us."

"There are no girl clans," said Pinch. "Everyone knows that."

"I know, but think about it. It doesn't make any sense."

"Come on," said Moth, looking at Leonardo. "These two will be here all day."

Leonardo grabbed his boots and followed Moth up the trail, leaving Pinch and Strato to their theories.

"Where *are* all the girls, do you think?" asked Moth, as they passed through the smaller clearing.

"Hiding from them," said Leonardo, jerking his thumb back at the trail.

In truth, he had no idea. He'd thought about it before. Probably more than he should've. It was a common topic of debate in the clan, and the popular conclusion was that there had to be girls too, they were just far away.

In the old stories, Raven Clan commonly sailed all the way to the end of the river, where it met the sea, and none of those stories mentioned girls. There was always upriver, but that involved travelling through Hawk Clan territory and being pelted with slingshots.

Maybe it was time to start exploring again…maybe after Aleksander got old. Aleksander was obsessive about protecting his territory, and it was too long since Raven Clan left their own waters.

CHAPTER 8

Leonardo was allowed back on patrol the next morning. The Fox Clan boy they had almost caught was big news in camp, and yesterday's morning patrol had apparently sat on the Fox Clan border for half an hour, with not a glimpse of the other boat.

Leonardo was at point-watch as they rowed there today. A lot of boys thought they should sail right to Fox Clan's camp and demand an explanation, but Aleksander was smart enough to know that rowing down Fox Clan's narrow, bramble-edged streams would be asking for an ambush.

Is that what they want? wondered Leonardo. *Are they trying to lure us in?*

They held at the border, above the tiny waterfall and the smooth black rocks. They waited for twenty minutes, and then, to everyone's surprise, the fox-headed prow of a longboat glided around the bend downstream.

The fox boat stopped there, as usual, with only the front end of the boat exposed and silent as Aleksander tried to communicate with them. After a few minutes of Aleksander shouting, the two oars they could see dipped into the water and the boat slid back out of sight.

Aleksander swore and kicked a bench. They stayed in place for another ten minutes, then Aleksander swore again and ordered them to get moving. Leonardo watched the bend in the river as they back-paddled out of the bowl.

Something isn't right here. And if we don't find out what it is—and soon—it's going to wind up on our doorstep. He knew these woods too well to think otherwise.

Raven Clan had the central territory, and any trouble that flowed over their neighbours' borders washed up on their banks first.

Aleksander knew this just as well. He told Leonardo to meet him in his quarters when they pulled the boat up on the bank.

"I need to talk to you about Fox."

"Now?" asked Leonardo, one foot over the side of the boat.

You want to discuss Fox with me?

"No, not now," snapped Aleksander. "Come up in an hour."

An hour later, Leonardo crossed past the armoury to a circular platform around the trunk of a thick tree. Ladder steps were nailed to the trunk, leading up to Aleksander's treehouse in the tallest tree. At the top, Ajax sat outside the door, reclined in a rawhide sling chair with one leg folded over the other.

"Go in," he said when Leonardo walked up.

Leonardo pushed through the curtain. Aleksander looked up from his desk as it fell shut. The 'desk' was nothing than a piece of slate over two stumps, but the effort alone it had taken to get it up this high made the piece valuable. Of course, Aleksander had only supervised the process, while other boys struggled with the ropes.

Aleksander had twenty-four pebbles arranged on the surface, each representing a member of the clan. He'd gathered them into groups and lined them up by patrol and assignment. It was a foreign language to Leonardo and, in his opinion, trying to remember what rock represented each boy would be more confusing than it was helpful.

"Leonardo."

"Aleksander." Leonardo wondered which rock was his.

"You didn't do anything wrong this time. You can relax."

It was probably the chipped one, grey and lumpish with a crack down the middle. Aleksander wouldn't waste one of the interesting rocks on him.

"Sit," said Aleksander, gesturing to a rawhide sling chair. Leonardo sat. All of their furniture came from the nearby Native tribe, whom Aleksander and his se-coms met with twice a year—or as close as they could gauge in their fluid time—to trade for supplies. It was a longstanding agreement from the early clans. The Natives didn't like the clan boys—they never had, apparently—and Raven Clan's end of the bargain was simply to keep out of their way. In return, they supplied the boys with everything from chairs to weapons.

Aleksander regarded him across the slab of rock. He had a funny little smile on the edge of his lips. A private smile, for himself

66

only. He liked the control. He liked that Leonardo had no idea what he was here for.

Leonardo was content to wait. This was far from new, and he knew an explanation would come eventually.

"You're probably wondering why I summoned you," said Aleksander, after an extended pause.

Leonardo inclined his head.

"Fox Clan has been acting suspicious," said Aleksander. "I believe an attack is imminent. That Fox in our territory was likely an advance scout, and the incompetency of our patrols allowed him through. I'm adding two new patrols to solve the problem."

"In the woods?"

"On the river. The main patrol will continue to use the long-boat, and the new patrols will use the three-person clinker boats."

"Are those still usable?"

"They've been rotting in the weeds too long. It's time to get them back on the water."

"But will they float?"

"If they sink, it will be up to the new patrols to repair them."

"And I'll be on one of these—"

"You will command one."

Leonardo stared at him. *Two promotions in four days?* That was more reward than he'd seen in his entire time in the woods.

"Ajax will command the other," said Aleksander. "You may choose two members to finish your patrol. I'll expect your choices by mid-afternoon, and you'll take your first patrol during the evening meal."

Leonardo frowned, trying to discern some kind of catch.

"Dismissed," said Aleksander.

When Leonardo didn't move right away, Aleksander half rose out of his seat.

"Going," said Leonardo. He pushed himself up and crossed to the door, as Aleksander lowered back onto his rawhide throne.

CHAPTER 9

An evening breeze stirred the reeds on either side of the
river. Leonardo watched dragonflies weave through
them, sitting on the rear bench of his new clinker boat.
Moth and Pinch had been the obvious choices for him, and Moth
worked the oars while Leonardo and Pinch scanned the banks.

"He promotes me to point-watch," said Leonardo, "Then not
even a week later, he takes me off the main patrol and gives me
my own boat. Explain that."

Pinch tilted his head, knees crammed in the front bench.

"You're sure there's no catch?"

"Maybe he's hoping this thing will sink and I'll drown." Leonardo pressed on a spongy board with his heel. "I have no idea."

"It's a possibility," said Moth, eyeing a bead of water on a
crack.

A shadow moved between the trees on the bank. Leonardo
squinted at it. A moment later, the golden bird launched itself out

of the underbrush and flapped over the river. Leonardo kept watching the trees. What he'd seen looked bigger than a bird.

Nothing else moved, and Leonardo slowly moved his gaze on to the rest of the river.

"Couldn't we have eaten first?" asked Pinch. "I'm a fast eater. Five minutes, and then you can ship me off whenever."

"I think that's the point," said Moth, working the clinker's only set of oars. "He's testing us."

"For what? Our ability to starve?"

"Your ability to follow orders," said Leonardo. "And mine to enforce them."

"What?" Moth and Pinch said in unison.

"I think he's testing me," said Leonardo. "He knows he doesn't have much time left. What if all these promotions are because he's trying to see if I could be leader after him?"

The shadowed stretch of trees slid out of sight. Nothing else moved.

"Um..." Moth frowned.

"He hates you," said Pinch.

"I know," said Leonardo. "But think about it: Aleksander is so possessive, he must despise the thought of anyone else running the clan. But I have his blood...If I took over, it would still be like a piece of him is in control."

"That certainly sounds like something he'd think," said Moth. "Did he say anything about it to you?"

"No." Leonardo shook his head, scraping a stubborn clump of moss off the top edge of the boat. It smelled strangely sweet as it came loose and plunked into the water.

"Well, be careful," said Moth. "I don't trust him."

"Don't worry," said Leonardo. "I learned not to trust him a long time ago."

"If you're leader, can I be se-com?" asked Pinch.

"Shut up, Pinch," said Moth.

"I'm serious! I could make Cato carry me around everywhere. It would be hilarious."

"He'd throw you off a rope bridge in three seconds."

A spider came scurrying out from under Leonardo's bench. He flicked it in into the footwell. It landed on a growth of bluish fungus.

We're definitely going to die in this boat, thought Leonardo.

"I could be wrong about Aleksander," he said, quelling Pinch's jokes. "And besides, I don't even know if I want to be leader."

"Of course you do," said Pinch. "Who wouldn't?"

"Life isn't a game, Pinch," said Moth. "This is serious."

"*This is serious.*"

"Can you not mock me?"

"When did I do that?"

"Just now!" said Moth.

"*Just now.*"

"You're doing it again!"

"Guys." Leonardo gripped the sides of the boat. Slime smeared under his hands and he let go.

"What?" said Pinch.

"We're out here for a reason," said Leonardo. "Let's just focus on that, ok?"

"Sorry," said Moth.

"We're coming up on Fox," said Leonardo. "We need to stay alert."

***

The Fox Clan border was quiet, as was Bear Clan's and Hawk Clan's. It wasn't until they were rowing back for camp that they caught their first sign of life, on a rocky stretch of coastline overhung with willow trees.

Pinch rowed, Moth sat in the back, and Leonardo rode up front in the bow. As they rounded a bend in the river, Leonardo spotted movement on the far bank.

"Hey, what's that?" said Moth.

"I don't know," said Leonardo, squinting.

It was in the shadows now.

"An animal?" Pinch let his oars drift as he turned to look.

"There!" said Moth. A shape moved down onto the rocks.

"It's a girl," said Pinch.

"A Native girl," Moth amended.

"What's she doing by the river?"

"They live near the river," said Moth.

"*Alone*," said Pinch.

Leonardo wondered the same thing. He'd only ever seen the Natives in groups, especially the younger ones. Unlike the clan boys, they actually had adults, and those adults trusted the boys like the boys trusted Aleksander. They didn't let their youth anywhere near them. The girl looked no older than him or Pinch, in a beaded leather dress, her hair braided down each side.

"I don't know," said Moth. "Maybe the rest are coming and she just went ahead."

Leonardo frowned, watching her.

"She looks lost," said Pinch.

Leonardo tilted his head. She didn't seem *lost* to him. More like hesitant. Or afraid.

"They live just up that trail," said Moth. "How could she be lost?"

"Why don't we ask her?" said Pinch.

Leonardo half-twisted to ask him if he'd lost his mind, but Moth beat him to it. "You're not suggesting we go over there?" he demanded.

"Why not?"

"Because she's a *Native*, Pinch. And they have men, with bows and arrows—"

"Not this again."

"It's the truth!"

"Guys, she's watching us," said Leonardo.

The girl had moved back between two trees, and her dark eyes followed them from the shadows. She placed a hand on each trunk and her beaded dress hung still, unmoved by the breeze. There was something ominous in her expression, and a chill ran up Leonardo's spine.

All three boys fell silent, unsure what to do. The girl glanced back into the shadows, and the hairs stood up on Leonardo's neck.

The current carried them down the river, drawing closer and closer to the big flat rocks, dark and slick and suddenly sinister.

"Let's go," said Moth.

Pinch made a noise of assent and took up the oars again. Leonardo continued to stare at the girl as they paddled past. She stayed on the riverbank, all alone and watching them. She glanced over her shoulder again, then turned and ducked into the trees, gone as suddenly as she'd been there.

***

Back in camp, they relayed the details of their patrol to an attentive Aleksander. When Leonardo described the girl on the bank, he stopped him.

"Where was she? On the flat rocks, you said?"

Leonardo nodded. "Near the big bend in the river."

"She looked lost," said Pinch.

Aleksander gave him the *you're all idiots* face. He drew a line in the dirt with his boot, representing the river. "This is where you saw her," he said, tapping a spot on the line. "This is their camp." He dragged his toe in a short line away from the spot, then made a circle.

"We know," said Leonardo, "but—"

"You didn't make contact?"

"No. But Aleksander—"

"Good," said Aleksander. "If you see her again, keep sailing."

"She was acting strange—"

"Am. I. Understood?" said Aleksander, stepping on his drawing.

Leonardo sighed. "Yes sir. Understood."

"Good. Dismissed."

Moth caught Leonardo's eye as they walked away.

"Leo," he asked, keeping his voice down. "What were you going to say? 'She looked like she was...'"

"Afraid," said Leonardo.

***

They took another patrol that night, and another in the early morning. The flat rocks were empty both times, and they didn't meet a soul besides the frogs and the kingfishers. The next evening, on their fifth patrol as a trio, they spotted a boat in Fox territory, but it came no closer than any fox boats ever did.

"How much do you wanna bet Aleksander is overreacting about this whole thing?" Pinch asked, leaning over the side to drag his fingers through the water.

Leonardo wasn't so sure. *Something's going on.* He was sure of it.

"Your hat," said Moth. "And get your hand out of the water."

"Deal," said Pinch. "I win, you give me that creepy fairy carving."

"Why?" asked Leonardo, trying to find a fungus-free section of the oar handle.

"Pinch likes playing with dolls," said Moth.

"Screw off, butterfly," said Pinch. "I want to see if I can catch a bird with it."

Leonardo squinted at him, then glanced up as a bat whipped past, wheeling and flapping up into the darkening sky. He hadn't realized how late it was. The shadows between the trees deepened and hiding places formed along the riverbank.

"It's getting dark," said Leonardo. "Let's keep alert."

They looped up to the Hawk Clan border, the Tree Cliffs black and ominous against the navy sky. Moth switched in to row and Leonardo climbed into the front, leaning forward to watch the star-spattered river slosh gently against the bow.

When they passed the flat rocks, a shape moved into the moonlight.

"She's back," he said quietly.

"Native Girl?" Moth stopped rowing and turned to look. She

stood in the exact same spot as last time, a hand on each tree trunk. Watching them.

"What does she want?" said Pinch. Suddenly, he jumped up in the front of the boat. "HEY! GIRL! WHAT DO YOU WANT?"

Leonardo, Moth, and the girl all flinched at once. She looked around in panic, shrinking back into the shadows. Leonardo jumped forward, grabbing Pinch's arm as Moth snapped, "Pinch! What are you doing?"

Leonardo dragged him down and Pinch crossed his arms.

"What was that?!" demanded Leonardo.

"I wanted to know what she wanted."

"Clearly!" said Moth.

"I didn't know she'd be shy!"

"Shy? You screamed at her," said Leonardo.

"Don't exaggerate."

"I don't know what the big deal is," said Pinch.

"*SHE'S NATIVE,*" said Moth, speaking slowly. "We don't mess with them."

"I'm not afraid of her."

"She's not the one I'm afraid of."

"And Aleksander said no contact," said Leonardo.

"He said 'keep sailing.' He never said not to speak to her."

"*I say* no speaking, no waving, no blinking in her direction," snapped Leonardo. "Understood?"

"Yes *commander.*"

Leonardo sighed. "Moth, oars. Let's get home."

He turned to look back as they paddled away. The bank was empty.

When the Raven Clan beach came into sight, Leonardo spoke to the other boys. "I'm not telling Aleksander."

"You're not?" asked Pinch.

"If I tell him, there's fallout for all of us."

I'm not doing it for you. There's a reason that girl is showing up, and now we might never get to know.

"Oh," said Pinch. "True."

CHAPTER 10

That night, Leonardo couldn't stop thinking about the girl. He flipped over on his bedroll and stared up at the moon, wide awake like him.

Twice now, she'd been standing there, alone, watching them. *Are you trying to tell us something? Do you need help?*

Unlikely. The Natives were more than capable on their own. But she was there for a reason.

If he knew one thing about the Natives, it was that they knew more than the clan boys. Aleksander certainly grumbled about it enough; *they're not telling us everything. They know why we're here, and they hide it from us.*

Leonardo wasn't sure how much of that was Aleksander's paranoia, but he believed they had more knowledge than they offered. Their elders had spent a lifetime in the woods after all, learning its magic and its secrets. Some boys believed the Natives could come and go from the woods as they pleased, but Leonardo tended to think otherwise. The woods were too possessive to offer such an easy way out. If there was one, he imagined it would be hard to find the first time, and impossible to find again.

But maybe she'd learned something, like one of the woods' darker secrets, and was trying to get away from it.

Is that why she's alone?

Maybe she'd been shunned from her camp.

Or she's hiding from her camp. Maybe she's living in the trees at the edge of the river, trying to get our attention to tell us she needs help.

Leonardo rolled over, studying the dark lumps of his clanmates on their bedrolls.

Your imagination is running away. Try to think logically.

But if she is in trouble…

Strato snorted in his sleep, and someone slapped an arm on the floor—it sounded like Puck. Leonardo pushed himself up, looking around the room. Pinch and Moth were out cold, and he was fairly certain they'd stay that way until morning.

Maybe his theories were dramatic, but he couldn't just leave her if she needed help.

He stood and quietly crossed to the door. The night was cool, edged with a breeze that rustled the leaves and rattled the lanterns, making them swing on their branches.

Leonardo crossed a rope bridge and descended one of the ladders to the ground. He'd gotten an idea. It wasn't a very good idea, but his mind was spinning and he needed to put it to rest.

He dropped to the dirt and started toward the beach, ears

tuned for both lions and Aleksander. He wouldn't put it past his brother to walk the camp at night, just to make sure no one else was.

He reached the beach without incident and paused just inside the trees, leaning out to see the guard. He lay slumped against a big rock. Sleeping? It looked like Nym. Stepping quietly, Leonardo walked around the shale and stopped at his side. Nym gave no reaction, which confirmed Leonardo's suspicions.

You're lucky it's me and not Aleksander, he thought, then retraced his steps and crossed to the pair of clinkers tied off in the water. Leonardo's and Ajax's patrols used old ropes to secure them to the roots of an upturned tree.

Silently, Leonardo untied his boat's lead and dropped it into the bow, then followed it over. A glance up the beach showed that Nym was still asleep.

Good. He climbed to the middle row, dipped the oars into the river, and guided the clinker away from the beach. Ajax and his patrol choices, Snout and Rugby, were scheduled to leave in about an hour and a half, although Leonardo would be willing to bet that a lot of their 'patrols' consisted of simply rowing to the nearest patch of wild blueberries and killing an hour in the bushes.

Regardless, he had to be back before they cast off. If there was anything that could motivate Ajax into actually doing something, it was the chance to get another clan member—especially Leonardo—into trouble.

By the time he reached the river bend, the oar handles were slick with his sweat, and Leonardo's heart pounded. The branches rattled overhead and the leaves rustled in the black of the woods.

The crickets and frogs sang an urgent chorus in the reeds. His thoughts of Ajax had been replaced by the Natives and what they would do if they found him.

The smart thing to do would be turn around and row right back to Raven Clan. Forget the whole thing. But Leonardo needed to see. Just to make sure.

The bank appeared quiet, so he rowed over, moving the clinker upstream of the rocks and guiding it back behind a boulder. The current held his boat in a niche, so Leonardo could stand and peer into the trees.

He listened for any sounds at all—breathing, the rustle of clothing, the snap of a twig. Nothing. He placed a hand on the nearest rock and climbed out of the boat.

He checked to make sure the clinker wasn't about to drift away, but it was pinned by the current, slipping between smaller gaps and offering no backwash to push it out. Content that he wasn't going to lose his only escape, Leonardo straightened and picked his way over the rocks towards the trees.

Blood pounded in his ears and every hair stood on end as Leonardo crept closer. He scanned the trees constantly, searching for the slightest sign of movement. This was a bad idea. But he'd known that from the beginning. It wasn't going to stop him now.

Leonardo stopped on the last rock before the bank. The moonlight illuminated a trail, leading back into the trees. The Native camp was at the other end of that, he knew. He hoped it was a long way in.

Taking a deep breath, he rethought his plan for the dozenth time, then called into the trees, his voice barely over a whisper.

"Hey! Is anyone there?"

He got no response. That was a bit of a relief, but it meant he needed to try again. "Hey! Are you in there?" he called, a little louder, eyes on the trail.

"Hey!" he called a third time. "Are you—"

A footstep.

Leonardo's stomach leapt into his throat.

"Hello?" he called again.

The leaves rustled to the right of the trail. Leonardo took a step back. The branches parted and a face emerged through the leaves, a foot off the ground.

A fox stepped out, its ruddy fur caught in the moonlight. Leonardo released his breath. A fox. A red fox.

The girl wasn't there. Leonardo felt slightly ridiculous, but at least he'd checked. He called out one more time, just in case, and even took a few steps up the trail, but the woods held its secrets tight. He sighed and left the fox on the bank, picking his way back to the boat.

It had rotated three quarters of the way around and didn't take much effort to get out into the river. Leonardo watched the bank as he rowed away. The fox was still visible, a spot of moonlit orange against the dark underbrush. He felt strangely disappointed. It was nice to know that she hadn't been shunned from her tribe, but he realized that a part of him had been excited at the idea of it all.

Helping her escape, bringing her back to camp or hiding her somewhere nearby. He could steal food for her from the cooking pits when no one was looking, sneak it out to her hiding place. It would be exciting.

He cast one last look at the bank. The rocks remained empty, mottled in moonlight. Disappointed, he started to row around the bend.

Then something moved. A darker shadow in front of shadowed trunks.

Leonardo paused, water running off his oars. He started to turn the boat, fighting a current that forced him back around the bend, out of sight of the rocks.

Leonardo got the boat half twisted before reality caught up with him. He'd been gone a long time. If he went to the rocks again, there was a good chance he wouldn't make it back to the beach before Ajax came down for his patrol.

Leonardo swore.

A little more time… That's all I need.

The risk is too high.

But—

A shadow, that's all you saw.

No. It was her. He had no doubt about that.

In the end, the logical side of Leonardo's mind won out, and he rowed the clinker back into the current.

Tomorrow night.

When Leonardo came up on the Raven Clan beach, he saw the slumped form of Nym, still sleeping. Ajax's empty clinker bobbed by the fallen tree.

Thank you. Leonardo guided the clinker to shore, lowered himself into the ankle-deep water, and tied off the lead rope. He looked up the beach to the trail. It wasn't a long walk, just an exposed one, with a lot of loose shale.

Leonardo made it halfway before taking a wrong step. But it

was a big one, and it sent a shower of pebbles down the sloped beach. Nym stirred, making a noise, and reached up to rub his eyes.

Dammit. Leonardo raced up into the bushes. He ducked behind a tree and leaned against the trunk, heart racing for the hundredth time that night.

An owl hooted overhead, making him jump. It crouched and took off, rattling the branches as it swooped down over the river. Leonardo slipped through the trees, hoping that Nym would be distracted. He stopped just before the trail, pausing to listen.

This time, he didn't find an owl, but rather a two-legged predator. Footsteps came down the trail, a thin wall of underbrush between them. Based on the walker's soldier-march, he guessed it was Aleksander. A few seconds later, that guess was confirmed.

"Nym," barked Aleksander.

"Sir."

"Anything suspicious?"

"No, nothing. It's a quiet night."

If he wanted to get out, now was the time. He had no idea where Aleksander would go after this, and making it back to his treehouse would become increasingly treacherous with Aleksander roaming the camp.

He inched around a bush and peered down the trail. Aleksander's back was partly visible, but he faced the other way, and that was all that mattered. Leonardo stepped onto the trail and sprinted to the clearing, blood thumping in his ears.

He scrambled up the ladder, pulling himself up onto the platform just as Aleksander appeared through the trees. Leonardo ducked behind a clump of branches, then edged around the platform and hurried across the rope bridges to his treehouse.

Moth glanced up, mumbling something unintelligible as Leonardo pushed the curtain aside.

"Bathroom," Leonardo whispered back, and Moth rolled over.

Leonardo walked to his roll and lay down, staring at the ceiling as he waited for his pulse to slow down. The moon still watched him through the window, and if he didn't think about it much, it felt like he'd never left, and the whole thing was just a strange, tense dream.

***

The next morning, Leonardo gripped the edge of the hatch and pulled himself up into Moth's workshop, looking around the mess of wood shavings and the tiny army of carvings. A square of golden sunlight painted over them as the first rays crept through the window, and Leonardo's eye was drawn to Moth's lion.

Just then, hands and feet scuffled on the ladder rungs outside.

"Morning," called Leonardo.

"Who is it?"

"The fairies."

"Ha ha." Moth's head appeared through the opening. "Morning."

Leonardo looked at the stump Moth was shaping into a raven. "What do you think he wants that for?"

"Beats me," said Moth. "Maybe he'll put it on the beach, scare off Fox Clan."

"Pinch is really convinced they're not coming."

"Pinch is a halfwit. And he's afraid to lose his hat."

Moth picked up his knife and the fairy on the window ledge, studying her eyes.

"That was a piece of poetry, eh?" he said. "Getting Pinch to take the bet?"

Leonardo didn't answer. He was staring at the lion carving again.

"Hullo?" said Moth.

"What?"

"Where'd you go?" Moth followed his gaze to the lion.

"Isn't it strange," said Leonardo. "That right after you carved that, the first lion in years shows up?"

"Oh yeah, I know. I wish I'd carved it after. I did its ass wrong."

"I'm serious."

"Sorry," said Moth. "Do you still think it's an omen?"

"I don't know," said Leonardo.

"I wish more people had seen it."

"Everyone on patrol saw the fur," said Leonardo.

"Still," said Moth, placing the fairy back on the sill. "So long as Aleksander says 'Bear', no one's going to argue with him."

"Who cares?" said Leonardo. "Everyone believes you."

"*He* doesn't." Moth picked up two more fairies, examining them.

"Why does that matter? Since when do you care what Aleksander thinks?"

"I don't. It's just…" Moth sighed. "He treats me like I'm completely useless, and I know I can't fight or do anything valuable, but—"

"Hey now." Leonardo took the carvings from Moth. He'd unconsciously twisted the tip of his knife into one's back.

"No, listen," said Moth. "I can't fight, I'm a weak rower, and my eyes aren't as good as yours and Pinch's. I can carve wood, but I can't hunt, or fish, or do anything that's actually useful to the clan. Stop trying to argue, I'm making a point."

Leonardo closed his mouth.

"I'm bad at more things than I'm good at. I know that, you know that, Aleksander knows that, and I don't care. It's who I am. What I care about is being treated like an idiot. I know what a lion looks like."

"He treats everyone like they're stupid," said Leonardo, looking for a place to put the fairies.

"He thought I'd confused a bear. Or a wolf. I mean, seriously, Leo. A wolf."

"If he'd seen it with his own eyes, he would've blamed a mirage from the sun on the leaves." Leonardo put them on the sill, pushing the dozen already there into a tighter jumble.

"I know, I know, he's insane. It's just irritating. It feels like he picks on me especially."

Leonardo would've said the same thing about himself.

"God, I can't wait for the day he disappears," said Moth.

"Amen."

"Come on," said Moth. "His Majesty will be back soon. If we splash some water in our hair and go stand near the woodpile, he'll think we've been working. You can hold the axe, I'll grab some wood."

CHAPTER 11

The girl wasn't there during either of their next two patrols. When they passed the rocks that evening, Pinch spoke up.

"Looks like Native Girl found something more interesting to do than stalk us."

Or I scared her off, thought Leonardo. *If that* was *her.* In the logic of daylight, he wasn't so sure anymore. A lot of things cast shadows in the night.

He watched the bank until it curved out of sight, an empty jumble of rocks in the setting sunlight.

"What do you think she was doing?" asked Moth.

"She looked afraid," said Leonardo.

"Of what?" asked Pinch.

"You!" said Moth. "You and your yelling!"

"No," said Leonardo. "I'm talking about before that."

He thought about the expression on her face when she'd glanced back over her shoulder. And then she'd run away.

Something was in those woods, and it wasn't just foxes.

He needed to find her again.

"Leo?"

Moth and Pinch both frowned at him.

"Sorry." Leonardo shook his head. He realized that Pinch had answered his question, but he hadn't heard a word of it.

"Are you ok?" asked Moth.

"I'm just tired," said Leonardo. It wasn't a lie. "I didn't sleep last night."

And he wouldn't tonight either.

***

His plans to sneak out again were interrupted when a storm rolled in, causing Aleksander to suspend all patrols. Leonardo sat inside his treehouse with Moth, Pinch, Puck, and Strato, listening to the rain pelt the roof and sizzle through the leaves outside.

Even if he tried to weather the storm, he doubted the girl would be out in this downpour. And besides, how would he explain his absence? He didn't want to tell the other boys about his theory yet, or his late-night escapade. They would only complicate things, and things were complicated enough as it was. He needed to find the girl himself.

The rain continued into the morning, but the brunt of the storm had moved on. A rapping on the doorframe woke Leonardo.

"Woodpeckers," Pinch mumbled in his sleep.

"Get rid of them," said Moth, flipping over on his bedroll. "It's too early."

Leonardo sighed and pushed himself up. "Who is it?" he asked, crossing to the curtain.

"Nym."

Leonardo stepped outside. The sky was still dark, and the rain fell in a gentle shower just beyond the overhanging branches. The smell of the pines hung rich and pungent, bows swinging in the rain.

"What is it?" Leonardo asked, rubbing sleep from his eyes. It felt like he'd slept ten minutes, tops.

"Cato sent me. Sorry to wake you so early. Aleksander wants you in his quarters."

***

Leonardo found his brother at his desk, behind his pet rock collection. His pet humans were there too.

Cato and Ajax looked up from the table when Leonardo walked in. Aleksander slid two rocks to a different pile and sat back, regarding Leonardo.

"What's he doing here?" asked Cato.

"Being late," said Aleksander. "Sit down, Leonardo. You look half-dead. I don't need you collapsing when we go to the Native camp."

Ajax and Cato gaped at Aleksander. Leonardo froze. He was wide awake now.

Aleksander frowned at him. "You look petrified. I'm not sacrificing you to them. Sit."

Leonardo didn't move.

"What's wrong with you?" asked Ajax, squinting at Leonardo. Cato copied him.

Leonardo swallowed. *This is bad.*

"Never mind," said Aleksander. "Stand, sit, we've wasted enough time on you. A Native warrior came this morning. Their chief wants to speak with me."

"About what?" asked Ajax.

About me.

"He didn't say," said Aleksander. "The rain is letting up. We'll go as soon as it clears."

Leonardo's mind raced. *What if the shadow wasn't the girl after all.* If one of the warriors had seen him…

"Wait. Is *he* coming?" Ajax pointed at Leonardo.

Aleksander gave him a *don't ask me stupid questions* look.

"Why?" Ajax's eyes flashed with betrayal.

"Because he's a patrol commander."

"So?" spit Ajax. "Since when do we need four people to visit the Natives?"

"The Native Chief requested he be there. And it won't be four. Just two."

Aleksander walked to the curtain and looked outside.

Ajax and Cato's mouths fell open.

This is very bad, thought Leonardo.

"You're taking him and not me? Not *us*?" Ajax corrected quickly.

"I need you to run the camp while we're gone," said Aleksander. "Surely you haven't forgotten the duties of a se-com."

"Of course not," said Ajax. "But—"

"Good," said Aleksander. "Leonardo, get your sword and meet me on the beach. Dismissed," he added to all three of them.

Leonardo followed Cato and Ajax out, trying to stop his hands from shaking. Whatever punishments he'd been imagining last night were gone. He'd take any of them over this. There were stories of what happened to the boys who tried to sneak into the Native camp; it didn't happen often, but none of them ended well.

Ajax and Cato held up for Leonardo at the bottom of the ladder from Aleksander's quarters. When he stepped off the last rung, he found Cato with his big arms crossed and Ajax clenching his fists. That was the better arrangement; he could survive a hit from Ajax.

"What's going on?" demanded Ajax. "Is he planning to name you successor?"

"What?" said Leonardo. "No. I don't... How would I know?"

"You're stuttering," said Ajax, eyes narrowed in suspicion.

"You're stupid," said Cato, attempting to contribute.

"I have no idea what Aleksander wants," said Leonardo.

"He hates you," said Ajax. "Why would he want you as a successor?"

Because I'm his brother? Even still, Leonardo tended to agree with Ajax. The promotions glared in contradiction, but Aleksander did a lot of things that didn't make sense.

"He probably doesn't," said Leonardo. "I'm sure he's just waiting for the right moment to name you the next leader."

He didn't mean to say it as such a jab, but it came out before he could stop it.

Ajax's eyes widened. He stepped towards Leonardo, glaring down at him from his lanky height. Behind him, Cato punched his other palm with enough gusto that both Leonardo and Ajax jumped.

"Ask Aleksander." Leonardo stepped around Ajax. "I need to get my sword."

He stiffly crossed the rope bridge, waiting for them to come running after him. They didn't, and he made it, hands shaking, to the armoury.

He paused inside the old treehouse, drawing a deep breath, then strapped on his sword and pushed back outside.

If the Natives are angry…if they know I came looking for the girl…will Aleksander stand by me or will he just leave me with them?

Leonardo wanted to believe the former, but in truth, he had no idea. The Natives could be just as angry at Aleksander for not controlling his clan better. That wouldn't resonate well at all with Aleksander's pride.

On the beach, Aleksander supervised while Bates and Robin bailed out a clinker. Ajax stood on his other side, arguing something—it wasn't hard to guess what—while Aleksander mostly ignored him.

He looked up as Leonardo crossed the shale. Tense lines strained his freshly-shaven face. He glanced upriver, and he didn't look quite as commanding as he had last night.

Ajax huffed. "Cato can watch the camp."

"Cato is an idiot," said Aleksander.

"Ok, but still," said Ajax. "It's not like he's going to burn the place down while you're gone." He glanced bitterly at Leonardo. "You're choosing him over me."

Aleksander whipped around, all of his attention now fixed on Ajax. Ajax took a step back, fear flashing across his face. Leonardo paused on the shale a few meters away.

"As I've told you twice now," said Aleksander. "The Native Chief requested him. I am simply appeasing his request because I don't want to deal with his temper. Leonardo, you're rowing," he said, waving Bates and Robin away.

Leonardo didn't move, and Aleksander snapped at him, "Before tomorrow, preferably."

Leonardo swallowed and crossed to the boat. Bates and Robin shuffled out of the way, their expressions mirroring his thoughts.

What is Aleksander taking me into?

CHAPTER 12

When they reached the Native beach, it was as quiet as always. The rocks and bushes gleamed dark and wet, the trail less appealing than ever. Heavy clouds hung overhead, and the sun formed a weak bulb somewhere behind all the grey. The air still smelled like rain as Leonardo climbed out of the boat.

Aleksander already strode up the rocks and Leonardo hurried after him, slipping and struggling across the slick boulders. He caught up on the bank, grateful to be on dirt again, and followed Aleksander into the trees.

The first thing Leonardo smelled was smoke. Campfire smoke, and it got stronger as they walked up the trail. They rounded a bend and passed a stand of birch. Voices whispered through the trees, then a warrior suddenly materialized out of the shadows. He was the same height as Aleksander, but his bare chest rippled with muscle, making him seem much larger. He carried a feathered spear, and the hilt of a long knife stuck out of his belt.

"Aleksander." He nodded in acknowledgement, serious and guarded. His eyes were the colour of a cold, moonless night, black and piercing.

"Dakota," said Aleksander.

"You're here to see the chief?" His accent glinted as dark as his eyes, inflected with the very fibres of the woods. Leonardo couldn't explain why he thought this, but it was the image that came into his head when Dakota spoke.

"Yes," said Aleksander.

"This is the one?" Dakota examined Leonardo suspiciously.

Leonardo straightened, closing his palms so Dakota couldn't see the gleam of sweat on them.

"Yes," said Aleksander, brusque. He turned a distasteful eye on Leonardo.

Dakota wore a matching expression, but it was directed at Aleksander.

The tension that hummed in the trail was enough to force out the air, making it hard to breathe. Leonardo had always heard about the Natives' lack of affinity toward clan boys, but he'd never expected it to be this intense.

Why do you hate us so much? he wondered.

Finally, the warrior spoke again, his voice heavy in the weighted air. "Follow me."

He led them into a clearing ringed with tipis and a dozen fire pits. Native women brought racks of pelts out of one of the tipis and set them up to dry around the fires. The grass was wet from the rain and water dripped from the branches around the clearing.

The women paused what they were doing to watch the clan boys pass. He looked for the girl, but he couldn't see her. A few kids milled around, but they were mostly younger. They glanced at their mothers and scrambled out of sight, peeking out at Leonardo and the others from behind tent folds.

A boy Leonardo's age paused with an armful of firewood. He glared at them through narrowed eyes. Leonardo looked away. Two girls peered out from the doorway of a tipi and for a second Leonardo thought one of them was her, but no, still not.

The men-with-bows-and-arrows-and-spears were just as silent as the rest, hands on the hilts of their weapons. One warrior sat on a big rock, stringing a longbow taller than Aleksander. His eyes followed them.

No wonder Aleksander doesn't bring the clan here, thought Leonardo. He got the feeling one wrong step would set off a fight.

Dakota stopped outside the largest of the tipis and told them to wait while he ducked inside. The outer shell of the structure was made of animal skins sewn together, stretched over big posts and folded open at the top, where a wisp of smoke curled into the sky.

The animal hides hung wet and heavy between the support posts. Leonardo reached out and ran his fingers down the stitching. It was well sewn, better than anything the Clan boys would've been able to do.

No wonder we trade for everything from them.

Aleksander batted his hand off, giving Leonardo an *are you stupid?* look.

Dakota said something inside the tipi. It was muffled by the skins, but Leonardo thought it might've been in another language. He said something else and backed out again.

"Ok. You can go in."

Aleksander was already crouching down to duck inside. Leonardo started to follow him, then a girl stepped out of a tipi across the clearing and Leonardo stopped, recognizing her braids. She froze, eyes wide. She looked around quickly and the warrior with the longbow frowned at her.

"Get in here, Leonardo," snapped Aleksander, voice muffled inside the tipi. "What are you waiting for?"

"Nothing, coming."

He ducked through the opening, into a dark space strung with beads and feathered rings. A fire burned in the middle of the tipi, popping and crackling and throwing strange light and shadows on the walls. One shadow seemed to detach from the rest, stretching long and menacing up between the poles, then it plunged back down with the others.

A Native man with heavy wrinkles sat behind the fire, watching them with slitted eyes through the haze of smoke. Aleksander sat across from him, folding his long legs as he stared at the old man over the flames.

"Raven Clan," the chief said slowly. "Welcome."

His voice rasped with the same quality as Dakota's, as if the life of the woods were woven right into it. It was an ancient voice, weathered and reminiscent of the fire crackling in front of him. He kept his dark eyes on Aleksander, and Leonardo didn't like what he saw in them. If he were to make a guess off that look, he would say that the chief despised his brother.

Then he looked at Leonardo and Leonardo felt like he'd been hit with an electric current.

"Who is this?" asked the chief. "He has not been here before."

Didn't he request to see me? thought Leonardo.

"This is Leonardo," said Aleksander warily. "You wanted to see him." He looked at Leonardo, a warning in his eyes.

Leonardo shifted uncomfortably.

"Yes," said the chief. "I did. Now, *who* are you?" he asked Leonardo.

Leonardo stared at him.

"We don't have time for riddles, Tokala," interrupted Aleksander. "Why did you summon us?"

"How much longer have you in these woods, Aleksander?" asked Tokala, his voice chiding. "A wise man does not pass on with impatience and war in his mind."

"I don't know what you're talking about, old man," said Aleksander. "But I already told you——"

Tokala slowly drew a pouch from his robes and removed a black piece of what looked like bone. He tossed it into the fire, sending up a cloud of sparks. "My people are the guardians of these woods," he said, half obscured by the heavier smoke that now swirled over the fire.

"I know that," snapped Aleksander.

"I'm telling him," said Tokala, returning the pouch to his pocket and nodding at Leonardo.

A black flame licked through the fire.

Leonardo tilted his head, studying the old man. *What do you guard it from?*

"We have been in this corner of the woods for a long time," continued the chief. "The four clans of the Darkwoods have always required our closest attention. You kill each other faster than the clans of the Cove, the Redwoods, and the Highland combined. Did you know that?"

The Cove. That was where Lion Clan used to rule. He didn't know much about the other two places, only that they lay somewhere off in the vast land of the woods, miles away from their own tiny corner they called the Darkwoods.

Aleksander cut off Leonardo's chance to respond. "So? The Darkwoods is a war zone. It always has been." A sharp undercurrent edged his words.

He's hating every second that the chief talks to me and not him.

"It would not be," replied Tokala, "if the ones starting the wars stopped."

Aleksander raised an eyebrow. "I told you, I didn't ask for Fox Clan's attack."

Tokala shook his head, slow and weary. "And I have told you many times, the choices of your past write the consequences of your future. You cursed the Darkwoods with war long ago. It will not be gone until you are."

Aleksander sat back, and Leonardo witnessed a rare thing cross his face. Fear.

"Are you threatening me?" he demanded.

"Encouraging you," said the chief. "Move on. Leave this place."

"No," said Aleksander, sharp enough that Leonardo flinched. Aleksander shot a glance at him. Tiny beads of sweat glistened on his forehead and he licked his lips, nervous. He couldn't like that Leonardo was seeing this. Leonardo wasn't even sure what he was seeing.

The chief rummaged in his robes and removed a brass pocket watch. The hour, minute, and second hands sat frozen in a neat bunch just before twelve o'clock.

Neither the object nor the moment felt as mundane as they should've, and Leonardo had a strange thought.

Do they keep track of how long we're here?

He wondered what the purpose would be.

The chief examined the watch's face, then slipped it back into his pocket. "You have resisted the woods a long time," he said to Aleksander. "That is a great feat. Only a handful of boys have ever had enough willpower to do so. But such things have consequences. If you continue to resist, more damage will follow."

Leonardo had always joked that Aleksander would stay in the woods on willpower alone, but he'd never truly thought that could be the case. Hearing it from the chief, he had to admit it made sense. He'd never met anyone as single-minded as his brother.

He wondered what 'more damage' meant.

"The woods are calling us elsewhere," continued Tokala. "To a great danger." The black flame stretched taller in the fire. "The Darkwoods cannot continue on this path."

"And?" said Aleksander. "What do you want me to do about it?" His knuckles pressed white against the floor.

"There will come a choice," said Tokala. A second flame grew taller than the first and he slowly turned to Leonardo, dark eyes glinting in the firelight. "Ensure you make the right one."

Leonardo stared at him.

Aleksander whipped from Tokala to Leonardo, incredulous. He opened his mouth to speak, but Tokala settled his gaze on him and Aleksander seemed to forget whatever he was about to say.

101

"You may leave now," said Tokala, the embers in his voice cold and dark.

That's it? Nothing at all about the girl? About his nighttime visit to the bank?

Aleksander turned and shoved out of the tent. Leonardo scrambled after him, glancing back at the chief. He turned his fire-lit gaze on Leonardo, expression grave.

As he retraced his steps through the camp—nearly running to keep up with Aleksander—Leonardo searched for the girl. Halfway to the trail, he caught movement between two tipis. She stood in the shadows, watching him.

CHAPTER 13

Aleksander kept utterly silent on the trip back to camp, leaving Leonardo with a thousand unanswered questions.

There will come a choice. Ensure you make the right one. You have resisted the woods a long time. That is a great feat. If you continue to resist, more damage will follow.

Tokala's words tumbled over and over in Leonardo's head. And then there was the girl. At least he now knew she hadn't been shunned from her camp, though it brought him no closer to knowing what she actually wanted.

Leonardo followed Aleksander up the beach trail, glancing at the big gold bird on its familiar branch overhead. It croaked at him, shoulders hunched and feathered head cocked in the unnerving way of all the birds here. Leonardo stepped around the bend into the clearing.

Moth and Pinch stood waiting in the shadow of a hackberry tree, Pinch leaning on the trunk and Moth examining a broken branch, doubtless sizing up his next carving.

Leonardo split off from Aleksander and crossed the damp clearing, avoiding a big mud puddle below one of the treetop platforms.

He held up in its shadow, waiting until Aleksander crossed the rope bridge overhead, creaking and rattling as he stormed for the ladder to his quarters, coattails flapping behind him.

Overgrown branches hid the ladder from Leonardo's position, and as soon as Aleksander passed out of sight, Leonardo hurried across to Moth and Pinch.

"Bates told us you went to the Native camp," said Moth.

"The chief had a message for Aleksander...and me," said Leonardo.

Pinch straightened and Moth tossed the broken branch with the other deadfall.

"For you?" said Pinch.

"Let's go into the woods," said Leonardo.

They took one of the hunting trails out of camp, ducking under tall ferns and dodging arched, twisted roots. A giant, heavy-winged butterfly lifted off from a stump covered in bright red mushrooms. Leonardo paused as it flapped through the trees, wingbeats like billowing flags rustling the leaves and the underbrush. Big blue false eyes challenged the woods from the back of its wings, and Moth shuddered next to Leonardo.

"Those things creep me out," said Moth. "Butterflies shouldn't be that big."

"And moths shouldn't be such babies," said Pinch.

"Yeah?" Moth put his hands on his hips. "Well, pinches shouldn't be...shouldn't be...youknowwhat, just shut up."

"Come on," said Leonardo. He stepped around the mushroom-covered stump and led the way up the trail. The events at the Native camp spun around his mind, leaving no room for banter.

Moth and Pinch fell in behind him. Eventually, they stopped in a hollow overhung with more mushrooms, growing from the tree trunks overhead. These ones were a strange variety, extremely dry and filled with a fine dust. The younger boys liked to fire slingshots at them, sending up clouds of smoke. Holes pockmarked their ribbed undersides, and dozens of fallen pebbles lay nestled in the dead leaves and pine needles around the hollow.

Safely out of earshot from the camp, Leonardo described the encounter to them.

"It was really weird," he finished. "It was almost like—"

"The chief wants you to be the next leader," finished Moth.

"I don't know," said Leonardo. "I couldn't figure out *what* he wanted. He didn't like Aleksander, that was for sure."

"What do you think he meant, 'there will come a choice'?"

"Means he'll have to pick between something or the other," provided Pinch, plucking a piece of long grass and feeding it between his teeth.

"Thanks, smart-ass," said Moth.

"I think it has to do with ending the war," said Leonardo. "The chief said the Darkwoods can't continue on this path."

"You could do that as leader," said Moth. "Aleksander hasn't named a successor yet."

Pinch scoffed. "You really think—"

"He's not picking me," said Leonardo. "You didn't see the way he looked at me back there."

"Well he'd better pick someone quick," said Pinch. He spit out the grass stalk. "That tastes like shit."

"Where do you think he'll go?" asked Moth. "When he disappears, I mean. I know we've talked about it before, but if Aleksander is so afraid of it…"

Moth jumped at a noise in the trees behind him. A squirrel raced across a forked branch and leapt into the next tree.

"It can't be somewhere bad," said Leonardo. He could see that Aleksander's fear was making Moth afraid. "I don't think the woods mean us harm."

The shadows seemed a little darker than they'd been a moment ago, and he hesitated. A branch creaked somewhere behind all the foliage, slow and deliberate.

There's a new danger in the woods, the chief had said.

He said it was far away, thought Leonardo. *In some other corner of the woods.*

An icy breeze whispered through the hollow, making all three boys shiver. Leonardo wasn't so sure anymore.

He frowned as a dead branch swung overhead. The rest of the tree was dead too, and he tried to recall if it had been a few minutes ago. A lot of trees clustered around this hollow, but he thought he would've noticed such a big one being dead. It was a maple, sap dried on its trunk and its expansive canopy devoid of even a single leaf.

"I suppose that's true," said Moth. "The woods wouldn't send us somewhere bad."

Leonardo didn't hear him. He caught movement in the

bushes, big and slow. His nerves buzzed and the shadows looked even darker than before.

Then Cato's chubby face peered out through the leaves, completely oblivious to the blatancy of his hiding place.

"Get back, idiot," hissed Ajax's voice. "They'll see you."

Or we'll just hear you, thought Leonardo.

"What was that?" Pinch turned in a circle, hand on his sword.

"Probably just the wind," said Leonardo. He raised an eyebrow pointedly, and Moth's eyes widened. Pinch caught on a second later, distracted as he scanned the underbrush.

"Come on, let's get back to camp," said Leonardo, trying to keep it from sounding forced.

They filed out of the hollow. Pinch glanced over his shoulder and Leonardo kicked him in the shin.

He wondered how much they had heard.

***

Leonardo, Moth, and Pinch stepped into the clearing at the exact moment that Ajax and Cato slipped out of another trail, Ajax strolling with false nonchalance and Cato looking immediately toward them.

"Just act natural," Leonardo said to Moth and Pinch under his breath. He led the way to one of the cooking fires and crouched, stoking the embers with a stick.

"Who's on hunting duty today?" he asked Moth.

"Snout, Puck, and Robin, I think," said Moth.

"Right," said Leonardo. Across the clearing, Ajax and Cato lingered near one of the ladder trees, trying not to look obvious. They made a comical pair; Cato and his bulk, with blonde hair cut razor short, next to Ajax's lanky frame and long, flat, dark hair.

Listen all you want, thought Leonardo. *You're not going to learn anything else.*

It took another minute of pointless conversation between him, Moth, and Pinch for Ajax to come to the same conclusion. He said something to Cato, then they quickly left the clearing, disappearing through a stand of trees and up another hunting trail.

Leonardo held up a finger to Moth and Pinch. *Not yet.* They waited another minute, then the three boys jogged across the clearing.

They stopped at the edge of the trail and Moth opened his mouth to argue, but Leonardo and Pinch each held a finger to their lips. Leonardo stepped onto the trail, leaned around a mossy tree, and confirmed the path ahead was clear. A songbird let out a warning shriek and took flight as Leonardo crept up the trail, waving for Moth and Pinch to follow.

He knew Moth was itching with protest, but Leonardo kept his attention trained forward as he listened for the se-coms' voices. A few minutes up the trail, he heard them, hushed but carrying around the next bend. He held up his hands, warning Moth and Pinch, then carefully moved up to the big tree blocking his view.

He placed each foot with the utmost care, then pressed his back to the trunk and edged around just enough to make out their words.

"...and once he disappears, that bastard is going to put Leonardo in charge," said Ajax.

"What bastard?" asked Cato.

"The chief! Weren't you listening?"

"No."

"No?" said Ajax.

108

"I saw a bird," said Cato.

Leonardo closed his eyes, exasperated. *How does Ajax even work with him?*

"You...never mind." Ajax took a breath and let it out. "The point is, Tokala wants Leonardo to be the next leader. He can control him, and people will follow him since he's the idiot's brother."

"He's the chief's brother?" said Cato, shock in his voice.

"No, idiot," said Ajax. "Aleksander's brother."

"Oh."

Leonardo tilted his head, studying the pines across from him. *Control me? Why, because I'm weaker than Aleksander?*

"I want you to listen very closely," said Ajax.

"Ok," said Cato.

"Aleksander is going to disappear soon. Why else would the chief have told them all that?"

So you were listening for a while, thought Leonardo.

"When he disappears," continued Ajax, "I'm going to declare myself leader, and I have an even more important job for you."

"What is it?" asked Cato.

"Leonardo will argue. He'll try to steal my right as leader, and his little band of halfwits will stand with him. We can't have rebels in Raven Clan, so I'm going to name you my executioner."

"Your exit...?"

"Executioner. It means you get to kill anyone who stands against me."

Leonardo drew a sharp breath, and up the trail, Cato cracked his knuckles.

Leonardo stepped back from the tree, filled with horror. He

caught his foot on a root and nearly tripped, then stepped on an empty nutshell. It cracked under his boot.

Shit.

Up the trail, Ajax fell silent. Down the trail, Pinch swore.

"Who's there?" called Ajax.

Cato's heavy footsteps crunched the leaves and Leonardo took off. He, Moth, and Pinch tore down the trail, ferns whipping at their ankles as they ducked around corners. Leonardo jumped off a steep embankment, stumbling and staggering around the next bend.

They burst into the clearing, where Snout, Puck, and Robin were just returning from their hunt, toting rabbits and a big pheasant. A few other boys lingered around the clearing, shouting and jostling. They all looked up as Leonardo, Moth, and Pinch ran out between the trees.

Leonardo waved urgently for them to look away. He slowed to a walk, heaving for breath and trying to assume a casual gait. Moth and Pinch did the same, trying their best to blend in with Rugby, Will and Bates, who slowly returned to debating whether a bear or a shark would win in a fight.

"Definitely a bear," said Pinch loudly, as Cato and Ajax exploded into the clearing. "They can fight on land *and* in the water."

"Yeah, but sharks have more teeth," argued Bates.

Ajax narrowed his eyes and Leonardo turned away, holding his breath. Next to him, Moth coughed. Leonardo nudged him and they moved to a ladder, leaving Ajax and Cato in the clearing. Pinch stayed behind, now fully engrossed in the shark/bear argument.

Ajax can't become the next leader. Leonardo needed to talk to Aleksander.

And if he doesn't pick a successor? If he disappears and Ajax claims leadership?

Then I'll challenge him for it.

The alternatives frightened him too much to consider.

CHAPTER 14

T hat night, Leonardo, Moth, and Pinch took their regular clinker patrol. Leonardo looked out over the dark water as Moth rowed and Pinch reclined in the bow, both of them vague silhouettes in the blackness.

They checked the Fox Clan/Bear Clan fork first, then back-tracked up a long, narrow, and deeply shrouded stretch of river. The branches of massive, leaf-packed canopies met overhead, choking out the moon and any glimmer of starlight.

Frogs and night birds sung from the reeds, loud and invisible in the blackness, and a cool breeze whispered over the surface.

"Pinch, can you take your foot off my back?" said Moth.

"Why?"

"'Cause it hurts?" said Moth.

"So?"

"Guys," said Leonardo. "Let's focus."

Ajax and Cato had been on his mind all day. He couldn't relax, knowing Ajax's plan. *Executioner.* It sounded so harsh. And so purely Cato.

There's going to be a fight when Aleksander disappears. And it'll just be the start. As soon as Hawk, Fox, and Bear find out, they'll rip each other apart trying to get to us first.

Maybe Bear Clan will hold back. They do like to protect their 'friend-ships'. But they won't defend us. That would mean fighting their other 'friends'.

Behind him, cloth rustled as Moth twisted, followed by a thump.

"Ow!" said Pinch. "I would've moved it. Sheesh——" he suddenly cut off. "Boat!"

Leonardo spun around. At the end of the tree-tunnel, the river turned sharply to the left, down towards the fork. The canopy opened above the corner, and a beam of moonlight illuminated a longboat rounding the bend, oars churning down either flank. A second later, the sound of sloshing reached him and the clatter of oars rolling in oarlocks.

"Go!" Leonardo yelled at Moth, who was already hauling the oars back and leaning forward for another stroke.

At first Leonardo thought it was Bear Clan, then he caught the flash of orange on a shield and was even more surprised.

"It's Fox," said Pinch, half-standing in the bow.

"Get down," said Leonardo. "They might not have seen us yet."

"They're gaining," said Pinch.

"Obviously," snapped Moth. "You're heavy."

Leonardo glanced at Moth. "Switch with me," he said, already reaching for the splintered shafts. Moth relinquished the

113

middle bench, moving into the stern while Leonardo climbed over, fumbling in the dark. He dropped onto the bench and leaned forward, digging hard into the water.

They traveled light in the clinker; no leather armour, no cumbersome shields, and only a sword per person. He was grateful not to have the extra weight, but he felt virtually naked with the Fox boat on their tail. An enemy boat in Raven Clan territory, in the middle of the night, could only mean one thing: Fox Clan was finally making contact, and it wasn't to talk.

He didn't stop the Foxes from gaining—not even Cato could move enough water to do that—but he did slow their approach. And he kept their tiny clinker in front until Raven Clan's shale beach finally came into sight.

The Fox boat loomed just behind them now, bearing down with every sloshing, clattering stroke. Boys filled the benches, crammed together and shouting in very un-Fox-like behaviour. Pebbles flew from slingshots, splashing in the water around Leonardo's tiny patrol and thwacking against the stern of the clinker. A few found their mark, and Leonardo winced as one glanced off his knuckles on the oar handle.

Pinch had his own slingshot out and fired back while dodging shots at his head.

The point watchman stood in the bow, skinny and rat-faced like Ajax, but even more so, if that was possible.

"Is it just me," asked Leonardo between breaths, forcing the blades through the water, "or is Fox Clan bigger than the last time you saw them?"

"There must be thirty of them in that boat," said Pinch.

The last time he'd seen them in full force, in an attempted

attack on Raven Clan last year, Fox Clan were the smallest clan in the woods with barely twenty members.

Thirty. Raven Clan barely had that many. *How did they get so big?*

"Beach coming quick," said Moth.

Leonardo ran the boat right up onto the shale, the keel grinding into the rocks. They piled over the side and ran for the trail, where Strato—tonight's beach guard—was gone from his post. Leonardo hoped it was because he'd run at first sight of the Fox Clan longboat.

They tore down the trail and burst into the clearing. Leonardo looked up into the canopy and let out a relieved breath. A mass of boys gathered above the ladder and more ran over the bridges to join them. Aleksander was already halfway down, followed by Cato, a sword in each of their belts.

Leonardo, Moth and Pinch sprinted past Aleksander as he jumped to the dirt. There were half a dozen ladder trees scattered around the clearing, and they took the first empty one they reached. Pinch scrambled up, followed closely by Leonardo and Moth, who was puffing to keep up.

Something's wrong with this, thought Leonardo. They raced over a rope bridge and around a tree deck, onto another bridge.

That's why they've been hiding at the border, he realized. *So we wouldn't know how big they'd gotten.*

Leonardo followed Pinch into the armoury, grabbing a wooden shield from the wall and pulling on his leather vest. Moth burst in, staggering to the wall to grab a shield from the dwindling supplies.

Still, this attack is a bold move, he thought. *Even at night, no one's ever defeated us in open battle. Last time, at least they tried to be clever by sneaking in on foot.*

But that was over a year ago, and if the rumours were true, Fox Clan had a new leader now.

How did he gain members so quickly?

Clans only grew when the woods dropped new boys in their territory, and that didn't happen often. If their numbers were truly in the thirties now, that meant they'd been finding a new boy every four or five weeks.

Leonardo tied the last string on his leather vest and rushed outside, where the flames in the swinging lanterns burned tall and bright, the torches crackling with anticipation. Shouts filled the air and the clang of swords already rang through the trees below. Leonardo scrambled down the ladder and jumped the last few feet to the ground, drawing his sword as he hit the dirt and ran after the others.

The bushes rustled to the right of the trail and the rat-faced point watchman crashed into the clearing. Leonardo twisted and intercepted him, their swords ringing out. Leonardo took a swing that glanced off his shield, taking a chip out of the painted fox, and the boy slashed back. Leonardo blocked it and lunged again. They hacked at each other, fast and violent, until Rat Face took a wild swing at Leonardo's head. Leonardo ducked, then rammed his shield up into the Fox's body, throwing him back into Pinch, who slashed him two-handed across the back. The boy dropped, hitting the dirt with a thud.

Leonardo stepped back, breathing hard. The image of the sword coming at his head was still there when he blinked; cold and silver behind his eyelids.

Boys couldn't die in these woods, but instead vanished at the moment of a killing blow. Whether that was the same thing, Leonardo had no idea. All he knew was that he didn't want to find out.

"Go, I got him," said Pinch. He slid a coil of rope off his shoulder.

Leonardo shook himself out of it and ran for the trail while Pinch tied up prisoner number one. He'd drag him back near the ladder for Moth to guard.

Leonardo sprinted down the beach trail, to where a wall of Ravens battled attackers in the opening to the beach. Leonardo stopped a few feet back, looking around. Some Foxes had decided to try cutting through the trees instead, and Leonardo watched Cato chase one down in the moonlight. He slashed the runner across the back, his sword cracked against his leather padding, and the boy went sprawling in the underbrush. To Leonardo's horror, Cato stopped and raised his sword over his head.

"Cato!" yelled Leonardo.

Cato hesitated, sword suspended in midair.

"Prisoners!"

Cato squinted at him through the dark.

"Tie him up."

Cato kept staring at him.

"Pinch," said Leonardo as he ran up.

"Yes sir."

"Go tie up Cato's prisoner."

"Aye aye cap'n."

Pinch high-stepped through the underbrush, rope slung over his shoulder. Cato's eyes widened. He lowered his sword,

117

incredulous, as Pinch pushed in front of him and set to work tying up the Fox. He was Raven Clan's unofficial prisoner-collector. No one had ever escaped his knots. Cato, on the other hand, preferred a more violent approach to prisoner control. The huge boy was virtually a magician, with all the boys he'd made disappear.

He looked ready to take off Pinch's head for stealing his prize, but another Fox took his attention first and Cato barrelled off through the trees again.

Someone shouted as an attacker broke through the wall of Ravens, throwing Puck aside and sending him tumbling into the bushes. The boy was big and he came at Leonardo hard, rattling his shield with a massive swing. He had lost his own shield somewhere in the melee, and Leonardo tried to attack his exposed side. He missed and the Fox slammed him again, then again, with crushing blows that Leonardo barely got his shield in the way of.

Shit. Shit.

Shit.

Leonardo stumbled back and ducked under a slash, then took a swing that the Fox batted aside. Nearby, Puck detangled himself from the vines and came running as the Fox raised his arm to bring down another blow on Leonardo. Puck charged in first and drove his sword through a gap in the boy's padding. The Fox froze, sword suspended over Leonardo, then he vanished. His sword fell on Leonardo's shield, clattered, and rolled off, landing in the dirt at Leonardo's feet.

Puck fell forward at the sudden lack of resistance. He looked at Leonardo, eyes wide. "I didn't mean to do that."

"I'm glad you did," said Leonardo. There wasn't a drop of

blood on Puck's sword. Wherever the boy had gone, it was better than bashing Leonardo unconscious. For Leonardo, at least.

Leonardo rolled his shoulder, trying to get the numbness out of his arm.

"Come on," he said to Puck. "Let's finish this."

Fox Clan may've had equal numbers, but Raven Clan was a well-trained machine, and the inexperienced Foxes began crumbling, retreating backwards down the trail.

They never stood a chance, thought Leonardo, joining the mob as they walked the Foxes out onto the shale, hacking and slashing at orange-painted shields.

Their leader should've known that. Their odds weren't anywhere near enough to survive a head-on attack.

The fight spread out beside the river, and a Fox Clan boy came running through the lines, screaming at the top of his lungs. Leonardo awkwardly deflected his overhead cleave, then took a swing that forced the screamer back. The boy went silent, crouching low with his sword and shield extended like a ninja.

He was taller than Leonardo, with blonde hair that he'd tied back using a piece of string, and the strange appearance of a boy who'd aged faster than he should've. Leonardo had only seen a few like him, and they were an unsettling type; a mix of children's eyes and teenage bodies.

So the woods are giving Fox extra members and *accelerating their growth?*

Someone shouted nearby. The blonde kid glanced at the noise and Leonardo lunged. Blondie threw up his sword, blocking Leonardo's strike, and they slammed shields together, teeth rattling. Leonardo grunted as he pushed against the kid's shield, swords crossed over their heads. The pebbles shifted beneath them and both boys scrabbled for footing. The Fox spit in his face and Leonardo flinched, staggering back. Momentum brought Blondie with him and Leonardo gritted his teeth, digging his heels into the shale and forcing them into a deadlock. He blinked hard, trying to clear his vision.

The kid shifted and his sword screeched, sliding up Leonardo's blade.

Shit.

Leonardo pushed harder, grinding the metal together.

Another shout distracted the kid and Leonardo ducked out. His combatant fell forward and Leonardo whipped his shield around, slamming the edge into the back of his head.

The kid dropped instantly, blood welling up through his blonde hair. For a second, Leonardo thought he'd swung too hard, but to his relief, the boy didn't disappear. Leonardo sagged, exhausted.

"Leo!" shouted Puck. "Look out!"

Leonardo looked up as another Fox ran at him. But before he could get within reach, Pinch tackled him from the side, completely blindsiding him. They slammed into the ground, Pinch's hat flew off, and they rolled. The Fox came out on top, punching Pinch in the jaw. Pinch rolled away from his second blow and the Fox's fist slammed into the shale. Pinch threw him off, scrambling on top and throwing two punches before he could react, then two more, before the Fox could grab onto his wrists. It was a weak effort, and a moment later Pinch had fought free and wrestled him onto his stomach, shoving his knee into the kid's back.

Muffled curses came from under him and Pinch pushed on

the back of his head, pressing the Fox's mouth into the gravel. He glanced over at Leonardo, grinned and gave a clumsy salute, then picked up his hat and jammed it back on his head.

It was at that exact moment that Aleksander strode up. He frowned at Pinch.

"Fight's over," he said to Leonardo. "All the Foxes that weren't captured have surrendered."

"They surrendered?" asked Leonardo. Clan boys didn't surrender. They were far too proud for it.

"Correct," said Aleksander. He nodded at the blonde kid, still unconscious and bleeding all over the rocks. "Someone clean that idiot up and get him with the other prisoners. Drag him if necessary."

"You," he added, kicking the Fox under Pinch's knee. "Get up and surrender. Tie his hands first," he said to Leonardo, then spun on his heel and walked away, sword swinging at his hip.

CHAPTER 15

All of the Fox Clan members were gathered and lined up in front of their boat. Aleksander strode toward Leonardo, hands behind his back as he crossed in front of them. A victorious general on show for his prisoners.

"Where is your boat?" he demanded, stopping in front of Leonardo.

"What?"

"Your clinker," said Aleksander. "Did you swim here?"

"Oh," Leonardo looked down the beach. It was nowhere to be seen. "We didn't have time to tie it up."

"So you beached it."

"Yes."

"Then why is it not on the beach?" Aleksander's voice rang out at its maximum level of insufferability. Even his broken moral compass wasn't warped enough to justify killing the twenty remaining Foxes, so keeping up impressions was now priority number one. And Leonardo knew Aleksander's paranoia wouldn't take well to their prisoners witnessing the kind of incompetence that lost a boat.

Raven Clan's reputation was on trial, and Leonardo was in the hot seat.

"It must've floated away," said Leonardo. He didn't feel like playing along.

"Or it was taken," said Aleksander. He paced back toward the Foxes. Somehow, the accusation still seemed pointed at Leonardo, even as Aleksander strode away from him, surveying the battered ranks.

"Who is your leader?" asked Aleksander.

"I am," said an Asian kid in a bloodstained shirt. He looked fifteen-ish, with longish black hair and a boldish expression on his face. He was a very '-ish' sort of boy; not quite this and not quite that.

"What's your name?" demanded Aleksander.

"Hero," said the boy.

Aleksander crunched across the shale and stopped in front of him. "That's a big name," said Aleksander.

"I run a big clan," countered Hero.

"*Ran* a big clan," corrected Aleksander. "You lost a third of your members."

The tied-up Foxes hung their heads. Most of them would've lost friends, maybe siblings, in the battle. Leonardo and Aleksander weren't the only set of brothers in the woods.

"What did they expect?" asked Pinch under his breath. "Did they think they'd beat us?"

"I don't know," said Leonardo quietly. "Maybe they over-estimated their advantage."

Meanwhile, Hero shook his head. "We'll grow again," he told Aleksander. "The woods have been giving us new members ever since the last time we attacked you."

"Why?" asked Moth quietly, joining Leonardo and Pinch.

Leonardo didn't answer. His mind replayed Chief Tokala's words; *Such things have consequences. If you continue to resist, more damage will follow.*

He wondered if this could be what Tokala referred to. If the woods stacked the other clans with new members, Raven Clan would be outnumbered at every corner.

"Fox Clan has been passive too long," Hero continued. Defiance radiated off of him, from his bound wrists to the lock of sweaty hair across his forehead. "It's time we made our name in these woods. That's why we attacked you."

Aleksander tilted his head, and Leonardo realized he was smiling.

"I don't believe you," said Aleksander.

Hero frowned, and so did Leonardo.

"I'm going to ask you a simple question," said Aleksander. "And I want a simple answer."

"I think I already answered it," said Hero. He shifted in his bindings, confidence wavering for the first time.

Aleksander didn't respond.

"Ok, you win," said Hero. "Why the attack? Why now? I'll give you an answer, but it's not simple."

Aleksander remained silent for a few seconds. He stood a head taller than Hero, and his wavy hair hid most of his expression from Leonardo.

"Did you steal our clinker?" he finally asked.

Hero looked surprised. Leonardo wasn't. Aleksander liked to change the pattern of interrogation to keep people on edge. He'd done it many times to Leonardo. He'd return to the subject of the attack once he gained everything he could from this.

"No," said Hero. "How could we? We're all here."

"Are you?" asked Aleksander. "One Fox could've stolen the boat and we'd never know they're missing."

"We didn't steal your boat," said Hero, and Leonardo believed him. Weakening Fox's force—even by one boy—seemed too brash even for a leader like Hero.

Aleksander wasn't so quick to buy it. "We'll find out," he said, then he left Hero and walked back to Leonardo.

"Go find the boat."

"Right now?" Leonardo wanted to hear the rest of the interrogation.

"Yes, right now," said Aleksander. "There's another clinker right there. If you can manage to hold onto that one, take it and go find the other one."

"I'll need help to bring it back."

"Then take help. But get out of here. Even if they didn't steal it, if it gets over the waterfall, you've just given Fox a new clinker."

Leonardo glanced at all the Foxes standing on the beach, tied up and stranded.

Aleksander read his mind. "If you try to navigate the streams below that waterfall, we'll have to send another patrol to find *you*."

"So if it's in their territory, you want me to leave it."

"I want you back on this beach with two boats."

"But you just said——"

"Build one! I don't care!"

Leonardo nodded. When Aleksander got like this, there was no point arguing with him.

"And be quick about it. Ajax," he called, marching back up the beach. "Get these idiots moved into the clearing. We'll finish the interrogation in camp."

***

Leonardo rowed while Pinch scanned the riverbank.

"You know, it could have gone to Bear Clan too, depending which fork it took," said Pinch.

"True."

"They might give it back. They're pretty stupid."

"They're not *that* stupid," said Leonardo. The rusty oarlock stuck and he jerked it back into motion.

"All they care about is peace," said Pinch. "And friendship."

"You make them sound like six-year-old girls."

"That's not my fault."

"Bear Clan only cares about their 'friends' until it suits them not to," said Leonardo.

Something splashed into the river nearby, drawing both boys' attention.

"Muskrat," said Pinch.

A small dark head piloted out of the reeds, the surface rippling in its wake.

"Peace isn't a bad thing," said Leonardo. "If we didn't have

126

to spend so much time preparing to fight, we could explore. Find out what this place really is."

"Good luck," said Pinch. "The exploring stopped when your brother became leader and started a war with the entire Darkwoods." He chuckled ironically. "And after tonight, I don't see it ending any time soon."

They lapsed into silence. Leonardo listened to the slosh-clunk of his oars.

"What's the point in fighting if we're not doing it for peace?" Leonardo asked finally. "Are we just going to keep battering each other until we disappear?"

Pinch shrugged, reaching overboard to pull a stick out of the water. "It's worked so far."

"It just seems pointless," said Leonardo. "There has to be more than this."

"Croc," said Pinch, pointing to a spiny shape in a beam of moonlight, then he threw his stick at it.

They found the clinker caught on some rocks just before the fork. At first it looked ok, but when they got closer, they realized that one of the rocks had driven straight through the soft boards. The only reason it hadn't sunk was that it still sat impaled on the rock, water swirling around in the footwell.

"Well," said Pinch. "Fuck."

I want you back on this beach with two boats.

Aleksander was in for a disappointment. And Leonardo would face the consequences.

"If we take it off the rock, it's going straight to the bottom," said Leonardo, thinking aloud.

"We leave it then?" asked Pinch.

Leonardo shook his head. This jumble of rocks was in plain view of the Bear Clan border.

"If there's even a chance Bear Clan could steal this boat, Aleksander will skin us alive."

He shipped his oars and grabbed the edge of the damaged clinker. "So we sink it."

Pinch raised an eyebrow, then he nodded slowly. A grin spread across his face.

Leonardo sighed, imagining punishments. There was a bee-hive up one of the game trails. Aleksander liked the fresh honey sometimes, and he'd sent Leonardo to collect it more than once in response to infractions. If not that, he might be tasked with chasing out the family of badgers which had recently moved into their territory. Either way, Leonardo faced a painful day tomorrow.

Pinch would get off free—Leonardo formed a big enough target to distract Aleksander from any other offending parties. Pinch took hold of the damaged clinker with delight, oblivious to all of this and simply excited to sink the boat.

"On three," said Leonardo. "One...two...now!"

They shoved the near side down, lifting the boat off the rock, then Leonardo pushed it out into open water. The clinker responded sluggishly, water flooding up through the hole. It twisted in the current and started down towards the Bear border, filling up to the edge, then it slipped under the surface and out of sight.

Pinch took off his tricorn hat in mock solidarity. A pirate and a sunken ship.

Leonardo took hold of the oars again and pushed off from the rocks, wondering how many bee-stings he'd get this time.

When they got back to camp, everyone had moved into the clearing and Aleksander relieved the Foxes of all their weapons, shields, leather armour, and even their boots. They sat in a circle around one of the bigger tree trunks, tied together and bound at the ankles.

Leonardo and Pinch paused at the edge of the clearing, but Aleksander spotted them instantly.

"Well?" he demanded, sword swinging at his hip as he crossed towards them.

"We found it," said Leonardo. "But it hit a rock and sunk."

He left out a few unnecessary details.

Aleksander narrowed his eyes.

"The river isn't deep there," said Leonardo. "You'll be able to see it. I can show you tomorrow."

"Either way, the boat is lost," said Aleksander, curt and unforgiving. "I have an interrogation to finish. I'll expect you in my quarters tomorrow morning."

Great. Delayed sentences were the worst kind. They gave Aleksander time to think it through and perfect the punishment.

Aleksander marched away, shoulders squared and long legs striding over the hard-packed dirt. He commanded the clearing, and the Foxes looked apprehensive as he approached.

Leonardo wished he could eavesdrop. Whatever Hero hadn't told them on the beach, Aleksander was certain to root it out now. He briefly considered looping around through the woods and trying to get close enough to hear, but if Aleksander caught him...

You're in enough trouble already.

Leonardo followed Pinch to the ladder. Something else was at play, he could feel it, and he'd be sleeping with one eye open tonight.

CHAPTER 16

The next morning, Aleksander summoned Leonardo to his quarters again. He sat behind his desk, rolling a pebble under his hand.

"Sit," he said when Leonardo stepped through the curtain. "I need to talk to you about Pinch."

"Pinch?"

Maybe I won't be taking the punishment alone after all.

Aleksander rolled the pebble under his palm as Leonardo crossed the room and took a seat. It was one of his representative stones, each for a member of the clan. The rest were scattered in groups and lines across the table.

For a long minute, the only sound was the scraping of the pebble against the slate, as Aleksander watched Leonardo watch him. Finally, Aleksander scooped up the pebble and threw it at Leonardo.

It hit him in the chest and dropped to his lap.

Leonardo flinched. "What the hell?"

"Now give it back."

Leonardo stared at him. "Are you ins—"

"Give it back."

Leonardo picked up the rock and tossed it on the table.

Aleksander promptly threw it back him.

Leonardo ducked. The rock flew past his head and hit the floor, bouncing and skittering to the far wall.

"Go get it."

Leonardo looked at him, incredulous. "No."

Aleksander sighed. "That's Pinch's rock."

"Ok?"

"And every time I have it in my hand, it comes flying back at you."

Leonardo stared at him. "You've lost your mind."

"I should be throwing Moth's rock at you too, but at least he's smart enough to know who his real leader is. Usually."

"You think I'm trying to be leader?"

"According to that rock, you are." Aleksander pointed to Pinch's rock laying on the floorboards.

You're insane.

"I promote you to point watch," said Aleksander. "I promote you to patrol commander. And this is what I get for it."

"What are you talking about?" asked Leonardo.

"Tell me," Aleksander waved around at the room. "What's the point of all this?"

"This room?"

"The woods. Everything. Boys show up here, waste their

childhood trying to figure out where the hell they are, then vanish without a trace. You want to know the answer?" Aleksander stared him in the eye. "There is no point."

Leonardo frowned. *Waste their childhood? Is that how he feels?*

"The only purpose is if we create purpose," said Aleksander. "Lion Clan went down as the greatest clan of all time. Why? Because they conquered the Cove and ruled it. I've been trying to do that here since the day I set foot on the bank, but I've failed."

Leonardo opened his mouth but Aleksander cut him off.

"I won a lot of battles, but I never conquered. For a time, I was foolish enough to think you could carry on my legacy, finish what I've always been on the verge of starting, and turn Raven Clan into a greater power than Lion Clan ever was. I named you after them for Christ's sake."

Leonardo stared at him. *Named me after them?*

"The chief told you there would be a choice," continued Aleksander. "That choice will destroy the legacy I've spent my life building. Did you know that?"

Destroy the legacy…?

"How do you know that?" asked Leonardo.

"Because I know the chief," said Aleksander. "He speaks in riddles, but they're not hard to solve."

"But what if I don't make his choice? I could carry on your legacy."

Leonardo wasn't even sure why he said that. He didn't want to become Aleksander. He didn't want to conquer. But his brother stared at him with such intensity, such disappointment.

"I know you, Leonardo," said Aleksander. "I know what choice you'll make."

It could've been a tender moment, but the bitterness in Aleksander's voice soured it.

"Which is why you can never be leader," he continued. "And I have to deal with the problem of your patrol."

"My patrol?"

"Yes. I will not allow my clan to have divided loyalties. Last night, Cato was dealing with a prisoner when Pinch intervened. On your orders."

"Cato was—"

"I don't care."

"He was—"

"Cato is a se-com." Aleksander brought his fist down on the desk. The rocks wobbled. "He outranks you and Pinch both."

"He was about to kill a Fox." Leonardo shoved himself out of his chair.

"I'm changing your patrol members," said Aleksander, still seated.

"What?"

Aleksander reached out and straightened a few of the rocks, a bizarre calm falling over him. "Last night, Hero told me that we have a traitor in our midst."

His blue eyes glinted at Leonardo, searching.

Leonardo paused, one hand on the back of his chair. "What?"

"Apparently, a Raven went to Fox Clan's camp several weeks ago. He told Hero that if Fox Clan could kill me, Raven Clan would be theirs."

"That's ridiculous!" said Leonardo. "No Raven would ever join Fox. Who told him this?"

"He refuses to say. But he will," Aleksander added, his tone dark. "Apparently, this nameless Raven claims to have enough power to turn most of my clan to Hero's side. All he asks for in return is my death."

Leonardo shook his head. "How did they even get to Fox Clan? Someone would've noticed if a clinker was missing."

Even as he said it, Leonardo remembered his own late-night escapade. No one had missed the clinker then.

"This was several weeks ago," said Aleksander. "The clinkers were still back in the weeds."

Right. It could've been gone all night and no one would've known.

Shit.

"Do you think someone borrowed a clinker?" asked Aleksander, sliding a few rocks into a different pile.

Leonardo stopped, realizing the insinuation. "You don't think it's me, do you?"

Aleksander glanced up, his expression neutral.

"You're joking," said Leonardo. "*No.* It's not me. And it's not Moth or Pinch either, if that's your next question."

"Then who? Offer a name."

"Ajax." It came out before Leonardo could think. "I heard him talking to Cato yesterday—"

"Ajax." Aleksander smiled sceptically. "I highly doubt it's one of my own se-coms."

"But you'd suspect your own brother?"

The smile slid off Aleksander's face, replaced by cold distrust.

"I don't believe this." Leonardo shoved his chair into the desk and walked to the door.

"I can't trust you," said Aleksander. "I can't trust anyone until we find the traitor." He slid a rock across the desk, paused, then slid it into a different pile. "I need your eyes on the water, you're sharper than most of these halfwits, but Moth and Pinch's loyalty to you is dangerous. Report for midday patrol in two hours. And notify Cato and Puck that they'll be joining you."

"Cato?"

"Dismissed."

"You're joking."

"*Dismissed.*"

"I'm not the traitor," said Leonardo. "What if it's Cato? *Or Ajax*? Are you changing *his* patrol?"

"Do I need to dismiss you a third time?" asked Aleksander.

"This is ridiculous." Leonardo bent and picked up Pinch's stone. "Here." He threw it at Aleksander. It hit a pile of rocks, scattering them across the dark slate.

***

It was raining again, but Leonardo didn't feel it. He grabbed his practice sword from the armoury and climbed the slick ladder rungs to the ground, dropping and crossing to the edge of the clearing. He shoved through the branches, pushing deeper into the woods until he found an old tree with raven heads carved around its ancient trunk. Names were etched into the wood below each carving, representing all of Raven Clan's past leaders.

Leonardo took his sword in both hands and swung it at Aleksander's raven. The blade flew toward the carving, then Leonardo adjusted at the last second and his sword slammed into the wood above it. It stuck in the trunk, an inch over the raven's head.

Leonardo yanked it out. The carving's beady eyes mocked him.

He stood before the tree, breathing heavy, sword in hand.

There's a traitor in camp.

The reality hit him for the first time and Leonardo's anger began to dissipate, replaced by horror. He backed up, sliding his sword into his belt and running for the clearing.

Moth and Pinch were inside their treehouse quarters when Leonardo threw aside the curtain. Moth lounged in Pinch's hat, Pinch scowling at him.

"You like my hat?" asked Moth. "I think I'll go after his sleeping spot next, mine is—"

He faltered, seeing Leonardo's expression. "What's happening?"

"There's a traitor," said Leonardo. He relayed the details, missing some and backtracking.

"Who would do that?" demanded Moth.

"I bet it was Ajax," said Pinch.

Leonardo had thought the same thing, but now, hearing Pinch say it, he realized they were wrong.

"Ajax wants to be leader," said Leonardo. "Why would he give Raven Clan to Fox?"

"Maybe he lied to them," said Pinch.

"For what purpose? Aleksander is going to disappear soon anyway. He doesn't need to gamble with Fox Clan to get rid of him. Whoever did this wants to destroy Raven Clan."

"Why Fox?" asked Moth. "Hawk are better fighters, and Bear is bigger."

Leonardo had thought of that too. "No Raven—no matter how disloyal—would ever work with Hawk. There's just as much chance Gallus would kill them as listen to them. And Bear is too self-preserving. Lance would never take the risk. Hero, on the other hand, is a new leader eager to prove himself. The woods keep giving him new members and he wants to establish Fox as a superpower."

"That actually makes sense," said Moth.

"I bet it was Robin," said Pinch. "I've never trusted red-heads."

"Let's stop throwing accusations and actually think about this," said Leonardo. "Who would be cunning enough to do something like this?"

The rope bridge creaked outside.

All three boys froze.

Leonardo placed a hand on his sword as Strato stepped through the curtain.

"Oh, hey…" Strato trailed off. "What's going on?"

"Where have you been?" asked Pinch, his voice loaded with suspicion. "The past few weeks?"

"Um…" Strato frowned. "Here…? You've seen me."

"Nowhere else?" asked Pinch.

"Well, on patrol, I guess. Am I in trouble? Did Bates tell you something?" he asked, looking to Leonardo and Moth. "Because he's the one who broke it. I swear I didn't even touch it."

Leonardo released a breath. Whatever Strato and Bates broke, he doubted it had anything to do with Fox Clan.

But can we trust him?

Moth nodded ever so slightly to Leonardo, on the same line of thought. Meanwhile, Pinch continued to eye Strato warily, arms crossed.

Strato didn't do it, thought Leonardo. Strato was loyal. *Immature. Loud.* But loyal.

Leonardo drew a breath. "There's a traitor in camp."

He explained the situation a second time. Strato's reaction confirmed everything he already knew.

"Holy shit." Strato paced to the back wall. He snapped back. "Why is no one guarding the Foxes?"

"Nym is," said Moth.

"And Nym's not a suspect?" demanded Strato.

Nym wasn't at the top of Leonardo's suspect list, but he stepped towards the curtain anyway. "Let's go."

Outside and down below, the Foxes still sat in their ring, tied up around the tree. Nym sat on the low branch of a nearby tree, guarding them. A few of the Foxes had their heads tipped back, and Leonardo followed their gaze up to Aleksander's treehouse in the highest branches.

Aleksander stood against the rail, attention fixed on the makeshift prison tree.

"I don't think we need to worry," said Leonardo.

"Then let's go somewhere we can talk about this," said Strato. Leonardo wasn't used to seeing him so serious. "It's too easy to eavesdrop here."

They climbed to the ground and crossed the clearing to one of the game trails that led out of camp. Aleksander's eyes burned into Leonardo's back the whole way.

They passed Jack, staying out of the rain near one of the cooking fires.

He gave a two fingered salute, his clay-spiked hair entirely unaffected by the weather.

"Jack disappears all the time," said Pinch under his breath. "He should be a suspect."

"Is that your third or fourth accusation?" asked Moth.

Leonardo ducked under a giant fern, dodging a stream of water and thinking about Jack as he led the way up the trail. Jack was eccentric, that was for certain. But a traitor? Leonardo found it hard to picture.

"I just think it's suspicious," said Pinch.

"He disappears with Page," said Strato. "No mystery there."

"But Pinch is right," said Moth. "We can't cross him off the list. Everyone is guilty until proven innocent."

"How do we prove anyone innocent?" asked Leonardo. The trail got steep around the next bend, but thick roots grew like a staircase, curled with tiny sprouts. "The timeframe is too loose for alibis to mean anything."

"I suppose Aleksander is innocent," said Moth. "And we know we all are."

"*Is* Aleksander?" countered Strato. "He could've planned the whole thing for all we know."

"Planned his own assassination," said Pinch. "Right. Great thinking, Strato."

"I'm serious," said Strato. "The whole story could be a lie."

"For what gain?" asked Leonardo.

"I don't know. But we can't take it out of the equation." Leonardo sighed. He was right.

How have we gained more suspects?

They stopped in the same hollow where Leonardo, Moth, and Pinch had spoken yesterday, overgrown with giant red-capped mushrooms. The rain drummed on them like umbrellas high above, and the four boys took shelter on the dry soil below.

"What about Snout?" suggested Strato.

"He is a loner," agreed Leonardo.

"And he's always had a chip on his shoulder," said Moth.

"Idiot's name is 'Snout'," said Pinch. "He probably did it just to get a new name. Fox is clearly more generous with those than we are."

"Right," said Strato, "How does one even get the name 'Hero'."

"Maybe he did something heroic," said Moth.

"When he showed up?"

"You thought you were Superman when you showed up," said Leonard to Strato. "We could've called you Hero."

"And then he told us his name was Bob," said Pinch. "And Frank, and Joe, and Mohamed, and Stephanie—that one was odd—and Huang Fu…"

"Ok," said Leonardo, at the same time that Strato gave Pinch the finger. "Let's stay focused," he continued. "We need to figure out where Snout is. If he is the traitor, we can't let him anywhere near the prisoners."

Before any of them could say another word, footsteps sprinted up the trail and Nym rounded the bend, up the root-stairs.

"There you are!" he said, dodging around a puddle and jogging to a stop. "Aleksander just called a clan meeting."

CHAPTER 17

All of Raven Clan stood in the clearing, under the relative dryness of the thick canopy. Since it hadn't been a true clearing for many years, the branches grew dense together overhead, shielding the cooking fires and the cluster of boys from most of the rain.

"Where have you been?" demanded Aleksander when Leonardo, Moth, Pinch, and Strato joined the group. His eyes burned with paranoia.

"We…" Leonardo glanced at Snout. He stood between Bates and Rugby, the same mixture of confusion and wariness on his face as everyone else's.

"What's going on?" asked Puck.

Nearby, the Foxes perked up. They listened intently, tied-up in their circle around the tree.

"We were discussing the…" Leonardo trailed off.

Aleksander nodded.

"The what?" asked Robin.

"Raven Clan, there is a traitor in our midst," said Aleksander. He paced in front of them. "A Raven conspired with Fox Clan in an attempt to destroy us."

"What?" asked Jack.

"Who?" demanded Robin.

Voices rose in an outraged jumble of shouts and accusations. Sweat gleamed on the back of Aleksander's neck.

What is he afraid of? wondered Leonardo. *People knowing that a Raven targeted him personally, or knowing that there's an option to switch sides?*

"If anyone would like to put forward a name," said Aleksander, his voice cutting over them. "I'm listening."

He continued to pace before the group, analyzing each of their faces, his strategist's mind visibly working through the possibilities.

Leonardo examined Snout sidelong. He certainly looked baffled, but maybe he was a good actor. Leonardo didn't know him very well.

For a moment, no one spoke, then Rugby cleared his throat. "Yesterday, Bates bet me I couldn't climb a tree with my eyes closed. I could," he added proudly, "but when I got down, he was gone. I couldn't find him anywhere."

"I was hiding! It was a joke," said Bates. "Don't drag me into this."

"How about Pinch?" said Ajax. "When we went hunting for the lion...er, *bear*, he intentionally separated himself from the group. After you clearly told us not to. Then the Fox spy shows up. Seems suspicious to me."

"Shut up," snapped Pinch. "Leo got separated too."

Leonardo knew it wasn't meant to be an accusation, but all eyes shifted to him.

"Leo is the one who found the spy," said Puck. "Why would he…" He trailed off, realizing how suspicious that sounded.

"Snout didn't do a raven call last time we were at the Fox border," said Bates.

"I swallowed a bug, halfwit," Snout retorted.

"Enough," said Aleksander. "I will give the traitor until sundown to reveal himself. After that, we will begin interrogations. In the meantime, I'm going to have another chat with Hero. Dismissed. Leonardo, the rain is slowing. You'll take your first patrol now."

Right. Leonardo hadn't told Moth and Pinch yet. Or Puck and Cato.

He pulled Moth and Pinch aside as the gathering dispersed. They picked their way over fallen twigs and around a stand of skunk cabbage between the trunks.

"Aleksander disbanded our patrol," said Leonardo.

"What?" Both boys stopped in their tracks.

"Why?" asked Moth.

"Why do you think?"

If they didn't find the traitor soon, Aleksander and his paranoia would rip Raven Clan apart. *Which*, he realized, *is exactly what Fox and the traitor want.*

CHAPTER 18

The one upside to everything was that Aleksander seemed to have forgotten about the lost clinker. Or more likely, he'd just pushed it aside in the looming shadow of the traitor.

Either way, Leonardo's new patrol served as punishment enough. It was still technically his patrol, but se-com outranked patrol commander, so Cato felt no obligation to even reply when spoken to; an immovable weight in the stern that neither rowed, spoke, or helped look for threats.

Puck wasn't bad. Bossy. But not bad. Leonardo had no idea which of the three of them was actually in charge of the patrol.

Back in camp, the tension made everyone suspicious and irritable. The rumour mill spun at high efficiency, and by the end of the day, there was a case against everyone, and everyone denied it vehemently. Puck told Leonardo that Bates caught Strato sneaking out of camp a week earlier. Then Bates claimed Rugby was the one who caught Strato, and Rugby said it was actually Jack. Jack said he caught Bates sneaking out, not Strato, and by then, Robin was telling people that Snout was the prime suspect. Leonardo had yet to come up with a better suspect, but neither could he entirely justify a motive.

At one point, Cato cornered Leonardo on the trail to the smaller clearing and pressed a finger to his chest.

"I think you did it," he grunted.

"Yeah?" said Leonardo.

"Mm-hm."

"Well, I didn't," said Leonardo.

"Liar," said Cato. "You're a bigger liar than..." he paused, thinking. "...a big liar."

Leonardo raised an eyebrow.

"Admit you did it," said Cato.

"But if I'm a liar," said Leonardo, "then wouldn't admitting it mean I'm not guilty? Since I would be lying about admitting it?"

Cato frowned.

"And if I were to lie about admitting it, then I must be innocent. So it can't be me," said Leonardo. He left Cato standing puzzled on the trail. That dilemma would keep him occupied for a while.

Meanwhile, Aleksander paced the camp, searching for needles of motive in the haystack of accusations. Being Aleksander, he found dozens. The interrogations began at sundown, and Leonardo was relieved to get back on the water, even if it was with Cato.

Puck manned the oars, and when they reached the big bend, Leonardo glanced towards the rocks.

Empty again.

He examined the twilit bank, the canopy gently rustling overhead. *Where did you go?*

He was just turning forward again when something moved in the trees. Leonardo snapped back to the bank. Movement again, back in the shadows, but the height looked right, and—

"What the…" Cato shifted in the stern. "Who's she?"

"Who?" Leonardo pretended not to see.

"The girl, stupid. Go over there," he grunted at Puck.

"Now?" said Puck.

"No," said Leonardo before he could think. "Don't."

"Shut up," said Cato.

"Actually, I agree with Leo," said Puck. "It could be dangerous. What would Aleksander say?"

Cato grabbed the bulwark, rocking the boat as he leaned forward. Leonardo couldn't tell if he'd accepted their logic or was just distracted.

"*Keep rowing,*" he mouthed at Puck.

Cato leered at the bank, heavy brow furrowed. Leonardo tilted his head, watching the girl. She was staring straight at him.

Do you know something about the traitor? The thought hit him so suddenly that he almost voiced it aloud. He needed to get back here tonight. While she was still out. If he could get away from camp in the next hour…

Leonardo switched spots with Puck a short time later, rowing extra hard to get them through the rest of the patrol and back to camp. Darkness had long set in by the time they returned to the beach.

"You go ahead without me," said Leonardo, as they walked toward Nym and the trail back to camp. "I have to talk to Nym for a minute."

Puck and Cato carried on, and Nym straightened on the low branch where he sat.

"What's up?"

Leonardo waited until the boys were out of earshot, around the first bend, then he took a breath.

"I need to use the boat again, and you can't tell Aleksander."

"What?" Nym slid to the ground. "Why?"

"I can't tell you," said Leonardo.

He trusted Nym, but there were a hundred things that could go wrong with telling him. Nym could say it's not worth it and forbid Leonardo from going, or he could get suspicious, decide his duty was more important, and tell Aleksander. Or even let something slip by accident if Aleksander came down to the beach while Leonardo was gone.

"I know you took the boat before," said Nym. "Three nights ago."

Leonardo's mind lurched to a stop.

He was awake.

Shit.

"Look," said Leonardo. "I know it seems suspicious but—"

"I don't think you're the traitor." Wariness permeated his words. "But if Aleksander finds out I let you go, after everything..."

148

"I'm trying to help the clan," said Leonardo. "I might be able to figure out who the traitor is."

Nym chewed his lip.

"I'm going that way," said Leonardo, pointing upriver. Fox Clan's camp lay downstream. "I promise you—"

"Are you going to the Natives?"

"I…"

"Go," said Nym. He drew an anxious breath. "But be quick; I don't know what I'll say if he comes out here and finds the boat gone."

"Thank you," said Leonardo.

He rushed down the beach and climbed into the clinker, then worked out into the current and started rowing. He made twice the headway without Cato and Puck on board and quickly came upon the bend. Clouds of fireflies swarmed over the water, blinking like tiny stars over the real ones reflected in the river.

Leonardo took a long breath. *Are you sure you know what you're doing?*

No, he most certainly did not.

Leonardo rowed around the bend and caught his breath. A dark silhouette stood on the rocks.

He swallowed. *Here we go. Don't waste your chance.*

He needed to be quick. Aleksander rarely took long to realize someone was missing.

He drew another breath and rowed over to the rocks. As soon as he pulled alongside, the girl stepped out of the shadows, bronze skin painted silver in the moonlight. She blinked at him with dark eyes, carefully picking her way down to the water's edge.

Leonardo dried his palms and half-rose out of the boat. Being this close set his nerves spinning on end.

Her dress was made of a tawny hide, strung with tiny blue and white beads. It looked softer than anything the clan boys wore. She stopped on the rocks, studying him.

"Hi," said the girl.

"Um, hi…" said Leonardo. He glanced up at the tree line, with a brief thought that this could be some kind of trap.

"No one's coming," said the girl. "They're all asleep. I think."

"You think?" asked Leonardo.

She frowned. Her accent reminded him of Dakota and Tokala's, but brighter, intertwined with the river and the ferns, rather than the dark rasp of the ancient woods.

"Here." She took a step toward the boat, then paused, glancing at him. She looked over her shoulder, chewing her lip, then she nodded to herself and stepped down to the lowest rock.

Leonardo jumped up to offer his hand and the clinker almost tipped over. He dropped, grabbing an oar handle for balance and almost falling again when it gave out under his weight, the blade-end swinging up wildly. The girl jumped back and the wooden hull banged against the rocks, sloshing water near her feet. Leonardo swore and used an oar to steady the boat, gripping the bulwark for balance. When the rocking stopped, he glanced up and realized she was giggling.

Leonardo's cheeks heated up and he cleared his throat.

The girl composed herself and crouched down on the rock.

"Hold it steady," she said, then sat and swung her legs into the stern, sliding into the boat and onto Cato's seat.

"There." She folded her hands in her lap, her knees inches from his.

Leonardo's heart already pounded from the near boat-flip, and he swallowed, forcing himself to say something.

"I'm Leonardo," he said. "Leo."

"I'm Viola," said the girl. "There's a spot up the river." She pointed. "We can talk there."

***

The spot was an oak tree on top of a steep rise in the bank, its arching roots pushing back the surrounding trees and protruding through the face of the bank. Leonardo tied the clinker to a root that overhung the water and climbed up to the weedy grass on top, then turned to help Viola, but she'd already grabbed another root and pulled herself up. She straightened on the lip of the bank, brushed the dirt off her dress, and picked her way to a U-shaped branch that almost touched the ground. Leonardo dusted off his hands and followed her.

The tree was so ancient that these low branches brushed the earth, suspended like big, corkscrewed logs. Leonardo climbed onto the branch across from her, looking up into the canopy and thousands of leaves, dwarfed by the massive branches and parting to reveal an edge of the moon, less than full now, but just as bright as it had been the night of the lion hunt.

"You came back," said the girl. Viola. She tilted her head, studying him again. Her eyes shone a deep brown, like the darkest trees in the woods.

"No one knows I'm gone," said Leonardo. "If I'm not back soon, they'll come looking for me."

A timer raced down in the back of his mind. *Hurry up.*

"I thought you might be trying to tell me something," continued Leonardo. "Warn us...or..."

Her face went grave. "There's going to be an attack."

"You mean Fox Clan?" asked Leonardo. *She doesn't know it's happened yet.*

She nodded, bunching her dress in her fingers. "I'm not supposed to tell you. We're not allowed to interfere with the Lost Boys."

"Lost Boys?"

"Is that not what you call yourselves?" she asked.

"No."

"Oh." Viola sat back, examining him anew.

"The attack already happened," said Leonardo. "Last night—"

"No." She let go of the bunched material. "That was just a diversion."

"What?" His stomach dropped.

"The other two clans are going to attack you." Her fingers shook and she pressed them against the tree branch. "I'm really not supposed to tell you this."

"Both of them?" Leonardo's mind spun. Then he realized something. "They'll free Fox. They'll bring extra weapons."

Three clans have never joined forces.

We need to get the prisoners into the treetops. Somewhere that Hawk and Bear can't reach them.

"When?" he asked.

"Tonight," said Viola. "After midnight."

That gave him about an hour to get back and warn everyone.

Viola swallowed anxiously.

There's more, realized Leonardo.

"What else?" He itched to leap up and run to the boat, but he needed to know everything.

She took a breath, spinning a bead on her dress between her fingers.

"Chief Tokala planned it."

Leonardo stared at her.

"Your leader won't leave the woods," said Viola defensively. "He's holding on too tightly. All the war in the Darkwoods is because of him. He needs to leave before it can stop."

"And killing all of Raven Clan with him is the solution?" demanded Leonardo. "I thought you were supposed to be some sort of guardians."

"Your leader brought this on himself," countered Viola, fiercer than he expected. "If you step aside, they won't attack you."

If she believed that, she clearly hadn't met Gallus and the other clan leaders.

"How did Tokala even get three clans to work together?" he asked. The clans he knew would've ripped each other apart after three seconds.

"He promised to tell them where they came from," said Viola. "And what this place is."

He promised them…

No wonder they're working together.

"He lied, though," she added. "We're leaving. We'll be gone by the time they come looking for the answers. But it's for the greater good."

"Why are you telling me this?" he asked.

"I…" she hesitated, kneading her hands together. "I've been watching you."

"Me?"

"Your clan," she said, meeting his eye unashamedly. "You row past every day, and we're not allowed to talk to you, and I guess I've always just wondered what you're like, the Lost Boys. Where you live, what you do."

"Have long have you been watching us?"

She shrugged. *Long enough.*

"I've never seen you," said Leonardo.

"I'm good at hiding. I only started coming out on the rocks when I heard about the plan. I don't know the other Lost Boys, just your group. When I found out they were going to attack you…"

"You decided to warn us."

She nodded. Then she started twisting another bead.

Shit. There's more.

"I should've said this earlier," she cleared her throat. "They're already in your territory."

"*What?*" Leonardo jumped off the branch.

"During the battle last night, the other two clans sailed across your borders. Their boats should be hiding right now in a feeder stream near your camp."

"They've been there all day?" Leonardo's horror grew like an oil spill, spreading bigger and blacker every second.

"They've been moving into position all day, surrounding your camp…"

"While we were distracted," finished Leonardo. "Looking for

the traitor." All at once, the remainder of the oil flooded out in one realization. "There is no traitor, is there?"

Viola slid off the branch in front of him. "Tokala needed something to keep you all in camp. The lie was an easy way to do that. He planned the whole thing with my older brother, Dakota. Dakota met in the Backwaters with the Lost Boys and told them what to do, then he told me everything."

"In the what?"

"The Backwaters. There's a whole system of rivers and lakes behind these trees." She pointed behind her. "It ties into this river up beyond the Tree Cliffs and down past the fork."

Everyone's territory but ours.

If Aleksander hadn't forced them to spend their entire lives inside their territory, Leonardo would've known about that. His brother had always stressed that the other clans would swoop in the moment Raven Clan weakened its force by sending a party down the river. He'd accepted the logic, but their lack of knowledge was hurting them now.

Raven Clan, being the central territory, had always held the illusion of controlling contact between the clans. If they never let anyone cross their borders, the clans wouldn't even have the chance to conspire. Now with the revelation of the Backwaters, Leonardo realized how incorrect that belief was.

He realized something else, and he swore at himself for not seeing it sooner.

"Gallus won't have the patience to wait until midnight," said Leonardo. "He'll rush the attack, even if Ravens are still awake."

"Are you sure?"

Leonardo may not have known the woods like she did, but he knew its clans.

"Positive," said Leonardo, already ducking under branches and scrambling down to the clinker. Viola followed on his heels.

When they reached the flat rocks, Viola barely let him slow the boat before jumping up onto the wet stone. She landed with a poise that showed she'd grown up in these woods as much as he had.

"Good luck," she called as he rowed away.

"Thank you," called Leonardo. "For everything."

The weight of the night pressed down on him, dark and foreboding. Viola's silhouette stood atop the rocks, watching him go.

CHAPTER 19

L eonardo slowed the clinker as he approached camp. Something moved in the trees and he paused, oar suspended over the water.

A shadow darted between two rocks.

I'm too late.

He scanned the beach. Nym still sat at his watchman's post, and the Fox boat hadn't arrived yet. Nym raised a hand in greeting. Leonardo held his breath.

Ok. There was still time, but the woods hung in a delicate balance. If he rushed in to warn everyone, he could startle the ambushers into attacking early. Even bringing the boat ashore could spook them.

Leonardo dipped his oar into the water and began to turn the clinker, aware that more eyes than just Nym's followed him. He pointed the prow upriver and backtracked around the first bend, out of sight. He moved as far along the bank as he dared, boots pressed so hard into the boards that his heels might bruise, then he guided the boat into a muddy alcove and jumped out, scrambling up the bank.

Any further and it would take him too long to walk back to camp. Even starting from this far was pushing it, but he didn't want to risk coming ashore near an intruder.

Of course, that risk never went away, but he surmised that the further he got from camp, the less likely that would become. The gamble paid off, and Leonardo found himself alone in the trees.

He ducked low and began to creep through the underbrush. He knew these game trails inside out and near-sprinted over them in the pitch black of the woods. There was a reason they called it the Darkwoods, and it was nights like this, when the canopy completely blocked out the moon.

As he neared camp again, something moved in the bushes to his left. He slowed, peering into the leaves. A branch rustled somewhere behind. Pine needles crunched under a heavy footstep.

Shit.

Leonardo's nerves coiled themselves as tightly as his muscles, tense and flooded with adrenaline. He placed a hand on his sword.

A crash somewhere in the distance. A rustle in the direction of the first noise. He squeezed his fingers on the leather grip. A pine bow swung gently where it had been disturbed.

Leonardo slid his sword from his belt and stepped off the trail and into the trees.

Quietly. Slower.

It took all of his effort not to run.

Checking over his shoulder, he moved around a tangle of blackberries and down a sloped bank. He kept low, pausing every dozen steps to listen. The leaves hung utterly still, and every whisper of a breeze made him jump.

All of his senses amplified as he abandoned the trail. The smell of the earth permeated everything, and Leonardo's footsteps crunched through the ground-fall, tinting the air with the scent of crushed pine needles.

A flurry of noise overhead, but it was only a squirrel. It took a flying leap to the next tree and raced out of sight. Leonardo released his breath and started forward again, only to freeze around the next turn when he came across a shape laying in a small hollow, ten paces ahead.

A boy lay on his stomach, facing the other way. Leonardo checked behind him and moved back a distance, crouching down to watch from behind a nest of roots.

The boy was geared for war, with a sword, slingshot, and knife, leather armour, and a wooden shield propped in front of him.

As Leonardo watched, another boy appeared in the hollow, said something to the boy on the ground, and vanished back into the trees. The other boy picked up his shield and slipped after him. There was a bear painted across it.

Leonardo stepped out and started after him.

CHAPTER 20

L eonardo saw intruders everywhere. The closer he got to camp, the more frequent they became; glimpses of a shirt sleeve through the brambles, fresh footprints in the dirt, a snatch of whispered conversation.

Leonardo barely breathed.

He skirted around three more intruders in a stand of trees, then followed a slope down in the direction of camp.

He lowered himself down an embankment into a dry ravine. Moss covered a jumble of rocks that looked like they hadn't been touched for a hundred years. The roots of giant pines snaked out of the far bank.

Leonardo picked his way across, looking up at the vast bows that swayed overhead. These were the type of pines that grew on top of the Tree Cliffs at the Hawk Clan border. He grabbed the first root and scrabbled up the bank, rolling onto a mossy ledge.

He pushed himself up, wiping his hands on his legs. Pinecones the length of his forearm lay fallen in the dead needles, like the spiky eggs of some giant bird that Leonardo never wanted to encounter. He stepped around one and climbed over an arching root before he was stopped again, this time by a boy stepping into the open fifty yards in front of him. Leonardo ducked for cover. The boy carried his shield at his side, angled back enough that the hawk there was clearly visible.

Three clans. Tokala knew about it. Hell, he planned it. So did Dakota, when he led us to Tokala's tipi. Gallus probably knew about it when he told us at the border to stop worrying about Fox Clan. The Fox spy we lost in our territory was certainly involved, probably planning out hiding places.

The entire Darkwoods had ganged up on Raven Clan. Even the woods itself, according to Hero, had swelled tiny Fox Clan until they barely all fit in their boat.

And they lied to us. All of them.

It angered him. It scared him. But more than anything, it lit a fire in his blood. Leonardo wanted to defeat every last soul who thought they could flip the tables on him and his clan.

He waited until the boy was gone, then ran across the open ground into the dense bush where they had hunted for the lion. He needed to get back to camp, end the 'traitor' pandemonium, and warn everyone about the attack.

Ten minutes later, Leonardo pushed through the last of the bushes and stopped just out of sight, hidden in the shadows under a giant fern. The empty rope bridges swung in a slight breeze. The lanterns flickered in the treetops, and the cooking fires burned around the clearing, warding off animals in the night. The Foxes sat roped around the tree, awaiting their rescue. Cato sat on a stump nearby, guarding them, but even he wouldn't stand a chance against two full clans.

It was like the moment before a storm hit, when the whole world hung in static-charged suspense.

A twig snapped nearby, drawing Leonardo's attention to the dense line of trees and underbrush that encircled the camp. In that moment, he knew they were completely surrounded.

Before he could take a step toward the ladder, footsteps came pounding up the trail from the beach. Ajax burst out into the clearing, Nym a few seconds behind him, and sprinted to the nearest ladder. He didn't see Leonardo, and Leonardo took a breath to shout out, then he stopped.

There could be an attacker on the other side of this fern.

Ajax reached the top of his ladder and raced over the rope bridge toward the ladder to Aleksander's quarters in the highest tree.

Nym tore after him, shouting something that Leonardo couldn't make out from the ground. That was fine, Leonardo could guess the situation well enough; Ajax had come out on the beach and found the clinker missing, along with Leonardo.

Ajax reached the ladder and scaled it, then took off for Aleksander's quarters. Nym struggled after him, clearly arguing or trying to explain.

Leonardo realized this was his chance to move, while all the attackers stared up at Nym. He took a breath and raced out of the bushes. His hands slammed against the ladder rungs, vibrating with adrenaline. He expected the slingshots to start flying any second, but the Hawks and Bears held their fire as he climbed.

What are they waiting for?

Leonardo pulled himself up onto a deck platform and scrambled to his feet. A branch creaked high above and he looked up as Aleksander pounded down the ladder rungs, Ajax and Nym above him, and Bates following them, saved from his interrogation.

Boys emerged from their treehouses, woken by the noise.

"Get your weapons!" yelled Leonardo. "We're under attack!"

He ran for the armoury and shoved through the curtain, grabbing a shield off the wall as Moth, Puck, and Strato stumbled in.

"It's an ambush," said Leonardo, yanking on a leather vest. "Hawk and Bear have us surrounded."

The boys stopped, shields half lifted off the wall.

"Hawk *and* Bear?" asked Moth.

Leonardo nodded. "Plus Fox, once they free them. The Natives orchestrated the whole thing."

"What?" demanded Strato.

"How do you know that?" asked Puck.

"Later," said Leonardo. He took a step toward the door. "Oh, and there's no traitor. It's all a lie."

"What?" said Strato.

"Does Aleksander know?" asked Moth.

"No," said Leonardo. "I'm going now. Tell the others. Don't let them go down the ladders."

Leonardo rushed back outside. All of Raven Clan was awake now, running along the rope bridges.

Aleksander marched across one bridge, Ajax, Nym, and Bates in his wake, and Leonardo sprinted to meet them.

"It's an ambush," he shouted.

Aleksander frowned. "Ajax," he said over his shoulder. "I thought you told me Leonardo was missing."

"He was, I swear," said Ajax. He glared at Leonardo, as if he'd reappeared just to spite him. Nym let out a breath behind them, relieved. He and Leonardo were both in the hot seat.

Leonardo relayed the details of the attack a second time.

Aleksander's eyes went dark. "How do you know this?"

"I…" There wasn't time for lies. "I met the Native girl. The one from the bank. She told me—"

"You did *what?*"

"She told me that about the attack. The Natives are trying to get rid of you. Chief Tokala organized the whole thing."

Aleksander's eyes widened. The same fear he'd shown in front of the chief played through them.

"He promised he would explain the secrets of the woods to them," said Leonardo. "But he lied. The Natives are going to leave before they get the chance."

"RAVEN CLAN!" shouted Aleksander, his voice like a whip over the shouts and boots on bridges. "NO ONE LEAVES THE TREETOPS!"

He stepped around Leonardo, striding up to the armoury platform.

"FORTIFY THE LADDER PLATFORMS. NO ONE—"

A shout split the air below and the sound of five dozen slingshots whisked through the leaves.

"GET DOWN!" shouted Leonardo. He threw himself to the boards, flinching as pebbles clipped off his elbow, his head, his back.

Hundreds of pebbles rattled against the boards, and boys shouted out in pain. Below, both clans crashed the clearing, flooding out around the beach path and the entire perimeter of camp.

They fired as they ran, pelting the treetops with a reverse rain of flying pebbles. The Foxes were freed in seconds and joined the Hawks and Bears sprinting for the ladders, painted shields swinging at their sides. Leonardo rolled, angling his own black raven shield at the shooters as he jumped to his feet.

Pebbles clicked off it as he ran, hunched over. One deflected off the back of his head. Leonardo ducked, swearing. Another drilled him in the ankle.

Leonardo stumbled, half-diving onto a ladder platform. A Fox started to pulled himself up and Leonardo stomped on his fingers. The boy cried out, let go, and a pair of stray pebbles hit him in the head.

The Fox started down, climbing faster than he'd come up.

Pinch ran onto Leonardo's platform, leaning over the rail. It looked like he was counting.

"All three?" he asked.

"All three," said Leonardo.

"We're outnumbered four-to-one," said Pinch.

"I think it's even more," said Leonardo, flinching back as a pebble flew past him.

The chaos up top was as bad as down below. The rope bridges swung wildly, Ravens shouted, and the thwack of slingshot pebbles peppered the underside of the boards.

Moth, Puck, Robin, and Will joined Leonardo and Pinch on their platform.

Good. He liked to have Moth and Pinch nearby during fights.

Moth was entirely helpless with a sword, and Pinch was so reckless that Leonardo didn't know which of them to worry about more.

Another pebble whisked past Leonardo's head and he leaned over the rail to see a group of Bears aiming at him.

"Put your shields around the edge," said Leonardo, ducking to his knees and propping his shield against the rail. The other five boys did the same, creating a wall. There were holes, but it gave them something to hide behind, and a steady stream of shots popped against the wood.

More flew through the ladder hole in the centre of the platform, whizzing past into the treetops. The boys crouched well back from it.

Pinch grabbed a few of the loose pebbles that landed on the boards and fired them back through the opening. A barrage rattled the platform in response. Pinch stumbled back, clutching his hand.

"Be careful," said Leonardo.

"How many stones do they *have?*" demanded Robin.

"Not as many as us," said Bates, running up behind them. He dropped one of the pebble baskets from the armoury on their platform, then ducked and ran across the bridge to the next ladder, lugging three more baskets.

"Hell yeah," said Pinch. He pulled out his slingshot. "Have a taste of this, halfwits."

He grabbed a handful of pebbles and started firing down the hole, dodging the return fire.

Robin had a slingshot too, and he joined Pinch. Will started grabbing stones and throwing them through gaps in the shields, and Leonardo followed suit.

By the time they'd half-depleted the basket, the incoming fire had mostly dropped off, and only perimeter shots thwacked off the shields.

"Hold up," said Moth. "We shouldn't use all of our ammo."

Leonardo nodded. Pinch paused with a rock drawn, fired anyway, then tossed the slingshot near what was left of the stone pile.

"Ok, so now what?"

"We wait for Aleksander," said Leonardo.

Pinch groaned. "That's your plan? Wait?"

"What's Aleksander waiting for?" asked Puck.

"I don't know," said Leonardo. "Be patient."

Easier said than done. He peered over the shield wall at the army of boys below, talking in fast voices and eyeing the treetops.

"So Hawk Clan, Fox Clan, and Bear Clan are all attacking us?" asked Robin.

Leonardo nodded.

"Has that ever happened before?"

"Not that I've heard of," said Leonardo.

Robin's response was cut off by Aleksander's voice ringing out over the clearing.

"WHERE IS GALLUS?"

Here we go.

Leonardo half rose to see him.

Aleksander stood in the centre of the rope bridge, over the highest concentration of attackers. Ajax stood off his shoulder, regarding the clearing in his best Aleksander-impression.

"Right here." Gallus rolled the 'R' as he stepped out into the open. "How did you know I was the mastermind behind this?"

Mastermind?

"Lucky guess," said Aleksander.

"Didn't you say the Natives planned it?" whispered Moth. "Does Aleksander know?"

"Yes," said Leonardo. "He's playing into Gallus's ego."

And it was working, though Leonardo wasn't sure to what gain.

"Here, meet my friends," said Gallus.

Lance, the leader of Bear Clan, moved to join him, followed by Hero. Hero's bravado was dwarfed next to Gallus, who's arrogance filled half the clearing by itself. Lance alone appeared nervous. He was tall like Aleksander, but blonde, with an instantly dislikable face—astoundingly fake and so stiff that it threatened to crack. He wore an ill-fitting brown shirt, with the same snags and unpatched holes as every time Leonardo saw him. He shuffled his feet, eyes darting. Bear Clan had long sustained the idea that they wanted friends over enemies.

Well, thought Leonardo. *They can't say that anymore.*

"You think that three clans will be enough to take down Raven Clan?" asked Aleksander.

"Oh I know it," said Gallus. "You know why?"

"Why?"

"It's all up here." Gallus tapped his head. "Inside the melon."

"Indeed," said Aleksander.

"I got an idea," said Gallus, grand as a showman. Hero frowned at him, and Lance tilted his head. They knew the truth even better than Leonardo. "Three clans stand together, defeat the bully of the woods—that's you," he added to Aleksander. "And then the rest of us can live in peace. Hero and Fox Clan were eager to prove themselves. I gave them the noble job of creating a diversion."

"The sacrificial lamb," said Aleksander. "And yet you stand again. I commend you."

"We outnumber you by at least four to one," said Hero. He looked depleted; twenty-four hours of capture hadn't treated him well, but he spoke with defiance. "Have you trained your Clan for anything like that? Did you ever expect the entire Darkwoods would turn on you?"

Aleksander smiled. "I began to prepare for that before you ever set foot in these woods."

Really? Leonardo frowned. *Like what?*

Hero faltered, then he recovered. "Did those preparations involve allowing traitors in your clan?"

Aleksander smiled bigger. "You actually thought I believed that?"

"He didn't?" asked Will.

"There's no traitor," said Leonardo. "I just told him."

"How do you know?" asked Robin.

"Trust me," said Leonardo. "I'll explain after." He didn't want to miss anything.

Down in the clearing, Gallus grinned, cocky. "He's bluffing," he assured Hero. He glanced up at Aleksander. "Afraid of what the melon cooked up this time. And what it cooked up is a choice: an ultimatum, really."

He held up a chubby finger, addressing all of the Ravens on the ladder platforms. "Option one: you hand over your leader. We are not unkind. We will allow you to dissolve into the other clans, if you promise no funny business." He added a second finger.

"Option two: we grab some sticks from those fire pits and burn your camp to the ground."

Whispers filled the treetops, panicked and urgent.

"We have to go down and fight them," said Puck. "They'll burn us alive."

"What about—"

"No one's handing over Aleksander," said Leonardo, cutting off Will. "Even if anyone tried to; he, Cato, and Ajax would put up too big of a fight. If we start fighting each other, we're just doing their job for them." He nodded to the Hawks, Bears, and Foxes below, swords gleaming in the moonlight.

Finally, Aleksander spoke again. "May I converse with my se-coms?"

"Of course. But the choice is for your entire clan." Gallus smirked, crossing his arms and watching Aleksander and Ajax step together. Cato lumbered over from a nearby ladder platform. Then Aleksander looked across at Leonardo.

Leonardo frowned.

"What the—" started Pinch.

"I'll be right back," said Leonardo. He stepped out onto the bridge. It creaked under him, overloud in the watchful silence of four clans.

Ajax glared at him, hissing a question under his breath at Aleksander. Aleksander ignored him.

"Listen and don't talk," he said quietly as Leonardo reached him. "I have a contingency in place, but I can't get to it without alerting our enemies. I need you to go instead."

"Him?" demanded Ajax. "Why?"

Me?

"The location is secret," said Aleksander. "It has been passed down from leader to leader since the beginning of Raven Clan."

"But..." Now Leonardo was truly confused. "You said yesterday..."

"You'd never be leader?" said Aleksander. "I was testing you. After Fox Clan's attack, I guessed something like this would come, and that I might not be able to get to the contingency. I needed to give someone else the location."

"What are you talking about?"

That was a test? And I passed?

In the clearing below, a Fox shouted something crude, then a dozen Ravens responded from the treetops.

"Listen to me," said Aleksander. "Remember the rock I told you was Pinch's?"

The one you threw at me? Leonardo nodded.

"It's not Pinch's," said Aleksander. "I want you to do what I did with it, but vertically."

Throw it?

Leonardo had no idea why Aleksander insisted on speaking in riddles right now. Aleksander hated riddles. He'd made that very clear at the Native camp.

Aleksander worded the next part carefully, an eye on Ajax. "Then go where I put it the second time and..." he paused, visualizing. "Move three toward me."

He doesn't want Ajax to understand, realized Leonardo. *He's making sure his own se-com could never find this 'secret contingency', yet he's telling me, the one person he hates more than anything.*

It made no sense at all.

And neither did the riddle. *Move three toward me. Three what?*

171

"Go," said Aleksander. "Take a torch down. Light them all."

"Down?" said Leonardo. "I don't know what you're—"

"Figure it out," snapped Aleksander. Catcalls flew back and forth from the ground and the trees. "I have work to do."

"Time's up, Aleksander," called Gallus. "Let's get this show a-moving."

CHAPTER 21

Leonardo moved along the rope bridges, trying to keep the urgency from his pace.

"I have a few questions," said Aleksander, back on the central bridge. "Before we surrender."

Moth, Pinch, and the others looked for an explanation when Leonardo approached them, but he shook his head.

"Be ready," was all he said. What for, he had no idea.

He stepped around Moth and started across the next bridge.

"Tell me, Gallus, Hero, Lance," said Aleksander. "After you defeat us, how do you plan to divide our territory?"

"Why do *you* care?" asked Gallus.

"I'm just curious," said Aleksander. "The river forks down to Bear and Fox. Hero and Lance can each claim the hundred yards down to their borders—maybe fifty on the Bear side—but they'll find a tough decision where the forks meet. One will have to stop there, unless they plan on sharing the rest of the river."

Silence.

Leonardo passed into the leafier branches, where the canopy hid him from the clearing. Safely out of sight, he abandoned his casual pace and ran.

"And then there's Hawk," said Aleksander. "Have you asked how much Gallus is planning to take? Maybe you won't have to worry about who gets the fork after all. I suppose that's the easiest solution, Gallus takes three-quarters of our territory, and you each get the eighth down your end of the fork."

"Quit stalling," called Gallus. "You're just wasting everyone's time."

Leonardo wished he could see the other leaders' reactions. Hero was still new enough that standing up to Gallus would seem intimidating, but Lance on the other hand... Leonardo guessed Aleksander's words were starting to find their mark. He cared just enough about his self-interests for the doubts to take root.

"Gallus deserves more territory," said Aleksander. "He did orchestrate the whole plan, after all."

More silence.

Leonardo reached the ladder to Aleksander's quarters and started up.

"Or...wait," said Aleksander. "He's lying about that, isn't he? I forgot"—his tone said he very much had not forgotten—"it was Chief Tokala who planned everything, wasn't it?"

"How do you know that?" asked Hero.

"The same way I know that he lied to you when he promised to share the secrets of the woods. He and all the Natives will be gone before you get the chance to claim your reward for killing me."

Leonardo reached the top of the ladder and climbed onto the deck.

He grinned despite himself. Aleksander had just flipped the entire situation so that Hawk Clan and their allies seemed like the ones being played. He was trying to drive a wedge between them.

And if it doesn't work? Leonardo wished he knew the plan. Or at least his part of it.

He ducked through the curtain and rushed to Aleksander's slate desk on its twin stumps. The thirty or so Raven Clan stones sat grouped into lines and clusters, surrounded by about eighty black, brown, and orange pebbles.

Leonardo stopped, frozen by the eery accuracy of it.

Aleksander knew this was coming. He predicted the attack.

Then Leonardo spotted the smooth black rock that Aleksander had thrown at him. It sat in the exact centre of the 'Raven Clan' stones. Seeing it now, he realized it looked completely different than the other representative stones.

He told me it was Pinch's so I wouldn't suspect anything, but I'd be able to recognize it later. He wondered if that explained Aleksander's throwing it at him. So he'd remember it.

Leonardo picked up the pebble, smooth and heavy for its size.

He wondered at the implications, the *consequences*, of learning the secret. If only Raven Clan leaders could know it, then Leonardo would have to become successor.

Then Leonardo had a dark thought. *What happens if he changes his mind?* Aleksander sent Leonardo because he had to. He couldn't leave without alerting Gallus, so he'd been forced to incidentally name a successor. If they survived the battle and he decided Leonardo wasn't worthy after all…

Leonardo shook his head. His clan was in danger and he needed to act, regardless of the consequences.

Leonardo eyed the stone.

Do what I did with it, but vertically.

That could only mean one thing. Leonardo tossed the stone up in the air, unsure exactly what this would achieve.

He opened his palm to catch it, but instead of the black stone, a brass key landed on his hand. Leonardo stared at it.

Scrolls of fine metalwork curled along the shaft of the key and in the big circular thumb piece.

How…?

Leonardo looked around for the stone, knowing the whole time that he wouldn't find it. He'd experienced the magic of the woods before, but never this directly.

Outside and far below, someone shouted, then someone else shouted louder. Leonardo snapped back to the urgency of the moment.

What did Aleksander say to do next?

Go where I put it the second time…

The second time, he'd thrown it past Leonardo, against the far wall.

Leonardo remembered the exact spot where he'd picked it up. He'd been angry about the accusations, and he'd thrown it back at Aleksander before storming out.

Leonardo went to the floorboard and knelt down, examining the old wood for a keyhole. Then he remembered the third instruction; *move three toward me.*

Three boards. Aleksander was sitting at his desk yesterday, so…

Leonardo shifted to the correct board. Immediately, he spotted a knot in the wood and reached his finger inside. He found a catch, which released the entire board. Excitement jolted though his fingertips. He lifted it away, revealing the top of a hatch door.

The next board came up easily now, and the one after it, until the hatch was completely exposed. A keyhole gleamed next to the handle, and Leonardo slid the key in, fingers shaking with adrenaline. The shouts outside grew louder.

The lock clicked and he slipped the key into his pocket, then pulled the hatch open. The smell of raw wood filled the air. Underneath, a circular passage led straight down what had to be the centre of the tree, hollowed out, with ladder rungs nailed to the interior of the trunk.

Leonardo leaned over the opening, peering into the darkness.

All the times he'd been up here, and he'd never known. It seemed impossible; the key, the hatch, the tunnel. He had no idea.

Take a torch down, Aleksander had said.

Leonardo jumped to his feet and rushed back outside, where a pair of torches burned in the night, lodged in slots on the rail. He surveyed the clearing below, visible through a gap in the branches. Gallus, Lance, and Hero appeared to be arguing, while their armies began to size each other up. Hawks, Foxes, and Bears shuffled apart, swords and shields raised a fraction.

Aleksander's stalling was working. But for how long?

Leonardo pulled out a torch and ran back inside.

He didn't hesitate, flipping around and starting down the rungs, holding the torch in his left hand. Claustrophobia clamped around him inside the tree, and a few of the nailed rungs wobbled when he stepped on them, but Leonardo kept descending. He tried not to think about the fact that this was the tallest tree in the clearing, and the fall would be a long one.

The torch crackled above him, throwing shadows on the smooth wood.

He wondered who carved it out. *It must've taken ages.*

His breaths echoed in the hollow trunk, and the smell of wood hung heavy and rich. He took extreme care to hold the torch way from the sides. Lighting the tree on fire was the last thing he needed right now.

When Leonardo finally reached the bottom, his back slick with sweat and muscles protesting, he found himself in an underground cavern, with dirt walls and a ceiling of thick roots.

He switched the torch to his other hand and rotated his shoulder. He shone the light around the space, taken aback by the size of it. Passages split off from the main chamber, snaking away into the dark.

These caves must span the entire clearing.

Voices echoed down one of the tunnels and Leonardo frowned, holding the torch ahead of him as he pushed into the darkness.

He found a smaller chamber with a fire pit in the centre, surrounded by a circle of big stones, the wood already arranged and ready to burn. A rope dangled directly above it, tied to a bundle of plants and rope half-exposed in the dirt ceiling. The roots of another tree arched across the far end of the chamber, letting in a few slivers of moonlight through mouse holes in what would be the base of the trunk, high above.

Hero's voice carried down through the openings.

"...but Gallus, you're guaranteed territory no matter what. Lance, can we talk about the fork?"

It felt strange, being 'under' enemy lines. His clanmates were high above, and Leonardo was alone, a few meters below an army of clan boys.

"We'll make a compromise," said Lance. "We're all friends, yes?"

"But there is no compromise," said Hero. "The forks split from one river. My clan risked a lot in this attack. Both attacks. We deserve the extra territory."

He's more tenacious than I gave him credit for, thought Leonardo.

"But our fork is shorter," said Lance, his tone falsely amicable. "Why would my clan risk their lives for fifty yards of territory?"

While he listened, Leonardo examined the rope and the bundle in the ceiling. It didn't look like an escape route, instead, it appeared as though the rope was intended to catch fire once the stack of wood below was lit.

Why?

He held up the torch to better see the bundle half-buried in the dirt ceiling.

"You won't need to risk your lives," said Gallus. There was some concern in his voice for the first time. "They're surrendering."

"Oh, did I say that?" asked Aleksander, his voice distant from the treetops. "My mistake."

Sticks, leaves, and mushrooms made up the bundle, bound tightly with rope. Leonardo recognized the red caps of the

179

mushrooms from the forest hollow, the ones that the younger boys fired slingshots at to release clouds of smoke.

These ones had clearly been here a long time, but if anything, it just would've made them drier, the fine powder inside more volatile.

The plan slowly came into focus.

The branches and leaves looked to be from eucalyptus trees, rare to find in the Darkwoods, but Aleksander had to have chosen them for a reason.

Up above, the leaders continued arguing. "Who cares about territory?" tried Gallus. "The Native Chief—"

"Tokala lied," interrupted Hero.

"So says Aleksander," countered Gallus.

"You think he's lying about the lie?" said Lance. "Come on, Gallus. Why would the Natives suddenly tell us everything? This makes far more sense."

"But—"

"Bear Clan has been friendly with Raven Clan for a long time," said Lance. "Without the promise of information, I see no gain in destroying them. And I'm not interested in a new territory war with Fox Clan."

Leonardo remembered that Aleksander was waiting on him. The whole clan waited on him, they just didn't know it. He ran down the next tunnel, just far enough to see another fire pit and another bundle in the ceiling.

"But the plan!" Gallus sounded desperate now.

"If the Natives want Raven Clan to burn, they can do it themselves," said Lance. "Bear Clan, with me."

Bits of dirt rained down from the ceiling as half of the boys in the clearing marched out, following Lance down the trail to the beach. Leonardo checked the fourth and fifth chambers, then returned to the first one.

The caverns may have been an ancient secret, but the smoke bombs had his brother's name written all over them. If the mushrooms did what Leonardo expected, the entire cavern system would fill with a thick, impenetrable fog as soon as the fire reached them. And thanks to the mouse holes, that fog would come spewing into the clearing a few seconds later, blanketing their attackers' vision and allowing Raven Clan to descend the ladders.

This is what he meant, when he said he'd been preparing.

"Even without Bear, we have your ladders surrounded," shouted Gallus. "Surrender, or we'll burn you up there."

Show time.

Aleksander's last instructions played through Leonardo's mind.

Light them all.

The idea of starting fires on the ceiling, so close to the tree roots, made him hesitate, but he had to trust Aleksander's planning. Leonardo took a breath and held the torch to the fire pit. The dry wood caught immediately and he rushed into the next chamber.

This had better work.

Leonardo lit all five fires, then tossed the torch in with the last one and ran out to the main chamber, under the tallest tree.

A strange sense of pride raced up his chest. Clan pride or brotherly pride, he wasn't sure, but all he wanted to do was get topside. The other clans thought they were in for an easy victory, but Aleksander, Leonardo, and Raven Clan were about to prove them wrong.

The genius of the fire pits was that they created a delay, allowing him to escape before the bundles burst into smoke. None of the ropes had even caught yet, but the flames grew taller and he knew it was only a matter time.

Leonardo scaled the ladder rungs inside the tree and pulled himself up into Aleksander's quarters. He kicked the hatch shut, but left the floorboards scattered as he rushed outside and descended the ladder to the rope bridges.

He found Aleksander, Gallus, and Hero no further along in their argument. Aleksander's ability to stall ranked alongside his prowess as a battle commander. And a bomb maker.

"…you really thought you could walk into our camp and burn it down?" asked Aleksander. "Put down that torch, or we'll be forced to attack."

"You think I'm afraid of a bunch of Ravens in a tree?"

"You should be," said Aleksander.

Leonardo rejoined Moth, Pinch, Puck, Will, and Robin on his ladder platform.

"Where have you been?" hissed Pinch. "Bear left. Aleksander literally talked them out of the fight."

"I know," said Leonardo, breathless. "Listen, you all need to be ready. Aleksander built smoke bombs out of mushrooms and eucalyptus branches. They're going to—"

"Eucalyptus?" said Robin. "I thought the last eucalyptus tree in the woods exploded."

Leonardo stopped. "What?"

182

"Last year," said Robin. "Remember when the lightning started that bushfire? The last eucalyptus caught, and apparently the oils are really explosive or something. Puck was telling me about it—"

Suddenly, a bang split the air. Smoke exploded from a hole in the ground, sending Foxes flying. Another bang, and Hawks shouted as the earth blasted apart beneath them. The smoke shot like geysers, straight into the air.

Flames raced up a boy's sleeve and he screamed, throwing himself to the ground. Another boy grabbed desperately at nothing as he fell through a hole, into the waiting fire pits.

No, thought Leonardo, horror paralyzing him. *No, no, no...*

He'd completely misgauged the purpose of the bundles. They weren't smoke bombs, designed to fill the caverns and escape through mouse holes; they were real bombs, ripping through the ground like landmines.

The last three went off in rapid succession, sending Hawks and Foxes sprawling and burying the clearing in a wall of white.

Screams of pain and confusion pierced the smoke.

I did that, thought Leonardo, sick with the realization.

"Raven Clan, attack!" shouted Aleksander, and someone shoved Leonardo's shield into his hands. He stumbled, nauseous, and came face to face with Moth.

"Leo?" said Moth. "Are you ok?"

"I'm...I just..."

"He just set off Armageddon," said Pinch. "Of course he's not."

He grabbed Leonardo by the shoulders. "Leo, you need to wake the fuck up. Bombs or not, we're badly outnumbered and both of those clans are trying to kill us. You can confess your sins later, do a rain dance or some shit. Right now, you need to fight."

"Ok." Leonardo pulled himself back to the present. "I know."

Under the billowing smoke, fifty-some Foxes and Hawks waited to kill his friends. Bombs and morality aside, Leonardo wasn't going to let that happen. He swung onto the ladder and threw himself down the rungs into the clouds of smoke.

Pinch followed a second behind him, trailed by Puck and Will. Leonardo glanced down, blinking against the stinging fog, and judged the distance to the ground. He scrambled down another dozen rungs, then jumped off backwards, landing and stumbling on a flaming stick, which he quickly danced away from, stamping his foot to kill the flames.

Something whirred past his head and hit the tree trunk. Leonardo ducked, throwing up his shield as the other three Ravens dropped behind him.

"Attack!" Puck charged the nearest silhouette. Leonardo ran at a pair of shadows with slingshots. A stone pinged off his shield. The other shot got lost in the smoke, and then Leonardo was on them. They scrambled to draw their swords and he crashed into them, shrouded in milky white.

The boy on the right, a gangly kid that looked like a skeleton in the smoke, managed to get his sword in the way of Leonardo's first swing and stumbled back as their blades rang out. Leonardo hooked his ankle and yanked it out from under him, then twisted to meet silhouette number two. He hacked hard and fast, threw the kid off balance, then smashed his shield in his face. He turned back as Gangly got to his feet and took a swing. Leonardo blocked it and slashed under his shield, hitting the leather padding on his stomach and driving the wind from his lungs.

Two down. Fifty to go.

Leonardo spun to the right, flashing his sword in an arc that forced back two boys who'd come running. The only features he could make out were their fox shields.

The pair of Foxes charged him and Leonardo gritted his teeth, fighting both at once. That was the most important part of Aleksander's preparations—he'd spent years training Leonardo and the other Ravens to be an elite war machine. Leonardo hacked and blocked and took a sword in the side before he managed to dispatch the Foxes, thoroughly enough that one of the boys vanished.

Shit. He hadn't meant to do that.

Leonardo stumbled back, pain radiating from his side. He panted, staring around as boys ran through the smoke, the smell of burning leather and burning mushrooms clogging the air. Swords clanged, shields cracked, and voices yelled through the mess of it all.

A Hawk came charging though a plume of smoke, his face red and sweaty and his sword raised. Leonardo threw up his shield and the boy crashed into him. They fought, cutting and slashing and stumbling away from each other, throwing blind swings and grunting as they wrestled in a violent circle.

It was a messy thing, in no parts graceful, and finally Leonardo managed to shove the boy off balance and kick him in the midsection, where his leather vest stretched over his stomach and his breath expelled in one, "Oof."

He fell to one knee and Leonardo bashed him over the head with his shield.

Leonardo stepped around him, breathing heavy. Suddenly, a wall of pain slammed into his back and Leonardo dropped. His palms hit the dirt, then he was on the ground. He rolled onto his back and a Fox stepped above him, sword raised over his head. Leonardo threw his shield in the way and *crack*, the impact shook every bone in his arms. He didn't realize he had dropped the shield until it hit his face, the corner catching him just under the eye and flooding his vision with tears.

He blinked back the pain and scrambled to pick up the shield again. The Fox raised his sword and Leonardo tensed for the impact, but it never came. The Fox didn't see Cato until he barrelled through him, like a tornado against a woodshed. One moment he was standing over Leonardo, the next he was flat on his back, Cato and his fists on top of him.

Leonardo gritted his teeth and rolled over, pulling a sharp breath. Sometimes—on very rare occasions—he was grateful for Cato. This was one of those times. He shoved his shield out of the way and struggled to his feet. The ground was littered with boys, unconscious or in worse pain than him. Nearby, Puck sliced through attackers, Cato had finished with Leonardo's attacker and Pinch fought a Hawk, his hat sliding more cockeyed with every slash.

The smoke was already thinning as the holes in the ground slowed their output, transitioning to the thin, black smoke of the fires below. Leonardo limped to the ladder, choking on the heavy air, and started climbing, cringing every time he lifted an arm. He took in a lungful of smoke and coughed again, nearly falling off the ladder.

By the time he reached the top, Leonardo was drenched in sweat and it took all of his effort to roll up onto the platform.

The rope bridge clanked and he glanced up to see Moth hurrying toward him. Leonardo shifted onto his back and closed his eyes.

"Leo!" said Moth as he jogged up. "Are you ok?"

"Fantastic," Leonardo told the back of his eyelids.

"What happened?"

"Sword across the back."

Moth rolled him enough to see under his vest. "You're not bleeding."

It just felt like bruising. Maybe lung bruising, if that was a thing.

"Can you stand? We'll get you inside."

Leonardo opened his eyes, shifting so Moth's head blocked the sun. "I'm not leaving this fight."

"You're not going to fight like this."

"Just have to breathe…through it." Leonardo winced. "I'll be good in a minute."

"Right."

"Where's my sword?" Leonardo scanned the platform.

"Right there." Moth nodded to his right hip.

"No, that's my spare one."

"Oh. Well, in that case…" Moth leaned over the railing. "It's right about…there."

Leonardo groaned.

"Come on," said Moth. "There are more in the armoury."

They made their way over the bridges, freezing at one point as a pebble deflected off the railing and flew into the treetops.

Leonardo looked over the side. "Who's still shooting rocks?"

He spotted the kid just as he loosed another one. Leonardo ducked back as it whistled past, hitting a branch overhead and falling in front of them. It clattered on the boards and rolled down a crack, dropping back to the clearing.

"Him, apparently," said Moth.

Someone from Raven Clan spotted the shooter and came at him with a raised sword. Leonardo and Moth took advantage of the chance to get away. At the armoury, Leonardo took a new sword and shield, and tried a test swing on the platform. His back still hurt, but he could ignore it. And he could mostly breathe again.

Leonardo rubbed grit from his eyes. "I should get back down."

"Are you sure you're good enough?" asked Moth. "You don't look good."

Leonardo straightened his back, clenching his teeth.

Moth's eyes flicked over his shoulder and his face blanched. "Um, Leo, we've got…"

He started to draw his sword and Leonardo turned around. Two Hawks had scaled one of the ladders and were rising to their feet on a platform a dozen trees away.

At the same moment, Leonardo caught sight of movement to his left and turned to see Aleksander pulling himself up another ladder, sword in his hand and eyes on the Hawks.

CHAPTER 22

Leonardo ran to join Aleksander as he started toward the Hawks. His back gave a twinge as they sprinted over the bridges, but Leonardo ignored it and kept running.

They reached the platform at the same time and crashed together with the Hawks, swords clanging beneath the overhanging branches. The boy on the right was tall, with a mess of brown hair sticking up over his bandana. Leonardo blocked a swing with his shield and took a slash at him, but it was weak and he deflected it easily, lunging at Leonardo's side. Leonardo jammed his shield in the way and took a swing that the Hawk caught on his sword.

Leonardo was breathing heavy already, and he realized he might not have been ready to rejoin the fight yet after all. He clenched his teeth and pushed against the Hawk's sword. The Hawk pushed up and Leonardo gasped, pain lancing down his back. His grip faltered and he ducked as the Hawk's sword sliced past his face.

Leonardo stumbled back and threw his shield up, absorbing another rattling blow. Beside him, Aleksander had the other Hawk on his heels. His sword flashed in and out, cracking against wood and leather and singing against metal.

Leonardo's Hawk came at him again and Leonardo fought to hold him off.

His vision pulsed red around the edges and he swore, grunting with every bone-rattling block.

Leonardo's Hawk stepped shoulder-to-shoulder with Aleksander, each hacking in opposite directions. He was so focused on finishing Leonardo that he missed the movement. It happened so fast that Leonardo barely registered it. The pommel of Aleksander's sword flew sideways, striking the Hawk in the head. He crumpled instantly, falling at Leonardo's feet. Aleksander was already back on his own Hawk, and three hacks later, he was on the ground too.

Aleksander stepped back and glanced at Leonardo, who grimaced, a hand on his back.

"Are you hurt?"

"Earlier."

Aleksander nodded, catching his breath.

"Thank you," said Leonardo.

"For what?"

Leonardo kicked the Hawk with his toe. "He would've had me."

Aleksander swept his curled locks off his face, then he used his sword to flip over the Hawk's shield, hiding the insignia from view.

"I never gave up on you," he said finally. "You know that."

Leonardo had spent a lot of years pursuing those words, but hearing them now, he realized it might be too late. They no longer meant what they used to.

"I can't be what you want me to be," said Leonardo. He thought about the screams when the bombs went off and felt sick to his stomach.

"Try," said Aleksander. He looked pained, blue eyes searching. "That's all I've ever wanted."

"That's all I've ever done," said Leonardo. "But I'm not a conquerer. I never will be."

Aleksander opened his mouth to say something else, but it was lost as Moth came running over the bridge, yelling, "Behind you!"

Leonardo twisted to see another Hawk hurtling towards them. He recognized Gallus's second in command, Pistol.

Suddenly, Aleksander was back.

"Move." He shoved Leonardo out of his way and drew his sword, running to meet Pistol on the platform encircling the next tree trunk.

Aleksander dodged around Pistol's sword and forced him to twist and block a vicious backswing. Pistol stepped back, scrambling to defend as Aleksander rained blows on him. He lunged in and tried to disarm Aleksander, but Aleksander was quicker. He slammed Pistol's sword away with his shield and came at him with another barrage.

Pistol turned it away, and for a second, it looked like he was winning. But Aleksander hadn't reached the rank of legend by losing fights. He let Pistol lunge, then disarmed him with a flick of the wrist, bashed him in the face, and put his sword clean through him. Pistol vanished instantly. Aleksander sheathed his sword, face gleaming with sweat.

A scream rang out below and Leonardo looked down as Cato sliced his way through a group of Foxes, each one vanishing like a ghost at his sword.

The bridge rattled behind Leonardo and he turned as Moth ran up.

"Can you hear that?" asked Moth.

"What?" Leonardo strained to hear anything over the shouts and the clang of metal. "The fight?"

"No. Drums."

An instant later, Leonardo heard them, pounding in the distance and drawing closer.

War drums, beating a blood-chilling march.

The tempo of the battle stuttered, as boys stopped fighting and turned to gaze at the wall of trees that hid the river.

The drums got louder, paired with the slosh of oars.

Aleksander stepped down onto the rope bridge, frowning at the sound.

"Natives," he said.

Leonardo and Moth looked at him.

A moment later, shale scraped under boat keels, and the beat of the drums carried up the beach trail. Ravens, Hawks, and Foxes alike scrambled back from the opening.

Dakota led the way into the clearing, spear in hand, knife in his belt, and bare chest painted with green lines.

Behind him, a Native pounded on a deep drum, a tan hide stretched tight across the top. Dozens of warriors filed into the clearing, spreading out in a double line before the Lost Boys.

Some carried drums, all carried weapons, and all of them towered over the boys.

Are they joining the fight? It contradicted everything the chief had told them.

Last of all, Chief Tokala walked out of the beach trail.

He stared up at Leonardo and Aleksander on the rope bridge.

"What is the meaning of this?" shouted Aleksander.

"Aleksander," Tokala didn't shout, but his voice carried easily across the clearing. "I warned you there would be consequences."

"Are you here to kill me?"

Tokala shook his head, slow and weary. "I am here to set you free. Your fight is over."

Ten feet from Leonardo, Aleksander's breath came quick.

"Come up here and fight me, old man. Or better yet, send a few of those warriors of yours. Let them see how easy it is to get rid of me."

"You'll never understand, Aleksander," said the chief. "This place, these woods. They're not about war."

Suddenly, a crack split the air. Aleksander tensed, then the boards broke under his feet and Aleksander plunged out of sight.

Leonardo leapt for him, but it was too late. He hit the boards just in time to see his brother crash into the bushes, then the leaves swallowed him. There came a firecracker explosion of sticks snapping, then silence. Leonardo knelt frozen on the swinging boards, staring through the hole at the bushes.

"Ohmygod," said Moth. "Is he…?"

"I don't know." Everything felt like slow motion. Leonardo's mind slogged through the reality of it, the horror spreading dark and slick. "I'm going down there."

"Me too," said Moth.

They rushed down the nearest ladder, jumping off in the middle of a cluster of Hawks, Foxes, and Ravens. They all stepped back, and Leonardo went straight to the bushes—the tall ones that he'd avoided cutting out earlier that week—and started pulling apart branches.

He shouldered into the space between two bushes, ducking and climbing. A wall of twigs poked at his back, snagging in his hair and scraping down the back of his neck. He scanned every gap for a sign of Aleksander, and took more than one twig in the eye. He swore, blinking, and pushed in deeper.

He saw Aleksander's boot first. His right boot, propped up at a strange angle and caught in the fork of a branch.

Leonardo's breath caught. Heart sinking, he climbed toward it.

When Leonardo reached him, his first thought was, *He's dead.* But 'dead' didn't exist here. He should've disappeared. Instead, Aleksander lay in the dirt, his body twisted over the branches and his leg up in the air. A gash on his head bled down the side of his face, and his chest wasn't moving.

Leonardo stood staring at him, unable to move, unable to call out to Moth.

Aleksander was a thing to hate, an object to blame for any and all hardships, but Leonardo had no idea how to feel anymore. There was a lot more to Aleksander than bitterness and power. In his own, warped way, Aleksander cared, and he truly wanted Leonardo to succeed him.

What he'd done to the woods, the wars he'd started in his quest for control, Leonardo couldn't justify that. But he didn't blame Aleksander for struggling with the weight of it, trapped in a woods that forced him to grow up faster than he was ready for. His brother had been desperate to create purpose; manifest a meaning for the childhood denied to him.

Leonardo tore his eyes away from Aleksander's body and turned to call for Moth when Aleksander's hand twitched.

Leonardo snapped back to focus. He held his breath, eyes locked on his brother. Nothing happened for a long moment. Aleksander lay motionless and Leonardo started to wonder if he'd just imagined it. Then Aleksander gasped. Leonardo jumped. Nearby, Moth's rustling fell silent.

"Leo?" called Moth.

Aleksander shifted, dragging his hand through the dirt.

Leonardo's heart pounded in triple-time.

Everything went still, then Aleksander's eyes snapped open.

CHAPTER 23

Aleksander blinked at him, blue eyes vivid like ice in the filtered light. Next to the red of his blood and the green dome surrounding him, everything looked unreal, oversaturated.

Aleksander stopped blinking and focused on Leonardo. It was haunting in a way that Leonardo wouldn't forget for a long time. He looked older. Old enough that for the first time, Leonardo truly saw how little he fit here. Aleksander wasn't a teenager anymore. He was a man in a clan of boys. He wasn't *young*, and he wasn't *getting old*. He was *old*.

"Leonardo," said Aleksander. "Like a lion."

Leonardo heard Moth call his name and glanced behind him, calling, "Over here! I found him, he's—"

He turned back and froze.

Aleksander was gone.

CHAPTER 24

Disappeared.

A word that Leonardo had never fully understood until now. And after today, he understood it less than ever.

Aleksander was gone. *Disappeared,* and Leonardo was in a mild state of shock. He and Moth climbed out of the bushes, and Leonardo looked around at the faces of three clans. Boys disappeared all the time. Every year, every day, every night, a boy somewhere in the woods was at risk of disappearing. It had happened to hundreds, maybe thousands, but Aleksander was never really supposed to be one of them.

"He's gone," said Leonardo.

Shock rippled through the clearing. Hushed voices turned to louder ones, confused and afraid. Eyes turned toward the Natives, swords and shields lifting.

"These woods face a great danger," said Chief Tokala, his wrinkles deep in the flickering torchlight. "All of the woods. It watches us even now, from the shadows, from the darkness. Division will not help us in the days to come."

Hawks, Foxes, and Ravens stood transfixed, all their attention on the chief.

Leonardo wondered if the fight could be over this easily. Was losing Aleksander all it took to bring peace to the Darkwoods?

Then Gallus grabbed a short stick and stuck it in the flames of a cooking fire. Leonardo's blood froze, and around the clearing, two dozen Ravens started to move.

Gallus was quicker, and he lobbed the stick high into the treetops. It spun through the air, ablaze in the night, and landed on a ladder platform.

Flames licked at the old wood, quickly taking hold.

Someone shouted. Cato came running at Gallus, and suddenly boys were fighting again.

Leonardo whipped up his shield, blocking a swing from a Hawk. He slashed him back, then caught the flash of a sword in his peripheral too late. A piercing pain lanced his side, and everything went black.

Not black. Gold. He drifted in a field of a million firelit sparks. Leonardo looked around, down at his feet—he was floating. A quiet whine filled his ears, and he realized it was building, gaining volume, and he was moving, flying through a vacuum as the whine built to a scream.

Leonardo crashed back into the woods, stumbling and staring around at the battle, raging on as it had a moment ago.

The boy who'd stabbed Leonardo looked at him like he was a ghost, and Leonardo slashed at him, forcing the boy back.

What just happened?

He knocked the boy's sword out of his hands. The boy turned and ran.

Leonardo looked at Tokala and the chief gave him a look that said, *don't make me do that again.*

He brought me back, realized Leonardo. *I disappeared, and he brought me back.*

Tokala raised a hand and one of the warriors pounded his drum.

Boys faltered around the clearing, turning to look at the Natives.

A few swords found their marks and boys vanished.

Tokala didn't pull them back.

Why me?

The warrior pounded his drum again. This time, everyone stopped.

"The battle is over," said Tokala, directly to Leonardo. "Dark days are coming. Make the choice your brother couldn't."

He gazed up at the burning platform, dark eyes glinting in the firelight. The flames burst higher and Leonardo watched in horror as they raced across a rope bridge, faster than any natural fire should travel.

The inferno reached a treehouse and the entire structure exploded into flame.

Pinch, Bates, and Will took off for a ladder. Pinch reached the top first and sprinted into the first treehouse. He reappeared a second later, tossing an armful of sleeping rolls over the rail. Bates dove into the next treehouse and emerged with a basket of clothing.

"The battle is over," repeated the chief, calm while the flames reflected in his dark eyes.

Swords glinted in the firelight and Gallus took a breath to say something.

Dakota took a step toward him, feathered spear in one hand and the other on his knife.

Gallus paused. "Hawk Clan, we depart!" he shouted instead, as if that were what he'd planned all along.

"Stop them!" shouted Ajax.

"No," shouted Leonardo, louder. "No more fighting."

Gallus gave him a salute and ran into the trees, his Hawks sprinting after him.

"Fox Clan," called Hero, and they followed, leaving the Ravens alone with the Natives below their burning camp.

"The fire will die once this camp is burnt," said Tokala. "Make the right choice."

Then the Natives left. As one, they turned and filed out of the clearing, drums silent.

"Salvage what you can and get out," shouted Leonardo.

He took a step toward the pile of supplies, then stopped as a pine bow fell, igniting the leaves of a hackberry tree before it hit the ground in a rain of sparks.

The flames spread quickly, blackening the leaves and racing to engulf the entire tree. The pops and cracks in the canopy grew louder, and Leonardo flinched at an explosion nearby.

Three rope bridges smouldered, in tatters, and the bridges he and Aleksander had fought the Hawks on were completely on fire.

The flames spread faster every second and Leonardo realized that Pinch, Bates, and Will needed to get down immediately.

A booming crack cut his yell short, as a massive branch broke overhead and fell to the clearing. It knocked one of the bridges, sending it swinging, and crashed to the ground in an explosion of sparks.

Leonardo scrambled back, along with a dozen other boys. The ends of the branch lit a dozen more bushes that went up instantly. The temperature rose by the minute; the clearing quickly becoming an oven. Leonardo gaped at a swinging bridge, just in time to see a flicker of orange take hold of the ropes.

"Get down!" he yelled, and the other boys joined in.

Bates stuck his head out of the storeroom door. He saw the flaming bridge and his eyes went wide. He turned and yelled, "Will! Pinch! We gotta go!"

Will and Pinch emerged from two other treehouses, one of which was already starting to flicker, and everyone below held their breath as the three boys sprinted over the lurching, burning bridge. The flames grew and fire crept along the underside of the boards.

Come on, thought Leonardo, watching the fire outrun them. *Come on, come on—*

A board burst into flames in front of Pinch, and Pinch leapt over it, stumbling after the others. All three boys reached the ladder platform and scrambled down as the last unburned trees around the clearing began to catch.

201

"We need to get out," shouted Leonardo. Puck straightened nearby, supporting Rugby under the arm.

"He's hurt," he called. "Help me with him."

Leonardo ducked under Rugby's other arm and helped Puck get him to the beach trail. As they started down it, Leonardo looked up into the branches, hazy with smoke.

They half-ran, blinking through watering eyes, and burst out onto the riverbank.

Other boys raced past them, tossing bundles of supplies into the longboat. Leonardo helped Rugby over the side, then started back up the beach. Another flaming branch fell through the canopy, its crash lost in the roar of the fire. Further back, a tree trunk exploded like a gunshot.

Pinch came running out, carrying an armful of cooking pots and sleeping rolls.

"I'm the last one," he shouted at Leonardo.

"You're sure?"

"I'm sure."

Bits of ember floated through the air, glowing orange as they landed on the rocks. Leonardo crushed one under his boot, running after Pinch to the boat.

The regular rowers sat ready on their benches, and Moth glanced back at Leonardo, soot on his face. Leonardo grabbed the side of the boat and pushed it into the water with Cato, Jack, and Bates. He leapt over the side as the oars clunked into motion, dropping onto a bench and turning to watch the flames burn his home.

CHAPTER 25

They chose to camp for the remainder of the night on the bank directly opposite, back from the water in a hollow surrounded by small-leafed, smooth-barked trees.

Leonardo lay awake for most of the night, and based on the sound of their breathing, he guessed that everyone else was the same.

Aleksander never named a successor. He showed me the hidden chambers, but no one except for Ajax and Cato know what that means.

I can't let Ajax become leader. He'll kill us all. Or at least, have Cato do it.

It rained for two hours in the early morning. A hard, cold rain that had forced them back under the trees, scrambling half-awake to drag their sleeping rolls out of the downpour. They were a sullen group for its duration, but no one complained. With a rain like that, the fire across the river would be all but stamped out. Just as Tokala had promised.

Leonardo wondered at the point of it. He didn't understand why Raven Clan's entire camp needed to burn if this was just about Aleksander. Tokala could've helped them put out the fire Gallus started. Instead, he'd guaranteed not a floorboard remained for any Raven to call home.

None of it added up with Tokala or Viola's story, but Leonardo decided to put it out of his mind until daylight. He was tired and sore, and pondering their hopeless situation did nothing to improve any of it.

The tree roots grew so thick here that the only place to lay out their rolls was in the clearing, so once the rain stopped, they trudged out into the wet grass to find the least muddy spots.

The next morning, Leonardo woke from the little bit of sleep he'd finally caught and shifted painfully on his bedroll. At least the treehouse floor had been flat. Out here, rocks and sticks and bulging roots pushed into his back, leaving him bruised with stiff muscles and a sore neck.

Leonardo rose to his feet, grimacing as he stretched, and Nym glanced over from his perch on the lowest branch of a nearby tree. He'd been up all night and still looked wide awake. Leonardo picked his way around the other sleeping bodies. Twenty-four Ravens had survived the fight, and they all lay huddled in the tiny forest hollow. He nodded to Nym as he walked up.

"Morning," said Nym, as bright as the early sun rays.

"What's your secret?" asked Leonardo, clenching his jaw at a pain in his side.

"I'm sorry?"

"I actually slept for part of last night, and I'm ready to die."

"You took a beating yesterday."

"And you didn't?" A bruise bloomed under Nym's eye and a cut scored his forehead. Still, he sat up straight and resilient.

"We all did," Nym agreed, shrugging. Leonardo wondered if anything had the power to dampen Nym's optimism.

They were distracted as Jack shifted, groaning loudly. "It's official," he declared. "I quit."

Bates threw a pinecone at him and Page flipped over on his sleeping roll, shushing him and pulling the shirt he was using as a pillow over his ears.

Leonardo turned back to Nym. "Thank you," he said. "For trusting me last night."

If not for Nym, Leonardo never would've gotten to Viola in time for her warning.

"Thank you for saving us," countered Nym. "How did you find out about the attack?"

"I…" Leonardo hesitated. After everything last night, he felt leery to reveal any connection between himself and the Natives.

Nym tilted his head, elfish features drawn together in thought. He started to say something, then changed his mind.

"You know what, it doesn't matter," he said instead. "You found out, that's all I care to know."

Leonardo didn't know what to say. He couldn't imagine any other member of Raven Clan dropping it like that.

"It's not my place to pry," said Nym. A leaf fell from a higher branch and he caught it, examining the veins in the sunlight.

Thanking him would only make it look more like Leonardo had something to hide. He wasn't sure what he'd done to earn this kind of trust from Nym. He put his hands in his pockets and his fingers brushed a smooth stone.

Right. He'd forgotten about Aleksander's stone key. He supposed it wouldn't have much use anymore. Aleksander's tree-house lair and the underground cavern were almost certainly burnt black.

"Did you hear Ajax last night?" asked Nym, lowering his voice. "I heard him talking to Cato during the rain. He's going to claim leadership today, since Aleksander...you know..."

"Disappeared," finished Leonardo, thinking about Ajax. Ajax only said he'd kill the ones who stood against him. If Leonardo let him take the leadership, he might spare them.

Might.

If Ajax becomes leader, he'll be worse than Aleksander. There will be no such thing as safety anymore.

"We need to stop him, Nym," said Leonardo, almost whispering. "He's going to kill everyone."

"What?" Nym dropped the leaf, all his attention fixed on Leonardo.

Leonardo shifted so his back was to the clearing. He wished they could go out in the woods to talk, but he didn't want Ajax to wake up and find them missing.

"I heard him talking to Cato in the woods..." Leonardo relayed what he'd eavesdropped, talking so quietly that Nym asked him to repeat himself several times.

Leonardo's nerves coiled tight in his stomach as he spoke, listening to the other boys stir on their sleeping rolls behind him.

"You're Aleksander's brother," whispered Nym. He scanned the clearing over Leonardo's shoulder. "People will follow you."

"I'm not even a se-com," said Leonardo. "Ajax can argue that he's more qualified."

"So?" said Nym. "You have leader's blood. Besides, we all know how to run Raven Clan. Our jobs don't change, we just need someone calling the shots."

"Right." Leonardo took a deep breath, wondering if everyone else would feel the same way.

"Listen," said Nym, trying to lighten his mood. "You've got the best nightwatchman in the Darkwoods on your side. You can't lose."

Leonardo tried to smile.

"In all honesty, I don't know the other Clans' watchmen," said Nym. "But still."

"When you heard him last night," asked Leonardo. "Did he say when he was planning to crown himself?"

"He wants to go across the river first," said Nym. "Make sure everyone sees how bad the situation is."

"Then he'll swoop in and take control," said Leonardo.

"Exactly," said Nym.

"Ok…" Leonardo chewed his lip, thinking. "We need to make sure only half the group goes across. It should be easy, lots of people are hurt. You and Moth can stay with them, and while the rest of us are across the river, you start swaying them to our side."

"Got it," said Nym. He caught another falling leaf and frowned, looking up at the branches above.

"Ajax won't claim leadership until he has the whole clan in front of him," said Leonardo. "By the time we get back, hopefully you and Moth will have gained the numbers, and then we can…I don't know. Hopefully he'll back down when he sees he's outnumbered."

"What do we do if he doesn't?" asked Nym.

"I don't know," said Leonardo. He crunched a pinecone under his heel. "I don't want another fight."

"We'll figure it out," said Nym.

"I hope so."

He left Nym and walked around the clearing, out to the bank, where a thin mist had just begun to burn off. This was normally his favourite time of day, but Leonardo wasn't in a mood to enjoy it. The trees along the far side stood black and burnt, pencil thin, and Leonardo glimpsed bits of the camp further back.

Rebuilding would be a long process, even without the problem of a false-Aleksander attempting to assert himself.

How did things get this bad?

Leonardo picked up a stone and skipped it over the water. It broke the surface on the second skip and went under.

"Nice shot."

He turned to see Strato, sprawled out against a fallen log like a piece of the underbrush.

"Beach patrol," he explained, pointing a thumb at himself. "In case the nasties come back."

"Quiet so far?"

"Just me 'n the fishes."

Leonardo followed his gaze to the far side.

"It doesn't look good," said Leonardo.

"I'd be surprised if there's anything left."

Leonardo nodded.

Strato pried a piece of bark from the log and threw it down the bank. "When the Natives showed up..." he said, chipping at another piece of bark. "What did the chief mean, '*make the choice your brother couldn't*'?"

"I don't know," said Leonardo. "This is the second time he's told me that."

Strato pushed himself into a sitting position, cocking his head.

"He speaks in riddles," said Leonardo.

He especially didn't want to be associated with the chief. Gallus may have been the one to throw the stick, but it was Tokala's magic that turned the fire loose. And Aleksander's fall…Leonardo didn't need anyone thinking he was connected to that.

"There's going to be more fighting before this is over," said Strato.

"I know," said Leonardo.

"How did you know about the ambush?"

He should've seen that coming. He swallowed. "What?"

"The ambush." said Strato. He frowned. "You knew that Hawk and Bear were hiding in the woods."

"I saw them," said Leonardo. "They weren't hiding very well."

"Oh." Strato tilted his head, watching the river flow past. "Well that's lucky."

"It was," agreed Leonardo. He dried his palms, wondering how many more lies he'd have to tell.

***

As soon as everyone was awake, Ajax stepped up to the front of the clearing, knee-deep in long grass.

"We need to go survey the camp," he said, hand on his sword and shoulders squared. It could've looked commanding if his trench coat wasn't so rumpled, his dark hair hanging limp and flat. "I want everyone on the beach in five minutes."

"What about the injured?" said Leonardo. "The burnt camp isn't going anywhere. They should stay here and rest up."

"I'll stay and help them," said Moth. Leonardo and Nym had filled him in a few minutes earlier.

"Me too," said Nym.

"My back is stiff," said Puck. "I wouldn't mind taking it easy too."

Good. Leonardo was relatively confident Puck would join their cause. He could help Moth and Nym sway the others.

Ajax narrowed his eyes, straightening the lapels of his trench coat as he stepped out of the grass.

"Ok, then we'll send a party across," he said. "The rest can stay here."

Perfect. Now for the difficult part.

Leonardo joined Ajax, Pinch, Cato, and a handful of others in the longboat. Ajax whispered something to Cato as they climbed in, and Cato ground his fist into his palm, grinning.

We can't let it come to a fight, thought Leonardo.

Moth and Nym had better be convincing.

***

On the far bank, Leonardo leaned back, gazing at the skeleton trees over the beach.

"Smells fantastic," said Pinch, crunching a piece of charcoal under his foot.

"Did you expect better?" asked Strato. "It stinks from across the river. Just gonna get worse the deeper we go."

"Then stay away from me, everyone," said Pinch. "I'll collapse if I have to deal with all of your stink *and* the woods."

Ajax led the way up the trail, breaking fallen branches with his

210

sword. Black trees hung over them like charred claws, gnarled and menacing as the boys filed through the tunnel and into the clearing.

Or at least, what used to be the clearing. Now it looked like something out of a nightmare; the ground covered in a snowfall of white ashes, the treetops littered with broken boards and the burnt-out shells of treehouses. What was left of the rope bridges hung in tatters, and pieces of ladder platforms lay broken at the bases of the trees that used to support them. The giant tree holding Aleksander's quarters was burnt through, exposing the hollow core. Little bits of snowy ash floated through the air, contributing to the haunted, otherworldly quality of the place.

It stunk like something putrid, and a cold breeze blew heavy clouds across the wide-open sky. Overnight, their world had been transformed into a barren, hostile one, completely unfamiliar and utterly lifeless.

Leonardo stared at the carnage and thought, *This can't be fixed. Not even Aleksander could fix this.*

He struggled to imagine the clan in front of him, inexperienced and undersized, rebuilding anything like what used to be. The best they could hope for were a few shoddy structures in a hollow like they were camped in now. Any hope of resurrecting the old framework was swept away as he looked up at the treetops. This stretch of woods had become a wasteland, and it wouldn't be good for anything for a long time.

Without a fortress to stand in, Raven Clan would go from boy kings to creatures of the underbrush, hiding and cowering until their enemies rooted them out. If they didn't come up with something, they would be forced to absorb into the other clans. He imagined Gallus's face, smug and apple-cheeked, or Lance's, or Hero's. None of them were appealing.

It hadn't even been a great battle, just a well-timed one, where the mighty Raven Clan was caught on their heels and—just like their legendary leader—did the unthinkable.

They fell.

"Leo."

Leonardo blinked, realizing that Pinch had said his name several times. The other boys had spread out and were picking through the rubble around the clearing.

"What is it?"

"God you're deaf," said Pinch. "Look, I'm going to climb that tree. The platform up top looks sturdy. I think it would hold me."

"Why?" asked Leonardo, alarmed. Up above, the rickety boards creaked in the wind.

"Because the supply room isn't totally burnt, and I want something to eat besides apples."

"Whatever's up there is out there too." Leonardo pointed though the charred trunks to wherever the greenery started again. "We can go hunting or picking or whatever you want later."

"Why would I do that if there's food *right there*?"

"Because it's dangerous?" said Leonardo.

"You're turning into Moth."

"The tree is *burnt*, Pinch."

"Only a bit."

"Just leave it. We'll go looking for food when we're back on the other side of the river."

"But I'm lazy," argued Pinch.

"So you'll climb a tree."

"Don't argue with my logic."

Leonardo sighed. "Why are you even telling me this?"

"Because I need a spotter. It's a burnt tree, Leo. I could fall."

Leonardo rolled his neck. He had a headache already, and he hadn't even started with Ajax yet. "I'm going over there. Find someone else to watch you die."

"But everyone else will enjoy it."

Leonardo frowned, recognizing an old tree, exposed now that the underbrush was gone. He stepped around Pinch and crunched through the charcoal toward it.

"Hey!" called Pinch. "Come back here!"

Leonardo studied the raven faces carved into the old tree. Miraculously, the fire had somehow spared this one trunk, and Aleksander's name was only darkened with a little bit of soot, his raven still intact, along with the deep wound above it from Leonardo's sword.

Maybe all wasn't lost after all.

A boom rang out from above and Leonardo looked up. A charred branch cracked, and the treehouse atop it shifted with an ominous scrape, listing heavily to one side.

Boys scrambled out of the way in the ashes below. The broken branch fell to the blanket of white, throwing up a cloud of dust.

The treehouse groaned, tilting heavier. Something slid across the floor, high above. A lot of somethings, scraping over the boards, and then they flew out through a hole in the wall.

Moth's carvings, tumbling like a swarm of wooden dive-bombers. Charred fairies rained on the clearing, punching into the ash and throwing up explosions of dust.

213

Pinch, directly below the attack, ducked out of the way, arms over his head. When a bigger carving pinwheeled out of the sky, he dove clear of its path. The lion, as long as Leonardo's forearm, just missed him.

Leonardo released his breath, then the entire treehouse came down.

No! Leonardo leapt for Pinch as he scrambled to his feet. The structure crashed between them and he staggered back, twisting away from the flying ash.

Not this. Please, after everything—

Pinch's tricorned silhouette straightened in the dust and Leonardo closed his eyes in relief.

"Fuck." Pinch coughed and swore again.

"Let's get out of here," called Leonardo. "It's not—"

"Everyone to the beach," said Ajax, louder. "Move it."

Ajax's lanky form strode through the ash, wrapped in his soot-covered trench coat, as he ushered boys out of the trees.

Here we go. He didn't even have a plan yet for stage two. *What do I say when he names himself leader?*

Pinch ignored Ajax, stepping toward the broken treehouse and crouching down.

"What are you doing?" asked Leonardo.

Pinch straightened, holding the blackened lion.

"This fucker tried to kill me. I'm taking him prisoner."

"Naturally," said Leonardo. "Come on, let's go."

They returned to the boat and climbed in as Ajax stepped up onto the captain's platform. He placed a hand on the stem and gazed out over the river. He looked like an imposter. A rat dressed up in mink. He could cut his hair like Aleksander, and talk like

214

Aleksander, and stand on the captain's platform like Aleksander, but he wasn't Aleksander.

And neither am I.

He wondered if he could lead Raven Clan. Then he decided it didn't matter anymore.

It was time to act.

***

Back at the new camp, Moth glanced up as Leonardo walked over, binding a rag around a wound on Bates's leg. A few boys sat nearby and Moth gave Leonardo a warning look.

They're Ajax's? Leonardo wondered how many—if any—Ravens Moth and Nym had pulled to his side.

"Well?" asked Moth, falsely nonchalant.

"Burnt," said Leonardo, playing along.

"Completely?"

"Close enough."

"So, no chance…?"

Leonardo shook his head. "From scratch at a new site."

"Shit." Bates pushed himself up. "This camp sucks."

He wondered whether Bates was one of theirs.

"We'll find a better site," said Moth.

"You ever built a treehouse?" Bates asked Leonardo.

He's one of ours. Leonardo could see it in his eyes.

Leonardo shook his head.

"Me neither," said Bates. "Whoever built our camp knew shit. We don't."

"So?" said Moth. "We'll learn."

Bates snorted. "I don't feel like falling through the floor so one of these halfwits can 'learn' he has no idea what he's doing."

"Then what do you suggest?" Moth finished tying off the binding on Bates's leg, yanking it tighter than necessary.

"Ow! Shit, Moth, it's not a tourniquet."

Moth rolled his eyes and loosened the knot.

"ATTENTION!"

Ajax jumped onto a stump near the front of the clearing. Cato trundled up behind him and off to the side.

"Here we go," said Moth, climbing to his feet.

Bates did the same. The three of them stood near the edge of the clearing, fifty feet from Ajax. The rest of Raven Clan was scattered around the space, injured and uninjured alike turning their attention to him, voices hushed and talking fast.

Behind Ajax, Cato put his hand on his sword. Leonardo did the same.

"As you're all aware," said Ajax, addressing the clearing, "Aleksander is gone."

The clearing fell silent.

"Since he never named a successor, we must select a new leader ourselves. As second-in-commands, Cato and I have spoken and agree that I am the best choice to fill that role."

Cato glanced at Leonardo, rolling the pommel of his sword under his hand.

Leonardo drew a breath, then he squared his jaw and stepped forward.

CHAPTER 26

Ajax chuckled. "And here comes the prince. Planning to tell us that Aleksander named you successor? If he did, no one else heard it."

In the long grass behind him, Cato grinned, swatting at a wasp with his sword.

Actually, someone did hear, and it was you. The weight of the stone key pressed in Leonardo's pocket.

"No," Leonardo said instead. He kept one hand on his sword, an eye trained on Cato as he approached the stump.

"Regardless of what Aleksander did or didn't do, *I* don't think I could lead this Clan," said Leonardo. "I'm not my brother, and deny it all you want, but neither are you."

Ajax stepped off the stump, eyes narrowed. "Do you have a point?"

"Explain to me, Ajax," said Leonardo. "Why these boys should pick a leader who wants to be Aleksander so bad that he'll kill for it."

Ajax paused, one foot on a root, his grin matching Cato's. "That's your play? You'll have to swing a lot harder than that, Leonardo."

"I don't have a play," said Leonardo. "All I have is a warning."

Across the grass, Jack said something to Page, and Snout furrowed his brow, standing in the shadow of a hackberry tree. A nervous anticipation settled on the clearing.

"Ajax and Cato plan to kill everyone who stands against them," said Leonardo. "You'll never be safe with him as leader."

Behind him, Ajax laughed, too loud and slightly nervous. "Is anyone believing this? Gentlemen, I'd like to introduce you to the traitor."

"There is no traitor," said Leonardo. "You know that."

"Yes there is!" Ajax jumped back onto his stump. "There's something you don't know," he informed the listening Ravens. "Leonardo has been meeting with a Native girl. Reserve your shock, I'm not finished yet. He was out the night of the Fox Clan attack and led the Foxes right to our doorstep. He also snuck out, minutes before last night's ambush, and returned—*through the bushes*—just before they attacked us."

The attention shifted back on Leonardo. The sun slid behind a cloud, bathing the clearing in shade. The temperature dropped and a bird screeched somewhere in the treetops.

He's twisting it, Leonardo wanted to say. *It's all lies.*

But it wasn't lies, and the first retorts that came to his tongue

218

sounded weak and unconvincing. He hesitated, and Ajax took advantage of it.

"The Natives have corrupted him. They used one of their girls to seduce him, and now he's their puppet."

"That's a lie," said Leonardo. "Ajax—"

"Aleksander was in the way," Ajax cut over him. "So they took him out. They intend for Leonardo to become your new leader, so they can have a puppet to manipulate. Do you want a traitor puppet for a leader?"

"Leo?" said Nym. His eyes flashed with questions, and the desire to take Leonardo's side.

Moth and Pinch glanced at each other. Moth kneaded his hands nervously.

New tactic. "It's true," said Leonardo, stepping forward.

Shock rippled through the clan. The clearing fell so quiet that only the drone of mosquitoes pierced the tension.

"I met with a Native girl—once," said Leonardo. His voice sounded extra loud in the silence. "Last night, before the attack, she was standing on the bank and I thought she might know something about the traitor. That's all. It's because of her that I knew about the ambush."

Nym steepled his fingers. Leonardo could see their conversation last night playing through his mind.

And Strato. Leonardo had lied to him out on the bank earlier. Strato scratched his chin, quirking his mouth.

"Was that after our patrol?" asked Puck.

Leonardo nodded. "I had to go alone. There wasn't time to explain."

"What about Aleksander?" asked Snout, suspicion in his

219

voice. "Did you really know they were going to kill him?" The filtered sunlight caught half his face, silhouetting the oddly shaped features which had earned him his name.

"When we went to the Native camp, the chief told Aleksander his time was running out," said Leonardo. "And if he kept resisting the woods, there would be more damage."

Robin leaned over and said something to Will, pointing in the direction of the river, hidden behind a stand of heavy pines.

"Now we know what that meant," said Leonardo, nodding to Robin. "So here it is: I snuck out, I met with a Native girl, I knew that Aleksander's time was up, and I know the chief wants me to make some sort of decision. You heard him last night; he said the same thing to me two days ago. I don't know whether that decision is to lead Raven Clan, but whatever it is, my first—and only—allegiance is to all of you. Everything I did, I did it to protect Raven Clan."

"Liar!" snapped Ajax. "He's been scheming with them. He'll trade away your lives, just like Aleksander's."

"Shut up halfwit," yelled Pinch. "No one's listening."

"Why would the Natives want to destroy us?" asked Moth. He took a step forward, overcoming his nerves to challenge Ajax. "They want peace."

"We don't know what they want," snapped Ajax, forcefully enough that Moth staggered back. "All we know is that Leonardo met with them and never told anyone."

He marched into the centre of the clearing, stopping directly in front of Leonardo. His rat's eyes glared into Leonardo's while he addressed the clan.

"I don't know about you, but that sounds suspicious to me."

"He didn't have time to tell anyone!" said Puck. "He just said that."

Cato stepped forward. "Leonardo went in the bushes."

"Shut up, Cato," said Ajax. "Puck, are you really stupid enough to believe the words of a traitor?"

"He went into the bushes," repeated Cato. "When Aleksander fell."

"So?" said Ajax.

"Maybe he killed him."

Silence dropped over the clearing again and Ajax stepped back, as surprised at Cato's deduction as everyone else. It might've been the most intelligent thing he'd ever said, and at the worst possible moment.

"That's true," said Ajax, beginning to pace. A wind breathed over them, flipping the edge of his trench coat. "For all we know, Leonardo killed him in that bush. And conveniently, the Natives were all present, in case we figured it out and turned on Leonardo."

"I didn't kill him," said Leonardo, startled at the fierceness in his own voice. "He was my brother. I would never kill another Raven, much less my own blood."

"It's too late," said Ajax. "For the crime of betraying Raven Clan, I sentence you—"

"He didn't do it!" shouted Nym. A few more voices joined his. Moth, Pinch, Robin, Bates.

Cato turned on them, sword raised, and their shouts faltered.

"Enough of this. Let me hear you," shouted Ajax, trench coat flapping as he jumped back up on the stump. "Are you going to let this liar trick you and betray you again?"

Scattered shouts in response.

"Is Raven Clan full of cowards?" yelled Ajax. "I'll ask it one more time. Who wants to see Raven Clan rise again, under a real leader?"

The collective shout of, "I!" drowned out Leonardo's supporters like a wave, flattening them in one blow.

Then someone yelled, "You're no leader, Ajax!"

"You were nothing but Aleksander's snitch!" shouted someone else.

A sea of insults came hurling back.

Over Leonardo's shoulder, Pinch rolled up his sleeves. "Gonna be a fight," he crowed.

Others moved too, shuffling around as the clearing divided in two. Ajax's side outnumbered them by nearly double, and Leonardo realized exactly how it was going to play out.

Suddenly, Puck appeared in the middle of the clearing, waving his arms and raising his voice over the shouts. "Hey! Hey! Calm down! Half of you are hurt," he shouted. "The last thing we need is more fighting. Hey!" he yelled, as Snout shoved Nym into Strato. Nym, light and elfish, staggered into the sturdier frame of Strato, just as Bates grabbed Snout in a chokehold, sweat on his dark skin.

"Hey!" yelled Leonardo.

"What?" snapped Bates, fedora sliding over his eyes as he struggled to hold a swearing, kicking Snout.

"Listen to Puck!" shouted Leonardo. "We're barely standing as it is. If we turn on each other, Hawk Clan will come here and they'll flatten us."

Bates hesitated, then he released Snout, shoving him into the crowd. The rest of the clan edged apart, hands on their swords and mistrust radiating between them. Snarls and sideways glances flew in the close quarters of the clearing.

"Fight's over," said Puck, moving to jump up on the stump, then changing his mind when Ajax didn't budge. "We can debate this—calmly—later. For now, we need to get this camp in shape. That means food, water, shelter."

Ajax laughed as he jumped off the stump. Puck faltered, glancing back at him.

"That's exactly what you want, isn't it?" said Ajax. "That's what all of you want"—he looked at Leonardo and the boys standing around him—"Time. Time, time, time, to poison my clan out from under me. But we're not going to give them that, are we?"

Ajax strolled through the ranks of Ravens still poised to fight. Cato moved behind him, shoving boys out of his way.

"If anyone here wants to join this liar and his little band of halfwits, good riddance with you. Say hi to Aleksander for us. But if you want a real leader and you want to see Raven Clan rise again and burn every godforsaken inch of Hawk, Fox, and Bear territory up and down this fucking river, then you know who to follow. So"—he shoved Moth out of his way—"I want to hear it. Who's with me?"

Everyone shouted, except for the six boys standing around Leonardo.

"There." Ajax stopped directly in front of Leonardo. "Decision made."

He stepped around him, Cato in tow, and pushed between

Pinch and Bates. Their footsteps crunched away into the trees, leaving the clearing silent once again.

"Come on," said Moth, taking Leonardo's shoulder. "Let's get out of here."

***

Leonardo, Pinch, and Moth, along with Puck, Nym, Robin, and Bates, found a shaded hollow away from the main clearing, where one of the feeder streams ran through a jumble of mossy rocks, clear and cold as it tumbled over itself en-route to the river.

"He won," said Leonardo, furious at himself for losing the fight. *It happened so fast. I had them, then he just...*

"Shut up," said Pinch, kicking a pebble into the stream. "We're just getting started."

"No, we're not," said Moth. "We fight them, we're dead."

"I'm not following Ajax," said Pinch.

The second we oppose him, we give Ajax the green light to sic Cato on us. Leonardo saw no clean way out of this. "I told you *exactly* what I heard in the woods, right?" he said.

"The executioner?" said Puck, shuddering. "You told me about that too."

"If you were afraid of that, you should've joined them back there," said Pinch. "It's too late now."

"I'm with Pinch," said Bates, tense lines on his face. "Cato is probably looking for us already."

"Do we leave then?" asked Robin.

"Where would we go?" asked Nym. "Hawk Clan?"

"Gallus is just as dangerous as Ajax," said Leonardo. "Or close to." As far as he knew, Gallus didn't have an executioner.

"Bear would take us," said Robin, running a hand through his curls, fiercely orange in a square of sunlight.

Pinch climbed onto one of the moss-covered rocks, flicking a spider out of his way. "You want Lance for a leader?"

"Beats Ajax." Robin crossed his arms.

None of them are good options, thought Leonardo. *We'd be taking a big risk any way we turn.*

"What if we start our own clan," said Leonardo.

Everyone stopped. The stream continued rushing past, mirroring the speed of his thoughts.

Pinch is right; Ajax will kill us the first chance he gets. I pose too big a threat to him. The only option might be to get away as quickly as possible.

"The seven of us?" asked Moth. "We'd never survive on our own."

"It's better odds than we have here," said Leonardo.

"Let Ajax keep all the halfwits," said Robin. "Who needs them?"

"That's a lot of halfwits," said Nym.

He climbed onto a low branch, chewing his lip. "You want them as enemies?"

"They're already our enemies," said Pinch. "Weren't you out there just now?" He flicked another spider off his rock. "Shit, this thing is infested."

"Where would we go?" said Moth. "We can't live in Raven Clan territory—Ajax would just hunt us down. And there's no chance we're claiming a piece of another clan's territory."

"So we leave," said Leonardo. "We're rebuilding anyway. Who says we have to do it here? Gallus would be out of our hair, and if we go far enough, maybe we'll find a cave or something that we can turn into a camp."

"Leave?" said Nym. "And take the longboat? What about Ajax and Cato and everyone who didn't come with us? We'd just leave them here, helpless?"

"Sure," said Pinch. "It's what they'd do."

We can't just abandon them, thought Leonardo. *At least until they know what they're choosing between.*

"We'll give them a choice," he said. "From the safety of the water."

He paced to the edge of the stream. "Anyone who wants out can join us. As for the rest of them, the war needs to end. Taking the boat will cripple Raven Clan; they won't be able to patrol their borders or retaliate for last night. They'll have to negotiate with the other clans if they want to survive."

He remembered the chief's words. *Dark days are coming. Make the choice your brother couldn't.*

The choice is to leave all of this behind, thought Leonardo. *There is more to these woods than war, and Aleksander never understood that.*

Puck hadn't gotten a word in for over a minute and he looked ready to burst. "And how to you propose we get the longboat? Walk out and steal it? Sorry to break it to you, but there are a lot more of them than there are of us."

"Strato was on beach duty earlier," said Leonardo, pacing back from the stream. "If I can pull him over to our side, we might be able to take the boat before anyone realizes."

"Good luck," said Nym. "I heard him when he left the clearing. He called you a liar and um…" Nym cleared his throat. "Just like your brother."

Normally, that would've meant something, but Leonardo had more important problems to deal with.

"I'll talk to him," said Leonardo. "Strato is one of ours. We're not leaving him here with Ajax."

CHAPTER 27

The sun inched higher over the sheltered hollow and Leonardo's uneasiness climbed with it. They needed to get moving soon.

"Is everyone ready?" he asked. "Nothing will be easy from here on out."

"Yessir, leader-sir," said Bates, grinning.

Leader. Of a nameless, seven-person clan.

He shook the thought away. The second he let doubt creep in, the whole thing would come crashing down.

"We should pick a name," asked Nym. "If we want more members, we need to make it sound like a real clan."

"You're right," said Leonardo. "Ok, quickly, ideas?"

"Something dangerous," said Pinch. "Like Croc Clan."

"That's stupid," said Moth.

"You're stupid."

"Piranha Clan?" suggested Bates.

"That's worse than Croc Clan," said Nym.

"Shark Clan."

"We're not at the ocean."

The ocean. An idea struck Leonardo's mind. He remembered the carving Pinch had saved from the rubble, and its real-life counterpart they had searched for in vain, only days earlier.

"What about Butterfly Clan?" said Pinch, grinning darkly at Moth.

"Do we have to bring him?" said Moth. "Can't we leave him behind?"

"Lion Clan," said Leonardo.

"What?" said Moth.

"Seriously?" said Puck.

"Lion Clan," said Pinch, his tone pensive as he picked at a piece of moss.

"Yes," said Leonardo. "And..." He walked to the edge of the stream again, thinking. Six pairs of eyes followed him.

"According to the old stories, Lion Clan's camp was made of stone. Aleksander said no one claimed it after they fell."

"Shit!" said Bates, "Good luck burning a stone camp!" at the same time that Robin said, "How did Aleksander know?"

"Before Aleksander was leader," said Leonardo, "Raven Clan used to send parties all the way downriver. He's been to the Cove."

Leonardo's arrival in the woods came shortly after Aleksander became leader, and by then, the Darkwoods was in a state of full-flighted war.

"He used to talk about Lion Clan all the time," said Pinch, with enough superiority to remind them that he and Leonardo had both been around since the early days of Aleksander's leadership. "He said all the halfwitted clans in the Cove are afraid to take their camp. If Aleksander wasn't so petrified of lions, we could've done it years ago."

"Why are the other Cove clans afraid?" asked Robin.

Pinch shrugged. "They think the woods will punish them or something."

"And you want us to try?" asked Moth. "Leo, I really don't think this is a good idea."

"Normally, I'd agree—" started Leonardo.

"Use your brain, Moth," interrupted Pinch. "Lion Clan disappeared years ago, and so did the real lions. Now, out of the blue, you see a lion in camp, which no one else can find. Then, this ugly thing tries to kill me yesterday, and what is it? A fucking lion."

"Are you saying it's a sign?" asked Nym.

Pinch shrugged.

"I didn't know you believed in stuff like that," said Moth.

"I don't believe in *fairies*," said Pinch. "But if it means I get to be part of Lion Clan, I'll believe in all the hocus-pocus you want."

"Or maybe not a sign, but a call," said Nym. "Maybe the woods want Lion Clan back."

"I'm in," said Bates. His eyes gleamed under his fedora. "Shit, man! Lion Clan! This is gonna be awesome."

Gold light dappled the faces of Leonardo's clan through the heavy canopy. They looked excited, and they had good reason to be. Reviving Lion Clan would be an incredible thing, and getting away from this branch of the woods, which could only hold trouble for them, would be even better.

Aleksander's last words played through his mind. *Leonardo. Like a lion.*

Leonardo took a breath, then slowly released it, feeling the plan come together in his mind's eye. The path ahead was hazy, but through the mist lay a river, long and unknown, with a camp on the coast at the far end, made of stone and lost in a legend that needed to be re-awoken. Pinch was right; there had to be a reason for the lions showing up around them.

"We'll need supplies," said Leonardo. "And we'll have to be quick about it. Puck, Bates, I want you to grab as many swords and shields as you can, plus leather vests."

"Got it," they said in sync.

"Pinch, Robin; clothes, flint stones, cooking pots, bowls, and anything else you can get your hands on."

"Aye aye cap'n," Pinch botched a clumsy salute, which Robin echoed.

"Moth, Nym, you're on food. We can find more once we start travelling, but I don't want to leave with nothing. Grab a few baskets and run. Be careful, all of you. If Ajax really does plan to kill us all, we're in danger already. Get in and get out as quickly as you can."

"What are you going to do?" asked Robin.

"I'm going to get us a boat."

He met their determined faces around the circle.

A trickle of doubt tried to creep in. *Everything will be a challenge from here on in.*

Leonardo pushed it down. *Then we'll face each one.*

He squared his shoulders. "Ok, Lion Clan. Let's do this."

231

CHAPTER 28

Leonardo found Strato on the bank, hurling stones out over the water. Strato glanced back, then made a derisive noise and skipped another stone. It broke the surface half a dozen times before Leonardo lost count.

"Nice shot," said Leonardo.

"What do you want?"

"I came to apologize for this morning. I shouldn't have lied to you."

"Correct." Strato drew out the word, while simultaneously sounding like he couldn't care less.

"I know." Leonardo bent to pick up a stone and sent it sailing over the water. Strato flung one after it. It hit Leonardo's mid-skip, taking them both under.

Leonardo glanced at him. "I'm sorry."

Strato shrugged.

"I want to make up for it," said Leonardo.

"Good for you." Strato bent to free another pebble from the dirt. Leonardo did the same, wiping the soil off of it and fitting the smooth stone into the crook of his finger. He got his throw off before Strato, and Strato's took his down again mid-skip.

Do you practice that?

"Look, I know you're angry—" started Leonardo.

"Angry? Nah." Strato kicked a pinecone. "I get it. You didn't want people looking at you sideways. Ajax proved how these idiots can twist things."

Leonardo and Strato both bent to dig pebbles out of the soil. He let Strato throw first and tried to hit the skipping pebble. He missed by at least a foot and the corner of Strato's mouth curled in a hint of a smile. Then it dropped again.

"Thing is," said Strato, "I didn't believe any of Ajax's garbage. You know why? *Because I know you.* We may not talk all the time, but I've seen your face every day for what, six years? Eight years? Whatever a year even is here. You've got your issues, but all that traitor stuff is bullshit."

"He made a convincing case," said Leonardo.

Strato shook his head. "Didn't believe it for a second."

Leonardo pushed a rock into the dirt with his boot. A flock of swallows whisked by, hooking over the river and shooting skyward on an updraft. Leonardo wished he could escape his problems that easily.

"Get it now?" said Strato.

"You trusted me, after everything," said Leonardo. "And I didn't trust you back."

Strato shrugged.

"I'm sorry," said Leonardo.

"You already said that."

"I know," said Leonardo. "But I am. I was scared and I didn't think. I should've known you would believe me."

"You really would be a better leader than Ajax," said Strato. "If everyone wasn't too stupid to see it."

"I don't think a good leader lies to protect himself," said Leonardo.

"A good leader can make mistakes." Strato went to grab another pebble and stopped, glancing at Leonardo. "So long as they don't happen again."

"They won't," said Leonardo, as sincerely as he could. "I promise I'll trust you next time. I should have this time."

Strato shrugged. "It happened."

"We're good then?"

"Ancient history." Strato tossed Leonardo a pebble.

"Good." Leonardo sent it skipping over the water. "Because I need your help."

CHAPTER 29

Frogs and insects chirped an urgent harmony as Leonardo and the newly minted Lion Clan pushed the boat into the water, jumping inside and tripping over one another to get into position. Leonardo's hands shook with adrenaline as he climbed to the stern and took hold of the weathered wooden rudder.

The river glittered hard and bright, overexposed under a clear sky. Leonardo glanced at the tree line, expecting any second to see Ajax, Cato, and the others come charging out onto the bank. The keel scraped incredibly loud on the shale, and the oars sloshed as the rowers plowed the longboat out into the river.

The supplies lay piled in a heap mid-boat; Strato worked an oar alongside Nym, Puck, Robin, Bates, and Moth; and Pinch straddled his bench, slingshot loaded and poised to fire.

Despite all the rigid shoulders and white knuckles, it seemed like a clean getaway, which put Leonardo on edge.

This is too easy.

Nearby, a kingfisher plunged beneath the surface in a splash of droplets, labouring into the air a second later with a silver minnow flicking in its beak. A gust of wind whipped at Leonardo's shirt and fluttered thousands of leaves along the river. Except for directly across from them, where a collapsing graveyard of charred wood bared its blackened teeth, a burn wound on the evergreen face of the woods.

Leonardo tore his eyes away.

Stay focused.

The plan wasn't over yet. He couldn't live with the idea of completely abandoning his old clanmates; all the Ravens who'd stood beside Ajax. He needed to give them a choice.

From the safety of the water, of course.

Where are they? The beaten trail to the makeshift camp remained empty. *Six ex-Ravens just snuck in and stole supplies. Am I supposed to believe no one even noticed?*

And something else; the leaves around the trail weren't moving. Up and down the river, branches swayed and bobbed, rustling and whispering. But around the trail, the trees hung as if in a dead calm.

Leonardo tilted his head.

What the…?

"Leo," said Pinch, and the urgency in his voice made Leonardo whip around, just as a shape emerged from the burnt trees across the river.

"There's someone there!" said Bates.

"Shhh," hissed Puck.

It was a boy, maybe seven years old. He stumbled onto the shale beach, took two steps toward the water, then froze, gaze fixed on the boat.

Shit. Leonardo realized what was happening. *Now?*

Pinch realized at the same time. "No. Tell me he's not...The last thing we need is a new one."

"Well we've got one," said Leonardo. "Oars down. Take us over."

The newcomer stepped back as the longboat cut toward him, raven figurehead glaring over the prow. They pulled alongside the beach, scraping in the shallows, and Leonardo moved to the edge of the boat.

"Hi there," he called down, a few feet above the boy. The boy gave no response, staring back with wide eyes. He wore a paper-boy cap pulled low, wisps of blonde hair sticking out from under it. They all arrived young, but this boy seemed especially small.

"We're here to help you," called Leonardo. "You're probably pretty confused right now. Do you remember your name?"

The boy hesitated and Leonardo frowned, examining his face from the captain's platform.

He's very *little...* His features, his build. Almost delicate.

"It's ok," said Leonardo. "No one remembers their old name here."

The boy swallowed, taking in all of their faces. He had big eyes, green, like the trees behind him used to be.

"I'm going to come down, ok?" Leonardo placed a foot on the edge, and when the boy didn't react, he jumped down to the gravel.

The boy shied back a step as Leonardo hit the ground.

"I'm Leonardo," he said, offering his hand. "Everyone calls me Leo."

The boy hesitated, then he stepped out of the shadows, and the sunlight illuminated his features more clearly than before.

Wait...

Pinch spoke before he could, leaning on the forward bulwark. "That's not a boy."

"No," said Leonardo. "She's a girl."

***

"There's no such thing," said Puck.

"As girls?" asked Moth.

"As *clan* girls."

"Then what is she?"

"Is she Native?" asked Bates.

"Does she look Native to you?" demanded Pinch.

"She's one of us," said Moth. "There's no doubt about that."

The girl stepped backwards, small hands shaking. He guessed her a year or two older than his original estimate, maybe eight or nine. The wisps of blonde from under her cap gleamed gold in the sunlight, and everything about her, fair-skinned and petite, stood in stark contrast to the towering blackness of the burnt forest behind her.

"Guys," said Leonardo. "Enough. We're here to help you," he told the girl. "Every one of us went through what you're going through, and we want to get you to safety. Will you come in the boat with me? We'll take you somewhere safe, I promise."

You have no idea where you're taking her. Or the rest of this clan.

She nodded.

It doesn't matter. Anywhere is safer than here.

"Come here," he said, thoughts on Ajax and Cato again. "I'll help you up."

Where are they? They must know something is up by now.

Leonardo boosted her into the longboat, which took almost zero effort since she weighed nothing, then jumped up after her.

Everyone in the boat gawked at the girl, and Leonardo waved his hand at them when she turned her head. They snapped their eyes away.

"Where am I?" asked the girl.

"It's called the Darkwoods," said Leonardo. "Boys...er, *kids* have been showing up here for a hundred years. No one knows why."

"It's magic," said Moth.

"Like fairies," said Pinch.

"Shut up."

"You shut up."

"How do I get home?" she asked. Then her small features drew together, confused.

She doesn't know where 'home' is, thought Leonardo. He was all too familiar with that moment.

Before he could speak, a boom shook the woods.

CHAPTER 30

Everyone ducked, and the girl spun around, big eyes going to him as a blast of wind whipped over the bow. She grabbed her hat and Leonardo clamped a hand on her shoulder, bracing against the startling force of the wind. A loose shirt flew off the supply pile and Moth jumped to catch it. It plastered into his face, sending him reeling back. Pinch's tricorn hat came spinning backwards and Leonardo caught it with his free hand.

Branches swung wildly, leaves ripping off and flying into the air. And again, the bushes around the trail hung perfectly still, entirely untouched by the wind. Elsewhere, branches snapped and flying twigs joined the leaves in the air. Willow strands whipped, then, all at once, the wind died.

"What *was* that?" asked Robin.

"What the hell?" Bates jumped onto a bench, shading his eyes upriver.

A giant plume of white smoke curled out of the trees. It dissipated as Leonardo watched, like the last breath of a blown-out torch.

"The Natives?" said Leonardo, thinking of all the fires he'd seen when he visited their camp. But if this smoke came from a cooking fire, it had to be one the size of their camp.

It didn't look good, whatever it was.

Viola, he thought. She'd risked a lot to help them, and her warning had very possibly saved their lives. *If she's in danger now, we need to help her.*

"Oars down," ordered Leonardo. "We're going upriver."

"Seriously?" said Moth.

"What about the plan?" asked Puck.

"The plan can wait," said Leonardo. He glanced at the trail to the temporary camp, frozen in time. "I don't think they're going anywhere."

The woods are helping us.

So we could find the girl. And whatever waited upriver.

They rowed for the bend, Leonardo's fingers clamped tight around the rudder handle. Another kingfisher dove from a tree branch, lifting with a fish in its beak.

Leonardo paused to consider what he might be leading his clan into. He remembered the chief's warning: *these woods face a great danger. It watches us even now.*

Was it responsible for all of this?

For a stroke and a half, Leonardo contemplated telling them

to turn back, but they couldn't abandon Viola. Her warning had saved them. He refused to turn his back on her, even if it was dangerous.

So they carried on. Six rowers pushing the water as hard as they could. When they finally rounded the last bend, Leonardo leaned out to see—

Nothing.

The rocks were empty, entirely unremarkable.

"Bring us alongside," said Leonardo. "I'm going in to see."

"Into their camp?" demanded Moth. "Are you insane?"

"I'll be careful," said Leonardo. He couldn't shake the feeling that something was very wrong.

"You're not going alone," said Nym.

Puck nodded. "We'll all go in."

"Can we talk about this?" asked Moth, as the boat glided up to the rocks.

Leonardo forced the rudder over, bringing them alongside. "We're just going to look. If they're safe, we'll leave."

"And if they are in danger? Or worse…they're fine, and not happy to see us?"

Leonardo jumped out of the boat. He glanced back at Moth, as Puck and Nym scrambled out, tying a rope to the bowsprit and looping it around a sharp rock.

"We'll deal with it. Are you coming?" Leonardo examined the shadowed mouth of the trail, adrenaline buzzing through his fingers as he rolled his sword handle. He didn't have time to stand and debate.

"I'll stay here with…" Moth paused as the new girl climbed up onto the rocks.

"I want to come." She crossed her arms, challenging Leonardo.

Her boldness surprised him, but he didn't mind keeping her in sight.

"Sure, she's with us," said Leonardo.

"Well I'm not staying here alone," said Moth. He awkwardly vaulted out of the boat and stumbled up onto the rocks.

Good. Leonardo felt more comfortable with them all together. He started for the opening of the trail, still cloaked in morning shadows, hand on his sword. The other boys fell in behind him, barely breathing as they entered the trees.

The first thing he noticed was the campfire smoke, or lack thereof. The last time he'd been here, the smell reached him before he was halfway up the trail. Now, creeping along the hard-packed dirt, he smelled nothing but the forest.

When they came upon the bend in the trail before the camp itself, no guard moved out to intercept them. Leonardo recognized the bushes Dakota, Viola's brother, had met them at, and only a dragonfly whirred past now.

This isn't right.

He led the way through the opening into the clearing and his stomach dropped.

What the...

Every tree around the perimeter of the clearing stood dead, as black as if they'd been burned, though it didn't look like fire damage. Grass still grew around their bases. All the tipis, fire pits, and drying pelts were gone, replaced by patches of cracked dirt, and as he watched, a single leaf fluttered out of the barren treetops, swirling to the ground with the rest.

Leonardo walked out into the clearing, gazing around.

"Did they leave?" asked Nym.

"They were planning to," said Leonardo. "But..."

This is all wrong. The hairs on his arms stood on end.

"This was their camp?" asked Moth.

"It was," said Leonardo. He turned in a slow circle. The forest beyond that first ring of trees continued to bloom in shades of rich green, unaffected by whatever had blackened the ones before Leonardo.

What killed them? The blast could've ripped the leaves off, but the trunks...

"That had to be the boom, then," said Puck. "They disappeared."

"We don't know that," said Moth. "*We* don't make a boom when we disappear."

"Yes, but fifty of us don't disappear at once. What else could it have been?"

"What's that?" asked the girl. She pointed to a white lump poking above the grass.

Leonardo frowned and walked towards it. "I have no idea."

The other boys took notice and stepped up behind him. Leonardo stopped a few feet from it.

Roughly two and a half feet long, a crocodile skull lay in the exact centre of the clearing, bony and chipped, with a black line down the centre of its head. The line looked burnt, singed into the white bone.

"It's a croc skull," said Leonardo. He crouched, reaching out to feel the line.

"Don't touch it." He recognized Viola's voice and snapped his gaze up as she stepped out of the trees. She moved into the sunlight, in fur tufted moccasins and a beaded leather dress, twin braids framing her face.

Leonardo straightened. The boys around him tensed.

"Viola," said Leonardo.

"Back up," said Viola, watching the skull. "Don't let it see you."

"The skull?" Leonardo took a step back, looking at it anew.

She nodded. "The Dark is using its eyes. That's how it sees."

"The Dark?"

"The danger. *It.*"

Leonardo realized what she meant. "The danger the chief talked about."

"Yes."

A chill ran up Leonardo's spine. He took another step back and the other boys did the same, looking from Viola to the skull. She carefully skirted around behind it.

"It's called the Dark?" asked Leonardo.

She nodded.

"Like the *Dark*woods?"

"I don't know," said Viola. "My people say it was here a long time ago. I think the Darkwoods are named after it."

"Where are your people?" asked Leonardo.

"They're gone," said Viola. Her voice took on a strange tone. "The woods took them before *it* came."

The temperature in the clearing dropped. "And they left you behind?"

"The woods left me behind," she corrected, rapidly twisting a bead on her dress. "I had to run."

"Why?" asked Moth, before Leonardo could.

"Maybe this is my punishment for helping you. I don't know." The thread holding the bead snapped. She looked at it, surprised, then flicked it into the grass.

It's because of us.

He'd never even considered that possibility.

"I'm sorry," said Leonardo. "I never would've—"

"I knew I was breaking the rules," said Viola. "I wouldn't have done anything different."

"Will the woods bring your people back?" asked Moth.

"No," said Viola. "We were never supposed to stay in the Darkwoods this long. Even if they defeat the Dark, they'll go to the Redwoods or somewhere else. It will be years before they come back here."

"And this...*Dark*..." said Leonardo. "Will *it* come back here?"

"I think it's already here," said Viola. She turned her gaze on the dead trees. "It's everywhere."

Leonardo remembered the leafless maple he'd seen in the forest hollow, from under the mushrooms. It had seemingly gone from living to dead in the few minutes he stood talking.

What kind of thing are we dealing with?

"What is the Dark, exactly?" asked Leonardo.

"I don't know," said Viola. "It's a conscious being, like the woods, but it's a destroyer, not a creator. It will rip this place apart if it gets the chance."

"Great," said Pinch sarcastically. An undercurrent of alarm foiled his attempt to mask it. "Anyone here afraid of the dark? 'Cause it's fucking coming for you."

"My people will fight it," said Viola. "The woods sent them to the heart of it."

"And if they don't succeed?" asked Robin.

"Then we die, halfwit," said Strato. He ran his hands through his hair. "Shit."

"We're not going down without a fight," said Puck.

"You're going to fight *the dark*?" asked Pinch.

"Why not?" said Moth, surprising Leonardo. "We survived three clans."

"If it comes to it, we'll fight," said Leonardo. "But let's hope it ends before that."

Then Viola noticed the new girl.

"Who is she?" she asked, frowning.

"I just got here," said the girl, before Leonardo could introduce her. "I don't remember anything."

Leonardo tried to recall if he'd been this talkative so soon. Most boys took days to come to grips with their new situation.

"I see," said Viola, brow furrowed. "Well, welcome to the Darkwoods."

"I had a bad dream," said the girl. "A bunch of bad dreams, and then I was walking through the burnt trees, and I thought it was another dream, and then Lion Clan found me, and I realized I was awake."

"Lion Clan?" asked Viola.

Did I say Lion Clan in front of her? wondered Leonardo. He didn't think so. He couldn't recall anyone saying the new clan's name since they'd found the girl.

"It's a long story," said Leonardo slowly. "After the attack,

Ajax—one of Aleksander's se-coms—claimed leadership."

"He would've killed us if we'd stayed," said Moth.

"So a group of us are leaving," finished Leonardo.

Viola's whole demeanour changed. She crossed her arms, visibly pulling back. "Where will you go?"

"We're going to the Cove," said Leonardo. "To Lion Clan's old camp."

He wondered where *she* would go. Her people were gone, and apparently not coming back. He glanced at the other boys, trying to read their faces.

Should I ask?

Moth alone seemed to read his thoughts. He slowly nodded.

Leonardo had no idea what the other boys would think. She was Native; Ajax had already cast suspicion on Leonardo's relationship with them. But where else could she go?

He was leader. He needed to do what he felt was right.

"You can join us," said Leonardo. "If you want."

Pinch tensed in Leonardo's peripheral. The other boys shifted. Viola folded her arms tighter, defences on high.

"You'd be helping us," said Leonardo. "We need the numbers."

That wasn't wrong, but in truth, he didn't want to leave her behind. When he first went looking for her, he thought she'd been shunned from her tribe. That theory had proved initially wrong, but it was coming into reality now. He felt some responsibility to help her.

"We're leaving the Darkwoods," said Leonardo. "You're stuck in the Darkwoods. We can help each other."

"Without your warning, none of us might be here," said Moth. Nym and Puck nodded.

Thank you. Leonardo didn't know what he'd do if the boys objected to his offer.

"And like Leo said," added Moth. "Lion Clan could use another member."

Viola lowered her arms, glancing back at the skull and the dead trees.

"I've been suggesting this for years," said Strato. "I'm not arguing."

"Shut up, Strato," said Nym.

"What do you think?" Leonardo asked her, cutting over them. "Do you want to be a Lost Boy?"

Viola smiled a little. She straightened her dress.

"Welcome to Lion Clan," said Leonardo.

CHAPTER 31

The woods were noticeably worse for wear on the trip back. More branches stretched out, blackened and empty-handed, and several bushes virtually decomposed as he watched, shriveling smaller and more decrepit by the moment.

An eerie veil hung over all of it, like a filter on the sun; though to the naked eye, it shone just as bright as before. Leonardo couldn't quite understand it; the woods just felt *wrong*.

When they came in sight of the beach, all eyes turned forward in anticipation.

Whatever magic froze the camp before had broken now, and Ajax stood on the bank, sword drawn, with the rest of Raven Clan behind him.

"There they are!" shouted Rugby from the bank, one leg over the side of the clinker.

"Who are they?" asked the new girl quietly, not quite as bold anymore. She shifted half-behind Leonardo.

"Bad people," said Leonardo. "Some of them. We going to give the rest the chance to escape with us."

Leonardo stepped up to the rail and cupped his hands to his mouth.

"Ajax!" he called.

Ajax shoved Rugby out of his way and took two strides down the bank. "What is this?" he yelled. "I'm leader now, you're just digging your grave."

"We're breaking from Raven Clan," called Leonardo.

Ajax's mouth fell open. "You're...But..."

"Slow up," Leonardo called to his rowers. They forced their oars backwards in the water, bringing the boat to a halt twenty feet off of the bank.

"We're leaving the Darkwoods," said Leonardo. "Whoever wants to join us is free to do so."

Ajax laughed, stiff and slightly panicked. "You're leaving? Is this a joke? You can't—"

"Of course we can," said Leonardo.

"But..." For all his long hair and lanky body, he looked nothing like Aleksander, who wouldn't have gotten flustered if half the clan said they were getting on a rocket ship and flying to the moon.

"Where will you go?" called Jack. He stepped down the bank, tailcoat smudged with dirt from sleeping on the ground. His normally impeccable hair spiked up at strange angles.

"Somewhere safe," said Leonardo. "We're leaving all of this war and death behind. Join us and you won't have to fight anymore."

He thought about the Dark and wondered just how truthful that statement was.

Jack studied the ten of them, running a hand over his jaw.

"Who is she?" said Ajax suddenly, spotting Viola. "Or she?" he added, seeing the new girl.

"You have girls?" asked Rugby.

Whispers flew around the ranks of battered Ravens.

"Viola was left behind," said Leonardo. "Her people are off fighting the danger the chief warned us about—"

"She's Native! Traitor!" shouted someone behind Ajax. A few other boys took up the call.

"And this is the danger *I* warned you about." Ajax pointed his sword at Leonardo. "This puppet belongs to the Natives now. Anyone who joins him is sealing their own fate."

"Take me to the bank," Leonardo said to his rowers.

"What?" demanded Moth. He clutched his oar handle suspended, a bench ahead of Leonardo.

"Are you insane?" asked Strato, up near the bow.

"To the bank," said Leonardo. "Oars down."

His rowers responded hesitantly, and the Ravens on the bank bunched tighter, swords glinting in the sunlight.

This is a terrible idea. But I need to try.

Even with Viola and the new girl, Lion Clan needed members. Even one or two could make enough difference to tip the scales in their favour.

As soon as they scraped against the shale, Leonardo jumped to the beach. He landed in a crouch and slowly rose to his feet.

"Raven Clan," said Leonardo. Ajax held his sword out threateningly and Leonardo pushed it aside, stepping past him.

"Our camp is burned," he said, addressing the cluster of boys. "The Natives disappeared this morning. There's a new danger coming, called the Dark, and division is not going to help us defeat it."

The boys watched him with guarded expressions, but they were listening, and that was all he needed.

"If we stay here and try to get back on our feet, Hawk will just run over us again. And again, and again, until we're either dead or so broken that it doesn't matter. The only solution we can see is to—"

"Flee? Like cowards?" said Ajax, finding his tongue again.

"Start fresh," said Leonardo. "Raven Clan fell with Aleksander. Trying to bring it back would be as impossible as trying to bring him back."

A pebble came flying from a slingshot somewhere in the crowd. Leonardo ducked and it whizzed past his head.

"Who shot that?" yelled Pinch from the boat.

"Traitor!" someone yelled back.

Shouts exploded from either side, and Ajax smiled.

"Stop!" yelled Leonardo. "Blame me all you want. I'm not going to plead my case again. All I ask is that anyone who wishes to join us steps forward now."

Jack and Page spoke quickly in hushed voices, Will bit his lip, Snout and Rugby scratched their heads. Leonardo held his breath. A few boys started to step forward, then Ajax made eye contact with Cato and there came the sound of knuckles cracking.

Cato, almost a head taller than the boys around him and easily twice their weight, pulled his ugly face back in a grin as he ground his fists together. The Ravens paused, glancing at him, and all at

253

once the potential turncoats began to fade back into the crowd, their patriotism re-inspired and stronger than ever.

Leonardo's heart sunk. He looked at the longboat, and the nine faces looking back at him. Was that enough for a clan? Ten people?

Ajax took another step toward him, angling himself between Leonardo and the boat, sword pointed at his chest. Leonardo took a step back, placing a hand on the hilt of his own sword.

"Give back the boat," said Ajax. "Now."

Behind him, the mass of Ravens began moving, climbing down the bank to block Leonardo's path to the boat. A few of them moved as if to grab the boat, but hesitated without Ajax's direct order.

They're terrified of him already, thought Leonardo.

Some cast torn glances at the boys in the boat. Leonardo wished he could give them more time to decide. A chance to think without Ajax present.

But Ajax kept advancing and Leonardo kept backing up. He caught his foot on a rock and almost stumbled, but he kept his feet and staggered back to the edge of the water.

Will wouldn't look at him. He was a good kid, but too believing. If Leonardo could talk to him away from Ajax, and explain what really happened, he had a feeling Will would see things differently. And Jack. He and Leonardo had never been close, but he was a good one and he belonged on the right side of this split. Page too, and probably three or four others, if he could just get the chance to set things straight with them.

Unfortunately, Leonardo knew he wasn't going to get that

chance. He took another step back as the water lapped up against his heels.

Leonardo drew his sword. Ajax grinned, stopping in the weedy grass.

"You want a fight?" he asked. He sheathed his sword and turned his back on Leonardo. "Cato, kill him. Ravens, get me my boat back."

Cato had one talent in the entire world, and the entire weight of it barrelled towards Leonardo, another smile splitting his face. Every time they'd crossed swords in training, every insult and bruise and cut flashed before Leonardo's eyes.

It's all led up to this. One last fight. One final winner.

He took his sword two-handed and met Cato's first blow.

Meanwhile, the rest of Raven Clan splashed into the river, shouting and swearing, and the new Lions jumped to repel them. Viola, who'd never experienced their violence up close, took a step back. The girl staggered back with her, alarm on her small face.

The boys had no such pause. Pinch fired his slingshot like a machine-gun, taking down four Ravens before they got knee deep. Nym, Robin, and Moth used their oars to beat back the ones who made it through, and Strato, Bates, and Puck vaulted overboard, swords drawn.

Cato and Leonardo hacked at each other in a blinding battle, the blows heavier and more vicious than they'd ever been in training. Cato took a cleave that barely missed Leonardo's head and Leonardo stumbled away.

An inch closer and I'm dead.

Leonardo blocked the next attack with his sword, gasping at the pain of the impact. Their blades sang out in the cool air.

I have to end this fast. He couldn't sustain much more of Cato's weight pounding through his hands.

In the water, Snout grabbed the end of Robin's oar and dragged the boat offline, but a second later he was struck in the head with an apple, then another, and a third one glanced off his shoulder as he fell back, releasing the oar.

The duo of Viola and the new girl opened fire on the rest of the attackers, an open supply bag at their feet. Viola hurled an apple at Rugby and another at two Ravens trying to grab Moth's oar.

Ajax screamed orders from the bank, but the Ravens fell back, and Bates, Puck, and Strato scrambled back over the side, sloshing to their benches. A moment later, they had the boat lurching into motion and struggling up the bank toward Leonardo.

Pinch drew back a stone and fired, narrowly missing Cato. It gave Leonardo a window and he slammed the pommel of his sword hard into Cato's cheekbone, sending him staggering back.

Good enough.

Leonardo jumped up onto a rock in the water and leapt for the longboat just as the stern platform slid past. He hit the deck, grabbing the stem for support and keeping his feet. Leonardo twisted around, watching the Ravens who still chased them stumble to a halt in waist-deep water.

Cato stood on the bank, holding his face where Leonardo had struck him. Blood dripped between his fingers.

"Take us out," Leonardo ordered his crew, jamming his sword into his belt.

His rowers responded instantly, and the long, fast boat of Raven Clan peeled away from the bank, now the ship of Lion Clan, setting out on a journey to take up the mantle that had been set down long ago.

CHAPTER 32

The first challenge faced by the newly independent Lion Clan was simply getting out of the Darkwoods.

They elected to go through Bear Clan territory at the fork, for the obvious reason that Fox was the alternative, and if it was like everyone said, getting lost would be as much of a risk as getting caught. Leonardo halted them just before the border, stopping to rearrange his crew before they officially crossed into enemy territory. In truth, they were already in enemy territory, but Raven Clan had only a clinker now, so he wasn't too concerned about an attack from behind.

That didn't stop him from glancing back every few minutes, just to make sure the river remained empty, rippled by their wake and the tiny insects on the surface.

Leonardo wondered what Ajax would do about his boat situation. Like the treehouses, the boats had been there since

258

before anyone could remember. Leonardo doubted this was the first time a clan had lost their boat, but that didn't make the solution any easier. The most natural route would've been to go to the Natives and attempt to trade for a boat or have them build a new one, but the last of the Natives was sitting three rows in front of Leonardo.

Maybe they'd try to build one themselves, although it would never be as sturdy or watertight as the old boat. Leonardo placed a hand on the stem, thankful that his clan was on this side of the equation. He wondered briefly if it had been the right thing to do, or if taking the boat had sealed Raven Clan's fate for good. But no, everyone who'd stayed behind had known what they were signing up for. And he didn't feel a shred of pity for Ajax himself. Let him get a taste of actual work.

Leonardo sent Pinch to the point watchman's post and split Viola and the new girl on the two flanks. It wasn't ideal; neither had ever been on a patrol and one had barely spent any time in the woods, but nothing was ideal about starting a ten-person clan with nothing but an idea for a camp. They would all have to learn quickly.

Leonardo scanned the banks as they streamed through Bear Clan territory, a stiff wind blowing in his face. A lot of that wind was generated from the six-oar rowing team of Moth, Puck, Strato, Robin, Bates, and Nym, who dug hard to get them through enemy territory as fast as possible.

Despite all of their speed however, there was nothing they could do to avoid the Bear boat that materialized around the next bend. Pinch called out the warning from the bow, but Leonardo had already seen it, and the Bears had seen them. Shouts went up from the other boat, and Lance leaned out over the water, shading his eyes.

His blonde hair looked freshly cut, and deeply fake smile-lines stood out around his eyes and mouth. He was dressed in his usual ill-fitting brown shirt.

Leonardo swore inwardly. "Slow up," he called to his crew.

The Bear boat angled in to receive them, oars swinging up and out of the way of Lion Clan's flank.

"Friends," called Lance as they glided together. "This is an unexpected visit."

An electric undertone tinged his voice, an edge that told Leonardo he was just as tense as they were. Borders were a serious subject, and Leonardo's clan was well over Bear Clan's.

The boats slipped alongside and boys from Bear Clan grabbed the edge between Lion Clan's oars. Leonardo gripped the rudder, the wood slick with sweat under his palm. Bear Clan was the biggest clan in the Darkwoods, and this patrol alone outnumbered the entire force of Lion Clan. The longboats clunked together and every hand on either boat went to a sword, but Lance gave the slightest shake of his head and the Bears paused with their weapons sheathed. Leonardo released a little of his breath and opened his mouth to speak, but a voice cut him off.

"They have girls!"

"What are they doing there?"

Viola leaned back, indignant, as the Bear boat erupted into chaos.

"She's Native!"

"They're working with the Natives!"

"It's a trap!"

A few boys looked wildly toward the banks.

"We need to get out of here!"

"Boys. *Boys!*" shouted Lance. "*Enough.* Raven Clan are our friends. There has been no war between our clans, and they have no reason to attack us. Isn't that right, Leonardo?" The edge in his voice sharpened.

'No war' was a tenuous statement.

There was no war because Aleksander convinced you it wasn't in your best interest.

"There's no trap," said Leonardo. "And we come as Lion Clan."

Lance paused, then he laughed. "Lion Clan. So Raven Clan has died? Have you taken over, Leonardo?"

Leonardo shook his head. "Raven Clan is still standing. Ajax has taken over, but the old camp is burned to nothing. We decided to leave and start fresh rather than stay in the ashes."

"As Lion Clan, no less. A lofty quest. Who is Ajax?"

"One of Aleksander's se-coms."

"What happened to Aleksander?"

"He disappeared." There was no point lying.

"Really? Interesting. Who are they?" Lance nodded at the girls.

A hard edge on the rudder-handle dug into Leonardo's hand. "Members of Lion Clan."

"Indeed. *Lion Clan* is clearly looking for members wherever it can find them. How did a Native girl come to be a *Lion*, I wonder?"

"We're just passing through," said Leonardo. "We'll be out of your waters as soon as we reach your far border."

"Good answer," said Lance. "I would not share my secrets

261

either, were I in your shoes. Though I must ask…the other girl, she's not Native, is she?"

"May we pass through your territory?" asked Leonardo, more forcefully.

He wondered what he'd do if Lance demanded answers. He was inclined to play his cards close, even with seemingly benign information. Lance was a snake in bears' clothes. Leonardo wasn't even exactly sure what that meant.

I have to do whatever gets us out of here as quickly as possible.

Lance exchanged glances with a member of his clan.

"Is there a problem?" asked Leonardo.

"Depends," said Lance. "Will Lion Clan be setting up camp in the lake?"

"I'm sorry?"

"The lake." The amused lines deepened around Lance's eyes. "This leg of the river ends in a lake, just beyond our territory."

Leonardo stared at him. "This is the end of the river?" He'd always been told that it flowed all the way to the ocean.

"*This leg* ends," said Lance. "If you want to keep going, you have to go through Fox territory."

Leonardo swore inwardly again.

"That's going to be ridiculously dangerous," said Moth.

"I know," said Leonardo. The other boys in the boat started talking, and he thought about the narrow stream at the bottom of the waterfall, overgrown with brambles and bathed in shadows.

"Have you ever been in Fox Clan territory?" Lance grinned, the smile-lines curving around his lips. "You haven't, have you?"

Leonardo didn't answer and Lance grinned wider. His smile said everything that Leonardo already knew. Bear Clan had one allegiance; themselves, and while they may never be the ones swinging the sword, they'd happily feast on the carnage of every other clan in the Darkwoods.

They should be the ones named after ravens, thought Leonardo.

But then again, the name suited Ajax just as well.

"Raven Clan had so many enemies, you never had to cross borders for a fight," said Lance. "You don't really know the woods do you?"

"Some direction would help," said Leonardo.

Lance shook his head. "What if our Fox friends found out?"

Leonardo stared at him. *This is ridiculous.* "Oars down," he said to his rowers.

The Bears holding Lion Clan's flank looked back at their leader.

"Let them go," said Lance. Then he looked at Leonardo, still smiling. "It's a maze in there, be careful not to get lost."

Leonardo didn't grace that with an answer.

CHAPTER 33

"Are we seriously going down there?" asked Robin, gazing down the rocky steps of the small waterfall into Fox Clan Territory.

"What's the choice?" asked Puck.

Even on sunny days like today, Fox Clan's waters lived in perpetual shadow, the brambles growing under a thick canopy. Mosquitoes buzzed in swarms over the short stretch of visible river.

"It hasn't even been twenty-four hours since they attacked us," said Moth.

"Which means they'll be weak," said Puck.

"No more than us," said Leonardo. "We've now fought two battles since last night."

A wasp circled his head and Leonardo swatted it away.

"I was almost killed by a Fox," said Robin. "I don't feel like giving them another shot."

"No, it was a Hawk," said Pinch. He mimed a slingshot in the air. "A Hawk rock."

Next to Leonardo, the new girl observed all of this with the utmost attention, small features pulled together in concentration.

"Listen," said Puck. "Gallus was in charge. Fox won't do a thing without his orders, and he's a mile upriver with his Hawks."

"Bull. Shit." said Bates.

"Chief Tokala planned it," said Viola, drawing everyone's attention. "Not Gallus."

A beat of silence passed. Finally, Strato broke it. "Even better. He's on the other side of the woods."

This isn't about Tokala or Gallus, thought Leonardo. *It's about Hero and Fox Clan. And they've attacked us twice in the last thirty-six hours.*

"We can't go through Fox territory," said Leonardo.

"Why?" asked Strato.

"Because, halfwit," said Pinch. "See how dense those bushes are? They could hammer us with slingshots and we'd be lucky to spot one of them."

Robin unconsciously rubbed the back of his head.

"So what do we do?" asked Nym.

The Backwaters, thought Leonardo.

"The Backwaters," said Viola. "Behind my camp. We can use them to skirt around and pick up the river further down."

"*Back waters?*" asked Pinch.

"It's a system of lakes and rivers," said Leonardo. "East of here, behind the tree line."

"Why have I never heard of it?" asked Puck.

"No one has," said Leonardo. "In Raven Clan at least."

"If it lets us avoid Fox, then let's go," said Robin, lifting his oar to break rhythm from the back-paddling that held them above the waterfall.

"No so fast," said Puck, still working his oar. "Do we have to go all the way past camp again?"

"Further," said Leonardo, glancing at Viola. "The river ties into the Backwaters up past the Tree Cliffs."

"You want us to go into Hawk Clan territory?" said Strato. He missed a stroke and the boat began to twist toward the waterfall.

"The fork is just past the cliffs," said Viola.

"It's too risky," said Moth, fighting to get the boat in place again.

"How far past?" Leonardo asked Viola. "Twenty strokes? Forty?"

Viola scratched the back of her head. "I don't...I've never actually been—"

"Great," Pinch cut her off. "You want us to risk our lives for something that might not even be there. Good call bringing her, Leo, don't know what we'd do without—"

"Oh it's there," said Viola.

Pinch turned on her. "If you've never been there, you can't—"

"Yes I can," said Viola. "Trust me, I—"

"Trust you?" said Pinch. "Give me one reason why we should trust you on anything."

"*Pinch*," said Moth.

"I'll prove it," said Viola. "Right now."

"How?" demanded Pinch. "If you've never been there, you can't promise any—"

266

She closed her eyes, straightening her back and drawing a slow breath.

Pinch rose from his point watchman's bench. "Listen, girl—"

"Please stop talking." Viola neither opened an eye nor moved a muscle.

"Leo?" said Pinch.

"Give her a chance," said Leonardo.

Pinch made a disbelieving noise, betrayal on his face. He said something under his breath and sat back on his bench.

A second later, Viola blinked open her eyes.

"The fork is a hundred yards past the cliffs and the Lost Boys are in their camp, far upriver."

Every person in the boat stared at her.

Leonardo would've thought no brand of magic could surprise him anymore, but the woods kept tossing new ones at him.

"How did she do that?" asked the new girl, awe in her voice.

"Are you psychic?" asked Bates.

"Not exactly," said Viola. "They're sending a patrol in fifteen minutes. We have to leave now."

No one spoke. A flock of silver sparrows whisked over the water. The new girl gasped, experiencing her first of the woods' impossible creatures.

"Leo," said Viola. "We have to go."

"Ok," said Leonardo. *We can understand all of this later.* "Let's go."

"You have to be kidding," said Pinch.

"Do you have a better option?" asked Leonardo.

"You mean one that doesn't involve us getting killed?'

"Viola said they're in camp."

"And I say they're riding on the back of a giant goose waiting to kill us the second we stick our half-witted heads over the border."

"This is serious, Pinch."

"Then *be* serious, *Leo*. Native Girl doesn't know jack shit about what the Hawks are doing."

"Fourteen minutes," said Viola.

"Yeah," said the new girl, scrambling to pledge herself on Viola's team. "Fourteen minutes." She placed her hands on her hips.

"What?" said Pinch.

"They leave camp in fourteen minutes now," said Viola.

"How could you possibly know that?"

"Because, a minute ago I said they were leaving in fifteen."

Bates snorted.

"Yeah," said the new girl. "A minute ago she said they were leaving in fifteen."

He wondered if this was going to happen every time Viola said something.

"I say we go," said Robin. "It's the best chance we've got."

"I agree," said Moth. "Even if Viola's wrong, we have better odds of getting to the Backwaters through the edge of Hawk than trying to cross Fox's entire territory."

Viola gave Leonardo a *thirteen-and-a-half-minutes* look, mimicked a second later by the new girl. Leonardo nodded, suppressing a small smile. "Then let's go."

This time, all six oars reversed in sync.

***

He felt the change in his rowers the second they came within sight

268

of the charred Raven Clan beach. They were intruders now. Trespassers in their own territory. On the opposite bank, Rugby stumbled to his feet from the beach guard's log and sprinted into the trees.

"Pick it up a bit," said Leonardo, trying to sound calm. They slid past the stretch of bank where he had fought Cato earlier, then Ajax burst through the trees, shouting something unintelligible.

Everyone in the boat jumped and the oars faltered. Ajax strode down the bank and Cato exploded through the bushes behind him, an ugly purple wound marring his left cheek.

"Come here and fight, cowards!" shouted Ajax.

Other Ravens appeared through the trees, swords glinting in the sunlight.

The new girl shifted backwards, putting Leonardo between her and Ajax.

"Keep going," said Leonardo, hearing the tension in his own voice. The oars swung sloppy, out of rhythm.

"Keep going," he snapped as Ajax shouted something else from the beach. The oars cut harder on this stroke and the boat began to pick up again.

"Good. And...*Row*. And...*Row*. And...*Row*," he shouted, raising his voice over Ajax's screeching. He caught movement as three Ravens launched the clinker.

"Clinker in the water!" yelled Pinch.

"Eyes ahead, point-watch," shouted Leonardo. "Rowers, pick it up!"

Viola reached for the supply bags, then changed tactics and pulled one of the extra swords out from under the bench. Moth, Puck, Strato, Robin, Bates, and Nym bore down, launching

269

into one deep stroke after the next and pulling away from the clinker in their wake.

When it became obvious they weren't going to catch up, Viola returned the sword to its place.

She'll do fine here, thought Leonardo. *We'll all be fine.*

Then they rounded the bend from Raven Clan for the last time. It was a strange feeling, and after a moment he realized why. It wasn't a feeling at all. It wasn't anything. His family was in this boat with him, and without them, the forest meant nothing.

He turned his attention on the river ahead.

Tension rippled across the boat as they approached the Tree Cliffs, towering over the river in walls of sheer stone, tinted with moss and split down the middle where the water ran down from Hawk Clan territory. The giant pines that the cliffs were named after stood tall and proud above the opening, extending the wall another hundred feet toward the sky.

Leonardo's eyes locked on the opening between the cliffs, and the passage into Hawk Clan territory. "Keep rowing," he said as the oars slowed.

Up front, Pinch stretched to see through the opening.

"Pinch?" asked Leonardo.

"It's clear."

They cut between the cliffs and into the narrow, rock-walled tunnel, officially crossing into Hawk territory. Leonardo held the rudder steady, leaning out over the water to see around the bowsprit. Up front, Pinch braced against the bowsprit itself, back rigid as he scanned the far end of the passage.

The current rushed stronger between the cliffs and the oars sloshed loudly as Lion Clan's rowers dug in, all hesitation gone.

Safety now lay out ahead of them, down the fork that Viola had promised, and no one wanted to spend any more time than necessary getting to it. The stone smelled like pure iron, like blood, and the sunlight reflected off the ruddy walls of the tunnel, tinting their strained faces amber.

When they came out into the open, they found themselves in the base of a rocky bowl, filled with sand and gravel and the occasional scrawny bush, fighting for life in a crack between two rocks. The river sparkled, shallow and wide and empty of Hawks as it snaked through the dry land.

Leonardo breathed a sigh of relief. *She was right.* A hundred yards ahead of them, the bank cut back on itself, down another leg of the river.

"That's it!" said Viola, pointing. "That's the fork."

A hawk cry split the air.

The boat lurched as the rowers panicked and Moth's oar slammed into his stomach.

"Shit," Bates swore, half-standing in his footwell.

"Where are they?" shouted Robin.

The river remained empty, the plants stunted and offering no shelter. Red sand baked in the late morning sun, barren of even a footprint.

Behind the rocks, thought Leonardo. The craggy landscape offered one hiding place; the crevasses and boulders and sandy dips in the land itself.

"Relax, halfwits," said Pinch. "It's the real thing."

He pointed to a twisted tree, where a speckled hawk hunched on a leafless branch.

"Let's get out of here," said Leonardo.

They cut the corner with splashing oars and started away from the main body of the river, travelling fast with the current. A rabbit looked up from the sand, then bounded down a ravine, through a stand of spiny bushes. A dozen strokes later, all of it vanished from sight, lost around a sharp bend in the landscape.

"I told you it would work," said Viola. An undercurrent edged her words, aimed directly at Pinch.

"We're not out of Hawk territory yet," said Leonardo, still scanning the rocks and crags behind them.

"Yes we are," she said. "We're in the Backwaters."

Leonardo twisted around, along with the six rowers. Out ahead of them sprawled a delta, lush with oversized bushes and giant cattails, fuzzy tops as tall as a person swaying in the breeze. Lichen-draped trees grew right out of the water, forming sheltered alcoves where long, dark shapes lurked in the weeds.

Hundreds of birds, frogs, and insects sung from grassy islands, and a mile of lily-pads spanned out across the slow-moving water. A cocktail of heady flowers perfumed the air, mixed with the organic taint of the wetlands.

The river split into countless distributaries, and a disjointed symphony of waterfowl called out from around the delta.

A giant butterfly flapped past, stirring the water with the force of its wingbeats.

"Wow," said the new girl, peering out over the bulwarks.

"This place has been here the whole time?" asked Robin.

"We should just set up camp here," said Nym. "No one would ever know."

"Hawk Clan must know about this," said Moth.

272

"They do," said Viola. "This is where they came to meet with Fox and Bear."

"We have to go far enough that they can't find us," said Leonardo. "We continue on to the Cove. But I think we should stop here for a few minutes. We have some business to attend to."

It was time they chose a proper name for Lion Clan's newest member.

CHAPTER 34

They tied the boat to the trunk of a tree growing in the water, then shipped their oars and let it drift near a grass island, where a flock of red herons waded in the shallows.

"This is Moth, Bates, Pinch, Robin, Puck, and Viola," Leonardo told the new girl, pointing around the boat. "None of us remember our names from before—"

Puck opened his mouth to interject, pointing at Viola, but Viola stopped him with a subtle head-shake.

"…so we get new names when we arrive here," finished Leonardo. The girl would find out soon enough that she was an anomaly. He preferred her thinking that she and Viola were the same until she had time to fully acclimatize.

"Those are funny names," said the girl. Then she gasped. "Do I get one?"

She clasped her hands together, excited. Her green eyes shone hopefully, blonde wisping out from under her paperboy cap.

"Of course," said Leonardo, grinning. "But the tradition states that everyone else picks it. And if I were you, I wouldn't encourage something 'funny'. These boys are too good at that already."

"Ok." She laced her hands behind her back, then brought them forward again. She shuffled her feet, eagerly awaiting her new name.

"Any suggestions?" asked Leonardo, chuckling at her enthusiasm.

Robin cocked his head. "How about Greenie, because of her eyes?"

"Or Owl," said Bates, making his eyes wide.

"That's the dumbest name I've ever heard," said Puck.

"Better than Butterfly," said Pinch, grinning darkly at Moth.

"Shut up," said Moth.

"Smallfry," suggested Robin.

"Paperboy," said Bates.

"She's a girl," said Puck.

"Papergirl," Bates shrugged.

The girl made a face.

She's learning, thought Leonardo. Lesson one: never trust the clan boys. Regardless, he didn't intend to let them name her Papergirl.

"If we named people after their hats," said Puck, "Pinch would be Blackbeard and you'd be Sherlock."

"Do you see a hair on this chin?" asked Pinch. He reclined in the bow, head against bowsprit and boots crossed on the bench in front of him.

"Not the point," said Puck.

"Sherlock didn't wear a fedora," said Bates.

"Yes he did," said Puck.

"No he didn't. He wore a plaid hat, with flaps in the front and back."

"A deerstalker," said Moth.

"What?" asked Bates.

"How could you possibly know that?" asked Pinch.

"I do!"

One of the red herons squawked from the reeds, startling him.

"Right you do. There's your name," he called to Leonardo. "Deerstalker."

"Seriously?" said Leonardo.

The banter felt good. The attack, the fire, Ajax, the escape had all been laced with danger and tension. This easy, familiar energy was much needed. He was tempted to let it go on a bit longer, but his internal clock told him they needed to get moving again. Aleksander's assassination had been successful, after all— Leonardo swallowed the bitter thought. *Stay focused. He's still Aleksander, whether he believed in you or not. He still treated you like garbage.*

Either way, Hawk and Fox were due anytime to come into these waters seeking their reward of information.

"She needs a girl's name," said Viola. "What about Charlotte?"

Everyone paused. Next to Leonardo, the girl brightened. He guessed at least half the reason was because Viola suggested it, but if it worked for her, then he—

"Too... Je ne sais quoi," Strato waved his hands in the air.

"Wow, fancy words," said Bates.

"And it's too long," said Nym.

"Jane," said Pinch. "Short and it's a girl's name."

"Does she look like a Jane to you?" demanded Strato.

Leonardo closed his eyes. *Never mind.*

"Charley, then," said Moth. "It's short for Charlotte and it actually kind of sounds like one of us."

"What do you think?" Leonardo quickly asked the girl. He was ready to let her pick it herself if it meant they could get moving.

"I like it," said the girl, smiling shyly at Viola.

"So do I," said Viola.

"Good," said Leonardo. He placed a hand on the girl's shoulder. "Welcome to Lion Clan, Charley."

CHAPTER 35

The delta fed into a big lake, surrounded by giant pines and big, flat rocks like the ones on the Native beach. The water glistened, calm and still, and in the exact centre of the lake floated a canoe.

Viola gasped at the sight of it.

"Leo!" she said, her eyes sparking. "It's them!"

"Let's go," he said.

Leonardo eyed the canoe as they plowed toward it. A single figure rose up, lifting a longbow. He nocked an arrow and drew it back.

"Shit." Leonardo jumped up on the bench in front of him, waving his arms in a gesture that was hopefully non-hostile enough to make the shooter hesitate. Then Viola jumped up, scrambling to climb onto her bench.

"Dakota!" she yelled, cupping her hands to her mouth.

Leonardo squinted. *Is that Dakota?* The warrior raised a hand to shield his eyes.

"Viola?" he yelled back.

"Don't shoot," she shouted. "It's Raven Clan!"

He drew back his arrow again. His bow spanned all the way from the top of the canoe to a foot over his head.

Lion Clan's rowers hesitated.

"Move and I shoot," called Dakota.

"Stop!" yelled Viola, "I'm not in danger."

"Get down from there!"

"Hold up," Leonardo said to his rowers. They lifted their oars, which barely pushed water anyway.

"We come in peace," he called to Dakota.

They glided closer. Dakota watched him over the arrow.

"Permission to approach?" called Leonardo.

"Please, Dakota," begged Viola.

Dakota didn't speak for a long minute, then he released the tension in his bow and lowered it to his side. Leonardo breathed a sigh of relief.

"Permission granted," said Dakota.

Leonardo stepped backwards onto the stern platform. Viola stayed standing on her bench as the rowers guided them alongside, and Charley looked from her to the canoe and back again.

Pinch didn't stray from his position, never breaking in his constant scan of the banks beyond the canoe.

"What are you doing with them?" demanded Dakota.

"I thought you'd gone," said Viola. "Where are the others?"

"We did," said Dakota. "What you're seeing is an apparition of me. The woods brought me back here to intercept you. We've been taken far away from Darkwoods."

"Where?" she asked. "I'll come and find you."

He shook his head. "The woods left you for a reason. You must discover what it is."

"But if you tell me where you are—"

"That's not what the woods want," said Dakota. "I'm going to ask you again; what are you doing with them?" He turned his dark eyes on Leonardo as he said this, and not a shred of warmth burned in them.

"We're leaving," said Viola. "We're going to the Cove."

"No," said Dakota. "You will stay in the Darkwoods until the woods show you the reason—"

"Maybe the reason is to join them," said Viola.

"Stop acting like a child," said Dakota. His fingers clenched the wood of his bow. For an apparition, he seemed just as real as any of them, his arrow as sharp as their weapons.

The other boys made the same observation, and as Dakota's fingers twitched, Puck suddenly drew his sword. He stood, straddling his bench, and two rows down, Strato drew his own sword. Moth, Robin, Bates, and Nym did the same, while Pinch abandoned his post to fit a pebble into his slingshot. Leonardo placed a hand on his sword.

"Stop," ordered Dakota, eyes flicking to Viola. "Stand down."

He was afraid. *But not for his own safety*, thought Leonardo.

"Leo," said Viola. "Let's go."

"Viola!" said Dakota, pulling her attention back to him. "Don't do something you'll regret."

"That's why I'm leaving," she replied.

"You're angry. Or you're scared," he added, softer. "I understand—"

"No, you don't. We're leaving. Leo?"

"Viola. Listen to me," said Dakota. "You have a purpose!"

She folded her arms. "The woods brought them to me after you disappeared. The Dark hit the camp, did you know that? Right after you left. It's in the Darkwoods now."

"You don't know what you're talking about."

"I know exactly what I'm talking about." She turned to Puck. "What's your name? Puck?"

He nodded, eyes wide.

"Right. Puck, push us off."

"Leo?" asked Puck. Leonardo inclined his head, and Puck eyed the two hulls, bumping together. Before Dakota could react, he braced his feet and shoved the canoe with both hands.

It didn't move far, but a gap opened wide enough to fit oars in.

"You're sure?" Leonardo asked Viola. She set her jaw, her aesthetic something like a lioness cub; fierce and defiant despite her beaded dress and twin braids.

"Oars down," he ordered, and his crew quickly stashed their weapons and splashed their oars down into the water.

"You're going to regret this," said Dakota.

"I'll see you again, brother," said Viola.

And with that, they left Dakota behind, rowing for the river opening at the far side of the lake. A breath of wind gusted behind them, and Leonardo turned to see the centre of the lake empty. No trace of the canoe.

CHAPTER 36

That night, they camped on a grassy stretch along the bank. Nym took the night shift, and every time Leonardo woke and walked down to where he was sitting, Nym assured him that the river was right where he'd left it.

After the fifth or sixth time, Leonardo climbed the bank and stopped at the edge of where the rest of Lion Clan slept. Viola curled up close to where Leonardo had placed his own roll, and as he watched her sleeping, he had a memory of her the night before, painted silver in the moonlight as she warned him about the attack. A beam of moonlight caught her now, her face calm and serene for the first time all day.

He crossed to his sleeping roll and lay down on his back, staring up at the stars. Being the leader of a Clan, and becoming so in such a sudden and unexpected way, left him with a thousand unanswered questions. And it would've been enough on its own, but he had a second dilemma which had somehow established itself between all the running and fighting.

Every time she glanced his way, or smiled—or did anything at all, really—Leonardo found himself momentarily unable to focus on anything else. An electric current raced through his body and set off a feeling of desire that he couldn't easily suppress.

His mind drifted to the picture of her sleeping in the moonlight and Leonardo shook it off. He barely knew her. *She* barely knew *him*. They were travelling. They'd just survived two attacks. Her people had left her. He was leader. The timing was terrible for a thing like this.

And that last reason should've really been the first. *He was leader.* His new clan needed his attention before anything else. This ten had chosen each other and an uncertain road over the predictability of staying behind. It was a decision that bound them in ways that Raven Clan never could be, and Leonardo wanted to be the best leader he could for them.

That means no distractions.

Raven Clan wasn't his Clan, and it never had been. It was Aleksander's Clan, and Ajax's and Cato's, and everyone who wasn't named Moth, Pinch, Puck, Nym, Strato, Robin, Bates, or Leonardo. That was why they were here, because none of them belonged back there. For Charley and Viola, they'd never had the chance to be a Raven, but that didn't matter; they were as much a part of Lion Clan as any of the ex-Ravens. And that was what made the weight on his shoulders so much heavier. This was a true clan, a family, and Leonardo was the one responsible for getting them to safety, if such a thing existed.

CHAPTER 37

The next morning, Leonardo found Nym asleep in the grass, propped against a rock at his nightwatchman's post. Apparently, the events of the past few days had worn out even his tireless reserves.

Leonardo started to approach him, then paused. At first, he'd thought the darkness around Nym was simply the rock's shadow, but as he moved closer, he realized the grass itself had turned black. His mind immediately went to the trees surrounding Viola's old camp.

"Nym!" said Leonardo, rushing to shake him awake. The black grass crunched under his boots.

Nym didn't stir and Leonardo shook him harder, his pulse picking up until it slammed in his chest.

"What—" Nym blinked awake, squinting up at Leonardo.

"Leo. What's wro—" He tried to push himself upright and flinched, gasping in pain.

"What is it?" demanded Leonardo.

"Argh," Nym lifted his hands. Black streaked along the veins. Then he spotted the grass. "What the hell am I sitting in?" Nym jumped up.

Leonardo grabbed him by the sleeve. "Quick. Try to wash it off."

They ran down to the water and Nym threw himself to his knees, plunging his hands into the river.

The back of his shirt hiked up and Leonardo was relieved to see no black on his skin. It seemed to only be on his hands, which had been in direct contact with the grass. He was lucky he'd been propped up on the rock, his head away from it.

"It's not working," said Nym, rubbing his hands so hard in the cold water that droplets hit Leonardo.

"Keep trying," said Leonardo. The rest of the clan had begun to take notice, and they hurried down the bank. Viola pushed past Moth and Bates and crouched next to Leonardo, eyes fixed on the churning water.

Nym pulled his hands out of the river, splaying them to see.

"That's less," said Leonardo. Only a few of the black veins remained, snaking over his skin.

Nym jammed his hands underwater again, rubbing even harder.

"What happened?" asked Moth.

"Did you see the black grass?" asked Leonardo.

"It's the Dark," said Viola. "It's seeping in."

"To his body?" demanded Bates.

"To the woods," said Viola. "I didn't know it could go through skin like that."

Nym pulled his hands out, and to Leonardo's relief they'd returned to normal. Nym sagged, closing his eyes.

"Thank god," said Moth.

"Let's get moving," said Leonardo. "Get your sleeping rolls and packs to the boat, as quickly as you can."

Nym pushed himself up, examining his hands.

"Are you ok?" asked Leonardo.

"I think so," said Nym. "Thank you for waking me."

"Let's keep two night watchmen from now on," said Leonardo. "And be extra careful around the trees and grass."

***

The rest of the day went relatively smooth, until an hour after they stopped for the night. Nym was lounging by the fire when he suddenly cried out, jerking his hands as if burnt. The beginnings of black lines streaked his skin.

"Come on," said Leonardo, already on his feet.

"What's happening to me?" puffed Nym as they sprinted to the river. His voice, normally bright and unconcerned, cracked with fear.

Moth and Pinch and the others rushed to join them. Leonardo shared a troubled gaze with Moth, then Viola, who stepped around him and crouched next to Nym as he lifted his hands from the river, clean and free of the black again.

"It's gone," she said to Leonardo, dragging a finger along the surface of the river. "The woods are still strong enough to heal him."

"But for how long?" Nym asked quietly.

No one had an answer.

***

The river seemed to be the only antidote to Nym's condition, albeit a temporary one. The blackness returned an hour later, and then once more, until Nym finally opted to spend the night in the boat.

This seemed to halt the Dark's ability to spread from his fingertips, but Leonardo was well aware that Nym couldn't spend the rest of his life in a boat.

Nym kept a positive front. "It's ok," he kept saying. "Once Viola's people defeat the Dark, it'll go away. I just have to stay near the river until then."

Leonardo hoped so. He worried for Nym, and all of them. Things could turn bad very quickly if the Dark kept spreading like this.

After one long day of travel, they found a spot where the river split through dozens of tiny channels, forming miniature stepping-stone-islands covered in grass and moss. Nym discovered he could move about them safely, allowing him a respite from the boat.

Leonardo and the rest of the clan set up camp on the bank adjacent, where they could easily talk to him on the tiny islands.

A few of the boys suggested they simply stay here, but Leonardo gave the same answer he'd given in the Backwaters. To him, safety meant distance. They were still painfully small in numbers, and a few days outside the Darkwoods wasn't enough to let him sleep comfortably. Also, the idea of sitting tight until the Natives defeated the Dark didn't sit well with him. Too many things could go wrong. Staying in motion gave at least some illusion of control.

Plus, they'd spent their entire remembered lives on one stretch of river. Everyone agreed that they weren't ready to stop exploring yet, so they continued onward, the lure of Lion Clan's legendary camp filling their minds and much of their conversation.

Viola suggested that there might even be a cure for Nym there, although not even she could guess what that might be.

The clan seemed to be accepting her, and Charley was talking even more and starting to act like a real clan member. She'd imprinted firmly on Viola and followed her like a lost duckling. Viola told Leonardo she didn't mind, and spent the days showing Charley the many wonders of the woods. Pinch proved almost a better point watchman than Leonardo—*almost*—and the two girls quickly took to the jobs of left and right watchmen.

Even Nym seemed to improve as the days went on. The night after they left the stepping-stone-islands, he spent two hours by the fire before returning to the riverside.

The fact that everything was going so well made Leonardo nervous. He'd lived a lot of years in these woods—not as many as Aleksander; he didn't need to worry about that yet—and unless the balance of things changed dramatically a few days outside of clan territory, they were due for a turn. Maybe small, probably big.

Every smooth day put him more on edge. At one point, Viola called him paranoid, and when Leonardo tried to explain the unshakable feeling hanging over him, she just laughed and told him to relax.

Seeing her smile took his mind off things, for a while at least. His first two encounters with her had been tense and filled with danger; now outside the Darkwoods, she made for a bright presence in Lion Clan's ranks, laughing and integrating easily with the 'Lost Boys', as she continued to call them.

"Why do you call us that?" Leonardo asked for the fifth time.

She shrugged, grinning. It had become a bit of a game. He knew that she knew more than she was telling him. And she knew that he knew that she knew, and so on. The irksome part was that Leonardo actually wanted to know the answer, but he'd begun to suspect that some of her joking was an attempt to cover her own lack of understanding. Maybe she didn't know quite as much as he'd originally thought.

On the second evening, she joined him, Moth, Puck, and Pinch on a hunting party. Despite how well she was fitting in, the barriers took time to break, and she hadn't spent much time alone with any of the boys.

Moth eyed Viola like a wild animal that might attack at any moment. Pinch looked sullen, which had been an all-day event, Leonardo had no idea what about. And Puck was in another world entirely, in some sort of a trance as he watched Viola. This had been a two-day event, and if he didn't snap out of it soon, Leonardo was afraid the self-sure battle trainer would start drooling.

Move on already, Puck, he thought. *If I can control myself, so can you.*

He knew his bitterness was unwarranted, but watching Puck traipse after her didn't make it any easier for him.

"Do you hunt with slingshots?" asked Viola, looking first at Pinch's, then the one in Leonardo's waistband. They cut their way up a narrow game trail, swatting at insects in the muggy air. The evening pressed hot and humid and their skin gleamed with sweat.

"Yes—" started Leonardo.

"Mostly," said Puck, cutting off Leonardo in a voice nothing like his own. He sounded like the world's most pompous tour guide.

"It's the preferred weapon of the clans," continued Puck. "Along with swords of course. Back at Raven Clan, I was in charge of battle—"

"Why are you talking like that?" said Pinch, in a voice entirely his own.

"Like what?" demanded Puck.

"Like a halfwit."

"You're a halfwit."

"Guys," said Leonardo. He looked at Viola and said pointedly, "Yes, we hunt with slingshots."

She suppressed a giggle, ducking under a low branch.

Leonardo stepped over the bulging roots of the same tree.

"I thought it was usually you two who bicker like this," she said, looking at Moth and Pinch.

Both boys frowned at her.

"She used to watch us on the river," explained Leonardo.

"Oh good, our own stalker," said Pinch, kicking a pebble at Moth's ankles.

"Ow! What was that for?"

"Weren't you listening?" said Pinch, sharp with sarcasm. "Native Girl wants a show."

"Hey," said Leonardo sharply. "What are you so bitter about today?"

"Must've eaten some lemons." Pinch kicked another rock. Moth dodged it and Pinch shoved aside a branch, pushing out in front. "Shit." He slapped a mosquito biting his neck. "Fuck these bugs."

The other boys and Viola stared after him. Jagged branches swung in his wake.

Moth chewed a fingernail, his expression troubled.

"I'm sorry about him," Leonardo said quietly to Viola.

"Don't worry about it," she said back, just as quiet. Then, hesitantly, "Does Pinch dislike me?"

"I..." He waved his hand at a cloud of gnats, studying Pinch's back as he aggressively led the way through the underbrush. "I don't think so. I mean, he barely knows you. What reason would he have?

Viola nodded. The pensive tilt of her head said she wasn't convinced, but she didn't argue. Leonardo furrowed his brow, trying to recall anything that had happened between now and when they left the Darkwoods.

"What do your people hunt with?" asked Moth, overcoming his apparent fear of her in an attempt to diffuse the situation. He stepped in a gopher hole and stumbled. "Ow! Dammit!"

Leonardo caught his arm and helped him regain his balance.

"Bows and arrows," said Viola. "But only the warriors do it."

"You've never hunted?" said Puck.

"The girls gather plants and cook the meals," said Viola.

Puck stopped, gleaming with excitement under a layer of sweat from the humid air. "We should teach her how to hunt. She'd probably be good at it." He smiled at Viola, tour guide now replaced by a gentle soul.

Leonardo closed his eyes. It was going to be a long evening.

***

Leonardo and his hunting party came across a small flock of partridges in a hollow, big enough that they could position themselves around it without alerting the birds.

Leonardo waited for a count of three, then aimed and released the first stone. Pinch fired from across the hollow before his stone had even reached its target, and two partridges went down in quick succession. Leonardo already had another stone loaded, drawn, and in the air by the time the partridges could react, and he managed to take down a third as they took off, launching into the air on choppy wings and hurtling ungracefully out of the hollow.

Combined, they took down five birds, as Pinch's final shot narrowly missed and ricocheted off a tree trunk.

They collected the birds and divided them between the two bags Moth and Puck carried. Moth wasn't a hunter, and Puck had jammed his thumb building camp, so they played caddy while Leonardo and Pinch manned the slingshots.

The other five set up camp and built a cooking fire, while Nym tried fishing with a hook Moth had whittled. Leonardo had suggested Strato show Charley how to skip stones, to allow Viola a few minutes away from her shadow. Selfishly, he enjoyed the chance to talk to her without a small, blonde, high-output-question-machine in a paperboy cap taking both of their attention.

As they walked in search of more game, Leonardo fit a stone into the pouch of his slingshot and fired it at a tree across the path. The stone chipped off a big circular wound where a branch used to be.

"Can I try?" asked Viola.

The boys stopped to watch as Leonardo passed her his

slingshot, fishing a pebble from his pocket. Viola set her feet and eyed the tree.

"Like this?" She slipped the pebble in place and drew back the pouch.

"Just straighten the fork a bit," he said. "Aim with both hands. Like this." He took her shoulders and turned her slightly, so that the pouch aligned with the centre of the fork. Her dress was sleeveless, and his fingertips tingled where they touched her bare skin. Neither of them moved for a second, then Viola angled her head back to see him.

"Your hands are cold," she said.

"Oh," Leonardo pulled his fingers back. "Sorry."

She grinned and focused back on the tree, then shifted her angle. Squinting, she fired. The pebble smacked off the centre of the wound-turned-target.

Puck clapped.

Viola spun, offering Leonardo his slingshot with a flick of the wrist. He started to smile, reaching out to take it, then she whipped it away, grinning.

"Maybe I should keep this," she said.

"It's all yours," said Leonardo, and she slipped it through a leather band on her dress.

She walked past Pinch and took the lead. "Come on, show's over."

Leonardo suppressed a grin. She sounded more and more like a 'Lost Boy' every day.

Pinch fired a pebble into the dirt. The expression on his face said, *She doesn't come hunting again.*

Leonardo gave him a look and followed Puck and Moth down

the trail. He had no idea what had gotten under Pinch's skin, but whatever it was, his attitude was getting old fast.

They rounded off their hunting trip with two rabbits and a trio of grouse that had been standing in the middle of a game trail. Viola took down one of each. Pinch got his third shot off so fast that the last bird almost hit the ground before the first two.

For his sake, and the sake of everyone who had to live with him, Leonardo was glad that Pinch had gotten the extra kill this time.

***

The next morning, Leonardo got a chance alone with her while everyone else ate a breakfast of berries and plums that Robin found just outside their campsite. A wind had kept them up most of the night, so Leonardo allowed them a few minutes longer in camp before they hit the river again. He and Viola walked down the bank until they found an old oak, a few centuries smaller than the one near her old camp.

Viola jumped up onto a branch and Leonardo climbed up beside her. She still had his slingshot, hooked on the leather string around the waist of her dress.

"How are you doing?" asked Leonardo, with enough weight that she knew what he meant. She hadn't talked about her brother or her people since the first day.

Viola picked at a piece of bark beside her. She shrugged. "I don't know. I've been trying not to think of them." The tree bark came loose and she tossed it into the river. "I'm not doing very well at it."

"You'll see them again," said Leonardo. "The woods aren't *that* big."

She nodded.

"I told you my brother disappeared, right?" said Leonardo.

She nodded. "I'm sorry."

"He was old," said Leonardo. "It was his time."

"Do you miss him?"

Leonardo leaned back on the branch, thinking about it.

"We didn't always see eye to eye."

"I miss them," she said. "My parents, Dakota, my grandfather. You met him."

"I did?" asked Leonardo.

"Chief Tokala," said Viola.

"He's your grandfather?"

She nodded.

He thought about the strange, psychic ways of the chief, then he remembered how Viola had closed her eyes and somehow seen into Hawk Clan territory. How little he knew about this forest. He felt like an outsider in a world that knew itself far better than he ever could. And if he was an outsider, Viola was firmly local, a creature of the woods.

"They're not gone. Not like your brother," said Viola. "They're still here somewhere."

"Where is my brother?" asked Leonardo. "Do you know?"

"Um," she shifted on the branch. "No, not really."

Leonardo straightened. "But you know something."

"They never told me much," said Viola. "And I'm really not allowed to talk about it. I wish I could." She plucked an acorn off the tree and tossed it into the river.

"You told me about the attack..." said Leonardo.

"That was different. And just because I broke the rules once, doesn't mean…" Her tone turned slightly defensive, then she kicked her feet at the air, closed her eyes, and drew a slow breath. Her lashes fanned out on her copper skin. Then she blinked them open again and Leonardo glanced away.

"I don't know what to do," said Viola. "I wish I could talk to my grandfather. I don't know why we're supposed to keep these secrets. He always said it was extremely important, like something bad would happen if you knew."

"What kind of bad?"

"Leo…"

"Right." Leonardo sighed. "Sorry."

"I don't know much more than you." She fixed deeply vibrant eyes on him, earnest and apologetic. "We don't learn what being a 'guardian of the woods' means until we're older."

"Forget I said anything," said Leonardo. The impossible-to-focus thing was happening again, and his stomach tied itself in knots. "I'm sorry you're alone here. I wish I knew where your people went."

She looked down. "So do I."

"But like you said, they're not gone. We can go searching for them once Lion Clan is settled."

Her gaze traced his face, eyes soft and dark, contrasted against the hard glitter of sun on the river behind her. "Thank you. And I'm not alone," she said, giving him a small, shy smile.

Leonardo's heart staggered a few beats.

Calm down, he told himself.

He cleared his throat. "So you're a Lost Boy now. Or…" He frowned. "A Lost Girl?"

She grinned. "We're taking over your clan. You boys have run the woods long enough."

"I'm sure Charley would jump right in on that," said Leonardo. "Did you notice her carrying a slingshot around this morning, after she saw you with mine?"

"I noticed," said Viola. "It's a good thing. Better than her feeling alone in a clan of boys."

He nodded, pulling an acorn off the branch above. It made a satisfying pop as it broke from the bark.

"Where do you think she came from?"

Viola shrugged. "Same place you all come from."

"Which is?" Leonardo flicked the acorn into the river.

"I'll admit it's strange though," said Viola, pretending not to hear his question.

Leonardo sighed. *Why is it all such a secret?* He wished he knew what could be so bad about simply knowing something.

"I don't think there's ever been a 'Lost Girl' in the Darkwoods," she continued.

"None of our stories talk about it," agreed Leonardo.

"The woods do everything for a reason," said Viola. "Leaving me behind, giving you Charley. I don't think it's a coincidence that it's at the same time the Dark is coming."

"And this Dark, it's here...consciously...right?" asked Leonardo. "To attack us?"

"Yes," said Viola. "I just don't know how or when. Like I said before, they never told me much."

"What if it's coming to the Cove?" asked Leonardo.

"It's coming everywhere," said Viola. "But my grandfather

says if you kill the heart, it will die everywhere. That's where the woods sent my people, to the heart."

"Maybe the heart will be in the Cove."

"Maybe," said Viola.

"We could fight alongside your people."

"Yes, we could."

He blinked, surprised, and she crossed her arms. "What? You think I'm going to live with you all and not learn to fight? I'm not cooking and sewing anymore, I've done enough of that for a lifetime. Sometimes, when I used to watch your patrols pass, I'd sneak into the woods after and practice fighting with a stick."

Leonardo imagined that, in her fur-tufted moccasins and braids.

"Take that look off your face," said Viola. "I'm a good fighter."

"Why do your people hate us?" asked Leonardo. It came out more abrupt than he meant it.

"What?"

"We weren't allowed to go anywhere near you," said Leonardo. "Did you know about the trade agreement? Your grandfather gave us weapons, and shields, and rope, and all sorts of supplies, in return for us staying away."

Viola shook her head. "They don't hate you. My grandfather has strict rules not to interfere with you unless we have to. I suppose it's easier not to do that if you're not interfering with us."

"And the best way to guarantee that," said Leonardo, understanding now, "is to make us think you wanted nothing to do with us."

Viola nodded. "Plus, the elders think you're a bad influence."

"What?" Leonardo shifted on the branch to see her better. "Why?"

"The elders don't want our boys turning wild like you Lost Boys, and well…I suppose they don't want the girls near you for other reasons."

She glanced away, blushing, ever so slightly.

"And what would that reason be?" asked Leonardo, feeling daring. The knots in his stomach twisted, buzzing with electricity.

"Well," said Viola, staring intently at an acorn, "They might be worried that some girls could get swept up in how exciting your lives are, *the Lost Boys*. Life is quite dull in our camp, we just cook and sew and gather plants." She glanced at him. "I suppose they're worried one of the girls might get distracted by a Lost Boy and mistake all the excitement for something more, and then after she realizes it was just the excitement—you have very exciting lives—things would be complicated."

"Of course," said Leonardo, with the same nervous energy. "And I guess that could go both ways. A Lost Boy could have feelings for one of the girls in your camp, and your elders wouldn't want that."

"No," said Viola, quickly. "They think you're reckless."

"We are," agreed Leonardo. "Think of Pinch."

"I don't know him very well," said Viola.

"He's very reckless," Leonardo assured her.

She nodded and they lapsed into an awkward silence.

A rabbit took off from the bushes behind them, startling them both. It bounded away, down the bank and out of sight.

"I'm glad you found me," said Viola. "Before you left. I don't know what I would've done if I'd had to stay in those woods."

"You would've been fine," said Leonardo. "You're more capable than most of the clan boys."

"Alone?" She shook her head. "Without a camp, or anyone to talk to, or anything to do? It would've been miserable."

"There's always Gallus," said Leonardo, trying to joke. "And Hero and Lance and Ajax. I'm sure they'd make great company when they're not ripping each other apart."

"They've probably started already," said Viola. "Your brother caused a lot of war, but he prevented a lot too."

Leonardo tightened his lips, serious now. "It's going to be chaos without him to scare them into staying inside their borders."

"It's good we got out when we did."

"Yes," Leonardo agreed. "It is."

"And I want you to know," said Viola, twisting a bead on her dress, "I'm happy here. In Lion Clan. If my people aren't in the Cove, if we don't find them for a while, that's ok."

She smiled at him, then hesitantly placed her hand on top of his. Leonardo glanced down at her fingers, copper against his skin.

She blinked, slowly, and her fingers burned like embers on the back of his hand. He watched her lips, curved and slightly parted as she stared back at him.

The seconds raced past and his heart pounded a thousand times its normal speed and he'd later wonder why he just sat there, frozen, but a moment later the spell broke. They both glanced away, and Viola slid down off the branch, straightening her dress.

Leonardo jumped down after her.

"We should get back," said Viola.

Leonardo nodded. "We can't lose any more travel time this morning."

"No," said Viola.

Leonardo watched her braids bounce as she led the way back to camp, a tangle of emotions wrestling in his mind.

***

They rowed under a cloudless blue sky, a gentle wind at their backs, and the genius of putting Pinch at the front of the boat—the furthermost point from Moth—was becoming more and more obvious. Nym kept to himself, lost in a world of thoughts. He put up a false ease around the others, but Leonardo saw through it.

He chewed his lip, pondering the condition of his clan. The morale in general was beginning to flag. Questions bounced from one member to another, contemplating whether Lion Clan might just be a legend after all, and whether the stone camp they'd all heard of really existed. With all the empty wilderness they'd been sailing through, it was easy to imagine rowing for weeks and finding nothing but the same empty river.

Surprisingly, Moth was one of the few who never doubted their decision. He and Puck kept themselves busy putting down the other boys' doubts with a steadfast belief that their new home lay just over the horizon.

Leonardo watched the two of them, and Pinch, and the way that the other six began to turn to them for guidance. He included Pinch because of his confidence watching the river, and the knowledge he passed on to Charley and Viola, albeit in his typically dismissive manner. He gave them a lot of pointers without really meaning to, and Leonardo saw their ability to read the river and the banks improving.

All of this added another problem, and Leonardo wasn't quite sure how to solve it. When they beached that night, at a site

Charley had spotted, Leonardo waited until the Clan was settled in before pulling Moth aside.

They walked down the bank in silence as Leonardo tried to frame together a starting point. Moth kicked a pinecone and sent it spinning down to the water. It splashed on the surface, rolling as it floated away.

"What's on your mind?" Moth finally asked. "Something about Viola? You were staring at her all day."

"Really?" *All day?* "No, it's not about her."

Moth reached up to pull a green cone from a pine bow. It snapped from the branch, filling the air with the smell of evergreen. He threw it in the river, rubbing the sap off his fingers.

"I was thinking," said Leonardo. "And now that we're a clan, I should probably pick se-coms sooner than later."

Moth stopped in his tracks. "You're not thinking of me, are you?"

Leonardo had, of course, considered Moth. At first.

"Well, I did think of you."

"But..."

"Then I started looking at Puck and Pinch."

They resumed walking. A row of turtles covered a half-submerged log in the water, their shells dark and wet, painted with vibrant red and yellow patterns.

"Pinch?" Moth laughed. "Pinch wanted to be se-com so he could force Cato to carry him around, remember?"

Leonardo shrugged. "He's good in the boat, and he's a decent fighter. I think he'd be ok at it."

"So you are serious." Moth chewed his lip. "Maybe, I guess.

Puck is a good one, I agree with that. He's certainly bossy enough."

One of the turtles dropped into the shallows with a quiet splash. It piloted away, water streaming around its bright shell.

"I know it's a gamble," said Leonardo. "But we're a small clan; I don't have two dozen members to choose from. I don't even have one dozen."

"Aleksander had over two dozen and he picked Ajax and Cato."

"See?" said Leonardo. "You don't need perfection, you just need..." He trailed off, frowning.

"What *do* you need?" asked Moth. "I've always wondered what those two have that qualifies them to run a clan."

"Well, loyalty, for one. Neither of them would've ever turned their backs on Aleksander. And Ajax is smart-ish; I suppose brains are important. Cato is...well he's loyal."

Moth snorted. "I don't think Cato's vocabulary goes beyond the words, *sword, fist,* and *clobber.*"

"Fighting," said Leonardo. "That's important too."

Moth splayed his hands. "Another reason not to pick me."

"Loyalty, brains, and fighting then," said Leonardo. "Can you fault Pinch on any of those?"

Moth thought about it. He sighed, gazing out over the water. "No, I guess not."

A breeze stirred the leaves up and down the river, fluttering in every shade of green. Leonardo spotted a few barren branches, shrivelled black in a way that was becoming all too familiar.

The Dark. It's everywhere, Viola had said. He still didn't understand what that meant, but he was starting to see a clearer picture.

It's like a disease. But one that can think. And hunt? He thought about the crocodile skull in Viola's clearing.

That's how it sees, she'd said. And the black grass around Nym. Maybe that was how it hunted. The thought sent a chill up his spine.

At least Nym's on-shore time seemed to be going up, though he was still a long way from cured. Just last night, he'd stayed by the fire longer than he should've and wound up running back to the river with black veins.

"Well, he and Puck will be better than Ajax and Cato," said Moth. "I can tell you that."

"Now you're talking," said Leonardo, not really listening anymore. He had no idea if he was making the right decisions. Taking everyone to the Cove could be as big a mistake as it could be the right choice.

I could be leading us right to the Dark.

"Ok," said Moth. "If I give you my blessing, can we go and eat?"

Leonardo pulled himself back to the moment. "That's not why I asked you—"

"You weren't going to pick me and you wanted to make sure I was ok with it. I'm a big boy Leo, you don't need to do that."

"I know, but…"

"I wouldn't be a good leader. Or se-com. We both know that. The only thing I was worried about was that you'd pick me anyway."

"So long as you're sure."

"Pinky swear." Moth held up his pinky finger, still glistening with pine sap.

"I'll take your word for it," said Leonardo. "Let's go eat."

"At long last!"

"Oh, shut up."

Images of black hands and crocodile skulls played through his mind as they walked back to the others.

CHAPTER 38

The next morning, Leonardo was helping carry supplies to the boat when he heard a splash from downriver. The bushes grew high on either side of the break where they'd tied off the boat, and the rest of the bank was hidden from view of the clearing. Leonardo placed the bundle of sleeping rolls in the dewy grass and crossed to the bushes, his body tense. Visions of a bear or a crocodile played through his mind.

He'd known their luck wouldn't hold.

Whatever it was sounded substantial enough that Leonardo held his breath as he pulled the branches apart, rising on tiptoes to see over the bushes.

He found the source of the noise immediately and breathed a sigh of relief. Down the bank, a spit of shale stuck out into the river. Viola crouched near the edge, silhouetted in the morning rays as she splashed water over her hair. She bowed her head and ran her fingers through the tangles, loose and dark and gleaming with droplets in the morning light.

She had untied the beaded strings at the neck of her dress, and the soft leather was folded over itself, revealing a few inches of her back, smooth and copper between her tanned shoulders. Leonardo swallowed, knowing he should turn away. He wasn't used to having girls around camp; the clan boys didn't bathe very often—or ever, in some cases—but now, smelling his own shirt, Leonardo wondered if he should make it a more regular habit.

He stepped back, glancing around. Everyone else was busy preparing to leave and no one paid him any attention. Leonardo started to turn away, then turned back despite himself, glancing over the bush and getting one last look of her straightening up in a halo of sun and mist. She flipped her hair back and paused to look at something down the river, and Leonardo slipped away, not wanting her to catch him and think he'd been watching her the whole time.

He picked up the bundle of sleeping rolls he had dropped in the grass and carried it down to the boat, thinking about the differences in their clan now that they had Lost Girls too.

Lost Girls? He couldn't get used to it. It sounded even stranger than Lost Boys. Why were they lost? Sure, Charley had been lost when they found her on the bank, but she wasn't lost anymore, was she? She was a member of Lion Clan, just like Viola and himself and Pinch and Moth and all the others. He needed to ask Viola about it again and try to get a real answer of out of her this time.

But that could wait. They needed to keep moving. Wherever the Dark was, Leonardo wanted his clan safe behind the walls of

Lion Clan's camp when it came. The open river was far too vulnerable.

He gazed around the grassy bank, counting heads. He noted several absent, including Lion Clan's smallest member.

I'd better go look for her, he thought. *If she keeps chasing those butterflies, she's going to get herself actually lost.*

He found Charley back in a hollow partially sheltered from the main clearing. Pinch was there too, sleeping in a bed of moss—he'd been kept up most of the night by some sort of screaming bird that Leonardo had apparently slept through—and so was Bates, holding a finger to his lips as Leonardo stepped through the underbrush.

Leonardo frowned. Charley stood against the trunk of a willow, giggling uncontrollably, while Bates stood poised over Pinch's sleeping body, gesturing emphatically for her to be quiet. Charley wasn't wearing her hat, and blonde hair hung down to her shoulders. He realized a moment later that Bates was holding her hat, and attempting to swap it with Pinch's while he slept.

Leonardo grinned, leaning against a tree to watch. Pinch's tricorn rested over his face like a pirate who had somehow found himself in an old western movie, and Bates proceeded to place Charley's hat atop his own ratty fedora, freeing his hands to work. This launched Charley into a fresh wave of poorly-stifled laughter, and Bates wiggled his fingers, reaching for Pinch's hat with a great deal of ceremony.

Leonardo scratched his chin, skeptical at the chances of success. Pinch could be hard to wake, but that had more to do with not wanting to get up than being a heavy sleeper. Bates knew it too and raised a finger to his lips, winking at the younger clan member. He bent and took hold of two corners of the hat, took an exaggerated breath, and lifted it off of Pinch's face.

Underneath, Pinch's eyes were wide open. Bates jumped, stumbling back. Charley burst into laughter and Pinch blinked up at Bates. His hands shifted and Bates looked down, finding a loaded slingshot pointed at him.

Bates quickly placed the tricorn back over Pinch's face and Pinch pointed to the main clearing with his slingshot, then folded his arms back across his chest.

Bates backed away, eyes wide. Charley giggled harder than ever and Leonardo shook his head, grinning, as he turned and pushed his way out of the hollow.

Charley had found a home in Lion Clan, and Leonardo was happy as he crossed the clearing. His clan was coming together, against all odds, and Leonardo wondered if the apprehension he'd been feeling for the past few days was as pointless as Viola insisted.

***

They got away in record time that morning, leaving the grassy bank and the shale spit behind before the mist had even started burning off.

Pinch leaned over the bow, hat firmly wedged on his head, and Viola and Charley—paperboy cap back in place—sat on their bench mid-hull, watching the bank slide past. Puck counted aloud in time with his oar strokes, and Bates leaned back, rolling his eyes at Strato, but they followed Puck's tempo nonetheless. Leonardo would call him off in a while, for his own sanity if nothing else, but he'd wait until the rhythm pounded into their heads.

Puck's bossiness would reach new heights once Leonardo

made him se-com, but Leonardo still thought he was the right choice. Moth, sitting directly in front of Puck, might've come to a different conclusion. He mouthed, '*ohmygod*' at Leonardo after another period of rigid counting. Leonardo pretended not to see, suppressing a grin.

Pinch, in contrast, remained as silent as the raven carving over his head. He'd been acting strange lately; sullen, and Leonardo wondered if the role of se-com would help snap him out of it. He hoped so. Pinch in a bad mood was like Mother Nature in a bad mood; the clouds pulled together, the whole sky turned black, and anyone in the vicinity was liable to get electrocuted.

Viola knew this as well as anybody, and she looked surprised when Leonardo mentioned his plans to her later that morning.

"You want *him* as a second-in-command?" she asked. They sat in the boat, talking in low voices while the rest of the clan stretched their legs in a dirt clearing.

"He's not normally like this," said Leonardo.

"What's he normally like?" Viola folded her hands in her lap. "I wish I'd known all of you before this. I feel like I missed so much."

"Well…he's…" Leonardo hesitated, peering through the trees to where Pinch and Moth were talking. Pinch pointed up at something in the branches above.

"He's tough to understand. He doesn't trust easy, but he wants to. He's a good friend, he just puts up thorns to most of the world."

Leonardo studied a tangle of brambles on the bank. *Why do some things in nature feel such a need to barricade themselves?*

"How do you get him to take the thorns down?" asked Viola.

"I'm still trying to figure that out."

"I don't know," said Leonardo. "I've known him longer than anyone else here, and I still don't know exactly what lets him relax around Moth and myself. I've seen him give you and Charley some tips in the boat. That's a good sign, at least."

"Complained about my incompetence, you mean?" said Viola. She ducked as a dragonfly whisked past. "I'm sorry, I don't mean to be like that. His home just burned down, he has a right to be irritable."

"I'm sorry," said Leonardo. "I'll talk to him. Pinch is…" Leonardo looked through the trees again. "He's never played well with others."

Just then, Charley came running up.

"I caught one!" she said, out of breath.

Leonardo frowned. "One of what?"

Charley held up a squirming bundle of orange-faced fur, with black and white banded hind legs hanging out from under her fingers, scrabbling furiously at the air.

"Is that a hamster?" asked Viola, rising from her bench.

Charley nodded. "They're all over the place, and they're fast. I had to dive into a bunch of plants to catch him. I named him Lion. After Lion Clan. I twisted my ankle on a root chasing him."

Charley hiked up her pant leg to show Leonardo an entirely unremarkable ankle.

"Well, at least it doesn't seem too serious," he said.

"You must've made a miraculous recovery," said Viola. "To be running on it like you just did."

Charley missed the irony in her tone.

"Can I keep him?" asked Charley. "Please?"

"Keep who?" asked Moth, stepping down the bank.

"This is Lion." Charley turned to show him the hamster.

Leonardo was saved from having to answer as the rest of Lion Clan returned to the boat, climbing over the side with voices clashing and boots landing heavy on the planks. Nym checked his hands as he did so, but they looked clear to Leonardo. For now, at least.

Pinch glanced at him and Viola and rolled his eyes, annoyance radiating off of him as he climbed to the bow of the boat.

Leonardo frowned and returned to his stern platform, glancing at the bank and nodding in relief when Charley crouched down in the moss. 'Lion' could return to the bushes and they could get back underway. Whatever Pinch's problem was, it would have to wait. Each delay cost them valuable daylight, and on top of the Dark threat, the novelty of traveling had begun to wear off. Every day, the clan grew more restless, and Leonardo knew that tempers would grow shorter and patience thinner as the days wore on. The sooner they got to their destination, the better.

He planned to push them harder today. An extra mile or two could make a big difference. But first, he needed to attend to some business. He waited until Charley had rejoined the crew and everyone returned to their benches, then took a breath and addressed the boat.

"Before we cast off, I think it's time we made some decisions."

"What does that mean?" asked Strato, his mouth full of berries.

"Lion Clan needs se-coms," said Leonardo.

"Oh?" Now he had their attention.

"I've been thinking about it a lot," said Leonardo. "And I've decided on my choices."

"Who is it?" asked Bates. He rubbed his hands together, examining the candidates from under his fedora.

Leonardo looked at Puck, who sat back, surprised. "You've been in charge of battle training at Raven Clan for the past…two years?"

Puck shrugged. Time was impossible to gauge here.

"So you already have experience being in charge—"

"Plus, he acts like se-com already," said Robin.

"Shut up," said Bates. "Let him finish."

Leonardo knew his clan weren't the type for long speeches. That suited him fine. "Puck," he said, "Do you accept the role of second-in-command?"

Puck nodded solemnly. "I do."

"Shit Puck, you're not marrying the job," said Strato.

"Shut up," said Puck.

"And as the other se-com," said Leonardo. "I name Pinch."

Bates tilted his head and Strato scratched his chin.

"Me," said Pinch, blinking slowly. "That's the worst idea you've ever had."

"I'm banking on it," said Leonardo. "Do you accept?"

Pinch blinked again, deliberate as a cat, then he inclined his head and a small smile curled the edge of his mouth.

"Good." Leonardo dried his palms. He'd been worried how the Clan would take his decision, but the surprised expressions were turning to slow nods, and he released a little of his breath.

"Does anyone object to Puck and Pinch as second-in-commands of Lion Clan?" he asked.

Heads shook around the boat.

Viola gave him a small smile. Over from her, Charley fiddled with something between the benches, too distracted to care about se-coms.

"Then let's go," said Leonardo. "Oars down. Pinch, unite the bowline. Puck, set our tempo."

CHAPTER 39

Charley wasn't wearing her hat. Leonardo had noticed it while he named his se-coms, and a few hours down the river, she'd had yet to put it back on. Robin and Bates partially blocked his view of her, but he was fairly certain she held it in her lap.

A moment later, he found out why.

"Ow!" Charley cried out, and everyone in the boat twisted to look at her.

"Lion bit me!"

"Pardon?" asked Puck. He leaned to see her, incredulous.

"A lion bit you?" asked Bates.

"No. *Lion,*" said Charley. She now fought with the hat, which seemed to have developed the ability to move on its own.

"Her hamster," explained Moth.

"You let her bring one of those rats in the boat?!" said Pinch. "I almost got my foot chewed off back on that bank."

"He's not a rat!" said Charley. "Ow!"

An orange and black bundle flew from the hat, landing in the footwell. Charley grabbed for it, but the hamster moved faster, scrambling under the bench and out of sight. A second later, Puck jumped, somehow managing to get on top of his bench without dropping his oar. He peered into the footwell.

"Robin! Below y—"

"Ow!" Robin wasn't quite as graceful, dropping his oar so the current grabbed it and twisted it in the oarlock, slamming the handle into his stomach.

"There he is!" yelled Charley, diving between the benches as Lion doubled back. From the sound of her landing, Leonardo guessed she had missed.

"Shit, I kicked it," said Strato.

"Got him." Nym straightened on his bench, holding the hamster with both hands, the black from them vanished by the river. He'd stopped his oar handle under his leg, and 'Lion' looked downright docile in his grasp. Charley climbed over the benches to the front of the boat, hat in hand.

"Wait," said Nym, leaning to see under the benches. "There it is. Robin, pass Charley that basket. No, the empty one."

Charley paused, turning around as Robin fished the empty basket out from underneath his bench and tossed it to her. It was a deep basket, and Nym carefully placed Lion inside of it, then reached under his own bench for an old torn shirt, stretching it over the top and tying it underneath while Charley held it up in front of her.

316

"There," said Nym. "Now he can't escape. We'll come up with a more permanent solution when we camp tonight. If that's ok," he added to Leonardo.

"Please?" said Charley, wearing an expression of such dire seriousness that Leonardo almost laughed. She hugged the basket to her chest. "Pleasepleasepleaseplease—"

"Let her keep him, Leo," said Viola. "It'll be good for her."

"Hamsters are good for young people," Puck agreed, nodding wisely while glancing sidelong at Viola.

"Oh shut up, Puck," said Pinch. "Not this again."

"He is a *wild* hamster," said Moth. "He's not a pet. He could have rabies for all we know."

He's not wrong, thought Leonardo. *And we're traveling. Maybe when we reach our destination she can—*

"Rabies," said Viola, exasperated. "Did that hamster look rabid to you?"

"I don't know," said Moth. He crossed his arms, one eye on the basket. "I was too busy trying not to get bitten during his rampage."

"He doesn't have rabies," said Charley, big eyes pleading. "Please let me keep him."

Meanwhile, half the boat attempted to offer Leonardo their opinions at once, each entirely different than the next, and Puck continued nodding like an owl, wise and proud. He darted a glance at Viola every few seconds to see if she had noticed his wisdom yet. So far, she hadn't.

Viola tilted her head at Leonardo. *Are you really going to take away her pet?*

Shit.

Leonardo held up his hands, quieting his clan. "Ok," he told Charley. "You can keep him. *But*"—he interrupted her outburst of excitement—"you'll be responsible for feeding him and making sure he doesn't escape again. Is that clear?"

Charley nodded emphatically.

"Good. Then get back to your bench, right-watch," he said. "We're burning daylight."

CHAPTER 40

P uck and Pinch were in high spirits the next morning. "You know I'm going to be the worst se-com ever," said Pinch, as he and Leonardo walked the perimeter of the campsite. The rest of the clan packed the boat under the regal eye of Puck, who's feathers were freshly puffed since assuming his new position. He also seemed to have gained a new confidence in his chances with Viola, and the pompous-tour-guide from the hunting trip was back.

Leonardo could hear his voice from here, and for the dozenth time since waking up, he questioned his decision at giving Puck one of the two positions. He'd been watching the other boys' patience wear thin all morning, and he wondered how many of them regretted not suggesting someone else yesterday.

Stop worrying so much, he told himself. *He'll mellow. It'll be fine.*

Is this what being leader is like? No wonder Aleksander was so miserable.

319

"I mean, the absolute worst," said Pinch. "Imagine me ordering people around. Imagine them listening. It's ridiculous."

"I'm not expecting you to order people around," said Leonardo.

"No?" Pinch swatted away a wasp. "Shit." He ducked away from a second pass. "I swear these fuckers have a hit out on me."

"Everyone is an equal in Lion Clan," said Leonardo. "As soon as we start spitting out orders, I become Aleksander, and you become Ajax."

Pinch scratched his chin. "That's true." He looked toward the beach, where Puck's voice was still audible. "Maybe you should…"

"Tell him that? He just needs time."

Pinch made a skeptical noise. "He'd better do it sooner than that, or he'll be earning himself a black eye. And me a bruised fist."

"Just try to ignore him. He'll calm down."

"You think so?" asked Pinch. "He's been like this since we left the Darkwoods. Ever since Native Girl showed up."

"What does that mean? And she has a name, you know."

Pinch didn't say anything and Leonardo stopped walking. "What is your problem with her anyway?" As far as he knew, Viola hadn't done a single thing to elicit this treatment from Pinch. She barely even spoke to him.

"My problem?" Pinch chuckled, dark and musical. It was a laugh like shards of broken glass and it always put Leonardo's nerves on edge. "What's *your* problem?" he countered, stopping to face Leonardo. His expression radiated hostility in the shadow of his hat. "What's everyone's problem?"

"What are you talking about?"

Pinch stared at him a moment, then he shook his head. "Never mind." He stripped the leaves off a branch and started walking again.

"Hey." Leonardo took a stride after him. "You don't just get to walk away."

"No?" said Pinch. "I thought I was a se-com now."

"Stand here and talk to me."

"Is that an order?"

"It can be."

Pinch threw his handful of leaves on the ground. He turned on Leonardo.

"Ok, how's this? She's not a clan member. She doesn't belong with us. She should've stayed in the Darkwoods. But instead she's here with us and no one seems to have a problem with that. Shit, I'm surprised you didn't make *her* a se-com. Or do you have bigger plans for her? Are we going to carry her around on our shoulders now? I'm sure half the Clan would do it happily."

"Don't be an idiot," said Leonardo.

"Right," said Pinch.

"What does that mean?"

"Nothing." Pinch set his mouth in a hard line. The wasp buzzed back and he swatted it away without looking.

"Viola gets no more special treatment than you do," said Leonardo. "And she belongs here just as much as you and me."

Pinch raised an eyebrow. The space between them sparked with tension.

"What?" demanded Leonardo.

"She's an outsider."

"We're all outsiders, Pinch. If Raven Clan hadn't taken us in, you and me and everyone else would just be left for the crocs."

"That's the point though," said Pinch. "*We're* the same. We came from somewhere else and we go somewhere else when we get old. She was born here. She'll grow old here. And not what we call 'old', but actually old, like her chief. You might remember him; he burned down our camp."

"Gallus threw the stick," said Leonardo.

"And the old man turned the fire into a fucking inferno."

Leonardo caught movement in his peripheral as Moth crossed the clearing toward them.

"Oh great," said Pinch. "Here comes the cavalry."

"Seriously, Pinch," said Leonardo. "Enough already."

Pinch rolled his eyes as Moth walked up, stopping a few feet short of them.

"We're all packed," he said slowly. "The...black came back on Nym's hands, but he's in the boat now. Everyone's ready to go."

Leonardo sighed, pinching the bridge of his nose. He couldn't tell anymore whether Nym's condition was getting better, worse, or just sitting static, waiting for him to leave the water. He prayed it was the first or last. He had no idea what they'd do if it started getting worse.

"Thanks Moth," said Leonardo.

"What's going on?"

Leonardo started to say, "Nothing", but it wasn't nothing, and Pinch's rigid defiance promised it wouldn't go away any time soon.

Is this why you've been so irritable the last few days? Because of Viola?

"Pinch doesn't think Viola belongs in Lion Clan," he told Moth, aware of the anger in his own voice.

"Is that true?" asked Moth.

"Ever since she got here, she's all anyone cares about," said Pinch. "We can't even operate like a normal clan, because everyone's falling all over her."

"The only person doing that is Puck," said Moth. "And... yeah," he tailed off, glancing quickly at Leonardo.

"What?" asked Leonardo.

"Exactly," said Pinch, his voice sharp as glass. "*And him.*"

Leonardo pushed his hand down. "I'm sorry?"

"Oh, don't pretend you're ignorant. She's the only person you talk to anymore. In camp, on the river, at that fucking hamster colony."

Leonardo set his jaw. "Who am I walking with right now? Viola?"

Pinch snorted. "Oh, thank you great leader for gracing me with your presence."

Leonardo whipped around to Moth, startling him. "Is Viola the only person I talk to?"

"No," Moth answered immediately, then Pinch made an incredulous noise and he sighed.

"Look, Leo. She's not the *only* person you talk to *all* of the time, but she's the *usual* person most of the time. Is there any chance you've gotten just a little...distracted...since she joined us?"

Leonardo opened his mouth. He wanted to say that he had a thousand more responsibilities, they were travelling, and things couldn't be the same right now. Viola was still new, she didn't know anyone else very well, and he was already dividing his attention in a dozen directions. He couldn't even keep track of a hamster, much less the clan he was supposed to be running.

All of this was on the tip of his tongue when Moth stopped him. "I'm not saying things need to be how they used to. Everything's changed, and that's ok. None of us have the time to just sit around in the woods anymore, but maybe you could try to think of us"—*think of Pinch*, was what he meant—"a little more. Just a look, a conversation here and there."

Pinch glanced away, feigning indifference, and Leonardo saw it clearly for the first time.

Jealously was the wrong word, since Pinch certainly didn't want Leonardo's attention for the reason Viola had it, but maybe 'neglected' was a better one. Pinch was still like a child in a lot of ways, even though he tried his best to act the opposite, and Leonardo wasn't sure if he'd ever realized how much Pinch looked to him for approval. He was a piece that never fit in Aleksander's machine, but Leonardo understood him when no one else did.

Ok. So maybe I do have some fault in this. I have been occupied with Viola.

"I'm sorry," he said, his anger fading. "You two are my best friends. I'll try to do better."

Pinch unfolded his arms, and Leonardo saw that he was right. Actually, it was Moth who was right. Without him, Leonardo and Pinch would still be arguing.

"You have a lot on your plate," said Moth. "But we can help. You don't need to do everything yourself."

"Yeah," said Pinch. "Just tell us where the work is. I'll make sure Moth gets right on it."

"Ok," said Leonardo, chuckling. "Thank you." And he meant it.

Moth clapped him on the shoulder. "Come on, let's get moving."

Leonardo nodded, following him back to the beach. Pinch looked more like himself than he had since they'd left Raven Clan, shooting sideways comments at Moth, tricorn resting cockeyed on his head. Viola was right; Leonardo had been worried about nothing. He'd always had a bad relationship with luck, but maybe that only existed within the Darkwoods. Out here, there was no reason to think their streak of smooth sailing was going to do anything but continue.

CHAPTER 41

The sun sat at its highest point, glinting off the surface of the river, still enough to hold a clear reflection of the trees and the sky. Leonardo leaned over the side of the boat, gazing down through the water at the boulders as they dropped away. They'd been gliding over the big, algae-covered rocks for over an hour, and now they sloped down into the depths until Leonardo couldn't make them out through the gloom.

"The river just got *deep*," said Bates.

"I know." Leonardo placed a hand on the stem behind him. The way the bottom fell away made his stomach lurch. This was the widest point of the river yet, and Leonardo wondered just how deep it went.

He straightened back from the edge. His rowers leaned over between strokes, trying to see into the depths. Back in Raven Clan territory, there were only a few spots where the river bottom disappeared from view. They were used to being able to see what lay below them, and with the threat of crocs never far from their minds, shoulders stiffened and grips tightened down the boat.

Suddenly, Viola straightened. "Leo, something's wrong."

"What do you mean?" Leonardo yanked the rudder, steering them around a jutting rock.

"I…" she shut her eyes, concentrating. "I don't know. For some reason, I can't—"

"What was that?" Robin dropped his oar, shoving himself back from the edge.

"Where?" Viola jumped up, leaning out over the side.

"Over here! Where did it go?" Bates stopped rowing and craned overboard.

"Ohmygod!" Moth reeled back.

"What is it?" Leonardo stepped down off his platform, placing a hand on the hilt of his sword.

"It's back on this side!" said Charley. "There's another one!"

"Another what?" said Puck.

"Big white one under the bow," said Pinch.

"Big white what?" asked Leonardo.

"A fish?" said Nym.

"No way!" said Bates. "Have you seen it? There it is, quick!"

Nym twisted around.

"Did you see it?"

"That's no fish," said Nym.

"What is it?" repeated Leonardo.

"Oh. Oh shit." Strato yanked his oar in and stood up, shuffling back into the centre of the boat.

"Everyone, away from the edges," shouted Leonardo. Most of

the Clan had already shuffled back, their oars jammed at stiff angles in the oarlocks where they'd dropped them, but Viola, Pinch, and Bates hadn't moved.

"*Everyone,*" snapped Leonardo. "Back from the edge."

Viola was the first to give in, followed by Bates, then finally Pinch, rolling his eyes as he deliberately climbed over one bench.

"They're really big," said Viola.

"*What* are?"

She shook her head.

Just then, Leonardo caught movement. He whipped around as one shot past, just below the surface. It was white and scaled like a fish, bigger than him, and a fin flicked the surface as it plunged out of sight.

Leonardo drew his sword. Metal hissed as the rest of the clan did the same. Pinch and Viola both pulled out their slingshots. Pinch hesitated, started to draw his sword instead, then looked at Leonardo, swore to himself, and started fitting a pebble into his slingshot's pouch.

Leonardo nodded and his eyes went back toward the water. He had bigger things to worry about than Pinch being petty.

"Ok, everyone brace yourselves. I don't know what—"

Something knocked against the bottom of the boat.

Everyone froze, looking down between their feet. Leonardo's blood pounded in his ears.

It knocked again. Then again.

Knock, knock.

Knock, knock, knock.

The boat swayed.

KNOCK, KNOCK, KNOCK, KNOCK—

Pinch stomped his foot.

Bates and Puck both stomped in sync, then Charley and Viola, and Pinch again.

"Ok, ok!" Leonardo held up his hands. The knocking stopped. "That's enough. We don't want to provoke—"

Something tapped quietly, directly under Pinch's feet.

Pinch looked down.

Leonardo opened his mouth to stop him, but Pinch moved first, raising his foot and slamming it down on the boards.

The hull exploded with a pounding that threw him off his feet and sent him stumbling into the bulwarks. Leonardo dropped to his knees, shoving himself back from the edge. The percussion rang like a thousand cannonballs hitting the bottom of the boat, thundering and banging and popping like the boards were about to crack in two.

The eight other members of Lion Clan collapsed, falling over benches and into the stern, fumbling not to stab anyone—or them-selves—in the process.

Leonardo grabbed the nearest bench and climbed to his feet. He straddled it, bracing his knees on either side.

Moth did the same, crouching for balance as he looked at Leonardo. Water churned around the longboat, frothing and splashing against the sides.

"What's happening?"

Leonardo shook his head, then his blood froze.

A pale hand grabbed the edge of the boat behind Moth. Grey, jagged nails dug into the wood. Another hand appeared, scaly and soaking wet.

"Moth!" yelled Leonardo. "Duck!" Moth dropped to his knees

as Leonardo jumped past him and brought his sword down on the right hand. The clawed fingers released and the hand slipped over the side, leaving streaks of blood on the wood. Leonardo stumbled into the bulwark, grabbing the edge for balance.

Before he could move, another hand lunged out of the water, grabbing the edge right next to him. One finger caught the side of his hand, jagged nail digging into his flesh. Leonardo ripped his hand away, staggering back.

Blood welled in a long gash from his knuckles to his wrist. It stung like someone had dragged a razor blade through his skin.

He swore and lifted his sword as the creature pulled itself up on the edge. Blood dripped from the tip of its pale finger as it pulled its head up over the side of the boat.

Oh shit.

Leonardo didn't know what he'd been expecting, but the face that leered back at him was most definitely not it.

Her hair was white, iridescent like spun pearls. It hung wet and heavy around her face, her skin grey and sickly, and as she opened her mouth, a nest of long, pointed teeth gleamed in the sunlight.

A girl. A hideous girl. She hissed, pulling back her gums, and Leonardo scrambled backwards. Moth gasped and half-rolled, half-fell into the next footwell, taking Robin down with him.

The boat is too narrow, thought Leonardo. *We're going to—*

A splash behind him, and another blood-curdling hiss. Leonardo spun, blindly swinging his sword. It sliced through the dead skin of a second creature's face and she gasped, dropping into the water.

He spun back, taking an off-balance swing at the first one. He

330

missed and she lunged for him, nails clanging against his sword as he swung again in defence.

Puck hacked at her and she hissed, plunging out of sight just as two more creatures splashed up over the side. Puck and Bates jumped at them, swords flashing.

We're going to die here, thought Leonardo. He swallowed the panic, gripping his sword two-handed as the boat tilted under the weight of three creatures, water streaming off their scaled faces. They raised themselves above the bulwarks and he staggered back. They were too repulsive to call mermaids, but that was the closest word for them; naked from the waist up and hideous, with scaled grey skin that gave way to finned tails, pure white like their hair.

Pinch and Viola released their stones in sync, hitting two of the creatures in the head and dropping them.

Robin and Nym hacked at the third one, sending it after the first two.

More pulled themselves up every second. The pounding continued down below and the boat tossed in the water, making it impossible to balance. Water sloshed over the side, soaking them.

We can't keep up like this. His knee slammed into a bench and he swore, throwing himself away from a hissing mouth. A mixture of horror and terror coursed through his mind.

Then he scrabbled up and steeled himself. *No. We're not dying here. Not like this.*

Viola loosed a stone at the same instant that another one leapt up and dragged the side of the boat down. Her shot went wide and hit Puck in the back.

He stumbled, dropping his sword.

"Shit! Aim that thing, you half-witted—" He twisted and cut

off, realizing it was Viola and not Pinch. Then a demon-mermaid reared up two feet from him and he ducked, throwing himself out of the way.

Leonardo beat the creature back. Viola loosed a stone that connected with its face and it reeled back, plunging out of sight.

The sound of it all was horrifying. The hissing, the scraping, the splashing, the *bang, bang, bang,* on their hull. The desperate breaths of ten Lions, fighting for their lives in the middle of a soulless stretch of wilderness.

Suddenly, five mer-demons grabbed the starboard side of the boat and dragged it down, steep enough that Leonardo realized they were going to tip.

"Left side!" he yelled, hurling himself painfully into the bulwarks. Puck and Strato leapt after him, and their weight ripped the right side out of the creatures' grips. The boat swung back level with a splash, rocking crazily.

"Grab the oars!" he shouted, pushing himself up. "We need to row!"

To their credit, Lion Clan jumped to the task, scrambling to the nearest benches before their attackers could get a hold again. Leonardo grabbed an oar that was jammed through the oarlock and wrestled it free, then leaned forward and took a heavy stroke. Deep claw marks marred the wood beside him. Outrunning the creatures seemed impossible, but he was desperate.

Of course, as most desperate plans worked out, they made it only three strokes before the first oar ripped out of Puck's hands.

Nym tried to hold on to his, grabbing down below the stop for a better grip, but his hands slammed into the oarlock and he fell backwards, crying out in pain.

Leonardo braced his feet and yanked back on his oar, determined not to give in.

Not this time.

But his efforts quickly became desperate, frantically heaving on the wooden handle, the rope stop digging hard into his skin. He held out for a moment, gritting his teeth, but then he started to slide toward the wall and he understood that fighting it was pointless. There could be six of them on his oar alone.

He let go, and his oar shot through the hole until the stop slammed against the oarlock, leaving it hanging awkwardly out to the side of the boat.

Leonardo knew better than to pull it back in. It would just be yanked from him again, and he didn't want to test the stop a second time. The other five boys who'd gotten to an oar had the same thought, and they shuffled back into the middle of the boat for the second wave of attack.

CHAPTER 42

They didn't have to wait long. Twenty bodies exploded out of the water, grey fingernails breaking on the wood and hideous teeth snapping.

Lion Clan leapt into action, swords flashing and pebbles flying. Leonardo slashed at three mermaids in rapid succession, drawing blood from two and narrowly missing the third. She dropped anyway, losing her grip as she ducked away from him.

Viola reached in her pocket and hesitated, eyes wide as she realized she was out of pebbles.

He spotted a spare sword sticking out of a supply bag. It was a practice sword, dull and useless for cutting, but it would be perfectly serviceable for blunt force.

"Viola!" he called. She looked at him and he extended his own sword, leaning around Puck to get the hilt to her. She hesitated.

"Take it!" he yelled.

Viola grabbed the hilt and he let go, turning to yank the practice sword out of the supply bag and high-stepping over two benches back to the platform. Another creature pulled herself over the side, flopping right into the boat. Her tail was thick and muscular, shimmery with white scales that ended in a pair of smooth fins, curling to fit inside the boat.

A surge of water dumped off her body, soaking Leonardo's legs as it splashed over him. She twisted, hissing through bared teeth. Leonardo swung the dull sword as hard as he could and connected with her arm. Bone cracked and she screeched, lunging for him as she fell. Leonardo leapt back, tripping over a bench and falling into the footwell. His sword flew from his grip.

The creature dragged herself toward him with one arm and he gasped, scrambling to get out of the footwell.

From the bow, Strato shouted, "Pinch, the stern!"

Bates stepped on Leonardo's ankle and Leonardo cried out in pain. He fell into a bench. Yellow teeth opened a foot from his face.

In that moment, he knew he was about to die.

Then something slammed into the creature's forehead. Its body jerked and its eyes went blank, a pebble falling from a circular wound directly between them. A line of blood ran from the wound as it flopped across the benches, lifeless.

Leonardo twisted to see Pinch, standing on a bench near the bow with his slingshot still raised. He tossed it aside and drew his sword, hacking at a mer-demon as she tried to get over the bow.

Leonardo closed his eyes. *Thank you.*

He climbed out from under the bench, grabbing his sword and taking a swing at another mer-demon.

No others managed to make it over the sides, and when the last one dropped, the ten members of Lion Clan crouched, tense and ready to fight, for a long minute after she'd disappeared under the surface.

The silence blared around them. Leonardo could still hear the creatures hissing in this head. He wasn't sure if he'd ever forget that sound. His chest heaved as he scanned the water, frothy with bubbles and churned up foam. Blood coated the water too. He didn't think they had killed many of the creatures—aside from the one laying behind him—but they had injured a lot. Enough to make the creatures give up on what they must've thought was easy prey.

He looked back at the dead one. She would need to be dumped overboard. He was so exhausted right now that the thought wasn't even that repulsive. He didn't have the energy to be queasy.

Meanwhile, the rest of the boat came back to life.

"Well shit," said Pinch.

"Double shit," said Bates.

"What *were* those?" asked Robin.

"Mermaids?" said Puck.

"No mermaid I've ever heard of," said Bates.

"Did you see their teeth?" asked Charley, mimicking their chomping.

Leonardo glanced at her. She appeared surprisingly stable for someone who was still acclimating to the woods and its apparent horrors.

"Who couldn't?" said Robin.

Both boys glanced at the dead one. Leonardo followed their gaze and Puck followed his.

"Should we keep it?" asked Puck, lip curled back even as he suggested it. "Just until we can figure out what it is? Or find a weakness."

"I don't think it's particularly complicated," said Leonardo. The last thing he wanted to do was keep the stinking creature, which lay flopped across three benches, tail curled over in the stern.

"It has the same weaknesses as us," he continued. "It just also has claws and fangs."

"Not claws," said Nym, leaning to see. "Just really ragged fingernails."

"I say we get rid of it," said Bates. "Dead things creep me out."

Leonardo nodded. "Puck, Strato, Bates come and help me"

"Why me?" complained Bates as he climbed over the benches, grimacing at the creature.

"Oh god, she stinks," said Strato.

"They all stunk," said Nym, keeping to the front of the boat.

"I know, but she's worse," said Strato. "It's like rotting fish."

Leonardo stepped around the creature, trying not to breathe too deeply.

"Puck, grab the tail with me," he said as Bates and Strato positioned themselves near her head.

Grimacing, all four boys bent down and took hold of the creature's body. Leonardo and Puck had to try a few times, their fingers slipping on the slime-covered scales. They finally found a grip just above her fins and managed to wrestle her up onto the edge. Her tail was a deadweight, impossible to work with, and it took all four of them to get it up and over the side.

The creature's body hit the surface with a splash.

"Gross." Strato turned and started climbing back to his bench. Bates followed and Puck high-stepped back to his place.

Leonardo climbed up onto the stern platform, sloshing puddled water into the footwell with the side of his boot.

"Let's get the hell out of here," he said. "Oars down. Double time."

He glanced over the stern as they hobbled away, leaving a drunken wake of crimson froth behind, churned up by weak, uneven strokes.

He turned his eyes ahead, to the riverbank sliding past and his exhausted crew churning the oars. They'd been caught completely off guard. *He'd* been caught completely off guard.

They were incredibly lucky to have survived it. They'd banded together and fought off the danger, but Leonardo didn't feel victorious. His thoughts circled around next time, because he was certain there would be a next time.

If I let my guard down again, thought Leonardo, *I might not have a clan left to lead.*

CHAPTER 43

The next morning dawned murky and twilit. Weak light filtered through gaps in the grey, the air crackling with static energy.

Leonardo hoped the rain would wait until at least the afternoon before it broke loose. They needed to make a lot of ground today. He had no way to gauge how far they were from their destination, and he felt like they were falling behind schedule. His feet itched to get moving, to get out of this stretch of river.

"Viola," said Leonardo, as they finished packing the boat. "Yesterday…before the attack…you sensed the danger a few seconds before it happened, didn't you?"

Two benches over, Robin paused what he was doing.

The attention of everyone in earshot shifted toward them, while simultaneously trying to appear as though they weren't listening. Puck moved a stack of shields that had fallen into his footwell, gingerly placing them so they wouldn't clunk.

She didn't respond immediately, pushing aside a sleeping roll so he could wedge another one beside it.

"Just like back in the Darkwoods," pressed Leonardo. "When you knew that Hawk Clan was still at their camp. How do you do that?"

"I told you before, I'm not allowed to—"

"Viola, those things almost killed us yesterday. They could come back today, and who knows what else is waiting for us down-river. If you can see—"

"Look," said Viola. She lowered her voice to almost a whisper. "My people are of the woods, like the trees and the river. Because of that, we can use its magic sometimes. That's all. I'm not very good at it and I don't understand it. I—"

Thunder rumbled overhead and Viola broke off.

"Come on." She pushed the last sleeping roll under the bench. "Let's get moving before the rain starts."

Leonardo climbed back to the captain's platform, frustrated.

At least he'd learned something, but it wasn't enough.

Did she know about those creatures?

Does she know of any others?

Can she see how close we are to the Cove? He'd ask her as soon as her defences came down. Right now, Leonardo feared more questions would just close her up tighter.

We need to get off this river soon. The longboat was a terrible position to defend from, but he wasn't inclined to stay any longer than necessary at any of their campsites. He didn't know what other creatures lurked in the shadows, and he got a bad feeling from this stretch of the woods. He saw more dead trees every day, and the crocodile skull from Viola's clearing rose fresh in his mind. The feeling made him nervous for Nym. If the Dark was stronger here, was Nym in more danger? He made a note to suggest Nym shorten his on-shore excursions, for the time being at least.

He wasn't the only one with ominous thoughts, and a silent tension permeated the boat all day. The rain held off for the most part, until the sun began to set and the swollen clouds finally let loose. A stiff wind blew straight over the bow, and Leonardo squinted as the first drops hurled into his face.

Those first few quickly multiplied, and within a matter of minutes the surface of the river sizzled under the downpour as Leonardo's crew bowed their heads and rowed on, their clothes becoming spotty, then wet, then drenched and hanging from their shoulders.

Leonardo shielded his eyes, searching the banks for some-where to land. Walls of jumbled rock, tall and unstable-looking, bordered this stretch of river. A few boys leaned back to gaze up the left side wall, which was still relatively dry, and which they could probably climb to the shelter of the forest above.

If they reached a section that looked more stable, Leonardo might consider it. Right now, the rocks looked ready to fall with one wrongly placed hand, and streams of water ran down crevices into the moss. Leonardo held no illusions about how slippery those patches would be.

He took them in toward the bank for whatever bit of shelter it could provide—it wasn't much—but he didn't give the order that he knew they were hoping for. Pinch had come to that conclusion long ago, and he craned out over the bow like a statue, as though he could will a landing into existence.

Charley had completely abandoned her post to hide under an old shirt she had dug out of a supply bag. She held it up like an umbrella, laughing as most of the rain cut through anyway.

Leonardo let her be. Odds were, Pinch would spot a landing at the first possible second it could be seen, and Leonardo would see it a second later.

Maybe Viola can try to sense one.

He pushed the idea aside. She'd said it only worked sometimes.

She would've told us if this was one of those times. She's just as cold and wet as we are.

Communication was next to impossible over the sound of the rain on the river's surface. Leonardo's teeth chattered and his vision blurred as rain pelted into his eyes. At least the smell of fish was finally gone. Hundreds of nail marks scarred the bulwarks, both inside and outside, and he'd begun to wonder if the odour was permanently etched into the wood.

When Pinch finally raised an arm in the air and pointed straight ahead, Leonardo released a cold breath. Pinch didn't even bother to glance back and make sure he was looking. He knew Leonardo would have one eye locked on him at all times, and Leonardo squinted into the rain to see what Pinch had spotted.

It was two things. First, the bank finally sloped down to water-level, and second, a thicket of massive, wide-canopied trees took over from the scraggly ones they had been rowing alongside all day.

The branches met over the river, growing together into a thick ceiling that only a few streams of water managed to penetrate. It looked like the most blissfully dry space Leonardo had ever seen.

He pointed over the rowers' heads and they glanced back, following his gaze and picking up their pace for the first time in hours as they dragged the boat toward it.

A few moments later they slid into the tree tunnel and sighs of relief echoed down the boat. Dense, snaking vines and big leaves wove a canopy above them. Tiny, white, bell flowers hung from every branch, a product of either the vines or the trees, it was impossible to tell.

The quiet was as sudden as the dryness. A hundred feet in, the rowers shipped their oars and the water dripping off them was louder than the hiss of rain on the canopy above. Leonardo wiped a raindrop from his cheek and took a breath of the perfumed air. It hung heavy and humid, and the sound of his breath was hollow, echoing as though he were in a cave.

The boat continued gliding at a good clip, and the bit of light they'd had outside quickly diminished as they slipped deeper into the tree tunnel. The sides passed through the gloom, dense with underbrush and tree-trunks, and impenetrable to anything human-sized.

Smaller things however, like fireflies, had no problem. Swarms of them wove in and out of the branches, becoming more plentiful the deeper they got. They looked like sparks, flying from an invisible fire and swirling in the shadows overhead. The undersides of the leaves glowed yellow and tiny lights danced behind the bell flowers, but down at river-level it was getting too dark too see properly. Pinch became a vague shape up front and Leonardo decided that going any further was too dangerous without their own source of light. He started to give the order for his rowers to stop the boat when the tunnel started brightening.

Leonardo frowned as ranks of fireflies descended through the branches, joining the swarm and bunching together in such a high concentration that the light they threw expanded to hit the walls of the leafy tunnel and the longboat drifting below them. The water glowed yellow with their reflection, casting his clanmates' faces as if in candlelight. The air twinkled with even more of them, lifting out of the underbrush and rising to join the swarm.

They congregated over the boat like a chandelier, and as the boat drifted slower, so did the fireflies, mirroring its path in the air above. They bunched so tightly that Leonardo couldn't look straight at them. He squinted, focusing on the individual insects around the perimeter. He'd seen a lot of fireflies back at Raven Clan and these ones didn't look right. They were too big, and he wondered if he'd been too quick to label them. Maybe these were some bigger insect, only present this far south, that glowed like fireflies and clustered together.

And followed boats.

The individual ones in the air moved too quickly to make out details. Everyone in the boat spoke at once, and Leonardo glanced away from the not-fireflies as Moth's voice got louder, topped only by Pinch's.

"You think *that's* a firefly?" said Moth, pointing upward.

"I think *those* are fire*flies*," said Pinch.

"Don't you think they're a little big?" demanded Moth.

Both boys stood in their footwells, craning around to see each other.

"Maybe they just ate," said Pinch.

"What do they eat, birds?"

"It's better than your theory."

"You think?"

Meanwhile, Viola climbed to her feet and lifted a hand, palm up, toward the glowing mass. At first, nothing happened, except for Moth and Pinch having to stop and lean out over the water to see each other.

"For shit's sake, Moth," said Pinch. "They're not fairies!"

"Because why? You don't want them to be?"

"Because it's stupid."

"You're stupid. Look at them, they're as long as my thumb. Have you ever seen a firefly that big?"

Leonardo glanced between the two of them, wondering if he should step in. Then a single piece of the glow broke away from the mass and descended toward Viola's hand.

It looked even less like a firefly now that it moved slow enough to see more than just a light. It hovered down and landed on Viola's palm, on two legs, and looked at her with a face that was incredibly small, but undeniably human.

What the…?

"They're fairies," she said, glancing at Pinch.

Pinch cut off mid-sentence. He narrowed his eyes at her hand, then his mouth fell open.

"Wait…actually?" Moth gasped, stepping over his bench.

"So you two can stop arguing," she continued. "Moth is right, Pinch is wrong."

She couldn't have known the importance of this moment to Moth. She'd never seen the rows of carvings in his treehouse workshop. The dozens and dozens of attempts to prove that what he'd seen was real.

"Moth took another step toward her, transfixed by the tiny creature.

"The rest will be down in a few minutes," said Viola. "They're too curious not to."

"Wait," said Nym. "Have you seen them before?"

"Of course," said Viola. "They lose their way sometimes and wind up in the Backwaters. I've never seen this many in one place before. Here, Charley, do you want to hold her?"

Moth was right the whole time. A fairy must've gotten lost and found its way onto our riverbank. All those carvings, and no one ever believed him.

Just as Viola predicted, the fairies began descending on the boat after a few minutes, landing along the bulwarks, on top of the figurehead, and in single-file lines along the oar handles. Hundreds more hovered in the air, creating a luminescent dome around the boat.

At first, a lot of the boys flinched away from the tiny creatures, but as more landed and covered every inch of open space, they faced no choice but to share the boat with them. In a role-reversal, Moth seemed to be the only one who wasn't even a little bit uncomfortable. Aside from Viola, of course. But to be fair, this wasn't either of their first experience with fairies.

If they wind up in the Backwaters so often, why has only one ever made it to the river?

A fairy landed on the back of his hand and Leonardo flinched, surprised. She blinked up at him through vivid green eyes, frazzled chestnut hair hanging around her face and nearly transparent wings curling as she leaned back to see him. She wore one of the white bell-shaped flowers like a dress. It flared out above her knees, revealing slender legs and impossibly small bare feet.

Leonardo stared at her, rapt. She smiled, tiny lips pulling back to reveal tinier teeth, and gave a curtsey.

"Are they—" Moth paused. "Did someone—can you hear that?"

"Hear what?" asked Leonardo.

The fairy tilted her tiny head, examining him.

"Can't you hear them?" asked Moth.

Leonardo shook his head, straining to hear anything besides the whirr of wingbeats.

"You can't?" Moth looked around. "Can anyone?"

Heads shaking. Pinch stared at him like he'd grown a second head.

"What are they saying?" Leonardo asked in sync with Viola.

Moth closed his eyes, frowning.

"It's like they're talking in my head or some—" he stopped. "*Lost Boys*. I just heard *Lost Boys*."

CHAPTER 44

O
h, give it up—" Pinch started, but Viola cut him off.

"Anything else?"

"*Lost Boys,*" said Moth again. "They keep saying that, over and over."

"That's what Viola calls us," said Robin.

"It's what you are," said Viola, distracted.

"How do they know it?" asked Charley, her hands cupped and holding the first fairy.

"Wait," said Moth. "They're saying something else."

"What is it?" asked Bates.

"I don't know yet. Cork it." Moth closed his eyes. "Lost Boys…"

The clan fell silent, holding their breath as Moth concentrated. The only sound was the whirring of wings and the drip of water through the canopy.

Eventually, Bates broke the silence. "Well?"

Moth blinked open his eyes, looking up at the fairies. The expression on his face was one of pure fear.

A jolt of terror raced through Leonardo.

"What are they saying?" asked Robin.

Moth looked at Robin, then turned to Leonardo, his eyes drawing to the fairy on his hand. He swallowed. "They're saying 'dead boys'."

Steel hissed around the boat as swords were drawn and the fairies took flight, startled.

"No!" said Viola. "That isn't a threat!"

"You wanna bet?" said Pinch, swatting fairies away.

"Sounds like a threat to me," said Strato.

"It's not!" said Viola. "Put your swords away!"

The boat rocked as Lion Clan twisted and ducked, swords glinting in the fairy light. The fairies swarmed in the air, frantic and dizzying.

Viola turned to Leonardo, desperate. "It's not a threat!"

"No?"

"No!"

"Then what is it?" He glanced at the messy-haired fairy on his palm. She held out her arms for balance, wings flitting once.

"They're trying to help you," said Viola, raising her voice over the shouts in the boat. "They're trying to warn you—" a pack of fairies shot past her head. Bates took a swing at them, narrowly missing Puck's face. Strato's sword flashed past Robin's ear. Leonardo flinched away from Bate's sword on a second pass.

"Bates!" snapped Leonardo. "Watch it."

"They mean us no harm, I promise," insisted Viola.

Leonardo focused on the fairies and it took him seconds to realize she was right. The fairies weren't doing any of the attacking. His clan stumbled around, seconds from maiming each other, and the fairies simply scrambled out of the way. Charley huddled under a bench, next to her hamster, Lion, in his basket. She cupped her hands around the fairy Viola had given her, sheltering it from the swords and swinging arms.

"Everyone, calm down!" shouted Leonardo.

Panicked voices crashed together, swords and wingbeats and tiny bodies whirring through the air.

"This isn't an attack!" he yelled, louder. "Put your swords away!"

Then Robin cried out, clutching his arm. Strato dropped his blade in horror, the tip red with blood. Puck jumped up on his bench. "Stop!" he yelled. "All of you! Put your swords away. Hey! Put. Your. Swords. Away. Good, now Robin, sit down. Bates, go to your bench. Robin, what are you doing? Sit down, Robin. And Nym, put your hands out, they seemed to like you. Good. Charley, come out here and do it too."

Under Puck's direction, the boat slowly retuned to normalcy. Or at least, close to. The fairies stopped swarming and began to settle along the edges of the boat again, tiny feet touching down on the old wood. The members of Lion Clan watched them warily, hands near their swords.

Viola wrung the corner of her dress, soaked from the rain. She chewed her lip, clearly wrestling with something.

"Viola?" prompted Leonardo.

"You're all in danger," she said without looking at him. "The fairies are trying to warn you."

"What kind of danger?" asked Moth.

"Viola," said Leonardo. "You need to tell us. I know your people kept these things secret, but you're one of us now, and if we're in danger—"

"The Dark isn't here to attack the woods," said Viola. She twisted the hem of her dress tighter.

"Then what is it here for?" asked Robin. He pressed a rag to his arm.

"It's here for us," said Leonardo, understanding. "Isn't it?"

Viola let go of the hem she was twisting. "The night I warned you about the attack, Dakota caught me returning to camp. He told me everything. The real reason Aleksander had to leave, and how the Dark came here, and...I was afraid that if I told you, my people would find out. But you're right. You deserve to know."

She blinked at him through earnest eyes, a straggle of wet hair curling down her forehead. A rivulet of water ran from her braid, down her arm. Leonardo wanted to be angry at her for not telling them, but a different emotion pulsed at the front of his mind, completely unsolicited and unhelpful in the moment.

Another rivulet ran down her bare shoulder and Leonardo cleared his throat, trying to force his mind back onto the matter at hand.

"Wait," said Moth. "Might something bad happen if we know the secrets? What if that's why it's such a big deal?"

"Then we'll deal with that then," said Leonardo. He was tired of not knowing things.

"Ok," said Viola. She drew a breath and laced her fingers. "This place, the woods...it exists because you believe it does. The moment you doubt whether or not it's real, you begin to lose your hold on it. You return to the real world and you can never come back here."

"Are you saying this place isn't real?" asked Robin.

"Of course it's real," said Puck. "Look around."

The leafy walls of the tree tunnel glowed in the fairy-light, dark and shiny in the humid air. Streaks of electric yellow reflected on the black water and a silver fish darted past, just below the surface. As Leonardo and the other boys regarded their world, an idea took hold in Leonardo's mind. It was insane, impossible, completely unfathomable, but still...it fit perfectly.

Almost perfectly.

Another fish jackknifed under the boat.

"It's real," said Viola. "All dreams are real until the dreamer wakes up."

That's it.

"These woods are inside of our imaginations," said Leonardo. "We're all dreaming."

"That's impossible," said Puck.

"You're crazier than your brother," said Strato.

"Strato," said Moth. "You're surrounded by fairies. Yesterday we were attacked by mermaids. There's no such thing as crazy anymore."

"You think we dreamt this whole thing?" countered Strato. "At the same time? Or am I just imagining all of you? Because I'm certainly not imagining myself."

"It can't be like a normal dream," said Leonardo. "We go to sleep and wake up still here."

"And I dream every night," said Nym. "Am I dreaming within a dream?"

"If you pinch yourself in a dream, you're supposed to wake up," said Bates, pinching his arm for emphasis. "Nothin'."

"I had a bunch of dreams before I got here," said Charley.

Everyone began talking at once. Puck stood with his back to the water, preaching to anyone who would listen; Bates and Strato argued with Robin over what 'real' meant; and Charley had become a living lamppost, covered in fairies from her fingertips to the top of her hat. She spoke to each of them, not pausing to listen for an answer. Moth did that for her, brow furrowed deep in concentration.

"Aleksander let the Dark in?" he said aloud, more to himself than anyone else.

What?

"Shut up!" yelled Pinch.

The voices just got louder, so Pinch climbed up on top of his bench.

"SHUT! UP!"

Nine faces turned in his direction.

"I'm getting a headache from all this yelling," he snapped.

"One at a time," said Leonardo. Around the boat, the fairies shuffled, noticeably skittish. The last thing anyone needed was another situation.

"Starting with me," said Pinch, still standing on his bench. "Leo, how could it be all of our imaginations at the same time?"

Leonardo shook his head. "I don't know. Maybe—"

"And how the fuck did we get here in the first place?"

"It can't be common," said Puck. "Sometimes a year goes by between boys showing up."

"It's an accident," said Viola. "I know that much. I think…" She paused. "I remember my father once said, 'The problem with the Lost Boys is they have too much imagination; eventually it has no choice but to swallow them whole'."

That was a troubling thought, and all the boys paused, contemplating being swallowed by their imaginations.

"And then we end up here," said Leonardo slowly.

Aleksander let the Dark in? How?

Why?

Viola started talking again before he could ask.

"Dreams are very loose in shape," she started. "They can't fit on a map and they're not meant to be explored like the real world. Your mind can skip through them just fine, but when you actually step into a dream, the details change too quickly to keep up with. My grandfather told me that you get tossed from vision to vision so quickly that it all just blurs into one. Reality disappears and everything you used to know just gets jumbled up with all the dreams until it's too tangled to make sense of."

"That's how we lose our memories!" Charley glowed nearly too bright to look at, covered in fairies in tiny white bell flowers. "That's what you're talking about, isn't it?" she continued, and Viola nodded.

"There are no rules in the imagination," said Viola. "You could be a thousand different people in a thousand different dreams. Eventually you forget which one is real."

"So where are we now?" asked Robin. "Is this another dream?"

Viola shook her head. "I don't think so. This place is steady. I think it's like...what's the word, in the middle of a storm...?"

"The eye," said Leonardo.

So this is...

She nodded.

"This is the eye of the dreamworld," said Leonardo, regarding the dark foliage and the white flowers. "I think I understand." Another sliver fish darted past. "If what you're saying is true, then we all got so lost tumbling around our dreams that we eventually fell out here. And since this is the eye...maybe all of our imaginations meet here."

"Maybe," said Puck, scratching his chin. "It's possible."

"But what about the girls?" argued Strato. "Nice theory, but girls dream too. Explain where they all are."

Charley glanced up. A fairy attempted to land on her nose and she sneezed.

"Well, they obviously exist," said Pinch. "Example A." He pointed at Charley. "And obviously things can hide in these woods. Example B." He pointed at the fairies. "Maybe Charley just got more 'lost' than the rest of us and ended up in the wrong end of the woods."

"Maybe the woods did it on purpose," said Charley.

"Like a sign," said Nym. He steepled his fingers, pressing them to his bottom lip. "Or a message."

"Meaning what?" Moth leaned around to see him.

"Ow!" said Charley, distracted by her fairies again. "That's my hair!"

"I don't know," said Nym. "But I'm just saying, maybe it wasn't an accident she got 'more lost than the rest of us'."

Leonardo's thoughts still spun around Aleksander, and he interrupted their debate.

"Moth," said Leonardo. "What did you say a few minutes ago? About Aleksander letting the Dark in?"

"The fairies said it." Moth raised his right hand, where a fairy sat cross-legged. "I don't know what they meant. They just repeat the same things over and over."

"They understand the woods better than we do," said Viola. "They're helping you because they know how bad the situation really is. If the Dark kills you all, then all of this...all of *us*, ceases to exist."

"And my brother let this Dark in?" asked Leonardo.

"By accident," said Viola. "Only the imagination of a child can sustain the reality of this place. As you get older, you lose your imagination and fall back to the real world. Aleksander was afraid to leave, so he held on, even as his imagination faded. That opened a tear which let in a nightmare from the dreamworld outside."

"That's why Tokala needed him to leave," said Leonardo. "To close the tear."

"Exactly," said Viola.

"And what happens if the Dark kills us?" asked Bates. "If this is a dream, then what happens when we die?"

"You fall out. The reality breaks and you fall back into the open dreamworld."

"And if it kills us all, you'll disappear?" asked Charley, her teeth chattering.

"This place only exists because your imaginations sustain it," said Viola. "If you're gone, then so are we."

"That's not fair!" said Charley. "Leo, we can't let it—"

"We won't," he assured her.

She shivered again, her clothes still dripping wet from the rain and her lips a bluish purple. He was cold too. Freezing actually. He'd just been too distracted to notice.

"No one is going to die or disappear or anything," said Leonardo. "We'll make sure of it. We have a lot to discuss," he added, glancing at Viola. "Thank you for telling us. But we need to find a place to camp before we all freeze."

Heads nodded around the boat.

"Ok," said Leonardo. "Oars down."

CHAPTER 45

T he green-eyed, messy-haired fairy stayed with him as Leonardo scanned the sides of the tree-tunnel, listening to the slosh of oars and the whirr of wingbeats. The fairy-light illuminated the tunnel as well as any torch, and when Pinch spotted a hole in the greenery, which led to a sheltered hollow at the base of one of the massive trees, the fairies followed them in.

They settled on low branches around the perimeter, casting the hollow in a flickering glow as the boys of Lion Clan stripped off their wet shirts and hung them over the bushes.

Viola and Charley changed around the back of the tree. Leonardo found some spare clothes in the supply bags for them to borrow.

Meanwhile, the boys laid out their sleeping rolls between the roots of the giant tree and dug through what was left of their supplies for something to eat.

"We need to go hunting soon," said Puck as Leonardo walked up.

"As soon as the rain stops," agreed Leonardo.

"Do you think we're close?" asked Puck. "To Lion Clan, I mean."

"We are Lion Clan."

"I know," said Puck. "But the camp."

Leonardo squinted into the night. The fairy lights twinkled back. He nodded, slowly.

After days of empty wilderness, they had encountered life two days in a row. Either they were in some sort of forest oasis, or they had finally returned to the land of the living. If that was the case, they should start encountering new clans soon. Or the abandoned camps of old ones. That would be better.

"Yes," he said to Puck. "I think we are."

***

Leonardo passed Charley on his way back around the tree. The clothes hung on her a bit, but she didn't seem to mind hiking them up as she sprinted barefoot past him. He found Viola waiting for him in her new clothes behind the tree, her rawhide dress hanging over a root.

It was the first time he'd seen her in anything other than the dress, and Leonardo paused. She looked more like a Lost Boy than ever.

The fork of his slingshot stuck out of her back pocket, and she cocked her head at him, smiling.

359

"What is it?"

Leonardo blinked. "Nothing." He glanced away. Then, searching for something to say, he cleared his throat. "The clothes fit, then?" he asked stupidly.

"I don't know," said Viola. "I'm not the one staring at me."

She grinned and Leonardo's cheeks warmed up.

"It looks—You look good," he said, glancing away as she grinned wider.

"Thank you." She gave a little curtsy. "Do you want to sit down?"

Leonardo swallowed, his thoughts firing too fast to catch. He scuffed the ground with his boot, then nodded with false poise and climbed down next to her.

Neither of them said anything at first, and for a long moment they just sat there, listening to the fairies rustling in the under-brush.

"What do you think?" Viola finally asked. "About this place being in your imagination? I still don't really understand it; I was very young when my grandfather told me."

"It explains a lot," said Leonardo. "Although there still are some things that don't make sense."

She glanced at him quickly. "Like what?"

"Well, there's what Pinch said," said Leonardo. "How could we all be seeing the same thing—and seeing each other, for that matter—if we're just imagining it all? And even if this is some crossroads where our imaginations meet, someone would've had to imagine all of it in the first place, wouldn't they?"

Viola rolled a piece of bark under her fingers.

"Because all of it already existed when we got here," he

continued. "So how could we be the ones imagining it when we know nothing about it? If we were the ones imagining it, I should be able to think, 'there's a cake under that bush,' and then go under the bush and find a cake. Since I can't do that, I can't be the one imagining it."

Viola didn't answer.

"Viola?"

"Oh, sorry." She looked at him. "Repeat that?"

Leonardo frowned, still staring at her. "Who imagined all of this in the first place?"

"Oh. Um…What about the first Lost Boys?" She had a strange tone in her voice.

"You mean the first ones ever?" asked Leonardo.

She nodded. "Maybe they dreamt it up. Because if this is all…imagined"—she swallowed hard—"then it wouldn't have existed until they imagined it."

"I guess that's true." Leonardo nodded. "So then—"

She sniffed, staring hard at the ground.

"Is everything ok?"

She didn't answer, and Leonardo shifted to see her better. "Viola, what's going on?"

She bit her lip, her gaze firmly locked on the ground. She ran her thumb over her knuckles, faster and faster.

"Viola," said Leonardo.

"It's stupid." She shook her head. "Sometimes I just wonder…"

"You can talk to me," said Leonardo. "What it is?"

"Am I real?" she asked suddenly, looking straight at him.

"What?" Leonardo stared at her.

361

"If everything here is imagined, then what am I? What are my people? Are we just some...figment of your imagination?"

"Of course not," said Leonardo automatically.

"You're..." he was going to say, '*no different than us*', but that wasn't true, was it?

"Exactly," said Viola.

"No," said Leonardo. "Listen, you have to be real. Because..."

"Because what?"

"Well..." Leonardo struggled to think.

"See?" said Viola, biting her lip harder.

"How could I be talking to you if you're not real?" said Leonardo.

"Haven't you ever talked to someone in a dream?"

Leonardo frowned.

"Right," Viola crossed her arms.

"Ok, well...what about..." Leonardo stared at the darkness between the branches, searching for any sort of answer. But the bushes held no more answers than the rest of the night, and just the fairy-lights gleamed back at him, flickering behind the leaves. He knew they were imagined, just like the woods and everything else, but they seemed so real. He wondered if 'Imagined' was the wrong word.

Did everything in his imagination have to be *imagined*?

He noticed a bead of red on Viola's lip. She'd bitten so hard that she'd drawn blood, and all at once, Leonardo had an idea.

"Give me your hand," he said.

"Why?" She hesitantly held out her right hand while Leonardo dug through the leaves beside him until he found a thorn. Viola furrowed her brow and Leonardo paused. He changed tactics and pricked the thorn into his own finger, drawing a bead of blood.

Viola pulled her hand away and Leonardo held up his finger.

"A thought can't bleed," he said. "Only living things bleed. What use would something not-real have for blood?"

Viola reached up and wiped her lip with the back of her hand, then looked down at the spot of red on her skin.

"See?" Leonardo wiped his hand in the leaves. "If you can talk, dream, and bleed, then you must be real."

She gave a small smile—an, *I wish it were that simple*, type of smile—and started to push herself up. "Thank you, Leonardo. I—"

"Think about it," said Leonardo, jumping up. "Even if this whole place was imagined, it would've been a long time ago. I'm not the one who imagined it, because I didn't make the rules. And neither did Aleksander, or he would've imagined a world he could conquer. Whoever the first Lost Boys were, this place stayed after they disappeared, so clearly, it's real enough to support itself. All the new trees and bushes would've grown from the seeds of the imagined ones, which means that no one actually imagined them; they grew naturally, like real trees."

He picked up a pinecone and broke off one of the wings, showing her the seed underneath.

"And it's not just the trees," he continued. "Even if your ancestors were imagined, their children would've had to been real, right? And their children after them. You can't re-imagine something once it exists. And if something exists, doesn't that mean it's real?"

A drop of rainwater ran down Viola's neck. The plaid shirt bunched up near her collar and she stood so close, her breath reached his skin. Emotion glistened in her eyes, and this time, it was because she believed him.

"Your ancestors might have been imagined," said Leonardo. "But you have to be real."

Suddenly, she leaned forward and kissed him, and nothing in his life had ever felt so real as she did in that moment. She pulled back a second later, blinking at him in the fairy light, and Leonardo took a breath.

"Say that again," she said. "About the trees."

Leonardo couldn't remember a thing he'd said before she kissed him.

"You're real," he said instead, energy vibrating in his chest. Her energy; the rush of the river and the dew on the morning ferns and the breeze that played through the tangled branches. She was all of those things, tied together in a pair of dark eyes and twin braids, copper skin and shallow breaths as she parted her lips.

He pulled her closer and kissed her again. Electricity shot through his veins with every thump of his racing heart, sizzling where his fingers touched her skin. When they pulled apart, it took all of Leonardo's effort not to lean forward and kiss her again. Viola smiled, eyes locked on his and fingers clenched in his shirt. "I wanted to...before..." Her words jumbled together, breathless. "But I wasn't sure..."

"What?" asked Leonardo. "You mean if...I liked you, too...like that?"

Viola nodded. "I was too nervous to say anything. I thought you might know already."

"I…" Leonardo flushed. "Well, I was hoping, but I…I didn't know if you…"

"Well I did. I do." Viola leaned forward, peering around the curve of the tree's immense trunk. "I'm surprised no one's come looking for us."

"It's a big tree," said Leonardo, not looking at it. Being so close to her, all he could focus on was the fan of eyelashes on her skin, the press of her fingers through his shirt, the part of her hair, almost black and still damp from the rain.

"Like the oak," said Viola.

"Sure." Leonardo kissed her, and it was like a century had passed since their last one. Somewhere high above, the rain pounded down, but an endless canopy of sweeping branches carried it away, leaving them safe and dry in their fairy-lit hollow, deep in the woods of their imaginations.

CHAPTER 46

If Leonardo had expected the change in his and Viola's relationship to be a big deal around camp, he was mistaken. He was fairly certain everyone knew; Viola made it her mission to hold his hand every possible second, and more than a few eyebrows raised as the boys around camp took notice. But aside from a handful of sideways comments—piloted by Pinch, Strato, and Bates—the reaction was consistently underwhelming.

Which was more than alright with Leonardo, although he took it as a sign of travel fatigue setting in. They had left Raven Clan territory a week ago, and it was beginning to feel like a lot longer. Especially with the way the last few days had gone.

Puck barely looked up from shoving supply bags under the benches of the boat as they walked up. Bags that looked very depleted to Leonardo's eyes. He grunted a greeting, which

Leonardo and Viola both returned. Leonardo had no doubt the news would've reached him long ago. Last night, probably, if he knew this clan.

Puck's reaction was hard to read, but Leonardo hoped that seeing them together was enough to push him the rest of the way back to normalcy. Puck was practical. He wouldn't keep his head in the clouds for long.

Leonardo put it out of his mind as he climbed up to the captain's platform. He could see the light up ahead, sparkling on the water at the far end of the tree tunnel, and he knew they had to be close to *something*. He just hoped it was the something they were looking for.

"I've been trying to ask the fairies about Lion Clan's camp all morning," said Moth, moving to his bench. "They're not very good listeners. But they said a few things that make me think we're close. A day's travel maybe."

A sense of weary optimism filled the boat as the rest of the clan piled in. They were a tattered flag, but flying nonetheless. Aside from Charley of course, who looked fresh and ready for a day of sailing. Her hamster, Lion, slept in his basket, nestled between supply bags under the bench.

Over all of it hovered a new sense of apprehension. They understood the woods now. They knew why they were here and why they disappeared, and no one felt entirely stable in their world anymore.

Will I see Aleksander again once I…

He'd asked Viola about it late last night, but she didn't know whether leaving one's imagination had the same effect as entering it. If it did, none of them might remember each other after this. Leonardo couldn't bear the thought of never seeing her or Moth or Pinch or any of them ever again.

There has to be a way around it. It's just that no one's found it yet. You sound like your brother now. And how did that turn out?

Then maybe there's a way to come back. She said there wasn't, but still...

The fairies had stayed with them all night, and apparently had no intention of doing otherwise this morning. As they pushed off from the bank, the air whirred with hundreds of tiny wingbeats. Leonardo felt something touch the back of his hand—the green-eyed fairy from yesterday. Her wings slowed to a stop and she held out her arms for balance, looking up at him. She still wore the white flower for a dress, and she'd tied her hair into a small fountain on top of her head. She smiled, pulling back her lips to show a row of tiny white teeth.

Viola glanced back, covered in fairies herself, and Leonardo smiled despite the dilemma on his mind. His rowers worked into a rhythm, eyes on the sunlight up ahead, and he lifted the tiny fairy to his shoulder. She stepped off and sat down, kicking her bare feet and reclining to watch the end of the tunnel approach.

Two of them attempted to sit on the edge of Pinch's hat, and he took it off, swatting at them until they finally flew away, only to loop around and set down on the back brim after he placed it on his head again. Leonardo got Moth's attention and nodded at Pinch. Moth twisted around and grinned. Leonardo placed a hand on the rudder, taking a breath of the morning air and listening to the oars clunk in the oarlocks, water sloshing against the hull.

I'll find a way. Even if no one else has, I won't let myself forget all of this. These woods, these boys—and now the two girls—were the only life he remembered. He didn't intend to leave it all behind.

When they rowed out of the tree tunnel, they found a cloudless blue sky and a wide, sparkling stretch of crystal-clear river. They made double-time that day, rarely breaking stroke and only stopping when absolutely necessary. Only as it rolled into late afternoon did they start to slack off, lulled by the sun and their own depleted energy. Leonardo let them rest, watching the underbrush pass by. The trees had changed. It had been happening steadily the whole journey, but today things took a dramatic turn as the foliage went from lush and leafy to dark and tropical.

Leonardo didn't remember much of his past life, but he knew that no river anywhere could carry you from deep in the woods to the middle of a jungle paradise in the space of a few hours. But this wasn't any forest; it was a place of pure imagination, and complete swings in climate were perfectly logical here.

They had traveled to a different world from the pines back at Raven Clan, and the weather changed with it. The sun burned hotter, the air more humid, and Leonardo could almost taste the ocean on the breeze.

The birdsong warbled more vibrant, the ferns rustled louder, and when something leapt over the river, crashing into the treetops on the far side, it took Leonardo a moment to realize it was a monkey.

Everyone spoke at once, heads swivelling to take in their new surroundings. Leonardo let the chatter roll over him, too distracted to take part in it. A screech split the vivid greens and he spotted a parrot on a vine. Down below, colourful fish streamed just under the surface, darting away from Lion Clan's oars.

Bigger fish passed in the opposite direction, deep down below. He hadn't realized the river was so deep here. The water rippled a cut-glass shade of turquoise, hazy a few meters down, and he caught the flick of another big fin as it darted past.

Then Pinch called out, "Longboat!"

They'd spent so many days in empty wilderness, everyone knew exactly what that meant, and they stiffened.

We're in clan territory again.

A longboat rounded the next curve, the gaping wooden mouth of a viper leading the way as eight oars churned the water on each side.

Definitely Lost Boys.

"Snake Clan?" said Robin, excitement and fear mixed in his voice.

"One would assume," said Strato.

"What are they doing?" asked Charley, standing to see over Strato.

All along the Snake Clan boat, boys pulled up grey hoods. Their backs faced Lion Clan as they rowed, and not one of them turned back to look.

"Sit down, Charley," said Leonardo. He placed a hand on his sword. Up front, Pinch pulled out his slingshot, loading it out of sight, below the bulwarks. Viola did the same.

Why weren't we more careful? We knew we were close. I should've realized we could run into a clan.

Lion Clan was grossly under-equipped to fight a full, rested patrol in their own territory.

All at once, every fairy on or around Leonardo's boat took off, flying up into the trees and out of sight.

That's a bad sign.

"Where did they go?" asked Charley.

"They'll be back," said Viola. "They're hiding."

"From what?" asked Leonardo. "Do you know them?"

"No," said Viola. "My grandfather never talked about them."

The other boat's oars pulled in as they approached, and Leonardo ordered his crew to do the same. The boy standing at the rear of the Snake boat wore a darker grey cloak than the others, his face hidden in shadow.

"Announce yourself, intruders," he called. His voice carried a sharp quality, like the edge of a knife. It grated on Leonardo's ears, and Bates made a face at Puck.

"My name is Leonardo," called Leonardo. "Leader of Lion Clan. We come in peace."

The cloaked leader of Snake Clan paused. One of the hooded rowers leaned over and said something to another, both of them shapeless grey ghosts in their cloaks.

"Lion Clan," called the leader. "What is that then, on the front of your boat?"

"A lion," said Leonardo. He was aware that it didn't look much like one. Moth insisted that he wasn't finished yet, but a part of Leonardo wondered if more cutting and shaving would just make it look more perplexing. As it was, the carving appeared to be a bird with no beak and a frill around a too-narrow head.

"It used to be a raven," he explained. "From our old Clan."

"Raven Clan," said the cloaked figure.

"Yes," said Leonardo. "You've heard of us?"

"No. You're from the North?"

371

"Yes. The Darkwoods."

"That, I have heard of," said the voice under the cloak. "You've traveled a long way from home."

"Yes," said Leonardo. "It's not our home anymore."

"Tell me, Leonardo," said the snake leader, sleeve sliding down as he pressed his hands together. "In the Darkwoods, do clans come and go unannounced through other clans' territories?"

"We weren't aware that any clans lived here," said Leonardo. "We apologize for crossing your border."

"Good answer. We will accept your apology—this time. But you won't get that excuse again. What are you doing here, so far south?"

The prows of their boats met, point watchmen glancing sidelong as they glided past one another. Leonardo finally got a look at the snakes' faces. Each wore a matching scar on his forehead, a circle with a vertical line through it, resembling a snake's eye. The boys sat absolutely silent, faces shadowed under their cloaks.

A chill raced up his spine.

"Our leader disappeared," said Leonardo, remembering to answer the question. "The new one isn't fit to run a clan."

"So you bailed while you had the chance."

"Yes."

Do they give themselves those scars? Is it some kind of initiation?

"And now you're Lions," said the leader. He wore the same scar.

"We intend to revive Lion Clan from the legends," said Leonardo.

"Indeed," said the Snake leader. "A lofty quest. I would hate to be the one to delay you. Row on, *Lion Clan*. The far end of our territory is marked by a big white rock. The Cove is just beyond that."

A lofty quest. Leonardo had heard those words before. Miles upriver, a week earlier, when Lance, the leader of Bear Clan, sent them off to the Fox Clan border. Even the inflection matched. A perfect impression of something said miles away.

Leonardo tilted his head as they glided fully past the Snake boat and the stranger gave a theatrical bow, smiling from hollow cheeks.

"Welcome to the jungle, Leonardo," he said, straightening. "My name is Caliban. Leader of Snake Clan. I hope our clans can be friendly."

Leonardo nodded slowly, hairs standing on end. "As do I."

Caliban nodded from under his hood as their captain's platforms passed, and Leonardo realized his eyes were different colours; one green and one blue.

The Snake boat continued to drift, the boys' hooded faces motionless in their perfect rows, coiled and watchful like a nest of real snakes.

"Oars down," said Leonardo quietly. "Get us out of here."

The hairs on his neck didn't lie down until they passed the white rock at the far end of Snake Clan's territory, and Leonardo made sure to burn the image of it into his memory. If Lion Clan's camp was nearby, Caliban and company were going to be their neighbours. Leonardo didn't want to cross them again.

The foliage grew bigger, brighter and more tropical the deeper they went, until they sailed under leaves which spanned the width of the river, massive and shiny, with waxy stalks as thick as a person.

Peering into the water, Leonardo caught another glimpse of one of the giant fish from earlier, then another one. When a third passed below them, Leonardo got a better look at it, and he frowned. Through the haze in the water, it didn't really look like a fish anymore. The tail fanned out horizontally, like a dolphin's, and the long fins on either side of its body didn't really look like fins at all. They almost looked like—

Leonardo's blood went cold.

A fourth and a fifth darted past, then a sixth and seventh.

"Oars up!" yelled Puck. "Get back from the edges."

"Now," snapped Leonardo, drawing his sword.

His crew scrambled to drag in their oars. In the bow, Pinch leaned out over the water, holding his hat to shade the surface.

"Pinch," snapped Leonardo. "Inside the boat."

"Mermaids," said Pinch, pointing at the water.

"I know. *Inside the boat.*"

Pinch complied, jamming his hat in place as he climbed back over the benches.

"I counted seven," said Leonardo.

"I'm at nine," said Puck, sword in hand. The rest of the crew backed into the middle of the boat, drawing their weapons. Viola pushed Charley behind her.

Even if they fought off the creatures again, Leonardo held no illusions that everyone would survive it. The claw marks on the wood testified how close last time had been.

Leonardo reached out and took a shield from Moth.

Don't let it be Moth. Or Pinch.

Or Viola.

Or little Charley.

Or any of them. His stomach knotted at the thought of any member of his strange family leaving the woods. *Back into the dreamworld. Where the Dark came from.*

"Do you have pebbles?" he asked Viola. "For the slingshot?"

"I've been gathering them at every stop," said Viola.

"Good. Try not to hit Puck this time," he said, trying and failing to make a joke.

Viola nodded, serious.

Then the boat lurched.

CHAPTER 47

Brace yourselves!" yelled Bates.

Leonardo crouched, pressing his boots into the boards of the first footwell. He raised his sword and shield, ready for the first of the creatures to come launching over the side. The rest of Lion Clan did the same, backs to the centre of the boat and swords pointed out from behind their shields.

For a long moment, nothing happened. And then—

"Are we moving?" asked Nym.

Leonardo looked down, the boat lurching beneath him. He glanced overboard. The water streamed past, splashing against the hull.

"They're pulling us," said Robin, panic flushing his face as red as his hair.

"Everyone calm down," said Leonardo. "We need to—" The boat lurched again, and he stumbled as they picked up speed.

Moth and Bates barely dodged butting heads and half a dozen swords swung wildly as the arms holding them pinwheeled for balance.

"Put away your swords," yelled Leonardo, jamming his own into his belt. He kept his hand on the hilt, ready to draw it at the first sight of clawed fingers over the bulwarks.

The boat cut faster by the second, and staying upright became more and more difficult. Nym fell into Viola, taking her hard into Puck's shield. Charley fell into the footwell, hat rolling under a bench and hair flying loose behind her.

"Hold onto something!" yelled Leonardo, shouting into a wind that now whipped over the bow. Water splashed up behind them, spraying high where tail fins broke the surface.

Pinch yelled something from the bow and Leonardo squinted into the wind. Pinch pointed over the bow and Leonardo followed his gaze to the river ahead. It turned sharply at the next bend, where a wall of greenery awaited the speeding longboat.

Shit.

He gritted his teeth as the boat bucked under him. Water sprayed out from under the keel like a powerboat. Leonardo looked briefly at the oars, but the wake ripped too strong. Any oar that touched it would be torn from the rower's hands.

Diving overboard wasn't an option; the claws in the water scared him far more than the tree trunks ahead, although a crash at this speed wouldn't end much better. And any chance of making the corner diminished with every second they hurtled straight toward it.

The bank flew toward them and Leonardo braced for impact, then all at once they swung to the right. He fell into the bulwarks as the mermaids dragged them into a turn. Moth slammed into an oar handle next to him and Bates crashed into the footwell, piling hard against Leonardo's legs.

We're still alive. That was all that mattered.

But for how long?

The boat fishtailed, throwing a massive wave onto the bank, then they rounded the bend and began picking up speed again.

Leonardo detangled himself from Bates and used the benches to climb away from the others.

He wondered *why* they were still alive. A straight leg of the river ran out before them, no different to his eye than the one before it.

"Is everyone ok?" called Moth.

"I think so," said Leonardo, grabbing Puck's hand and helping him up.

Puck winced, grabbing his leg, and Moth held his shoulder. A few other boys had fallen on oar handles and got up gingerly, but it didn't appear as if they had sustained any serious injuries. Viola appeared unhurt as she climbed out of the pile, and Charley was more concerned about getting to her hamster than nursing any bruises of her own.

Whatever speed they had lost in the turn was regained by the time Leonardo's clan got back into position, straddling benches and crouching in footwells as water sprayed over the bow. They swung around a pair of shallow turns, through a thicket of bamboo, and under more giant leaves that blocked out the sunlight for a long stretch.

It became obvious the mermaids were taking them some-where, and Leonardo had visions of the crocodile nests back in

Raven Clan territory, only with far more dangerous inhabitants. There had to be a lot of them just pulling the boat, with the speed they were going. If there were more lying in wait wherever they were going…he didn't want to think about what could happen.

They cut around another turn and the banks became sandy to either side, and wider, pushing back the trees until the river cut through the middle of a sprawling sandbar. A moment later, he saw the sea.

It happened fast, flying down the last stretch of river as the trees peeled back, giving way to a sheltered cove surrounded by tan sea cliffs. One second, they shot over the river, the next they careened down one of a dozen forked channels and plowed out into the Cove. In the open water, they got even faster, pounding over the surface as sheets of saltwater flew back over the bow.

"They're going to drown us!" someone yelled, their voice ripped away by the wind.

"Hold on!" yelled Leonardo, turning away from the spray as they crashed through a wave. They ramped up over the trough, taking flight for a stomach-lurching moment. Then they hit the surface, twisting, and Leonardo felt the keel of the boat go under. He had a split second to realize they were going to flip and yelled "Let go!", then he slammed into the surf. The boat rolled in an explosion of spray and Leonardo plunged underwater.

He fell through a cloud of rushing bubbles, his breath knocked out from the impact. He rolled over and kicked his legs, following the direction of the bubbles to the surface. He burst through a wave and gasped for breath, blinking at the blurry shape of the longboat hurtling over the water in a runaway barrel roll, then another wave crashed over him and Leonardo plunged back underwater.

He forced open his eyes, searching for his clanmates. The bubbles streamed past his face, obscuring everything but the hazy outline of their bodies, merging together and impossible to distinguish. He prayed they had all let go. If anyone held on when the boat flipped...

Something swished past underneath him and Leonardo's heart stopped. He kicked his legs and broke the surface again, blinking back saltwater as he looked around desperately for the boat.

He spotted it, laying on its side, far enough away that his last bit of hope sunk with their scattered supplies.

As soaked heads popped up around him, Leonardo tried to get a count. It took him three tries, but he finally confirmed that everyone had bailed, and everyone had survived.

It was a fleeting relief.

His clan coughed and gasped for breath, swearing as they realized how far the boat was. He locked eyes with Moth and he saw his own hopelessness reflected there. Then Viola's eyes flashed.

"Swim!" she shouted, kicking her feet and starting for the overturned boat.

"You heard her," shouted Pinch. "Move it, halfwits!"

He rolled over and kicked out after Viola. Leonardo took a breath and kicked after them, knowing that they would never make it. It took less than ten seconds before the first shape glided past underneath them, crisscrossing with a second, then a third and a fourth and a fifth and a dozen more, weaving below them as they crawled to safety.

His arms dragged, heavy as the surf, and his legs weighed double. A mermaid streaked past just feet below him, moving so fast she could probably swim to the far side of the Cove and back before he reached the boat.

She streamed out ahead of him and Leonardo gave an exhausted stroke, his sword a deadweight on his hip. Swimming was pointless. They would die here or they would die a hundred feet from here. The boat might as well have been on another planet for all the hope they had of reaching it.

He watched the mermaid disappear from sight, and then he realized something.

Her tail had been turquoise. All of their tails were turquoise. Not white. The same with their hair; black, blonde, red. Never white.

He didn't know what that meant, and he didn't know if it mattered. He took another laboured stroke, then swallowed a mouthful of saltwater and spit it out, rolling upright and choking as it burned his throat.

Viola hesitated, twisting in the water to see him. Other boys struggled too, and their inching progress ground to a halt. Leonardo saw the recognition on Viola's face, a mirror of his own, that this was as far as they would get.

Then the mermaids broke the surface. They rose in a ring around Lion Clan, making no more noise than the waves. Their hair hung in wet tangles, and as they blinked away the saltwater, intelligence gleamed in their eyes. Eyes entirely different from the bloodthirsty, bloodshot ones still burned into his nightmares. These mermaids were young, and they looked nothing like the half-dead, haggish creatures from upriver.

Maybe...maybe it's not over yet, after all.

Suddenly, Charley shouted, "Lion!" and pointed past the mermaids. The mermaids twisted to look, but the only thing in sight was a tightly woven basket, rolling over the top of a wave.

"He's going to sink!" she shouted.

One of the mermaids ducked underwater. A moment later, she surfaced next to the basket.

"She's going to eat him!" screamed Charley, but the mermaid simply peered through the top of the basket, took hold of the handle, and swam back toward them, pulling it behind her. When she reached the circle, she stopped and pushed it toward Charley, sending it drifting to where she could swim to intercept it.

Lion Clan's youngest member stretched to see inside the basket, relief on her face, and Leonardo wondered again if he'd been too quick to decide their fate.

One of the mermaids smiled at him. "You're new," she said, moving forward. Blonde hair tangled around vivid blue eyes. "All of you are new." It came out half question, half statement. Another mermaid with dark hair and sharp features nodded, drifting into the circle.

Leonardo became aware that they were as unclothed as the ones from the river, except that their skin was less of a deathly grey and more of a warm tan, kissed by the tropical sun. Only the tops of their shoulders came above the water, but it was clear water, and it took a lot of concentration to keep his eyes from drifting.

Not all of Lion Clan had the same reservations, and a few feet over, Viola snapped, "*Strato. Bates.*"

"Who are you?" asked the dark-haired mermaid, drawing strangely sharp brows together. "We thought you were Snake Clan."

"They're upriver," said Leonardo. "We just met them."

So far, he wasn't sure which of the Cove's inhabitants he trusted more. *Neither* was a safe answer.

"That doesn't answer my question," said the mermaid.

"We're from the north," said Leonardo.

"Are you at war with Snake Clan?" interrupted Viola. "Is that why you crashed our boat?"

The mermaid eyed Viola down her nose. "We don't concern ourselves with the bickerings of Lost Boys."

Viola didn't blink. "Then why were you trying to crash Snake Clan's boat?"

The dark-haired mermaid simply pursed her lips.

"We protect Lion Clan territory," said a third mermaid, drawing a look from the dark-haired one. "You crossed the border. We had to do something."

The blonde who had first smiled at Leonardo spoke again. "Which of you is the leader?"

"Him," said Pinch, jerking his head at Leonardo.

"Oh good," She shook back her hair, heavy with saltwater. Something about the motion wasn't right. Something intrinsically non-human.

She swam forward, past Pinch, Strato, and Nym, and stopped directly in front of Leonardo. She was younger than the dark-haired one, no older than he was, and her eyes glittered in shades of turquoise, even more vivid up close. The colour of the sea. Her nose and cheekbones followed a soft curve, in contrast to the angled lines of the other mermaid. All of her features were subtle, but in an exceptionally attractive way, as guilty as he felt for admitting it.

He had to remind himself to keep his eyes up, focusing anywhere other than where the wet tangles fell across her bare shoulders, glistening with water droplets in the sun.

"What's your name?" she asked.

Something brushed across his knee and he recoiled, thinking it was a fish. He looked down out of reflex, then snapped his eyes back up, his cheeks going warm.

She grinned and something swept across his leg again, soft and feathery, and he realized it was her tail.

"Your name?" she prompted.

"Um…Leonardo. Leo," he said, trying to figure out where to look.

The dark-haired mermaid swam a stroke toward them, her expression sharper than ever. "Adriana," she said, a warning in her voice.

"What?" Adriana sighed, crossing her arms. "Who are you, Leonardo? You said you're from the north. What are you doing here?"

He hesitated. "We um…" *Lie or tell the truth?*

She blinked, faster than a regular person. *The speed is what's different*, he realized. They made every movement a gear quicker than human reflexes. Her tail brushed his leg again and he faltered, fighting to keep treading water.

Stay focused. She's trying to get information out of you.

"Our clan broke up and we had to leave," said Leonardo. "So we decided to travel south and…look for a new place to live."

"They were bad people," said Charley. "But we fought them."

"Is that so?" asked Adriana, smiling at Charley.

Charley nodded emphatically. "I threw apples; I hit a boy in the head with one." Then she clutched her floating basket. "Thank you for saving Lion. He's our mascot, since our name is Lion Clan."

Dammit. He should've realized Charley wouldn't think to hold anything back.

Adriana shifted back in the water, regarding Leonardo. "What?"

A wave rolled through them, lifting the Lions and mermaids and gliding them down in the trough. Leonardo kicked, struggling to tread water in his saturated clothes. His arms burned already and he wondered how long they could last if the mermaids didn't allow them to get to their boat.

"All she means is…" started Leonardo.

Charley coughed, swallowing a gulp of water.

"The woods sent us on a quest to become Lion Clan," offered Robin. "We're looking for their old camp."

"We're just looking for a place to live," interrupted Leonardo, desperately attempting to play it down. "Our old leader always said that Lion Clan's camp was abandoned, so we thought—"

The dark-haired mermaid held up a hand. Her fingers looked strange, her nails pointed and the skin ever so slightly webbed between them.

"This will require some consideration," she said. "But now is not the time; your muscles will begin to give out soon. We will allow you to go ashore, although you may not like the outcome."

"What does that mean?" asked Puck.

"It means they'll kill us if they change their minds," said Strato.

Adriana's expression told Leonardo that that was *not* what it meant. Neither did it tell him what it *did* mean, but right now, all he cared about was getting his clan to dry land.

"Thank you," said Leonardo, cutting over the other boys. "We appreciate your consideration."

"What consideration?" said Strato. "They just want to warm us up on the rocks before they eat us."

"Shut up," hissed Moth.

"It's more than the last ones gave us," said Robin.

"*Robin*," snapped Moth.

"What do you mean, 'the last ones'?" asked the dark-haired mermaid. Another wave rolled through them. Leonardo felt like pushing Strato and Robin under it and holding them there until this discussion was over.

"We were attacked by mermaids a few days ago," said Bates, and Leonardo swung around to look at him. "They almost ate us, but we fought them off."

Leonardo gave him a *stop now* look.

Bates' eyes widened. "They didn't look anything like you though," he added, as if that would fix anything.

Leonardo caught Moth's attention, a few feet from Bates, and mouthed, *shut him up.* Moth nodded and turned toward Bates.

Meanwhile, Adriana grinned. "Sirens," she corrected him.

386

"*Mermaid* is a storybook word. What 'almost ate you' were freshwater sirens, and I'm surprised you survived."

"Freshwater sirens," echoed Moth. "So what are you, saltwater sirens?"

"No," said the dark-haired siren, brusque. "We're just sirens."

"We all start the same," said another, with a trio of white shells in her hair. "But the sea gets jealous when we go upriver. If we push her mercy and stay away too long, she will try to kill us when we return. The ones you saw were an example of that. The sea would've started killing them the second they tried to returned to her. She kills their brains too. So they flee upriver, barely alive, and live out their days as monsters."

Bates cocked his head, incredulous. He swallowed a gulp of seawater and coughed violently. "So... you're saying at one point," he demanded, still choking. "Those creatures looked like all of you?"

The siren with the shells in her hair nodded.

"Well shit," said Bates. "Stop going in the river!"

"Oh, and they can't sing either," said Adriana, turning to Leonardo. "The sea's favourite punishment is stealing our voices. See, I'll show you; we were upriver today, so my voice feels like sandpaper." She took a breath.

"*Adriana*," said the dark-haired siren.

"What?" demanded Adriana. "They're already in the water. And they can swim. It's completely safe."

"No singing."

"I told you, my voice is rough. Nothing bad would happen."

"It's not an option, Adriana."

Charley swallowed another mouthful of water and coughed.

Leonardo's limbs weighed as much as his sword, dragging down on his hip.

"If you end up staying," Adriana told Leonardo, looking pointedly at the other siren, "come down to the water one night and I'll sing for you."

"Can we get moving?" snapped Viola.

"Yes," said Leonardo quickly, ashamed the offer tempted him. *What are you doing? Stop it, you idiot.*

"Will you let us get our boat?" he asked stiffly.

"Of course," said the dark-haired siren. "We'll take you there."

"Hold on to my shoulders," said Adriana, turning her back to Leonardo.

Shit.

He hesitated, glancing at Viola. She wouldn't look at him, and Adriana glanced back, impatient.

Leonardo swallowed, reaching out and placing his hands on the tanned skin of her shoulders, smooth and soft with seawater. Viola took hold of another siren's shoulders.

Good. She was doing it too. Everyone did it. That was a good thing, because...because...

Right. It meant he wasn't the only one. It wasn't quite so wrong. And it would be wrong because... He struggled to remember. He knew there had been something wrong. Something he was doing? Something he'd done earlier? His mind felt kind of fuzzy right now, and he realized that Adriana was humming, quietly, so that only he could hear it.

CHAPTER 48

It was a nice melody, with unexpected lilts and notes that dipped like the waves. He wanted to ask her to sing louder, but he didn't want to interrupt and miss a note, so he stayed quiet.

She kept humming as she started swimming, and Leonardo almost didn't notice they were moving, he was so lulled by the song.

Everything looked a little fuzzy, too. Adriana's hair turned gold in the late sunlight, and the surface of the water gleamed impossibly dark and glassy as they cut through the waves.

They reached the longboat far quicker than seemed possible, and Leonardo blinked up at it, struggling to focus and still partly distracted by Adriana's tangles. She stopped humming and let him slip off her back, and Leonardo immediately missed the sound, like a piece of the sun had just vanished. She smiled at him, swimming away to join the other sirens as they collected Lion Clan's scattered supplies.

Leonardo's senses slowly came back to him as he treaded water, and the truth of what had just happened hit him. It felt like he'd been drugged, and he remembered Adriana's words, *My voice is rough. Nothing bad will happen.*

Now he knew why the other siren had been arguing. He splashed water on his face, trying to clear the last of the haze from his mind.

Then he remembered Viola and guilt washed over him.

"Viola," said Leonardo.

She looked away. "The boat's ready."

"Viola."

She swam away.

Leonardo swore, rolling over and kicking toward the boat. He pulled himself up over the side and looked for her, climbing to her left watchman's bench mid-hull.

"Viola," he said, taking a step and stopping as Puck rolled into the boat, blocking his path, then Bates and Strato sloshed over the side.

Viola glanced back. "Later, ok?" she said, barely making eye contact before she settled onto her bench.

Leonardo sighed, swearing at himself again, then climbed back to his captain's platform as the rest of the clan dragged themselves onboard.

Miraculously, most of the oars had survived the barrel roll and just took a little un-jamming to get into use. The sirens tossed Lion Clan's sodden supply bags, shields, sleeping rolls, and the burnt lion carving into the boat, where they were shoved under benches and out of the footwells, which were now an inch deep with water. Charley kept the hamster basket in her lap, and all three of Pinch, Bates, and Charley had recovered their hats, which sat dripping on their heads.

Looking around the boat, it seemed that the only things they had lost were a handful of extra swords, which had been tucked under benches and would've sunk straight to the bottom.

The dark-haired siren swam up next to Leonardo's platform.

"The camp is over there," she said, pointing.

Leonardo followed her gaze to one of the cliffs, where three levels of pathways, bridges, and openings had been cut into the rock, glimmering with gold and marble. The mass of it hung over the water, old and wise. An ancient temple overlooking the Cove.

"That's the camp?" said Charley.

"No. That's the *palace*," said Moth, wonder in his voice.

The dark-haired siren cleared her throat, and Leonardo tore his eyes from the cliffside.

"Thank you," he said, glancing down at her. "We'll spend the night, and in the morning, if you want us gone, we'll move on."

So long as she believed those words, Leonardo didn't care how false they were. His clan was his first loyalty, and they needed time to talk in private and come up with an actual plan.

"Oh, it's not our decision," said the siren. "Did I say it was our decision?" Her sharp features drew together in an expression of mock innocence.

"Oh what, so you're allowed to have fun, but I can't?" Adriana scoffed. "Typical."

"I think you've had enough fun. We're leaving," she said to Leonardo, then she gave him a strange smile. "Good luck."

Leonardo frowned. He started to ask, "What for?" but she dropped below the surface before he could get the words out.

Why do we need luck? Who's making this decision?

The other sirens ducked after her. Adriana gave him a little two-fingered salute before she slipped under. He caught a flicker of teal fins and they were gone.

CHAPTER 49

Moth, Puck, Strato, Robin, Bates, and Nym guided the longboat alongside the dock, and Pinch threw a rope over the closest post. Leonardo took a rope from the stern and looped it over another post, tying it tight.

The cliff face towered above them, daunting and incredible. Even with a thousand things on his mind, Leonardo couldn't help but wonder at its majesty.

Switchbacking staircases connected the three levels of the fortress, and square windows watched the cove between the landings, chiseled out of the cliffside.

No Lost Boy's hands had carved this palace, that was clear. Only an imagination run wild could dream up something like this, and only a place as magical as these woods could bring it to life.

Leonardo realized he should say something before they got out.

"Well," he said, looking around the boat. "I'd like to say welcome home, but I don't think I can yet. We may still have a battle ahead of us—who knows what we'll find up there—but I can say with certainly that there is no clan I would rather be fighting beside. Regardless of what happens from here on out, we all know one thing, and it's that Lion Clan has returned to the woods."

"And we're here to stay," added Bates.

"No matter who tries to kick us out," said Puck.

"The sirens can't touch us on land," said Leonardo. "We have the advantage now."

He glanced at Viola while he spoke, but she still wouldn't make eye contact. He sighed, frustrated. Adriana was a *siren*; her entire purpose was to trick him. Was he stupid enough to fall for it? Apparently yes, and now Viola was mad, or hurt, or both, and not even a full day since they had kissed.

"I'm sick of sitting in this boat," said Pinch, bursting through his thoughts. "Can we get up there, or does anyone want to give an interpretive dance first?"

"I'm going to test the dock," said Leonardo. "It's probably old, I don't want to put everyone's weight on it at once."

He climbed over the side, putting one foot down first, then the other. The boards didn't even sag. Leonardo kicked, then stomped.

"It's solid," he said, and the rest of Lion Clan piled over the side, slinging their wet supply bags over their shoulders.

They ascended the steps to the first platform, and Leonardo could've sworn he felt the old Lion Clan's footprints under his boots. Mystique resonated from the powdery stone, cracked in the tropical sun and fringed with salt.

He stayed close to the rock wall; Raven Clan's rope bridges were nothing compared to the sheer drop down to the water.

Something flew past Leonardo's face, then something else buzzed around his legs, and he realized the fairies had returned. One of them landed on his shoulder, and he glanced down, already knowing that it was the green-eyed fairy.

At least you *don't hate me,* he thought. As soon as they were settled in here, he needed to fix things with Viola. He would apologize for not shutting Adriana down at the beginning. If he'd done that, none of the rest would've happened. And he would try to explain her humming, although he wasn't sure if Viola would believe him.

He looked out over the Cove, taking a deep breath. Things were going to be complicated here at Lion Clan, but Leonardo knew they could handle it. They had all grown, the eight boys and two girls behind him, and Leonardo believed that they were a stronger clan now than they ever had been back in the Darkwoods. If only he could patch things up with Viola, Leonardo was ready to face the full force of whatever this new jungle could throw at them.

And then they reached the top, and Leonardo stepped into a passageway under a vaulted gold ceiling. Marble pillars over-looked the cove, and all other thoughts were swept from his mind as he walked into the space, his footsteps echoing in the vastness of it. The passage was carved out of the cliff face, running parallel to the cove below and open along its entire length. A breeze blew between the pillars, rich with the sound of the waves and the smell of salt.

Pinch walked over to the back wall, coarse and craggy like the cliff face, and poked his finger through a small hole in the chalky stone. Leonardo frowned, looking closer and noticing dozens more, running in a straight line, chest high, for what appeared to be the entire length of the passage.

"What are they for?" asked Bates, watching as Pinch crouched down and pressed his eye to the hole.

"Arrows," said Puck, as confident as if he'd read the guide-book beforehand.

"That would've been nice when Hawk, Fox, and Bear attacked us," said Robin. "We could've taken half of them out before they even got a shot back."

Leonardo stepped up to one of the holes, bending to see inside. The thickness of the stone cut off most of his view, but he could still see a small room with tall woven baskets lined up along the back wall. There were hooks above the baskets, and a row of wooden longbows hung ready for use.

Leonardo wondered why no one had claimed this camp after Lion Clan fell. It seemed to him that someone would've moved in the second it was vacant. Fortresses like this didn't just sit empty. But maybe there was some fatal flaw that he wasn't aware of. Lion Clan eventually fell, after all.

Still, he thought, following the others to the end of the passage, *flaws can be repaired.*

A big stone door stood before them, carved with lions and palm trees. Moth ran a hand over the detailed work as Leonardo studied the gold lock.

Strato tried the handle but the door didn't budge.

"What now?" asked Robin.

"Anyone see a doormat?" asked Pinch.

Leonardo reached in his pocket, where he still carried the magic stone from Aleksander's treehouse.

I wonder...

Bates gave the door a tug as Leonardo pulled the stone from his pocket.

"What's that?" asked Charley.

"A key," said Leonardo. He tossed it in the air and a gold key, bigger than last time, landed in his palm.

It worked.

"What the hell?" said Pinch.

"Aleksander gave it to me," said Leonardo, fitting it into the lock. "It unlocked a secret passage in his treehouse. I thought it might—"

The lock clicked.

"We're in!" shouted Bates, his voice echoing in the vast space.

Did Aleksander know it did this?

Leonardo wondered where he'd gotten it from.

He removed the key and returned it to his pocket. Through the door, a second set of steps curved up into the sunlight. Leonardo led the way up; again, feeling the footprints of Lion Clan under his boots.

At the top, they found a natural terrace, open to the sky, with a stone rail along the front edge. The face of the cliff was set back, and square doorways cut into the rock wall, hung with blankets to keep out the sun. They were high up now and an incredible view opened out before them; the sun setting through a perfectly

397

positioned break in the cliffs, bathing the open ocean and the sheltered walls of the cove in rose light.

Behind him, Moth's voice called out, excited.

"Leo, come look at this."

Leonardo turned as Moth hesitantly stepped through one of the blanket doors. A feather had been carved into the stone above it, and as Leonardo stepped through, a wall of scent crashed his senses. Spices, herbs, and a hundred other aromas swirled together in the air, making his eyes water.

"What is this place?" he asked, coughing.

"It needs to be aired out a bit," said Moth. "Probably been sealed up for a while."

"No kidding."

"But look," he said, turning and lifting a long white object from a shelf. Leonardo frowned, then his eyes widened. It was a lion skull. Crystals had been fitted into the eye sockets, the teeth had been painted black, and every inch of bone was covered with intricately carved patterns.

"What the hell is that?" he asked.

"I don't know," said Moth. "But look at the rest of this stuff."

Talismans and coloured stones hung from the ceiling, a jar of feathers sat on a shelf, and a white animal skin stretched over a round drum, fringed with orange hair that looked suspiciously like the lion hair they had seen back at Raven Clan.

Dozens more strange items filled the room, and Leonardo stared around at it, dumbfounded.

"Did Lion Clan have a shaman?" he asked.

"How else do you explain all this?" asked Moth.

The room sprouted with more bizarre items than he could even begin to divine the purpose of.

He nodded slowly. "I think they did."

"So do I," said Moth, turning to put the skull back on its shelf. "Maybe I can find something to fix Nym's hands."

"It's possible," said Leonardo, studying the jars.

"But I'll have to understand it all first," said Moth. He kneaded his hands. "I was thinking...You know how I'm the only one who can hear the fairies? And I saw the lion back at Raven Clan when no one else could?"

"You want to be a shaman?" asked Leonardo.

"I don't know," said Moth. "If it's something that Lion Clan had before, then maybe it's something I can do, you know, to actually contribute something for once."

"You always contribute," said Leonardo.

Moth gave him a look.

"You pull your weight, Moth," he insisted. "If you can heal Nym, you should do it. But do you really want to get tangled up in the rest of this?"

The lion skull grinned at him with its black teeth and crystal eyes.

"Why wouldn't I?" Moth looked around the room, "This stuff is amazing. And I wouldn't just have to be the weirdo who believes in fairies anymore. It would be my job."

"No one thinks that anymore," said Leonardo. "Everyone knows they're real now."

"I know," said Moth. "But you get my point. And I *want* to do this."

"Ok." Leonardo shrugged. "It's yours."

Before Moth could respond, Leonardo heard his name from out on the terrace.

He turned to open the curtain as another voice cut in. A girl's, and it was neither Viola nor Charley.

"Who dares set foot in the camp of Lion Clan?"

CHAPTER 50

Leonardo pushed outside, Moth on his heels.

His clan clustered on the terrace, hands on their swords as a group of girls stepped around a stone outcropping, armed with slingshots, bows, swords, and shields embossed with gold lion heads.

Their armour gleamed with gold, and the girl in front held a ring-shaped blade, sharp along the entire outside edge. Strange symbols curled in gold along the metal.

She stood with feet apart, shoulders back and the ring poised to throw. She twitched her fingers, her skin a dark tan like Viola's, but with a South-Asian complexion. From her stance to her weapon, she looked straight out of a Bollywood movie.

"Are you the leader?" she asked. She spoke with an Indian accent.

"I am," said Leonardo.

She squinted one eye, lining up her shot. She wore a dot of red on her forehead, her hair loose and untamed. Half a dozen smaller ring-blades dangled around her wrists.

"What are you doing in our camp?"

"We didn't know anyone was living here," said Leonardo.

"Oh, of course," she said sarcastically, the words lilting on her accent. "Why would you?"

"It's the truth," said Leonardo, trying to sound like his heart wasn't slamming in his chest. "In the Darkwoods, everyone thinks this camp has been empty since Lion Clan fell. We had no idea—"

"Since *what?*" she demanded, still holding the circular blade in throwing position.

"Since Lion Clan fell," said Leonardo. "Can we talk about this peacefully?"

"No. What are you talking about?"

It's not very complicated.

"How long has your clan been living here?" he tried instead.

"A hundred years," said the Hindu Lion girl. "And I can't recall ever hearing about a time when we 'fell'."

Behind her, the other girls drew back bowstrings and raised their swords. Leonardo's Clan shuffled, tensing for a fight.

"How long ago did the original Lion Clan disappear?" tried Leonardo. He needed to keep her talking. Stop things from escalating.

"You mean the first members? How would I know?"

"Wait," said Moth, taking a step around Leonardo. "Are *you* the original Lion Clan?"

The girl scoffed, indignant. "How old do we look to you?"

"No," said Moth. "Not you specifically. I mean, was Lion Clan always girls?"

In the rose light of the sunset, a few of the Lion girls leaned over and whispered to each other. They looked just like the boys of the Darkwoods; mismatched and ragtag. Only, they wore gold armour and their weapons appeared a lot sharper.

"What else would we be?" asked the leader. She pushed a lock of black hair off her face.

"Boys," said Bates. "The Lions in the legends were boys."

"Then your legends are wrong," said the girl.

"But that's impossible!" said Bates. "All the legends say—"

"Who wrote your legends?" she asked. "They obviously weren't very good at it."

"Let me get this straight," said Leonardo. "Lion Clan never disappeared? It's been a clan of girls since the beginning?"

"Let *me* get *this* straight," she countered. "You believed we were boys, you were told we had fallen, and you thought a camp like this would be left empty? In this jungle?" She shook her head. "Things are clearly different in the Darkwoods."

She lowered her weapon and her clanmates did the same. A flock of seabirds with orange heads swung up over the terrace, screeching as they rode the wind.

"How were we supposed to know?" asked Leonardo. "The sirens didn't say anything about—"

"And you believed them?"

"They gave us no reason not to."

Behind him, Viola scoffed.

"And who is she?" asked the Lion girl. "She doesn't look like the rest of you."

403

"A member of our clan," said Leonardo. He had no interest in explaining Viola's presence to this girl.

"Yes," said the girl. "I can see that."

They stared at each other for a long moment, neither willing to back down.

Then the seabirds made a second pass and the Lion girl pulled a smooth, bent piece of wood out of a holster behind her back.

Is that a boomerang? thought Leonardo.

She gripped it at one end and hurled hard into the air. It spun over Leonardo's head and into the flock of birds, connecting with one and killing it instantly. Both the seabird and the boomerang clattered to the tiles at the far end of the terrace.

"Dinner," she explained curtly. "Isabella, do we still have apricots?"

"I believe so," said one of the younger girls, with light brown hair and armour that was a little too big for her.

"Good. Boil it with the apricots and ginger."

"The sirens said someone would decide if we could stay or not," interrupted Leonardo. "I now see they meant you."

He'd been dismissed enough times by Aleksander to recognize it. He didn't feel like listening to her dinner order while their fate remained uncertain.

"It's getting dark," he continued. "We're tired, and we don't know any of the clan boundaries. We can sleep in the passage down below, and we'll be out first thing in the morning..." Leonardo paused at the sound of footsteps. They drew closer, clattering up what sounded like another stone staircase, hidden out of sight behind the outcropping.

A few of the girls shifted aside as a young boy ran up. A too-big sword swung on his hip as he shuffled into the ranks of girls, armour tied on haphazard as if he'd missed the alarm.

Leonardo frowned. *They have boys too? Or is he the only one? Like Charley is with us.*

He seemed about the same age as Charley.

"Who is he?" asked Leonardo.

"Who is *she*?" replied the Lion girl, looking past Leonardo to where Charley had stepped around Puck.

"She showed up on our banks last week," said Leonardo carefully.

Could the woods have switched them?

"It seems the woods are playing games again," said the Lion girl. "What's her name?"

"What do you mean, games?" asked Leonardo.

"Pompey," called the girl. "Come meet your real clan."

"What's going on?" demanded Leonardo. He placed a hand on his sword.

"Mishti," one of the girls interrupted them, her voice urgent. She pointed out over the rail. The Lion Clan leader—Mishti—took a step around her, shading her eyes at the cove.

"Shit," she swore. "Shit shit shit shit *shit*."

A ship rounded the cliffs into the cove, black sails flying in the setting sun. A real ship, not a longboat.

"Where are the sirens?" snapped Mishti, marching to the rail. "Bitches. Protect our territory. Yeah right."

She spun back to Leonardo, eyeing the sword on his hip.

"Your boys know how to fight?"

Leonardo opened his mouth, but she cut him off. "Good. Follow me, and keep those away," she said, looking at Puck as he started to draw his sword. "You'll end up stabbing someone."

She turned on her heel and her clan parted to let her through. "Hurry up," she called over her shoulder. "Boats are fast."

"Who are they?" asked Leonardo.

"Pirates," she called, vanishing around the outcropping.

Leonardo turned to Moth, then Pinch, and Viola, who didn't look away this time. All three of them appeared just as uncertain as he did.

"Are you coming or not?" Mishti reappeared around the outcropping, looking out to sea and swearing again.

Leonardo drew a breath. "Pirates," he said to his clan. "Did anyone here sign up for easy?"

Head's shaking, jaws set.

"Good," said Leonardo. "I didn't think so. Then let's get moving, it's going to be a long night."

He started after Mishti, his clan falling in behind him. And Lion Clan—the other Lion Clan—fell in behind them. A pack of Lions, painted gold in the setting sun, running over the cliff as a ship rolled into the waters below them, sails billowing and black as the night.

The real fight is coming, thought Leonardo. The sails reminded him of storm clouds, and he couldn't help but see it as an omen. The woods liked to hint what lay ahead, and to throw one danger at Leonardo's clan just before a bigger one followed.

But the woods are on our side this time, he thought. He wondered if it would be enough.

Leonardo cast one last look over the Cove, new and strange, then he followed Mishti down a stone staircase, his clan behind him.

ACKNOWEDGEMENTS

First off, I have to thank my family. From the long walks problem-solving the Darkwoods, to putting up with the hours of writing and rewriting, and the weeks when I spend more time with the characters in my head than the ones living around me. Your support never wavers, and it truly means the world to me.

To my incredible Scottish-Cypriot Editor, Fiona. (And yes, that's how I describe you to people. I think it sounds much cooler than just 'editor'). Stephen King once said, "To write is human, to edit is divine." I fully understand that now. This book would be nowhere near what it is without you. Thank you so much for everything you do.

To Dan, my cover designer, who brought the Darkwoods to visual life and remained patient through all of my and Fiona's ideas and tweaks. In this case, I truly hope this book gets judged by its cover.

And to everyone in the non-writing parts of my life, who give me an excuse to step out from behind the laptop every once in a while. Especially the MCHS drama department, for allowing me to take off the 'writer' hat and become 'music director' for a few hours, a few days a week.

And finally, to my local community, which has been so amazingly enthusiastic about this book. Thank you!

TURN THE PAGE FOR
A SNEAK PREVIEW OF

THE COVE

BOOK TWO OF THE LOST BOYS TRILOGY

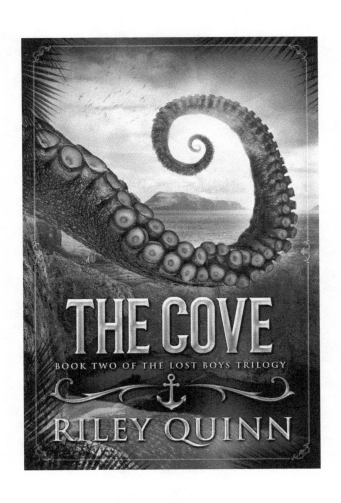

TWELVE HOURS AGO

Leonardo sprinted down stone steps, the rapid breathing of thirty other kids echoing through the stairwell behind him. Others rushed in front, swords swinging at their hips, shields clanging off the walls, and the leather straps of slingshots clutched tight in their fists. Dying sunlight flashed in stripes across their faces as they passed long slitted openings in the stonework.

Leonardo nearly missed a step and swore, grabbing an opening for balance as three Lion Clan girls shoved past him. He glanced through the tall window, watching black sails billow as a ship crossed the Cove.

Pirates.

"Let's go!" shouted Strato. He yanked Leonardo's shoulder on the way past. "I ain't fighting pirates alone."

Leonardo pushed away from the window, dusting salt off his hands. He gripped the handle of his sword as they reached a landing and hooked around a corner, then down another staircase.

Voices crashed in the confines of the tunnel, breathless and sharp with adrenaline.

Then the steps ended in a wide passage, only a few meters above sea level and cut with ornate openings that gazed out across the Cove.

Kids rushed to the openings, weapons sliding from their belts. A pair of girls released slingshots as another whipped an arrow from its sheath, fitting it to a bowstring. Leonardo watched the stones arc through the air and fall well short of the ship, then the arrow loosed with a snap, sailing out over the waves.

"Hold your fire," snapped Mishti, the girls' leader. "They're not even close yet."

"Sorry."

"Wait for my order. Is that too difficult to remember?"

Next to them, the boys under Leonardo's command leaned through the openings, staring as the ship approached. They hadn't been here an hour, and they were already under attack.

What else is new? Leonardo pushed through the crowd of girls, ducking past swords and arrowheads.

"Mishti," he called, dodging a girl with a spear. "Mishti, who's on that ship?"

"Pirates," she replied, without looking at him. She stood in her own opening, the wind of the sea snapping at her robes.

I know. You already said that.

"Are they other kids?" he pressed. "What are they doing here?"

"Yes, they're other kids," she snapped. "Were there anything other than kids in your corner of the woods?"

Leonardo stepped around two more girls and stopped behind Mishti's shoulder, both of their eyes on the ship. He hadn't realized quite how wide across the Cove was; in all the time it took to run down here, the pirates were only halfway across.

"They're like a clan," said a girl nearby, with strawberry blonde ringlets and a feather on a string around her neck. Unlike everyone else, she didn't carry a weapon or seem at all prepared to fight.

"They kidnap kids from other clans," she continued, her gaze darting out to sea between words. "The youngest, usually. They're here for Pompey and Charley."

"Charley just got here," said Leonardo. "How could they possibly—"

"You'll find the magic here is…different than anywhere else in the woods," said Mishti.

A splash sprayed up from the sea, and Leonardo turned as kids crowded toward an opening.

"Back up!" shouted Puck. "Back up!"

"What is it?" said Leonardo. No one answered, and he wove through the throng of kids, heart racing. Water sloshed and voices rose in pitch. Leonardo struggled to see anything past all their heads. He pushed his way to another opening in the wall and leaned out over the water, just in time to see Puck and Strato lean down, desperately grabbing for Bates, who treaded water an arms-length out of reach.

"Bates!" snapped Leonardo, "What are you doing?"

Bates neither replied, nor seemed to notice the boys trying to reach him.

"Halfwit just jumped in!" said Strato.

Then Leonardo froze as a faint breath of music carried on the breeze.

"Shh," he hushed the kids around him. He strained to listen, but the voices of everyone else drowned it out.

"Everyone quiet!" yelled Leonardo. This time both clans fell silent as a long note carried across the water. A second voice joined it, then a third, weaving and rising to chilling heights.

The song originated from somewhere near the pirate ship, and when Leonardo squinted, he thought he could see something in the water.

Sirens. Only moments ago, Leonardo and his clan encountered them upon reaching the Cove. He had no interest in doing so again.

"Get back from the edge," he ordered. "Puck, Strato, now."

"But Bates!" said Strato.

Leonardo kicked off his boots, tossing his sword on the ground. "I'll get him."

"Wait." Viola placed a hand on Leonardo's shoulder. "Look."

As the song grew louder, the ship began to turn; the bow swinging dramatically until the hull faced sidelong to the fortress. Kids crowded the rails aboard the ship. It continued rotating until it pointed back out to open sea, gold-framed windows peering out from the stern as it began to retreat across the Cove.

Silence filled the stone passage as the last wisps of music faded in the slosh of the waves.

"What just happened?" asked Leonardo.

"The sirens did their job for once," said Mishti. She glanced pointedly at Bates, still in the water. "The pirates can't stay, or they'll lose all their boys overboard. Now come on, get him out of the water. I've decided to let you stay tonight."

RILEY QUINN is a Canadian author and musician. He grew up in Western Canada, dividing his time between the Prairies, the Rocky Mountains, and the shores of the North West Coast. When he's not writing, Riley can be found performing and teaching music in his local community.
To learn more, visit: www.rileyquinnofficial.com

CPSIA information can be obtained
at www.ICGtesting.com
Printed in the USA
BVHW070457061120
592675BV00001B/1